Kill Talk

To Kup,

Thank you for all of the help that you have given me. I am extremely greatful for you doing the opening on my radio show, and very appreciative. I am also very indebted to you for mentioning me in your column so many times....

Your former partner in crime and old drinking buddy, my uncle, Irving Yergin always, loved working with you.

P.S. After you do or don't read this - take it to any bookstore, return Kill Talk, and get twenty bucks back —

Thanks Again
Kindest Personal Regards
M—— 9/8/02

Kill Talk

❀

Michael L. Yergin

Writers Club Press
San Jose New York Lincoln Shanghai

Kill Talk

All Rights Reserved © 2002 by Michael L. Yergin

No part of this book may be reproduced or transmitted in any form or by any means, graphic, electronic, or mechanical, including photocopying, recording, taping, or by any information storage retrieval system, without the permission in writing from the publisher.

Except in the case of brief quotations embodied in critical articles or reviews.

Writers Club Press
an imprint of iUniverse, Inc.

For information address:
iUniverse, Inc.
5220 S. 16th St., Suite 200
Lincoln, NE 68512
www.iuniverse.com

This novel is a work of fiction. Names, characters, places and events are either the product of the author's imagination or are used fictitiously. Any resemblance to actual occurances, places or people, living or dead, is completely coincidental.

Visit the KILL TALK website at www.killtalk.com Other works by the author include Wealth Building in the 90's—What Wall Street won't tell you © 1991, and Thoughts after the First © 1969.

ISBN: 0-595-21656-0

Printed in the United States of America

This book is dedicated to Stephen J. Cannell. Thank you for being my friend and mentor and believing in me. You are truly one of the good guys in Hollywood.

To Shannon Spencer, a great screenplay writer in her own right, who worked tirelessly, crafting my words and ideas in KILL TALK.

And Kristina Oster, assistant to Stephen J. Cannell, who spent many hours inputting this into her computer. And to my right arm, Janet Fleming, who kept telling me "Don't worry, I'll fix it." I would be lost without her.

And to Patricia Brickhouse, my publicist, and good friend, for bringing KILL TALK to the public's attention.

And to my parents, Babe and Archie Yergin, two very special people;

And the person who gives me the courage and insight to go forward, my wonderful son, Michael Patrick Yergin.

Contents

❁

Prologue 1
Chapter 1 WEDNESDAY NIGHT–7:00 P.M. 3
　CHICAGO, ILLINOIS
Chapter 2 WEDNESDAY NIGHT–7:05 P.M. 8
　CHICAGO, ILLINOIS
Chapter 3 WEDNESDAY NIGHT–AN HOUR LATER 13
　CHICAGO, ILLINOIS
Chapter 4 WEDNESDAY NIGHT–TWO HOURS LATER 16
　CHICAGO, ILLINOIS
Chapter 5 WEDNESDAY NIGHT LATER 19
　CHICAGO, ILLINOIS
Chapter 6 THURSDAY MORNING PREDAWN 23
　PROVIDENCE, RHODE ISLAND
Chapter 7 EARLY THURSDAY MORNING 27
　PROVIDENCE, RHODE ISLAND
Chapter 8 DEEMIS'S STORY 32
　PROVIDENCE, RHODE ISLAND
Chapter 9 LATER THURSDAY MORNING 38
　CHICAGO, ILLINOIS
Chapter 10 THURSDAY–SOMETIME 41
　SOMEPLACE
Chapter 11 LATER THURSDAY MORNING 42
　CHICAGO, ILLINOIS

Chapter 12 THURSDAY–EARLY MORNING 46
    CHICAGO, ILLINOIS
Chapter 13 LITTLE VENICE 50
    FORT LAUDERDALE, FLORIDA
Chapter 14 LATE THURSDAY MORNING 56
    FORT LAUDERDALE, FLORIDA
Chapter 15 EARLY THURSDAY MORNING 61
    PROVIDENCE, RHODE ISLAND
Chapter 16 THURSDAY–EARLY MORNING 64
    PROVIDENCE, RHODE ISLAND
Chapter 17 LATER THURSDAY MORNING 66
    PROVIDENCE, RHODE ISLAND
Chapter 18 THEN AND NOW 68
    FEDERAL PRISON CAMP–TERRE HAUTE, INDIANA
Chapter 19 WHY IT HAPPENED 71
    TERRE HAUTE, INDIANA
Chapter 20 HOW IT HAPPENED 75
    TERRE HAUTE, INDIANA
Chapter 21 THE PLAN 83
    FEDERAL TRANSFER CENTER, OKLAHOMA CITY, OKLAHOMA
Chapter 22 THE BIG HOUSE 92
    LEWISBURG PENITENTIARY, HARRISBURG, PENNSYLVANIA
Chapter 23 A MISERABLE PLACE 94
    LEWISBURG PENITENTIARY, HARRISBURG, PENNSYLVANIA
Chapter 24 CLUB FED 96
    ROBERT F. KENNEDY CENTER, MORGANTOWN, WEST VIRGINIA
Chapter 25 GETTING NERVOUS 98
    ROBERT F. KENNEDY CENTER, MORGANTOWN, WEST VIRGINIA
Chapter 26 NOT LIKE CAMP 100
    ROBERT F. KENNEDY CENTER, MORGANTOWN, WEST VIRGINIA
Chapter 27 THE MOB IS ALIVE AND WELL 104
    CHICAGO, ILLINOIS

Chapter 28 EARLY THURSDAY EVENING 113
    FORT LAUDERDALE, FLORIDA
Chapter 29 MOMENTS LATER 116
    FORT LAUDERDALE, FLORIDA
Chapter 30 JACK'S LETTER 118
    THE JUSTICE DEPARTMENT, WASHINGTON, D.C.
Chapter 31 THURSDAY NIGHT 120
    ALDERICE MANSION, FORT LAUDERDALE, FLORIDA
Chapter 32 EARLY THURSDAY NIGHT 122
    FORT LAUDERDALE, FLORIDA
Chapter 33 EARLY EVENING THURSDAY 125
    FORT LAUDERDALE, FLORIDA
Chapter 34 THE THURSDAY AFTERNOON DINNER
AT LITTLE MAMA'S 128
    CHICAGO, ILLINOIS
Chapter 35 THE DINNER CONCLUDES 135
    CHICAGO, ILLINOIS, AND WASHINGTON, D.C.
Chapter 36 LATER THURSDAY NIGHT 143
    FORT LAUDERDALE, FLORIDA
Chapter 37 AFTER THE DINNER AT LITTLE MAMA'S 145
    CHICAGO, ILLINOIS
Chapter 38 LATER THURSDAY EVENING 147
    CHICAGO, ILLINOIS
Chapter 39 THE PLOT THICKENS 151
    WASHINGTON, D.C.
Chapter 40 EVEN LATER THURSDAY EVENING 153
    MARK'S CONDO, CHICAGO, ILLINOIS
Chapter 41 THURSDAY 156
    KEY BISCAYNE, FLORIDA
Chapter 42 THURSDAY EVENING 158
    CHICAGO O'HARE AIRPORT
Chapter 43 LATE THURSDAY EVENING 160
    PROVIDENCE, RHODE ISLAND

Chapter 44 THURSDAY NIGHT 164
    THE CHICAGO BOARD OF TRADE (CBOT), CHICAGO, ILLINOIS
Chapter 45 THURSDAY NIGHT 172
    PROVIDENCE, RHODE ISLAND
Chapter 46 FBI HEADQUARTERS 176
    CHICAGO, ILLINOIS
Chapter 47 THURSDAY NIGHT 178
    UNDISCLOSED LOCATION
Chapter 48 THURSDAY EVENING 180
    PROVIDENCE, RHODE ISLAND
Chapter 49 THURSDAY EVENING 182
    PROVIDENCE, RHODE ISLAND
Chapter 50 SOMETIME 190
    UNDISCLOSED LOCATION
Chapter 51 THURSDAY EVENING POLICE STATION 191
    PROVIDENCE, RHODE ISLAND
Chapter 52 OH, FOR THE GOOD OLD DAYS 193
    CHICAGO, ILLINOIS
Chapter 53 THURSDAY NIGHT 198
    FORT LAUDERDALE, FLORIDA
Chapter 54 FBI 200
    CHICAGO, ILLINOIS
Chapter 55 THEN AND NOW 202
    DEERFIELD, ILLINOIS
Chapter 56 LEWISBURG PENITENTIARY 207
    HARRISBURG, PENNSYLVANIA
Chapter 57 THURSDAY NIGHT 209
    PROVIDENCE, RHODE ISLAND
Chapter 58 SHOW ME THE MONEY 214
    ROBERT F. KENNEDY CENTER, MORGANTOWN, WEST VIRGINIA
Chapter 59 A SOCIAL EVENT 218
    CHICAGO, ILLINOIS

Chapter 60 LATE THURSDAY EVENING 225
   NARRAGANSETT RACETRACK, PAWTUCKET, RHODE ISLAND
Chapter 61 EARLIER THURSDAY NIGHT 233
   AIRPORT FBI INTERROGATION ROOM, WASHINGTON, D.C.
Chapter 62 LATE THURSDAY NIGHT 236
   PAWTUCKET, RHODE ISLAND
Chapter 63 THURSDAY NIGHT 240
   CHICAGO, ILLINOIS
Chapter 64 THURSDAY NIGHT 242
   PROVIDENCE, RHODE ISLAND
Chapter 65 THURSDAY EVENING AFTER THE DINNER IN CHICAGO 244
   KEY BISCAYNE, FLORIDA
Chapter 66 THURSDAY NIGHT 246
   HOTEL, WASHINGTON, D.C.
Chapter 67 LEWISBURG PENITENTIARY 248
   HARRISBURG, PENNSYLVANIA
Chapter 68 THURSDAY NIGHT 250
   DINER NEAR PROVIDENCE, RHODE ISLAND
Chapter 69 THURSDAY EVENING 256
   FORT LAUDERDALE HOLLYWOOD INTERNATIONAL AIRPORT, FLORIDA
Chapter 70 FRIDAY 258
   ROBERT F. KENNEDY CENTER, MORGANTOWN, WEST VIRGINIA
Chapter 71 FRIDAY MORNING 263
   ROBERT F. KENNEDY CENTER, MORGANTOWN, WEST VIRGINIA
Chapter 72 FRIDAY MORNING 269
   ROBERT F. KENNEDY CENTER, MORGANTOWN, WEST VIRGINIA
Chapter 73 MOMENTS LATER 273
   ROBERT F. KENNEDY CENTER, MORGANTOWN, WEST VIRGINIA
Chapter 74 VERY, VERY EARLY FRIDAY MORNING 276
   MARRIOTT HOTEL, PROVIDENCE, RHODE ISLAND

Chapter 75 FRIDAY 284
    CHICAGO, ILLINOIS
Chapter 76 FRIDAY 287
    KEY BISCAYNE, FLORIDA
Chapter 77 FRIDAY 289
    WHITACRE HOUSE, RHODE ISLAND
Chapter 78 EARLY FRIDAY MORNING 291
    PROVIDENCE, RHODE ISLAND
Chapter 79 BEFORE FRIDAY'S MEETING 295
    MARRIOTT HOTEL, PROVIDENCE, RHODE ISLAND
Chapter 80 LATE FRIDAY AFTERNOON 298
    DR. BERNSTEIN'S OFFICE, DEERFIELD, ILLINOIS
Chapter 81 LATER FRIDAY 300
    WHITACRE HOUSE, PROVIDENCE, RHODE ISLAND
Chapter 82 FRIDAY 302
    FORT LAUDERDALE, FLORIDA
Chapter 83 FRIDAY 304
    NORTH MIAMI, FLORIDA
Chapter 84 EARLY FRIDAY EVENING 306
    WATER TOWER PLACE, CHICAGO, ILLINOIS
Chapter 85 FRIDAY–SHAREHOLDERS MEETING 308
    PROVIDENCE, RHODE ISLAND
Chapter 86 THE ALDERICE MANSION 321
    FORT LAUDERDALE, FLORIDA
Chapter 87 CHICAGO, ILLINOIS 324
Chapter 88 PROVIDENCE, RHODE ISLAND 331
Chapter 89 A FEW MORE WEEKS LATER 333
    CHICAGO, ILLINOIS
Chapter 90 A FEW WEEKS LATER 337
    THE SOUTH OF FRANCE
EPILOGUE 339

Prologue

❀

The first trial in the infamous Bre-X Minerals gold mining fraud, which wiped out billions of dollars in wealth, got under way Monday with a lawyer for former Bre-X Vice Chairman John Felderhof saying his client shouldn't have to take all the blame for many others involved.

—Chicago Tribune, *Tuesday, October 17, 2000*

🍁   🍁   🍁

Sammy (The Bull) Gravano, the former Mafia hitman who moved to Phoenix after testifying against the Gambino crime family Boss, John Gotti, was indicted last year and identified by police as a leader of the ring…a nationwide syndicate trafficking in Ecstasy pills…

—The Arizona Republic, *March 25, 2001*

🍁   🍁   🍁

"*The Corrections Corporation of America (CCA) is the industry leader in private prisons. It was the brainchild of a West Point cadet and*

Harvard Business School grad who received backing from the same investment firm that gave us Kentucky Fried Chicken."

—Paul's Justice Page, *April 2, 2001*

🍁   🍁   🍁

There is an ever-growing body of information that seems to substantiate the claim that Mob families may be involved in active terrorist activities, including the attacks on 9-11-01 in New York and Washington, D.C.

—*Anonymous CIA leak, January 1, 2002*

Chapter 1

WEDNESDAY NIGHT–7:00 P.M.

CHICAGO, ILLINOIS

Mark Goodwin opened the door to his condo and walked straight into hell. The bouquet of long-stemmed roses bought to surprise his new bride dropped from his hand and fell to the floor. He couldn't believe the wild scene unfolding in front of him in his own apartment.

"No! God, no! Stop it! Please! Goddammit, stop! What are you doing?" Mark screamed out. His body convulsed and shook uncontrollably as he watched the woman he married just ten days ago having sex with another man. Who was this man screwing his wife? Horrific, devastating, gut-wrenching pain engulfed him and intensified even more as he immediately felt the cold steel of the .38 caliber revolver pressed firmly to the back of his head by a strange woman who smelled of sex. Who was this naked woman behind him? Panic, fear, and total nausea immobilized him. "Stop!" he tried to scream, but he realized that no sound was coming out of his mouth.

The woman behind him held a gun to the base of his skull and pushed her breasts into his back. She thrust a knee between his legs and used her naked body to spread the stale smell of sex all over him. "You married an 'Outfit Cunt,' you pathetic bastard," she hissed into Mark's ear in a low, throaty mocking tone. "What are you, stupid? Did you actually believe that *you* were enough of a man to keep your blushing little nympho-bride from tasting my sweet juices and the hot cum of real men?" Disdainfully, she continued, "Your precious goddess may fuck you six nights a week, but each and every Wednesday night—*we fuck her!*"

Mark was in a state of utter disbelief. His heart pounded wildly. This couldn't be happening, he thought to himself. Was he dreaming? This had to be someone else's nightmare. Seeing his wife, Carole, naked on the living-room couch with another man, was agonizing. He was in complete and total shock. The woman holding the gun to his head continued to press her body into Mark's. His mind was racing furiously; he was confused and disoriented. What in the hell was going on? Then he remembered the strange phone message that Carole had left at the office earlier that day, and *now* things were starting to make sense.

🍁 🍁 🍁

Now Mark understood why Carole had been so adamant about supposedly needing time to spend with one of her girlfriends when she had called him at the office in the morning and left that message on his answering machine. He realized now that she had left the message because she didn't want to get caught. "Honey, you know I love you very much, but tonight one of my friends is coming by. She has some problems, so be a sweetheart and go work out at the East Bank Club, get a massage, have a drink, and come home around 7:00 tonight. I'll make you a nice romantic dinner," the message had said.

But Mark was not fully listening to her when he played the message. Smiling, he was looking at the pictures he had taken of Carole naked on the beach at the Hotel Ciboney in Negril, Jamaica, on their honeymoon last week. What a tremendous body she had, and what huge, perfect breasts! Even though the pictures didn't do her justice, he grew excited staring at those amazing nipples. Hard—they were at least a quarter of an inch in diameter, like erasers on a pencil. And that perfect ass. Without a doubt, Carole was the most beautiful woman he had ever seen. She was like a goddess. Mark had met Carole at a party on the Gold Coast of Chicago; she stood out from all the other women at the party. It was lust at first sight; Mark fell head over heels. More than just craving her, Mark was spellbound and instantly obsessed with her. She was enigmatically dangerous, orgasmic, wild-looking, and drop-dead beautiful. And she knew it. Every head turned when she walked into a room. Women at once hated her. She was the embodiment of perfection—Cleopatra, Helen of Troy—the type of woman men would kill for; let alone go to war for, leave their wives for, or risk their entire careers for, in a New York second. Mark was awestruck when he saw her. He knew immediately that he wanted Carole. He also knew she was trouble.

🍁   🍁   🍁

She was so hot. How had he been lucky enough to be noticed by this fiery, sultry, tempestuous, radiant specimen of a woman who gave men a hard-on merely by looking at her? Carole was a smaller, more petite, more erotically sensual version of a young Cindy Crawford, right down to the dimples.

When Mark had seen her at the party, all he could do was stare. The synergy between them was instant and explosive. Carole had walked up to Mark and said something that he hadn't understood. It didn't matter at the time. Mark was mesmerized. She seemed to look straight through him with her amazing, incredible cobalt-blue bedroom eyes.

He remembered how excited and weak-kneed he had felt when Carole took his arm as they walked out onto the terrace. Neither of them said a word. It wasn't necessary. The beautiful, cool summer night air charged them with intense sexual energy, and the clean, fresh breeze off Lake Michigan wafted over them as they made wild, passionate love. Mark had never met a woman who could have half a dozen orgasms in less than twenty minutes. They were totally lost and immersed in each other's unbridled sexual passion. Mark grew increasingly excited and started to come again. He was totally absorbed in the feel, scent, and taste of Carole. He vividly remembered the sheer fantasy that had overtaken him.

🍁 🍁 🍁

But now, standing there witnessing his wife having sex with some stranger in his condo, he realized that he had *not* been paranoid earlier that morning when he had listened to his answering machine upon arriving at his office. There was something immediately unsettling about Carole's message. He had just arrived at the office, which meant that Carole must have called within minutes of his leaving her at home. Why hadn't she told him then? As he listened to her message, he sensed that something wasn't right, although he didn't know what. He couldn't put his finger on it, but he had a sick feeling in his stomach. Maybe it was the tone of her voice. Did he believe her story about a girlfriend coming over to talk, or was she lying? Mark wasn't sure. Maybe he was just being paranoid for no reason; at least that's what he had thought earlier in the day. After all, Mark reasoned, he was the envy of every man. He got an almost perverse sense of pleasure at the way every man looked at Carole and fantasized about having her. But Carole was his and his alone.

In spite of her message, or perhaps because of it, he decided to go home early and surprise her with a dozen roses. She was an addiction, and Mark found it difficult to be apart from his lovely bride even for short periods of time. He was looking forward to surprising her—or was it paranoia, plain and simple? He wasn't sure. Perhaps there was still a lingering residue of mistrust from past failed relationships.

Maybe if Mark had known Carole more than two weeks before they got married, this ultimate betrayal wouldn't be happening to him now. Maybe he should have listened to what some of his friends had said about Carole: Too wild. Too mysterious. Too sexual. Too much. He knew they were right; why hadn't he listened?

Now, standing in *his* living room, Mark could not believe what he was seeing. A short, silver-gray-haired, good-looking, well-built man in his fifties, whom the gun-wielding woman called "Marty," looked up at him from between his wife's legs and said, "Watch me fuck your wife, and if you say one word…you're dead!"

Chapter 2

WEDNESDAY NIGHT–7:05 P.M.

CHICAGO, ILLINOIS

Standing dumbfounded in the middle of his living room, Mark tried to block out the present moment. His thoughts drifted back to pain of the divorce from his first wife, Patty. She had complained that Mark was working too much, and she was right. When Mark had been married to Patty, he was never home. He was always at one of the sales offices. Although married a little over a year, he didn't devote any time to their marriage; fifteen to sixteen hours a day, sometimes seven days a week, he was busy quickly building one of the most profitable condominium conversion companies in Chicago.

Mark was trying to remember the good times with Patty; were there really any? he wondered. At first, things seemed good. Only two years after graduating from college with honors, Mark, at twenty-three years of age, was grossing over $100,000 a week. And because of his age, became somewhat of a celebrity in Chicago. He appeared on the cover of newspapers and magazines at least twice a month. Patty and Mark attended all the right parties. Everyone liked Mark. He possessed all the right stuff; hardworking, smart, clever, funny, kind, generous, and honest. His dashing good looks perfectly complemented his dynamic personality. Rigorous daily workouts at the health club were therapy for the intense stress and pressures of his business, and he kept all six feet of his tanned, well-built body trim and muscular. Golden-brown hair accentuated one of his most striking features—deep-set, thick-lashed, hazel eyes that reflected a hint of the gentle nature of his soul. Seemingly unaware of the flirtations from all kinds of women, it never occurred to Mark to cheat on his wife. Ironically, his strong sense of values made him even more magnetic to females hoping to capture his attention. Mark was riding high, and then suddenly it all came crashing down. One Sunday night, he was hosting a charity ball for the Sloan-Kettering Cancer Foundation. On Monday morning, the Federal Reserve started raising interest rates. By Friday, the interest on his construction loan had almost doubled; his real estate career was over. In one week he had lost millions of dollars. Then he lost Patty.

Worse still, she had left him for his best friend. If he had not worked all the time and had given Patty more attention, he might have saved his marriage. Everyone made choices. Mark felt, with great remorse, that he had made his choice while still a young child. He thought that money and power would make him happier and less insecure. The truth was that he couldn't be happy and love someone else when he didn't even love himself.

🍁   🍁   🍁

Growing up in affluence in a big house on the lake in the northern suburbs of Chicago, breathing the rarefied North Shore air, Mark was most definitely a product of his environment—wealthy parents, loving but dysfunctional, a word no one used or understood back then. Being raised in and around money sat well with him. He not only was drawn to "the good life," but he had an insatiable craving for more. His father had always told him, "You're going to end up a millionaire." This was more an order than a statement. Mark was raised as a stereotypical "Jew." Money was the mantra, the measure of true success. He had succeeded financially at a very early age, but emotionally he was still a child. It took almost seven years, after losing his money and his wife, to make it back again. His portfolio was more diversified now. He was also a lot smarter and a lot wiser, except when it came to women. That's why he avoided relationships, and why he should have avoided Carole. What in the hell had he been thinking? Marrying someone he had just met, letting the little head control the big one; what a fool he was. How could one guy so consistently mess up when it came to women? Would he never learn? He wished he knew the answer to that question, but clearly he did not.

In a month he would be thirty and was again a multimillionaire. Big deal, he thought—money—but no brains—at least when it came to the opposite sex. Everything was good except his personal life. He had none. It was easier to ignore emotions, therefore allowing little chance for personal failure. Personal isolation ensured business success.

Mark was successful in business. His personal life was another story; no hobbies and no real friends, just work. Mark worked hard for his desires. He was not just a workaholic; he had built emotional walls around himself, too. It had cost him his first marriage with Patty. He even surprised himself when he said yes to marrying Carole. Mark had many regrets. Seeing his new wife, Carole, naked on the couch, he knew he had made a terrible mistake. He regretted how stupid he was, how little he really knew about life; he felt sorry for himself and angry at the same time.

The meaning of life, Mark had discovered long ago, was exactly what he wanted it to be. No more, no less. He had put a lot of work into his business success and was rewarded. He hadn't put any effort into his first marriage, and that's why it failed. Afterward, he went out with women when he had time but wouldn't even consider a serious relationship. He wouldn't know a good relationship if it bit him in the ass. Akin to being a spectator in life as opposed to a participant, he felt like an outsider looking in, and very lonely. He swore he wouldn't be hurt again. Why had he allowed Carole to penetrate his walls—his protection? He should never have allowed himself to try to love again. Or maybe, Mark wondered, with Carole, was it simply lust? Maybe Mark had never even really been in love. Maybe for some people it worked, but not for him. Why had he tried again? He knew that when it came to affairs of the heart, he couldn't win. Hell, the only relationships he understood were those of business. In college, his favorite singer/writer had been Paul Simon. "I am a rock. I am an island…," Simon had written. Let no one in and you couldn't be hurt; lonely—but safe; words Mark lived by when it came to women. Now the safe harbor of his self-imposed isolation was stripped away—lonely would have been a better feeling than the horror he was experiencing at this moment.

🍁 🍁 🍁

Watching his wife and "Marty" casually getting off the couch in the living room and sauntering into the bedroom, naked and smiling, was more than one man could handle. Mark's poor judgment when it came to relationships with women was confirmed once again as he viewed the wild scene in his living room. Although he had been educated at the best schools, there were no classes in relationships taught at New Trier High School or NYU.

"Excuse me, Hon, I best be getting in there before they call. And you better leave," the naked woman said to Mark, matter-of-factly, as she started walking to the bedroom, the gun still in her hand but lowered to her side.

Mark had a deep belief in the sanctity of a monogamous relationship. His first instinct was to divorce Carole—after he killed her. He should have never allowed himself to open up again. But an inner voice told him that he needed to find some answers. The whole scene seemed surreal. Although he saw Carole having sex with another man, he simply couldn't believe, or didn't *want* to believe, Carole's act of betrayal. Was he dreaming? Christ, they had just gotten married and were supposedly deeply in love or, at least in lust, and devoted to each other! Weren't they? With the roses scattered at his feet and the muffled sound of laughter from the bedroom echoing in his ears, Mark turned slowly and staggered toward the door. Although what he was witnessing was obvious, in no need of interpretation, he was too emotionally torn up to try and figure out anything right now anyway.

Mark couldn't handle this. One thing he was certain of, though, was that this nightmare was only just the beginning. Then he felt himself slipping into an almost welcomed, deeper state of thought-obliterating shock as he staggered into the hallway, pushed the button, and waited for the elevator to take him out of hell.

Chapter 3

WEDNESDAY NIGHT–AN HOUR LATER

CHICAGO, ILLINOIS

Mark was nursing his fourth Ketel One Gibson on the rocks, minus the little cocktail onions and the Vermouth.

He had driven almost four miles west of his apartment on Lake Shore Drive. He wanted to make sure he wouldn't run into anyone he knew. Surely no one would recognize him here. He had to think. Drinking was a rarity for Mark. If he had two dozen drinks a year, that was a lot. But now he desperately needed to calm his racing mind and his heavy heart. He was ruefully reflective, painfully running the scene with Carole through his mind and then replaying it over and over. He felt like shit. The dark, dreary, dimly lit bar was filled with a thick blue haze of smoke and the rancid, pungent odor of cigarettes, stale beer, vomit, urine, and disinfectant. If indeed, "misery loves company," then this was definitely the place to find it. Mark Goodwin's grooming and expensive attire contrasted sharply with his surroundings, and yet a common bond was instantly recognizable; in one way or another at that moment in time they were all "losers." A Merle Haggard-type song, in which some guy fell in love with his horse much to the chagrin of his jealous wife, and other moronic lover-loser songs, kept playing on the jukebox. "How many goddamned times are they going to play that crap?" Mark asked of no one in particular. Then another country tune came on:

> "You stole my pickup truck, you took all my money."
> "You took my wife and dog, you broke my heart and nose."
> "You smashed my guitar, but I'm too depressed to shoot myself."

The Westside Bar and Beer Garden was watering only green-toothed, unshaven uglies with vacuous expressions staring back at themselves in the old, faded smoke-stained mirror behind the bar. The shabbily dressed patrons were an assortment of bums, dope addicts, and dipsos that looked like the A-Team from the New York City Port Authority at two in the morning. Mark felt as bad as they looked, maybe even worse.

Hard as he tried, he couldn't calm down. What did he really know about Carole? he asked himself. He wondered what she really did for a living. Supposedly, she owned a boutique on Chicago's fashionable Oak Street. How could she afford that expensive apartment she had rented? And that silver Jaguar, the mink coats? Where did she get all her money? The scene kept playing in his head like a bad nightmare. Why was Carole screwing that old guy? And why in their apartment? Who was the naked woman who had held the gun to his head? Surely Carole had known that Mark would be home from the health club at any minute. Did she plan this just to hurt him? If so, then why? Or was Carole forced to take part in this orgy? Was she drugged and didn't know what was going on? No one acted surprised when he walked in. It was almost as if the whole event had been staged. But why? It simply didn't make any sense. And what was he to make of the woman's statement that Carole was an "Outfit Cunt?" "Outfit" in Chicago was an infamous moniker for the Mob.

"I'm so lonely I could die" appropriately played from the jukebox as Mark's anxiety attack produced a wave of nausea—he raced to the bathroom.

Chapter 4

WEDNESDAY NIGHT–TWO HOURS LATER

CHICAGO, ILLINOIS

Mark's head felt like someone had driven a six-inch nail straight through it. He hated drinking, and could no longer tolerate this run-down hillbilly tavern in which he had been a self-imposed prisoner for the last couple of hours. But he wasn't drunk. The booze was just making him more traumatized. All he felt was rage and anger. He made the decision to go back home.

"Fuck Carole!" Mark swore as he was driving back to his apartment. He finally knew what he was going to do.

He would pack some bags, get away to Fort Lauderdale for a few days, and leave a note for Carole instructing her to remove all of her belongings from the apartment and get out in forty-eight hours. Mark didn't want to discuss anything. He was not interested in any explanations from Carole. She could go straight to hell as far as he was concerned. He wouldn't allow himself to stay hurt. Mark tried to act tough, convincing himself that he would get over Carole and rationalizing that his feelings for her were really lust, not love, anyway.

Mark pulled his BMW into the garage of their apartment; no, he corrected himself, this was now *his* apartment. Yes, Carole was beautiful—he had never experienced such incredible sex. Yes, he was obsessed with her, but he would set his mind on forgetting her. Mark was actually crying; he hurt that badly. Did he really love her, he wondered? Probably just blinded by her beauty.

When he walked into the apartment, all the lights were on. No one was there. Good. She is probably out screwing someone else, he thought. As Mark moved from room to room, evidence of her guilt was everywhere. Carole's bra and skimpy silk panties were on the sofa along with other articles of clothing; empty champagne bottles lay strewn throughout the rooms. There were candles that had been left burning, casting a golden glow that lit the doorway to the bedroom. Mark nervously began moving slowly toward the beacon of light—the sound of his feet sinking into the plush carpet was almost eerie as he made his way down the hall. He could see the flickering of the clustered, tall ivory candles reflecting in the beveled mirrors that surrounded the black marble Jacuzzi in the spa room just to the left of the bedroom door. Mark gasped, "What the hell?!" The cloudy water of an abandoned bubble bath still filled the tub, and various sex toys dangled from the polished gold faucets. Another half-empty bottle of champagne and three crystal glasses lay on a mound of still-moist, fluffy white monogrammed towels that were piled in a heap on the floor.

Sickened by being forced to endure such personal invasion, his skin began to crawl, and Mark suddenly started retching violently. Stumbling over to the basin, he splashed his face with cold water. There were no words to describe the depth of the degradation that Mark experienced right now and nothing to prepare him for what was to follow.

Mark walked into the adjoining master suite. The familiar fragrance of Carole's favorite perfume and the sweet smell of the scented candles lingered heavily in the room like an opium haze. "Why…goddammit…why? I've gotta get out of here!" he cried out at the top of his lungs. He was not interested in any phony explanations from Carole. There was nothing left to the marriage—nothing she could say—nothing to discuss. "She can go to hell!" he screamed to no one.

Mark left Carole a short, terse, simple note telling her it was over and to get her stuff out immediately. He threw some clothes into his suitcase, went down to the lobby, and got into a cab. "Ritz Carlton, driver," Mark said.

Chapter 5

❀

WEDNESDAY NIGHT LATER

CHICAGO, ILLINOIS

The trendy restaurant was nestled among the exclusive boutiques of East Walton Street on Chicago's Gold Coast. The food was decent, but the prices were outrageous. Marty Serachi loved this place, and although he was short in stature, he was always treated like royalty, which made him feel ten feet tall. Table number one was reserved for him every Wednesday night at 8:00 P.M., and he loved the ritual that occurred upon his arrival. The staff catered to his beck and call each moment of every visit. The maitre d' brought two bottles of expensive wine over to the table, and the sommelier proceeded to uncork the first bottle: a 1982 Petrus. He removed the cork from the opener and placed it in Marty's hand. Marty ceremoniously brought the cork up to the light, studied it, then passed it under his nose, sniffing the aroma of the fine wine. He then smiled and motioned for the sommelier to pour a taster. He bit off a piece of a bread roll, chewed it, swallowed to cleanse his palate trying to emulate a class act; and then raised the glass of $1,000 wine with his thumb and two fingers, took a gulp, swished it around slowly in his mouth and swallowed, giving the maitre d' and sommelier his nod of approval. The other bottle, a $600 1990 Lafitte Rothschild, was opened so it could breathe and be just perfect for dessert. Marty loved being here with gorgeous young girls at his side. He was always aware that everyone in the restaurant would stare at them. He relished being the object of their envy or disdain; it was hard to tell which. But he really didn't care as long as all eyes were on him. His companion tonight was a knockout.

Marty Serachi was "connected," but he was also Jewish, which meant he was not and could never be a "made man," a designation reserved only for members of the Mob's elite "inner circle," whose true Italian heritage could be documented over hundreds of years. Growing up on Taylor Street in a Chicago neighborhood of Italians and Jews, he had changed his name from "Stein" to "Serachi" to sound Italian. Though he wasn't even part Italian, Marty, nevertheless, possessed the "Good Fellas" demeanor.

From running numbers to making book, he had risen through the ranks of the Chicago Outfit over the last twenty-five years. Marty was born street-smart, and he seemed to have a knack for being a crook. He never did well in school. That type of education had never interested him. His family was dirt poor, and he had started hustling at a very early age. After personally handling a hit for Meyer Lansky many years ago, he had progressed to the upper echelon of the Chicago Outfit. Marty had paid his dues and now, at fifty-five, he had it all, whatever "all" was. At this moment "all" was being the old guy with the young, hot chick. Being seen with gorgeous young women at his side was an important part of the ritual. The "sleeve jewelry" on his arm this particular evening, named Janet, was his favorite young possession. Marty's "Napoleon Complex"-commonly referred to as "short-man's syndrome"-was extremely intimidating to him. He was incredibly insecure about his stature. However, the fact that this young beauty was almost a foot taller than he was of no importance. As long as they were both sitting down, they appeared to be of similar height. He always would have the girl he was with be seated at the table before he would come over to join her.

"You look absolutely ravishing tonight," Marty said to this young beauty, as he toasted her with his wine glass. "A lot better than you looked earlier at your sister, Carole's, apartment."

"Thank you," Janet replied, forcing a smile.

"I hope you're feeling better," he offered.

Casting her eyes downward, Janet didn't answer. She was scared and was waiting for the right opportunity to begin, fully aware of Marty's violent temper. She thought that maybe after he got some wine into him—no, that wouldn't make any difference, she quickly reasoned; he was a killer whether drunk or sober. This was not going to be easy, but she didn't care. She had made up her mind. She took a sip of the Petrus to get her courage up.

"Marty, we need to talk," Janet began, setting her wine glass down, hoping to calm her slightly trembling hand.

"About what?" replied Marty.

"A lot of things."

"What things?" he asked, his face taking on a slight flush.

She could see that Marty was starting to get angry and continued cautiously. "Well, it's just that...uh...well...um... things have changed."

"Nothing's changed," he interrupted her coldly.

"But...," Janet attempted to continue before he angrily cut her off.

"But nothing!" Marty began, his voice rising, disturbing the people at the other tables, causing them to stare. "Listen, babe," he snapped back, reaching over and tightly cutting off the circulation in her hand, "we made a deal! We didn't come to you. *You* came to *us!* We have more than fulfilled our end of the bargain. So, you, my lovely, will not only continue to honor the terms of the agreement, but you'll do so with the same degree of willingness you displayed when you eagerly entered into it! You got that? A deal is a deal!"

"Whatever you say, darling." She batted her perfectly curled lashes in a fierce attempt to control the tears that were welling up in her eyes. She hated Marty Serachi, who had brought her into the Outfit. Janet had to find some way out, a compromise, anything to protect both herself and her sister, Carole, whom she loved more than anyone else in the world—and she had to find it soon! This evil, vicious man was in control of her life and—as she was all too aware—her demise; and now the life of her sister also hung in the balance because of what had happened in Mark's condo just over an hour ago.

"Where are you going?" Marty asked Janet as she suddenly got up from the table.

"Just to the ladies' room, dear. I'll be back by the time dessert comes." Janet, scared shitless, went toward the ladies' room to call her friend, Deemis Whitacre, in Rhode Island for help. Having done so, she snuck out the back door of the fancy eatery, grabbed a cab to the airport, and within the hour was on her way to Rhode Island. Marty would be furious—but Janet didn't care at this particular moment. Too much was at stake. Marty was holding Janet's sister, Carole, hostage, at least she hoped so—wanting to believe the lesser of two evils and praying that Marty had not already killed her sister.

Chapter 6

THURSDAY MORNING PREDAWN

PROVIDENCE, RHODE ISLAND

Marty was going fucking nuts. He still didn't know where Janet was. He had not talked to her since she had abandoned him at the restaurant, and her whereabouts were still unknown. Had he known that she had flown to see his associate Deemis in Providence, Marty would have probably had them both killed on the spot. Janet had been so scared after being forced to take part in the orgy at Carole and Mark's apartment and then being told by Marty later at dinner that her sister was being held hostage to erase any thoughts she might have about resigning from the Outfit. She hoped that maybe by seeing Deemis, he could help her; hence her flight to Rhode Island. She would use Deemis in any way she could. As soon as Janet arrived at Deemis's apartment in the heart of Providence, Deemis got Janet a joint and a drink from the bar. Janet inhaled the joint ferociously and slammed down three straight shots of tequila. Then they had two minutes of sex, and Janet smoked more pot and continued drinking. Deemis hadn't smoked pot since his father died. That was two years ago, and he was even now, unsuccessfully, trying to come to grips with his father's demise. He still felt guilty about not showing grief at his father's passing. Even at the funeral he felt remorse because he couldn't feel any emotions of sadness. He had loved his father, or supposed he had. At the least, Deemis didn't hate him anymore. He was relieved, not saddened, when his father had unexpectedly expired from a heart attack. Wilhelm Whitacre had been a successful surgeon, and he never forgave his son for his decision to turn down medical school in favor of becoming a lawyer. Wilhelm never told Deemis about his feelings of disappointment that he hadn't followed in his footsteps, but Deemis tacitly knew it.

"Why would you want to become a lawyer? There are too damn many already," his father had often told him, but Deemis had known even then that if he became a doctor he would never be as successful as his father. So, instead of living in the shadow of a great surgeon, he decided he would try to become a great lawyer. Deemis believed he could make his father proud. But Deemis realized, shortly after being fired from the first big law firm that he had worked at, that he didn't like being a lawyer. Deemis also realized that he would never be a great lawyer. He simply wasn't that good. However, after going to work for his wife's father, he realized that he could become rich and powerful by being a Mob lawyer. That, he thought, would gain his father's respect and love. He had been sadly mistaken. Now that the great surgeon was gone, he realized that he had wasted most of his life trying to gain the old man's love and acceptance. Deemis longed to finally be happy. Happiness and peace of mind had always eluded him and seemed beyond his comprehension, but Janet, he thought, at least sexually, might change some of that. Janet played Deemis like a fiddle. She was a consummate whore and knew how to drive him crazy. She had been introduced to Deemis by Marty, to "service him" whenever he would come to Chicago. Janet suspected that Deemis was pretty high up in the Mob's hierarchy and that maybe she could get some assistance from him. That's why she had just flown to his secret city apartment that his wife knew nothing about. Maybe Deemis could help her with her sister. On the phone in Chicago when Janet had frantically called Deemis just a few hours ago from the restaurant, Deemis, simply wanting to get fucked, had assured Janet that he could help her with her sister's plight and that she should get a plane out of O'Hare and meet him at his apartment in Providence. Janet always played a role worthy of an academy award with Deemis. He played along, totally aware of how full of shit she was. He knew that she was acting as if they were in some soap opera, trying to make him think that they were both risking their lives by turning against the Mob. Deemis's way of turning against the Mob, Janet thought, was by purposely leaking information to her in order to screw up a Mob racetrack deal, and Janet was doing her usual double-dealing, scamming and whoring. She thought she had Deemis totally pussy whipped. Janet thought that she made Deemis feel young and alive sexually. Janet, drama queen, skilled whore, acted like they were two lost souls who had both crossed the line into the nefarious world of the Mob and its power, money, sex, and sleaze. Hard as they tried, in their relentless search for the unholy grail, they had not found true happiness until they met each other—at least that's what Janet hoped Deemis thought. "Pussy Drama,"—that's what Janet had called it—she had created it to play with Deemis's mind. Men were so stupid, Janet mused. Deemis was not stupid. He had been around whores like Janet his entire life. He had told Janet about the racetrack deal because he wanted to screw up the deal to see his associates get in trouble. He used Janet simply as a conduit, a messenger. Contrary to what Janet thought—that Deemis trusted her and felt safe confiding in her about the race track—Deemis did not trust Janet one bit and knew by asking her to keep a secret she clearly would not.

"I missed you so much," Janet said, as she exhaled the thick whitish-yellow cloud of pot from her lungs. But that was a lie—she couldn't have cared less about Deemis.

"Me too, honey," lied Deemis.

"I've been so scared. Is my sister okay?"

"Carole is fine," Deemis lied again. He didn't know anything about her sister. Furthermore, he didn't give a damn. Just because he was fucking Janet he didn't feel he had to be honest. Deemis didn't even say goodbye to Janet; it was time to get back to his wife, but Janet was already so doped up and drunk that she had passed out before he could say anything. Deemis wanted Janet to believe that maybe he could intervene and help Carole so Janet would have a reason to continue fucking him.

Chapter 7

❊

EARLY THURSDAY MORNING

PROVIDENCE, RHODE ISLAND

Janet woke up at 3:00 A.M., alone and disoriented in Deemis's apartment. Where was he? Probably back home with his wife. Janet wasn't sure if she had been sleeping or had passed out from smoking too much pot, drinking tequila, or boredom from sex with Deemis. She grabbed her purse off the nightstand in the bedroom, pulled out a bottle of pills, opened it, and, to calm herself, swallowed two Xanex without water. Everything was happening so fast—too fast. She needed to get a grip, to calm down, and sort things out. Her big mistake in the past had been in being honest with Marty. What had she been thinking? She knew now that she never should have leveled with Marty about her life and trusted him, and then painfully remembered that she had once loved him. Janet had even been so naïve as to once think that Marty loved her. How stupid could she be? Her big mistake was to confide in Marty about how much she loved and envied her sister, Carole. If she had not talked about Carole to Marty, he probably never would have known about her. Marty was nothing but a wannabe high-class pimp, liar, thief, and murderer. He was a user. Months ago, when Janet had first told Marty that she wanted out of the Outfit, he had told her that she was nothing more than a high-class hooker but said he would think about her request. What a pig! He just wanted to make love to her; no, not to make love; Marty didn't know how to make love; he only knew how to fuck. Instead of being honest and telling the truth—that she could *never* get out—he lied and pretended to think it over so that he could continue to get fucked. Janet had no way of knowing that Marty was probably following her when she went to see her sister Carole, earlier that night. He probably had her phone tapped, too, to keep tabs on her. She had no one else to turn to except Carole. She had no friends to talk to, and she certainly couldn't tell her parents. They wouldn't understand or, for that matter, probably wouldn't even care. If anything, her father would probably be upset. Janet was giving him $1,000 a month cash. Instead of being appreciative, he came to expect it. Hours earlier, when she went to Mark's apartment, she was just about to confess and tell Carole everything when Marty and Renée appeared, seemingly out of nowhere. Renée was one of the hookers whom Janet had worked with. They had been in a ménage-à-trois with Marty more times than Janet cared to admit. Carole heard a knock at the door, and when she opened it expecting to see her sister, Janet, Marty and Renée forced themselves in. Janet was so confused; she vaguely remembered Renée putting some kind of foul-smelling rag over Carole's mouth and nose causing Carole to pass out—but she couldn't remember much more; everything was a blur. Janet began to scream out in her concern for Carole. But Marty had told her to shut up and moments later had explained that her sister had been escorted out in the service elevator. Janet knew enough not to question Marty and did as she was told. Marty had assured Janet that her sister was fine. He wanted to fuck Janet and Renée in Carole and Mark's condo. Janet had said no. But as usual, she had no choice. The most important thing on her mind was the safety and welfare of her sister. What was Marty up to? What had he done with Carole? And why insist on sex in Mark and her sister's apartment? She vaguely remembered

Carole's new husband, Mark, walking in on them. She had never met Mark, but recognized him from a picture in a real estate magazine she had seen. She knew that Marty was an exhibitionist, in addition to his other kinky perversions. Marty had fucked her while Carole's new husband was watching. He got off on it. Why was he doing this? She had taken a couple of Quaaludes right before she went to her sister's to calm herself down. One would have been more than enough. She was still kind of out of it and had trouble remembering exactly what had happened.

After the sexcapade was over, Marty and Renée told Janet to relax. When Janet went home, she immediately tried calling her sister's apartment, knowing she had been kidnapped. The line was busy. She was so drugged and confused, she wasn't even sure if she was calling the right number. She had to get ready to meet Marty.

Later, when Janet met Marty for dinner on East Walton Street, he made it quite clear that she could not get out of the Outfit, and that if she tried and did not come around and stop this crazy talk, her sister would be killed. Terrified, Janet managed to slip away from Marty and called Deemis on his cellular phone in Rhode Island, trying not to sound too hysterical. Janet hoped that Deemis was falling in love with her. She was a good manipulator but not that good. She also was sure that she didn't love, or for that matter even like, Deemis. She was just using him. He was powerful, maybe even one of Marty's bosses, although she couldn't be sure of that.

Deemis was already in his apartment when Janet was dropped off by the limo. The doorman, whom Deemis had told to expect Janet, let her in. Deemis greeted her at the door. Sometime after Deemis left, and she awoke from her drunken-drugged stupor, she called Marty, obviously waking him up.

"I don't know where the fuck you are, but if you're not in my office by noon, your sister's dead," Marty angrily told her.

Deemis obviously had no clout with Marty regarding Carole's safety.

"I'm out of town seeing a friend," she told Marty.

"I don't care where you are," Marty screamed. "I expect to see you by noon in my office, or…"

"Where's my sister?" Janet interrupted. "What have you done to Carole?"

"Don't worry your pretty little head. She's fine—for now anyway."

"If anything happens to her, I'll…"

"You'll what?" Marty fired back.

Janet paused and realized that threatening Marty was not smart, extremely dangerous, and would get her absolutely nowhere.

"Nothing. Look Marty, I'm sorry. But why are you taking your anger out on my sister? She didn't do anything to you. Why do you want to hurt Carole? It's not fair," she begged.

"Look kid," Marty told her, "I don't give a shit about your sister. I am only concerned about you. What the fuck is the matter with you anyway? I thought you were smart enough to know that you can't just up and quit the Mob. That's not the way it works. I thought your head was screwed on straight. I'm in a shitload of trouble because of you," he screamed on the phone. "You've made me look real bad to my people, like a fucking fool. You shouldn't have left me at dinner without telling me where you were going. I don't appreciate anybody making me look like a fucking idiot. Especially some crazy cunt," Marty snapped.

Janet hated that word, but she had tried to mollify Marty. "You're right. I've been thinking crazy. Forgive me, please Marty. I'm sorry," she begged.

"Well, that's better," Marty tersely told her.

"I don't know what's gotten into me lately. But please, my sister has nothing to do with this. Let Carole go and you won't have any more problems with me, I swear."

"Okay kid, I believe you." But Marty did not believe a word she was saying. The first meeting that required her expertise was tomorrow night in Washington, D.C. He needed Janet back in Chicago now to outline her role in tomorrow's operation. He also missed fucking her.

"I'll be back tomorrow, but I need to know that my sister is all right," Janet replied.

"Not a problem. She's all right. Trust me," Marty promised her.

Janet had no choice but to trust this pig. "But how will I know for sure?"

"We'll talk when I see you." Marty abruptly hung up the phone and went back to bed.

🍁   🍁   🍁

Dr. Bernstein couldn't sleep more than a few hours a night. He hated himself for what he was being forced to do to Janet—but he had no choice. The Mob had threatened him and his wife, and he was being blackmailed.

Chapter 8

❦

DEEMIS'S STORY

PROVIDENCE, RHODE ISLAND

Deemis Whitacre had been a lawyer for years. When he had graduated from Harvard Law School, he had a bright future ahead of him. He was tall, blond, and possessed deep blue eyes with an angular jaw and an infectious smile that women could not get enough of. He'd been captain of the swimming team and was always tanned from playing tennis in the spring and summer; the Wolff electric beach machine kept up his tan in the fall and winter. The tanning machine was in his second bedroom, with his weights, treadmill, and stairmaster. The ladies loved him, and this suited Deemis just fine. He had gone to work for Baxter & MacDemzie, one of the largest law firms in the country. Susan Attenborough, one of the managing partners in the Boston office, twenty years his senior, had taken a liking to his brains and body. As one of the firm's and the country's top environmental lawyers, she traveled the country extensively. Deemis was her apprentice, both in law and in bed. For her age, Susan Attenborough was a striking woman and relentless in the sack. She did not spend a lot of time conducting business in the office. Rather, she preferred to take care of business over three-martini power lunches at her favorite haunts, and Deemis was her constant companion. He loved the attention of being catered to by the owners and managers of the best restaurants in the country: Jesse Weiss Joe's Stone Crab in Miami, and now in Chicago, for the Bloody Marys and Stoners; Wolfgang Puck and Barbara Lazaroff at Spago in Los Angeles for the Jewish pizza and celebs; Wally Ganz's Palm in Los Angeles with Gigi; or in Chicago with Johnnie Blandino for the steaks. Chicago had great steak houses. Susan frequented all the best steak joints with Deemis: Gibson's, Mortons, Gene and Georgetti's, Eli's. Deemis and Susan were always given the best table in the house. When in New York, which was often, Susan always took Deemis to the famous LeCirque 2000. They were given special treatment by the charming proprietor, Sirio Maccioni, and enjoyed the extensive wine list. This was the true home of the power lunch. LeCirque 2000 always packed in the celebs and power brokers of the world.

But Deemis grew tired of Susan and the firm. He felt like a male hooker, always at Susan's beck and call. She was very possessive, even calling him at home on the weekends, ostensibly to discuss business but actually to check up on him. Everyone at the firm knew about Susan and Deemis's relationship, much to the displeasure of Deemis. The secretaries at the office in Boston would always refuse Deemis's invitations to go out because they were afraid of reprisals from Susan.

One day he was shopping for a suit at the Galleria in Boston, a few blocks from the office, when he first saw Penelope. Deemis, accidentally on purpose, bumped into her. He apologized profusely with all the charisma and charm he could muster, flaunting his good looks until Penny agreed to let him buy her a cup of coffee. She was stunning—a young version of Cybil Shephard. After three weeks of dating and no sex, then finding out that she was a virgin, Deemis proposed marriage to her. They decided to elope, then flew to Vegas and were married for $227 in an Elvis Chapel. Deemis was not willing to take any chances with Penny. Young and beautiful, a virgin, he snapped her up and married her instantly. Deemis believed that a prize like Penny would not be available for long, so he married her before someone else could. It was on their honeymoon, in a luxurious suite at Caesar's Palace in Las Vegas, that Deemis first suspected that perhaps he had made a mistake. Deemis assumed because of the instant attraction he thought they both had for each other that the sex would be fantastic, heightened even further because of Penny's past chastity. She was such a tremendous kisser. In fact, kissing was the only thing Penny seemed to be good at, and unfortunately, the sex was terrible. She didn't like sex at all. Penny would rather cuddle and kiss, and after three days of marriage, even that seemed more obligatory to satisfy Deemis than anything else. Deemis had hoped that maybe their sex life would improve after time, but he had a gnawing feeling in the pit of his stomach that this was as good as it was going to get, and this was not good enough for him.

Once back in Boston at Baxter & MacDemzie, Susan was outraged that Deemis had taken a wife and promptly had him fired from the firm. Deemis could easily go to other firms, but the idea of being low man on the totem pole, busting his ass, working seven days a week, trying to bill two-thousand-plus hours a year was not appealing. No Susan, no sex, no more great power lunches. He would be reduced to doing scut work, research, and kissing ass. His arrogance would not allow him to be a commoner. He wanted more, even if he was too lazy to really work for it. He felt that the world *owed* him.

Penny's father was a well-connected lawyer in Providence, Rhode Island, who had a small, although very prosperous, law firm catering almost exclusively to a handful of rich, old, and apparently Mob-connected clientele. Her father had offered Deemis $175,000 per year as a starting salary with a 10 percent yearly automatic increase in pay, plus bonuses. Deemis took the job. Why not? He figured no one else would pay him that kind of money for his mediocre legal mind, especially since his reputation was questionable after having been fired from Baxter & MacDemzie.

Deemis immediately disliked Penny's father. Deemis had only met him once during his three-week whirlwind courtship with Penny, but since this was to be the old man's last year before retiring, he figured that taking the job with his father-in-law was easier than starting over again at a big firm.

Penny and Deemis moved from Boston to Providence, where Penny found them a new duplex apartment, and Deemis promptly found a new girlfriend. If Deemis had just devoted to the law firm 10 percent of the time he spent chasing women, he would have made Penny and her father a lot happier. But he hated her father, and he disliked with a passion the rich, smug, and nefarious clientele he had inherited. He was also growing to hate Penny; sex between them was virtually nonexistent.

Monthly, he went to Chicago for the firm's business to meet Marty. Deemis would finish his boring business in one day then spend two days fucking his brains out before returning home. He liked Chicago because of the action and the abundance of beautiful women. Deemis always stayed in a suite at the Ambassador East Hotel on the corner of Goethe and State streets.

Deemis had made a lot of friends in Chicago; primarily young, luscious, easy, eager-to-please women. Located right in his hotel was the famous, plush Pump Room, totally restored to its original charm of the thirties by Rich Melman of the Lettuce Entertain You restaurants. It was a great place to pick up ladies and high-class hookers.

Within their first year of marriage, painfully aware of Deemis's infidelities, Penny developed a drinking problem. From morning to passing out at night, she remained in a perpetual drunken stupor, becoming fat, unkempt, and always wearing the same depressing landlady-green housecoat. One day, drunk as usual, she stumbled down the stairs, and as a result of the accident, became paralyzed from the neck down. They had to move to a ranch house so that Penny could get around in a wheel chair. Penny and her father blamed Deemis for the accident. They felt that if he had not always been cheating on her, she wouldn't have turned to drinking, and the accident would never have happened. Deemis felt guilty about it; deep down inside he blamed himself too. They were right; he was a piece of shit.

🍁 🍁 🍁

That was years ago and he was still feeling guilty about her accident. He knew he had wasted his life. Trapped in a situation with Penny and her father (unfortunately, still alive at age eighty-nine) Deemis had long ago given up hope for any semblance of happiness. He had total disdain and resentment toward everyone and everything—he was a crotchety old man—he had become what years ago he had hated in others. Even his myriad affairs no longer gave him any real satisfaction; however, the chance to see Penny, her father, and her father's friends and clients suffer—really suffer—brought a smile to his face and an excitement that had not been there for years. This is why he leaked the story to his new girlfriend/whore, Janet, in Chicago, about the Narragansett Racetrack in Pawtucket, located just outside of Providence, Rhode Island—a deal the Mob had been working on for almost two years. Deemis knew she would probably tell the wrong people; hopefully if someone else heard about it, bought the track, and kept it open, it would be subject to an audit and the board would be forced to undergo scrutiny of their books. As a result of this action, all of the current board members would then either commit suicide, go to jail, or be murdered—Deemis would have revenge at last! Oh! If only! he thought to himself. Deemis was visibly excited as he stared at his still-handsome face in the mirrored reflection of his shiny white Rolls Royce. Finally a way out! And an end to his lifetime of misery! They would all pay dearly, and they had it coming! They deserved to have their lives destroyed like his had been. But Deemis was not really thinking too clearly. Sure, he would get great satisfaction out of seeing a lot of people's lives ruined; he just hadn't thought long enough to consider the possibility that *he* could be one of those people, too.

Chapter 9

LATER THURSDAY MORNING

CHICAGO, ILLINOIS

Marty Serachi seldom felt nervous. He had power, money, and an abundance of beautiful women at his command. At one time he had had the world by the balls. So then, why was he sweating as he sat in his LaSalle Street office? Beads of perspiration dripped from his tanned forehead. His collar was moist and he could feel the dampness dripping under his arms. It was only 10:30 in the morning and Marty had already had two J&Bs (Jewish Booze) from his well-stocked bar built into the wall of bookcases containing books he had never read. They were there for appearance only. His boss, the Don, was coming to see him from Miami. The Don's private Gulf Stream Jet had already landed at O'Hare, and he would be here any minute. Marty knew he had committed major "fuckups," and he was very worried about how much the Don knew at this point.

Marty had a problem—a major problem that even he couldn't come close to getting a fix on. He knew that he couldn't be totally straight with the Don. He prayed that the situation with Janet wasn't that bad.

She had left him at dinner last night; she never came back for dessert after she went to the ladies' room. Marty had sat there for almost an hour before realizing that she was gone—he was still livid. But, how in the hell had the Don found out about Janet's disappearing act—who had told him? Marty knew that the Don must have been pissed off to no end. As he analyzed the situation for the hundredth time, he wished he could believe that it wasn't that bad. Marty, smart and raised never to trust anyone, had at least taken drastic action to hopefully minimize the potential for a greater problem—he had taken out insurance—life insurance—not on his life, but on Janet's, so to speak. It was far from a typical life insurance policy; Marty liked to think of it more as an "Outfit policy." If Janet didn't come around and straighten out, he would cash in on the policy, which meant that he would have her sister, Carole, whom he had arranged to be held hostage, executed. He felt certain that this "insurance" would do the trick. Janet knew him too well to risk crossing him. If not, Janet would also meet her demise, Marty had promised.

Such a regrettable waste of talent. Marty would definitely miss fucking Janet. He particularly loved that certain little "thing" that only she could do to him; it always triggered an explosive, ejaculatory eruption such as he had never been able to experience with any other broad. Nevertheless, business was business, and given his circumstances on this particular morning, if it came to his "getting paid back" by the Mob or "kissing off" her skilled, sweet pussy, there would be no question about his choice. Marty's own survival, as usual, was his utmost and only concern.

Marty had not trusted Janet for months, ever since she had told him that she wanted out of the Outfit, which was impossible. Janet knew this as well as Marty did. That's why he had planned last night's orgy involving Carole at the apartment when Mark walked in. Then, an hour later at dinner, he thought Janet would be firmly back in check after what had just occurred. Marty couldn't believe that Janet had the balls to "bolt" and leave him at the restaurant alone. He wasn't playing games and as promised, he would now kill Janet's sister, Carole and, without giving it a second thought, Janet, too. Marty continued to sweat profusely as he waited for the Don to arrive.

Chapter 10

❀

THURSDAY–SOMETIME

SOMEPLACE

Carole awoke and stared at the ceiling. How long had she been sleeping? she wondered. She felt groggy, like she had been drugged. Her mind was cloudy, confused, and fuzzy; she was disoriented. Where was she? How long had she been here? Wherever here was. All she could remember was a knock at the door last night; expecting to see her sister, she had opened the door. Marty and Renée forced themselves in with Janet. Then Renée put a rag that had an awful odor over her mouth and nose. That's the last thing she remembered. What kind of trouble had her sister gotten her into now? Carole hadn't even wanted Janet to come over to the apartment. She was nothing but trouble.

Now that Carole was madly in love and happily married, she had agreed to let her sister come over to see her one last time. She had planned to tell Janet never to call or visit again; she was through with her! She was finally going to use tough love. Carole started to cry. Where was Mark? Was he okay? God, how she loved him!

Chapter 11

❀

LATER THURSDAY MORNING

CHICAGO, ILLINOIS

Marty's boss glowered at him. "What the fuck is going on?" the Don barked.

"Well, things have gotten a little out of hand, but I think I've got it under control," replied Marty sheepishly. Janet had embarrassed Marty too many times—making him look stupid—being absent without permission or being out of contact for hours, even days, which enraged Marty. Janet would always tell Marty that she just needed to blow off a little steam, or get away, be by herself. Marty was tired of her disappearing stunts. But Janet's trip to Rhode Island last night was the last straw.

The Don was old, but there was no mistaking the look in his small, black, deep-set eyes; the eyes of a killer. Since he rarely left Miami anymore, Marty knew he was livid that he had to fly into Chicago. However, the Don would be back in Miami within a few hours and, hopefully, calmed down, Marty prayed.

"You dumb fucking Jew bastard!" he went off like a striking cobra. "We've been telling you for years to keep your dick in your pants, but no, not you, you don't fucking listen, you always got to be screwing the hired help."

"But…"

"But nothing, you stupid asshole. We've had enough of your stupid mistakes."

"Yeah, but I…"

"Just shut the fuck up and listen, you dumb kike. If you don't find that broad, Janet, by the end of the day, I'll kill you myself, you hymie bastard."

"She'll be back today," Marty said, trying to sound confident, "I talked to her late last night; she called a few hours after she left me at the restaurant."

"What the fuck makes you so sure she isn't lying?"

"Because we have her sister, Carole. We're holding her hostage."

"Where, you dumb piece of shit?"

"In a safe place where no one can find her. I'm telling you, don't worry, trust me, it'll be okay." Marty replied to the Don unconvincingly.

"Let's get one thing straight, you cock-sucker. I am worried, and I don't trust you, and the only way everything is okay is if *I say* it's okay, and right now *nothing's* okay, *do you hear me? Nothing!* I shoulda had you killed years ago!"

"But…" Marty stammered, trying to get the words out, sweating intensely. "We have her sister, Carole, and we are following the sister's husband, Mark, some rich real estate guy. They just got married, and by now he's got to be going nuts."

"What makes you so sure, fuck-face?"

"Because we made him go nuts. He saw me fucking his wife last night. We've been following him for months now, ever since Janet told us she wanted out. We even slipped him a note at the hotel he was staying at last night to scare the shit out of him. Don't worry, Boss." Marty realized he was starting to ramble. "Janet always comes back." Marty prayed to himself that that would be the case, as it had in the past.

"Comes back my ass, you dumb dickhead. If you hadn't been fucking the broad and just done what we were paying you to do, all this fucking shit wouldn't be happening now. And I would be back in Miami on my boat, relaxing, fishing, getting my dick sucked, instead of being here looking at your ugly fucking face."

"Look, I'm sorry, Boss, I really am."

"I told you to shut the fuck up! How much does this cunt know? I suppose you told her everything?"

"No, of course not," Marty lied, and *had* been lying to the Don about almost everything since their conversation began.

"Yeah, right. Knowing how you're always trying to impress pussy, you probably spilled your guts and told her everything. We should have never trusted a Jew. You dumb kike bastards think that this is some sort of fucking game instead of realizing that it's business."

"I told you, Boss, she doesn't know everything," Marty lied again, wondering if he would be alive by this time tomorrow.

"Does this bitch know what the real plan is?"

"No, of course not," Marty replied, feeling a little bit better that he hadn't told Janet anything. "Like everyone else, she thinks the purpose of the plan is to help get people out of jail, overcrowd the prisons, get more business for lawyers, loan money to cons and…"

"And you better be right, shithead," the Don interrupted, "or I'll cut your fucking balls off myself and make you eat them. Do you understand me, you asshole?"

"Yes, sir," Marty whimpered. "She knows nothing about the real plan of the Mob eventually taking over the privatization of prisons all over the country and becoming the biggest in the industry."

"Boss?" Marty tentatively queried.

"What, asshole?"

"Well, um…I know that it's none of my business…but how did you find out that Janet split on me last night?"

"You're right dickhead, it's none of your fucking business," the Don fired back.

Marty wondered if he was being followed. How else could the Don have known about Janet's leaving last night?

Chapter 12

❈

THURSDAY–EARLY MORNING

CHICAGO, ILLINOIS

The phone electronically chirped its dutiful wake-up call. Mark fumbled to reach the receiver. "Good morning, Mr. Goodwin. Would you care for some coffee and juice before your limousine arrives to take you to the airport?"

"Yes, thank you," Mark mumbled, still half asleep. Mark liked staying at the Ritz, especially on the concierge floor because of the extra perks. The price was more expensive than that of a normal room, but well worth it, he felt.

Mark had tried, to no avail, to block last night's scene with Carole out of his mind. He thought that spending the night in a junior suite would make him feel better. As usual, everything at the Ritz was up to par and very much to his liking. As he got out of the shower, Mark looked at the two plush white and blue hooded bathrobes with the Ritz-Carlton logo hanging on the bathroom door. He felt drained and empty, like the people last night at that god-awful bar. Something was missing. Namely, Carole. He longed for her to be there, or lusted for her, he wasn't sure which, but he wanted her and hated her at the same time. Mark wanted Carole to share the opulence of the suite but knew that was not to be. He still wished that what had happened last night was just a bad dream. How could he have been so wrong about her? In a moment of weakness he thought of calling her before he left for Fort Lauderdale. But what for? Was it pure lust or love? Hell, he wasn't sure if he even *knew* her. He had allowed himself to fall for her—to be vulnerable, to care. He hadn't done that since his first wife, Patty. Although he had loved Patty, he was never really "in love" with her. By nature, Mark was a very caring and concerned person, but his past experiences in the romance department had caused him to put up very solid walls. It took every ounce of willpower he had to keep himself from breaking down and calling Carole. He couldn't allow himself to forgive her or even try to understand what had happened last night; he needed to put her in the past. Fitfully tossing and turning all night, he had hardly slept a wink.

Wiping the steam from the mirror over the basin, Mark was suddenly taken aback. "My God!" he exclaimed out loud to the gaunt reflection that greeted him. He looked like death warmed over. The mirror told him he had been to hell and back, and it definitely showed.

Mark finished dressing and pulled the drapes in the bedroom open on his way out to the living room. He drank the fresh-squeezed orange juice in one gulp and placed the glass back on the sterling silver tray that had been brought in by room service while he was in the shower. He picked up the white and blue coffee cup and then noticed a small folded piece of paper on the saucer. Puzzled, he opened it, read the note, then reread it. "What the fuck is going on!" Mark uttered in exasperation. "Who? Why?" he yelled out. He folded the piece of paper and put it in his shirt pocket, grabbed his luggage, then quickly exited his suite, not bothering with the coffee, making a beeline into the elevator.

Nervously looking around as the elevator doors opened, Mark wasted no time as he made his way through the crowded lobby and out the front door of the Ritz. The chauffeur of the stretch limousine seemed upset that Mark had so quickly opened the car door, entered, and closed it before he had an opportunity to offer assistance. Mark felt a little better being hidden behind the gray-black tinted windows of the limousine. He pondered the note anxiously. It read:

"We are watching you. Do not call the police."

Who? Watching him for what? And why would Mark call the police? All these questions ran through his head as the limo sped toward O'Hare. His flight for Lauderdale left in fifty-two minutes. Mark wished he knew what the hell was going on, and he couldn't help feeling a bit sorry for himself, too. Why was all this shit happening to him? Not only did he not deserve it, he didn't even have any idea what all of this was about; much less what he was going to do about it. "Goddamned Carole," Mark mumbled under his breath in exasperation.

There was little traffic, and Mark quickly arrived at O'Hare; the chauffeur pulled right up to the curb at the departure area for American Airlines and quickly scurried around to open Mark's door. "Have a good flight, sir," said the chauffeur. "Thanks," Mark mechanically responded, forcing a smile.

He headed for the Admirals Club to wait in privacy for his flight to be called. The receptionist greeted him at the door and promised that his boarding pass and seat assignment would be made in ample time for his departure. Mark found a comfortable chair and a newspaper. He attempted, in vain, to unwind while he waited. Moments later, the receptionist arrived to escort him to the gate for "priority" boarding on his flight. Heading down the "A" concourse, he again thought, in a brief moment of weakness, about calling Carole before departing for Fort Lauderdale. Instead, he reached into his pocket and felt the note from the Ritz—a slight shiver pulsed through his hand. Nothing Carole could say now would make any difference anyway. Perhaps it would be easier for Mark if no one knew where to find him. He needed to think. Arriving at the departure gate, he tried to appear somewhat normal but felt like shit. He immediately boarded the plane.

After two Absolut Bloody Marys had been thoroughly absorbed into his blood stream, Mark again attempted to relax in his first-class seat. Sheer exhaustion, plus the combination of cocktails and air motion lulled him into a much-needed sleep. He wasn't sure how long he had dozed when he was awakened by an annoying tone, which turned out to be the "seat-belt alert" in preparation for landing. Through the window he could see the top of a Fort Lauderdale high-rise office building, easily recognized by its prominent eight-foot-high initials "IGBE," so he knew they were close to touchdown.

Twenty minutes later, he had his L.V. carry-on luggage in one hand and the keys to a Hertz convertible rental car in the other. Mark got into the car and put the top down; the bright, warm sun shining down on his skin normally would have invigorated him. However, with everything that had happened in the past twelve hours, Mark couldn't think of anything that would make him feel better at this moment, other than the hope that maybe he was still just having a bad dream, and that he would soon wake up and everything would be fine.

"Yeah, right—abso-fuckin-lutely," he sarcastically mumbled to himself.

All things considered, he actually thought he was holding up pretty well. Witnessing the disgusting scene with his new bride at their apartment last night, and then the disturbing note left at the hotel this morning, obviously had him reeling; other than his frequent glimpses into the rear-view mirror, he was trying very hard to put everything out of his mind. Mark knew that he had survived heartbreak before, and as long as he stayed strong, he could handle this, too. He knew that his convoluted way of thinking was pure bullshit. But, his attempt to be strong at least kept him from breaking down into tears and totally losing it again.

CHAPTER 13

❀

LITTLE VENICE

FORT LAUDERDALE, FLORIDA

Fort Lauderdale was one of twenty-nine cities in Broward County located between Miami and Palm Beach. Contrary to such movies as *Where the Boys Are*, which was first released in the sixties and depicted the city as the yearly destination for flocks of horny beer-guzzling college students invading the "Fort Liquordale" strip on spring break, Lauderdale in the new millennium was truly a world-class city. Little Venice, as it had been known for over seventy years because of the hundreds of canals with over 10,000 boats, was home to more luxury vessels—from sporty sixteen-foot water-ski boats to $5 million luxury cabin cruisers—than anywhere else in the world. After losing Disney World to Orlando years ago, the city leaders were spending millions of dollars to build a state-of-the-art cultural center. Downtown, the riverfront had completed a massive restoration process over the last few years. The boutiques on Las Olas Boulevard were on a scale equal to Worth Avenue in Palm Beach and Rodeo Drive in Beverly Hills, or Oak Street in Chicago. Fort Lauderdale attracted the wealthy, the educated, and also every con man in the world. "Scam capital of the world" was one infamous moniker Lauderdale would never elude.

Bill and Jim Alderice had migrated to Fort Lauderdale after graduating from high school in Tampa on the west coast of Florida. They thought it was the perfect place for their next scam. They acclimated instantly to the laid-back lifestyle, good-looking women, and abundance of cocaine, marijuana, and designer drugs that flourished in this get-rich-quick, incessant-pleasure, no-pain culture of "Snort Lauderdale."

The brothers started selling gold chains along the beach to tourists between Commercial and Oakland Park boulevards. They were earning thousands of dollars a day. The profit margin was incredible, and why shouldn't it be? The gold was fake—"fool's gold"—selling at top dollar to naïve tourists. By the time the visitors' wrists, ankles, and necks began turning green from the faux gold chains, the tourists would be back home in New York, Chicago, and parts unknown. What were they going to do once they were back home? "Caveat Emptor" jokingly became the credo of the lucrative Alderice brothers' caper. "Buyer Beware."

Incredibly, only a month later, they had saved over $100,000 and immediately opened a gold store in a little strip center on Oakland Park Boulevard, just west of U.S. Highway 1. Bill and Jim knew they were on their way to success. But no one could have possibly imagined, not even the brothers themselves, that very soon they would be raking in hundreds of millions of dollars, having successfully pulled off one of the biggest scams in Florida's history. Bigger than even the Bre-X Gold Mining scam in Canada. Michael Milken would have been proud; likewise Marc Rich, whom Clinton had pardoned before leaving the Presidency. Now, only a few months later, IGBE, International Gold Bullion Enterprises—as their empire was now known—had its luxurious headquarters, all four floors, 60,000 square feet, right-smack-dab in the middle of a white glass, thirty-story high-rise at U.S. 1 and Broward

Boulevard in the heart of the financial district. Hell, they *were* the financial district. They had even convinced the owner of the building to let them put their eight-foot-by-eight-foot illuminated logo on the tower—not just one, but four of the illuminated signs—so they could be seen for miles in every direction. So prominently were these landmarks displayed that flights descending into the Hollywood/Fort Lauderdale International Airport reportedly used them as a navigational reference. This was a source of intense pride to Bill and Jim as the helicopters hovered atop the tower for an entire day installing the huge signs displaying an American eagle replicating a $20 St. Gauden's gold piece with the initials IGBE prominently displayed under the wings.

The brothers quickly became one of the largest and best-paying employers in Fort Lauderdale. Granted, American Express was bigger, but it didn't offer the package that IGBE became famous for. The only qualification required for employment was that you had to be a friend of Bill or Jim's, or even a friend of a friend, and then you could start out making $1,500 to $3,000 a week and enjoy all the free drugs and booze you could consume. Walking through any floor of the corporate offices would yield an amazing scene: hundreds of twenty-year-olds, having been laid off from all the failing dot-com companies, were wearing $1,000 Armani, Ermenegildo Zegna, or Brioni suits with $5,000 Rolexes, Patek Philippes, or Cartiers adorning their wrists. Standard-issue, $300 Missoni, Hermès, or Valentino ties hung around their skinny necks, and a $500 Montblanc fountain pen attached to a marble pedestal replete with the IGBE logo rested atop each expensive ergonomically correct teak-and-leather desk and chair set. Any potential investor, or even small customer, couldn't help but be impressed when given a tour of the offices. They were truly magnificent, reeking of success. However, had anyone bothered to look beyond the visual trappings, it would have been obvious that no one was actually *doing* anything. At least not anything remotely relating to business. These "GQ" clones spent the bulk of their business day just hanging out, reading about themselves in major newspapers. Bill and Jim ran full-page ads in *The New York Times, The Wall Street Journal,* and *USA Today.* The Dow Jones was below 10,000. The carnage of failed dot-com companies was being felt. The stock market had shown too much volatility in 2001. Many people had suffered a serious financial blow to their lives, their retirement funds wiped out. The NASDAQ had lost 38 percent of its value in 2000 and 2001 was proving to be even worse, financially. People saw that this golden goose, aka the stock market, had started laying shit eggs. The signs were already there that the economy was going into a recession. Major layoffs were being announced daily—by big and small companies alike.

Clinton would no longer be president, despite Al Gore's repeated attempts at not giving up, and maybe because of the stupidity of some South Florida chad-impaired elderly people, Gore had lost. Increasingly, folks were getting very nervous that the stock market was going to fall apart. The S&P 500 suffered its third worst loss in history. Already President-elect George W. Bush was being blamed for the economic slowdown, possibly even a severe recession. Hard-money gurus preached hard assets, like gold and gold mining stocks. CDs were only paying 3 or 5 percent. Gold was the answer; solid tangible assets, not paper.

Bill and Jim sold all types and sizes of gold—ingots, wafers, maple leafs, cute koalas, bricks, nuggets; you name it, they sold it. Then Bill, the older brother and mastermind, devised a great scheme called *extended delivery.*

The concept was really quite simple: gold was heavy to ship and costly to insure and store. So, IGBE would store the gold in its impressive vaults and issue a certificate to the owner. The brothers spent $350,000 putting together a fabulous four-color brochure. A full five pages were devoted to pictures of the vaults, filled to the ceiling with gold bricks and impressive-looking uniformed armed guards diligently overseeing the gold. The only complication, a slight one as far as the brothers were concerned, was that the gold bricks were actually wooden blocks painted gold. Bill was going to put real gold in the vault as soon as he had enough money. Bill was losing $50,000 a day because, even though almost $500,000 was coming in daily, IGBE's expenses were about $550,000 a day.

Bill had started, or bought, thirty-eight different companies. He acquired a real estate firm, an advertising agency, a travel agency, a bar, a bank, and a plethora of dot-com companies for pennies on the dollar—Bill was building an empire—actually an empire of nothingness. The problem was that he wanted to be the richest man in the world but actually had very little, if any, talent for business. A Bill Gates, he was not. He had plenty of family and friends who would continually stroke his ego in a kind of fervent, supercharged, Amway-meeting atmosphere that was prevalent among the IGBE-ites, a nickname the boys had created for themselves. Enthusiasm and almost a cult-like loyalty to Bill was heightened by the fact that, by and large, unqualified people were being given outrageously high-paying positions and authority. No business acumen was necessary because no one did any business. Everyone was far too busy perpetuating the IGBE myth of success and endlessly snorting cocaine. Bill loved cocaine—but what the hell—so did the roughly one-thousand-plus employees who received it for free. Bill was to cocaine what Halie Saliese was to marijuana and Rastafarians in Jamaica. Ecstasy was also freely distributed to the employees.

Bill's favorite movie was *Scarface* with Al Pacino. The movie, which was over twenty years old, was shown once a week at his Intercoastal party palace, two adjoining houses that Bill had purchased for a million each, in cash, and made into IGBE's "party central." Bill modeled himself after Pacino's character, the fictional Cuban refugee crime boss. Bill and Jim may not have known how to legitimately make money, but they were experts at spending it. Their philosophy of spending money trickled down, in kind, to everyone in the firm. Of course, the wives and girlfriends of the guys who worked for Bill or Jim either loved all the newfound wealth or wished for it. They all envied Connie Cook, Bill's fiancé. Connie found this all somewhat amusing. She grew up in Brooklyn; she was Jewish, was nicknamed blimpie, was insecure, fat, flat-chested, had bad teeth, and mousy hair. That was her secret past. Through Bill's seemingly endless flow of money, her allowance of $5,000 a week had changed all that. She now had a personal trainer twice a day, six days a week, in the $100,000 gym she built herself in Bill's basement. Connie flew to Beverly Hills and successfully sought out the best nose-and-tit men and now had a lovely nose and very respectable 38D breasts, where previously there had been minimal buds. She also had her teeth capped. Her hairdresser moved from Palm Beach to Fort Lauderdale and now took care of Connie, his only client, on a daily basis. Despite the total makeover, at times she still felt somewhat insecure because of her former issues of low self-esteem, but she had a heart of gold and brains to match. Full of piss and vinegar, she also had a violent temper, especially when she caught Bill screwing around. Bill liked his woman. Connie would go nuts when she caught Bill being unfaithful. Tonight she was livid and would vent her spleen by causing thousands of dollars worth of damage to his expensive cars.

When the three squad cars arrived at Bill's Intercoastal mansion at 2:00 in the morning, Connie was at the helm of her new red Dino Ferrari, a Valentine's Day present from Bill, ramming it into Bill's black Maserati. The neighbors had placed several 911 calls to complain about the bizarre disturbance. By the time the police arrived she had also deliberately smashed into Bill's Porsche, his three new Caddies, and his Rolls Royce. It was a wild scene. The police thought they had seen it all before, but nothing compared to this expensive smash fest.

Mark Goodwin had never heard of Connie, Bill, or IGBE—other than seeing the logo on top of the Fort Lauderdale office high-rise—but he soon would. In fact, his whole life would change, as would Connie and Bill's.

Chapter 14

❀

LATE THURSDAY MORNING
FORT LAUDERDALE, FLORIDA

As Mark drove along A1A north to Ciel Bleu, he wondered if he should have called Raoul and Sylvia to let them know he was coming. No, it was better this way. He would surprise them. When Mark had bought his little house on Bougainvillea in Lauderdale-by-the-Sea years ago, he had hired Sylvia to clean and take care of the property. Sylvia and her husband, Raoul, had come to Florida from Cuba on the Mariel boatlift; they were hardworking and, above all, totally honest and dependable. When Mark had built five studio apartments adjacent to the house to rent out to tourists, he let Sylvia and Raoul Martinez move into the little house. They got free rent for taking care of his small hotel, Ciel Bleu, French for blue sky. Usually, when Mark came down, they would move into one of the studios so he could stay in his two-bedroom house that was part of Ciel Bleu. Since he was alone and didn't want to disrupt their plans, he planned to stay in one of the studios. There was always a vacancy. It sure wasn't the Ritz, but Ciel Bleu was clean, cozy, a block from the beach, and he owned this little hotel that he and his ex-wife, Patty had built, free and clear.

Mark was proud of Ciel Bleu. The house, although tiny, had been totally restored by Mark and Patty. Patty had a flair for decorating and had renovated Ciel Bleu with new electrical, new plumbing, central air, a new roof, two fireplaces—unusual for Florida—and an eight-person hot tub on the deck that was accessible through the sliding glass doors off the living room. The entire exterior of the house and the newly constructed studios were restored in cedar, again, rare for Florida. Most structures were built in stucco, a style Mark never liked. He preferred modern, not the Abner Mizner Spanish architecture that was so common in Florida. His neighbors hated this modern, cedar, skylighted, sleek-looking structure as much as he disliked their white and pink stucco dwellings. City code necessitated that he have a paved driveway, large enough for eight parking spaces. This seemed pointless, but he had no choice. To compensate for all the asphalt, Mark had planted an elaborate selection of flowers, bushes, philodendrons, and bougainvilleas on both sides of the driveway, running almost ninety feet from the sidewalk to the whirlpool in the front of the house. Mark found it very relaxing and somewhat cathartic to spend hours watering the flowers wearing nothing but a pair of Speedos and earphones, helping to maintain his great year-round tan, hose in one hand, Walkman in the other so he could continuously change channels. Mark thoroughly enjoyed watering the foliage as he watched the herds of beachgoers walking to the ocean or repeatedly circling the block trying to find a legal parking space. Sometimes, much to the dismay of his ex, Mark would let good-looking girls park their cars at Ciel Bleu. He was happy to do this, and it was certainly innocent enough. He never played around.

Sylvia and Raoul were outside washing their car when Mark pulled up at his hotel. Mark got out of the rental car and gave Sylvia a big hug and shook hands with Raoul.

"How come you didn't call to let us know you were coming?" Sylvia inquired of Mark, in her thick Cuban accent. Raoul spoke very little English.

"Where eez your wife, amigo?" Raoul asked.

Mark didn't feel like explaining. He didn't want them to feel sorry for him. And how could he explain? What could he say? Mark didn't understand the situation himself. Then he thought about the note found under his coffee cup at the Ritz. "I just came down by myself for a few days to take care of some business. I'll stay in one of the rooms."

"No, no, señor, we are going to drive to Key West for the weekend to see my cousin. You stay in the house. Everything is clean, even fresh sheets on the bed. We are leaving in about twenty minutes," Sylvia said.

"Fine, thank you," Mark replied, as Raoul carried Mark's Louis into the house. Mark changed into a pair of cut-offs, a tank top, and sandals. As he walked out toward a hotel on the beach, he told Sylvia and Raoul to have a good time. He didn't notice the white Ford Taurus parked in front of Ciel Bleu, although he should have. The man sitting in the car with dark sunglasses was poorly disguised to look like a tourist; he was costumed in a tropical shirt with polychromatic flowers, birds, and clouds all askew, white duck pants that were too tight, and black socks and sandals. The man who was supposedly reading the *Chicago Tribune*, which he had picked up at O'Hare Airport earlier that morning, was actually watching Mark.

Mark ordered a Bloody Mary. Since last night, he knew that he was drinking too much, but what the hell. He figured he was entitled after walking in on the wild sex scene starring his wife last night. This hotel on the beach was the preferred hangout for people of Mark's age group.

Lauderdale-by-the-Sea was one of the unique municipalities of Broward County. The town, bounded by Galt Ocean Mile to the south and Sea Ranch Lakes on the north just before Pompano Beach, allowed no buildings higher than four stories. It was a quiet, sedate, conservative town. The average age of the full-time residents was sixty-eight years.

Over a hundred small hotels and motels catered predominantly to the French, German, and Canadian tourists who wanted nothing to do with the tumultuous activity of Fort Lauderdale a mile to the south. The main attractions in town were the fishing pier and little souvenir shops. Thirty years ago, the main way to get to Lauderdale-by-the-Sea was to take a little boat from Stan's Restaurant and Bar on the southwest corner of the Intercoastal at Commercial Boulevard. After the Army Corps of Engineers had built the Causeway extending Commercial Boulevard over the Intercoastal into Lauderdale-by-the-Sea, the town became nothing more than a speed trap for people traveling through to get to the beach.

Mark sat at the oceanfront hotel bar that was originally Ho Jo's, watching the women in their string bikinis walking along the beach and oiling themselves up by the pool, careful never to get their bandage-sized bathing suits wet. Even though the poolside bar was in the shade, the sun was hot and beat down brilliantly, reflecting mercilessly off the blue undulating waters of the Atlantic. Mark put $10 on the bar as he got up to leave. The bartender thanked him for the generous tip. The girl across the bar, who had been semiflirting with Mark, gave him a big smile full of perfect white teeth. Mark, although definitely not in the mood, was flattered. He felt a little better, but was not instantly acclimating to the tropics as he usually did. He walked across the street to Publix to get some food for the house. Whoever was in charge of the air-conditioning in this supermarket must have been from Houston. The place was freezing within an inch of one's life. Mark hurriedly paid the cashier and with a plastic bag of groceries in one hand, and a one-gallon container of Buffalo Don's drinking water in the other, walked back to Ciel Bleu. He put the groceries away, changed into his Speedos, grabbed his Walkman, and exited through the sliding glass doors out onto the deck past the whirlpool to unroll the hose. The hotel was empty because it was off-season, but Mark didn't care. Ciel Bleu was not a moneymaker. He was contentedly watering the plants, trying not to think of

Carole, humming to the music from his Walkman when a red Dino Ferrari with a smashed front end came barreling up the driveway, crushing a bed of flowers and almost running him over. A very good-looking woman, expensively dressed, with a body to die for, jumped out of the car, in tears. She threw a handful of crumpled bills into Mark's hand after he had told her that there was a room available. Before Mark could stop Connie Cook to tell her that she had given him too much money, she sped away down the street, promising to be back soon. When he counted the bills later he found that it was almost $4,000 too much.

Chapter 15

※

EARLY THURSDAY MORNING

PROVIDENCE, RHODE ISLAND

As had been their custom for years, the eight board members of the Narragansett Racetrack in Pawtucket, Rhode Island, assembled at 7:00 A.M. in the conference room of K. Calden Rooley's law firm atop the Providence Bank and Trust Company building. The average age of the board members was seventy-six years old. To the casual observer, these regular informal Thursday morning meetings might seem like a mini-geriatric convention—not unlike the scene one might find any morning in the cafeteria of a senior citizens' home, replete with infirm, slow-moving gray-haired geezerly old men with their pants pulled way up over their bellies, drool dripping out of their mouths and down their chins. But the conversation this morning was not the morbific chatter one might expect among these dinosaurs. These men were a commixture of wealth and power beyond the average person's wildest dreams. They were all, to varying degrees, captains of industry: bank presidents, senators, and judges. Some had earned their fortunes and some had stolen them; some had "married right," while some had been lucky enough to be born into money.

Deemis Whitacre loathed these ruthless, crotchety old men who unabashedly cared only about their own personal gains. These were far from respectable men. They cared only about themselves. Deemis had not willingly agreed when asked to substitute on this particular day in his father-in-law's absence, but he had little choice. His father-in-law was also his boss at the law firm. Five minutes more and he was going to get the hell out of this "elder-fest!"

One of the truisms of greedy people who had wealth was that they always wanted more. There was no such thing as enough is enough. These men had been working for almost two years on an intricate scheme to sell the Narragansett Racetrack to the city of Pawtucket. The strategy of the plan was to convince the "powers that be" down at City Hall that the acquisition would be in the best financial interest of the community. On the surface it seemed like a good deal for everyone. The city would then officially shut down the track and develop the site into a mixed-use complex of residential homes and condominiums, shopping centers, and an industrial park. The project would be good for the city, creating jobs, bringing in new tax dollars, and new found prosperity. Of course, the board members and the 1,800 or so stockholders of the track would all make good money. But, these were not the real reasons that the board had pushed so hard for this deal.

The single most important benefit of the sale to the city, as the board members knew only too well, was plain and simple: they would all be spared the stigma of going to jail and would avoid the financial ruin and scandal that would ensue if the track were not sold soon! If the track stayed open, state law would mandate a financial audit. The board's years of skimming and stealing from the track would be revealed. They could not afford any delays.

Suddenly, one of the old boys began choking on a sweet roll he had been gumming. He couldn't catch his breath. The color was quickly draining from his face; he was turning pale and clammy.

"Help, help me. I can't breathe!" he gasped.

"Raise your hands over your head," someone nonchalantly offered.

"I can't...catch my breath...please...help me...call a...doctor!" the old man wheezed. He was frightened and was turning a pale shade of bluish purple, gasping for air as he choked.

"Is someone going to do something for him?" complained one of the members who was more interested in reading the latest edition of *The Wall Street Journal*.

"Why?" asked a man sitting directly across the table, obviously annoyed at the untimely interruption of the meeting.

"Because he'll die if we don't," came the retort.

"Good point...then there will be more money for us!"

The men sat and watched, fascinated, as the old board member twisted and retched in a fit of convulsion until finally his head pounded against the two-hundred-year-old conference table. Spewing blood and vomit before the death rattle in his chest finally quieted his feeble body, the old man collapsed in a pool of his own bodily fluids.

In an attempt to avoid soiling his expensive suit, K. Calden Rooley, chairman of the board, quickly recoiled from his seat of honor at the head of the table. "Someone call an ambulance and get him the fuck out of here!" he snarled in disgust. "And while you're at it...get the goddamned janitor in here to clean up this mess."

Deemis Whitacre wondered whether Janet was still at his apartment. He could use a good fuck. When she had arrived from Chicago late last night she was so fucked up that Deemis, not enjoying screwing a semi-comatose broad, had only had a couple of brief moments of sex before Janet passed out.

CHAPTER 16

❦

THURSDAY–EARLY MORNING

PROVIDENCE, RHODE ISLAND

K. Calden Rooley waited for the porter to finish pouring coffee for the board members—less one stiff—of the Narragansett Racetrack. When the porter had exited the conference room and closed the door behind him, Rooley spoke.

"Gentlemen, I think we may have a problem."

The other board members stirred uncomfortably in their high-backed leather chairs. Deemis Whitacre tried not to smile.

"There better not be," replied Pay Ratracha, Jr., the youngest member of the group.

Pay Jr. was the only one present who wasn't in his seventies. Yet, despite his lesser age, Pay was the most feared member of the group. His father, Pay Sr., had controlled the Mob in Rhode Island. Pay Jr. was an uncontrollably violent hothead and made the other board members very uncomfortable.

"Late last night," Rooley continued, "I received a phone call from an old friend of 'Little Nicky.'" Nicodemo Scarfo had been the Mob boss in

Philadelphia. Scarfo had also controlled Atlantic City after assassinating Angelo Bruno over twenty years ago in 1980. "It seems that someone—we don't exactly know who yet—will be coming into town tonight or tomorrow and offering our stockholders more money for the racetrack." The board members' faces fell to the floor. "Now, if this group plans to shut down the track, then we have nothing to worry about. In fact, we will all make more money," Rooley concluded.

"But what if they want to keep the track open?" one of the board members asked.

"Then we will eliminate them," replied Rooley.

When they all exited the Providence Bank and Trust Company building, no one noticed the two men in the black sedan watching them.

Chapter 17

❦

LATER THURSDAY MORNING

PROVIDENCE, RHODE ISLAND

K. Calden Rooley called another emergency board meeting to order. He seemed to have aged an additional twenty years in the last couple of hours. His eyes were sunk deeply into the mass of fat that was his face. "Gentlemen," he spoke slowly and deliberately, "I have just received confirmation that there will be at least two representatives arriving here to proffer a better proposal to our shareholders at our meeting tomorrow, and that they may be planning to keep the track open."

"Who are they? What family are they from?" asked one of the board members. The look of fear and dread was written all over his face. Rooley was sweating in his $3,000 custom-made silk suit.

"I don't know...," Rooley offered, his tone a mixture of defeat and anger. "I have put Plan B into effect. They will not be allowed to come to the meeting. In fact, we should have them eliminated the minute they get here and we find out who they are. Needless to say," Rooley went on, visibly shaken, "we must deal with this emergency without fail. Not only does it mean preserving our reputation and avoiding indictments, but if we don't get the money from the sale of the racetrack, we'll be unable to pay the next installment to the construction companies, much less the bribes to our guys on the House Judiciary Committee in Washington, which surely would slow down our acquisitions and continuing efforts at controlling the privatization of prisons." Rooley concluded, "If this happens, we're ruined, finished…and our lives are over." Deemis Whitacre held back his smile. Obviously Janet, as expected, had leaked the story to someone, and that 'someone' was Bill Alderice. Deemis had never seen his associates sweat. He reveled in their fear.

CHAPTER 18

❈

THEN AND NOW

FEDERAL PRISON CAMP–TERRE HAUTE, INDIANA

Jack was in an old dirty prison camp. He had been there for the past six months. Vividly, he recalled how he had felt the week before he arrived at the prison camp. It seemed like only yesterday that he was back at home in Chicago dreading his incarceration and feeling sick, scared, and close to suicide. He had wished, back then, that he had had the motivation to kill himself. But he had felt like shit. He was constantly dizzy, hallucinating, and scared to death. He remembered praying to God that he'd be able to make it through the day or even the next hour. He didn't think he would survive what he had been experiencing; it had been a living hell. He'd been running a high fever, yet he had felt ice cold; he had shivered violently and he remembered his gums beginning to bleed from the force of his chattering teeth. The combination of withdrawing from the drug half a year ago and the thought of what he would be faced with in the next week at prison had been more than he could handle. After he'd gone through another miserable hour of hot and cold flashes and vomiting, he remembered calling his psychiatrist. He was in excruciating mental and physical pain. The receptionist had told Jack that Dr. Bernstein was just finishing up with a patient.

"I'll hold," Jack remembered pleading with the receptionist.

He recalled feeling as if he were going to pass out. His palms at that point were sweaty, his breathing was labored, and his heart was pounding wildly as his anxiety escalated. He remembered feeling that the room was spinning. He had grabbed the sheets with white knuckles; filled with terror, feeling that his wildly pounding heart might explode before the doctor would get to the phone, he had tried desperately to breathe deeply, hoping to calm himself down. Unfortunately, he had not been successful.

"Help me God, please. I can't take this anymore!" Half a year later Jack still clearly remembered his screams of agony. He remembered lying naked on his bed in total darkness, awaiting help for what seemed like hours. The whole time he feared that he was having a heart attack.

"Yes, Jack," Dr. Bernstein, said, sounding annoyed after he had finally come to the phone. Jack remembered that six-month-old conversation like it was yesterday.

"Doc, Doc, I feel terrible," Jack had cried out in agony.

"It's to be expected with withdrawal from Valium," Bernstein had begun matter-of-factly. "After all," he had continued, "you've been taking three to four Valiums a day for the last four years…withdrawal is very tough."

"What should I do?" Jack recalled screaming frantically.

"Well, as I told you before Jack, going cold turkey has its dangers; cardiac arrest, seizures, in addition to other complications," the doctor had told Jack in a clinical monotone. "What I want you to do is take one Valium for two days, then half a Valium for two days, then a quarter for two days, gradually tapering off of the drug."

"But, but…," Jack had interrupted, his voice trembling.

"No buts!" the doctor firmly interjected, cutting him off. "I know how adamant you are about wanting to go cold turkey, but it's not working. I'll write a letter right now to make sure that when you get there next week, the prison doctors will have to keep you on the medication for a while. They don't want to be responsible for your dying." Dr. Bernstein had kept to his word of six months ago and had written the letter.

"Well...okay...okay, Doc," Jack remembered mumbling weakly as he placed the receiver down, swallowing the Valium, and waiting for it to work. Bernstein was right, Jack now realized. Going cold turkey and getting ready to go to prison at the same time was too much, even for him—Christ, for anyone! It had been hard enough getting ready to surrender himself for incarceration. There was no way he could have prepared to go to prison. Six months ago, he was scared shitless. His only experience with jail was from prison movies. Were there going to be big guys named "Bubba" hidden in every broom closet trying to rape him? he had wondered back then.

"Oh God! Oh dear God!" Jack remembered screaming uncontrollably until finally his tortured body had drifted into a drug-induced calm. He wasn't even supposed to be put away; this was all a terrible mistake. He had asked himself a hundred times how this whole drama had gotten so out of control. He remembered wondering if he would really be going to jail. Now six months later, sitting in this dirty, dreary prison camp, he thought that maybe he knew the answer to those two questions, but he still didn't know the real cause of it all.

Chapter 19

WHY IT HAPPENED

TERRE HAUTE, INDIANA

Jack Fleming was in the prison camp for credit-card fraud. He shouldn't have been there, though. He was set up because he had refused to cooperate with the government, and they were getting even with him. He would not roll over and become a snitch. He had misrepresented his income on some applications for Visa and MasterCard. He had hoped to get higher credit lines in order to pay some of the hospital bills for his dying mother. The insurance had run out, and she didn't have much time left. He needed quick cash to put her in a hospice. After his bank had turned him down for a loan, his loan officer, Jenny, had suggested that he exaggerate his income on his credit-card applications. It had not been his idea.

Jack waited in the visiting room of the Terre Haute prison camp to meet Pete, another inmate. He had volunteered to entertain the children of visiting spouses, so they would have some time to themselves. Jack wasn't sure how Pete was going to contact him in the visiting room. He had been told to volunteer for that day and that Pete would find him. Jack had been here for six months, and much to his surprise, he was no longer on suicide watch. His state of mind had improved. The prison doctor was slowly weaning Jack off the Valium with Klonopin, a drug similar to Valium, but approved by the Bureau of Prisons because Valium was considered "hot." The trepidation Jack had experienced about going to prison over the last few years proved to be unfounded. Life in the camp was not brutal; long days gave him plenty of time to read, play tennis, and get in shape, both physically and mentally. He was still angry that he was in prison, and he definitely did not feel he belonged here because the government knew that he had done nothing wrong, but he was forced to make the best of a bad situation. Jack felt badly that he had left the real estate business without even giving notice to his boss, Mark Goodwin. Mark had done many things for Jack in the past and surely would have helped him with this mess, but Jack was too embarrassed or proud (he wasn't sure which) to ask him for help. Jack was used to taking care of himself. His pride kept him from asking Mark for money.

Jack reflected on his situation; he was confused. He had been promised a million dollars over a five-year period after his release from prison, by his second lawyer, Donovan. Jack had already figured that with some well-placed investments, he would never have to work again. He was damn lucky or maybe being set up; he wasn't sure which. When he had been arrested, he surrendered himself and was out on an I-Bond within forty-five minutes; his first lawyer, Bill Sinclair, had explained that the chances of winning his case, if it went to trial, were slim to none. The government had a 98 percent conviction rate, but it was not because the government employed outstanding assistant U.S. attorneys—typically, the outstanding ones moved into private practice. Most of the high-powered criminal defense attorneys, like Bill Sinclair, were much better litigators than their government counterparts. Sinclair, in keeping with the profile of most criminal lawyers, was full of shit. At first, he had assured Jack he would never go to jail—then after he collected his retainer, everything had changed. Most criminal defense attorneys, including Sinclair, had started out as prosecutors, and worked for the government for a number of years before going into private practice. But as Sinclair knew, you could not fight the government. The state government, yes, but the Feds, no. They simply had unlimited funds, time, and resources. Clearly, the vast majority of cases never went to trial because a plea bargain was reached. If the Feds had it in for you, they would get you.

Sinclair had told Jack that if he pleaded guilty, he would get thirty-seven to forty months in prison. Sinclair suggested that if Jack were willing to testify for the government and "rat" on some associates, maybe the sentence would be lowered to eighteen months probation, with no jail time. But Jack would rather do thirty years than rat people out—he wasn't going to talk. However, he certainly didn't want to go to prison. Taking his case to trial and losing, which was almost a 98 percent certainty, could mean up to twelve years in prison. Neither option seemed great. In an attempt to do better, Jack fired his first ineffectual lawyer and instead hired Michael Donovan, a well-connected Mob lawyer, at the suggestion of Jenny, his loan officer, from his bank. Jack eagerly made a deal with the devil. He quickly accepted Donovan's offer before he had time to think about it. He neither cared nor had the time for moral balancing at this juncture in his life. The promise of easy money—and a lot of it—made for a quick decision. Donovan explained to Jack that he would be out in less than two years without "dropping a dime" on anyone and would also have a million dollars in cash to get his life going again. Well, sort of. Donovan had shown Jack a picture of Pete, an inmate who worked for Donovan, and told him that Pete would contact him in prison and explain what Jack had to do to fulfill his end of the bargain. Donovan, without giving any specifics, assured Jack that he wasn't going to have to hurt anyone or deal drugs. Jack's thoughts were suddenly interrupted by a stern voice over the intercom.

"All inmates immediately return to your bunks now, goddammit. Move, let's go!" the voice on the intercom frantically ordered.

Jack saw the Bureau of Prisons S.O.R.T. team charge into the room, dressed in black, like Ninja turtles, with their M-16s and nine-millimeter submachine guns aimed at the prisoners and visitors. As Jack was herded out of the visiting room into the corridor with the other inmates, women, and children, he saw Pete, the inmate whom he recognized from the photo Donovan had shown him six months ago. Jack was supposed to work with Pete to get some plan started and, in return, get the million dollars over five years; that was Donovan's promise. Pete was lying on the clean white linoleum floor with a pool of dark crimson surrounding his head. A look of panic was on everyone's face; tension and confusion permeated the air. There was total pandemonium as the guards tried to restore order. Like all cops, they hated shit like this—it meant there would be the necessary burden of endless paperwork.

"Shit," the lieutenant from the S.O.R.T. team said, angrily surveying the scene. "I only have one more month to retirement! I don't need this crap now!" he complained. Jack was no less upset.

What was he supposed to do now that Pete was gone? Why had he made that deal with Donovan? Why, he now thought in the clarity of 20/20 hindsight, hadn't he asked his boss, Mark Goodwin, for some money? Mark was a great guy, and Jack had been an integral part of Mark's real estate company. Mark would have been happy to help out. But Jack's mother had raised him the right way and instilled great values in her son; one of which was "never a lender nor a borrower be." What stupid bullshit. Yeah, his mother was a great lady. But false pride, ego, and not being a snitch for the government had landed him in the can.

Chapter 20

HOW IT HAPPENED

TERRE HAUTE, INDIANA

Jack went back to his eighteen-man cell, hoisted himself up on his upper bunk, closed his eyes, and reflected on how he got here. It was obvious that he was set up because he wouldn't cooperate with the government. He knew things about certain people from working in the real estate business for his boss, Mark Goodwin. He wasn't going to give out information about clients. Furthermore, they were good people—but the government wanted him to lie and make up shit; he told them to go fuck themselves. Jack never dreamt that he would really go to jail. Certainly not during the first three years when he began to hear rumors from friends that the government was investigating him. He thought that it was a joke—no big deal. But when the government people started calling him in, he realized this was serious and began to really get scared. Then he got mad, even indignant. How dare the Feds try to indict him because he wouldn't lie and cooperate—as for the credit-card charge, he was going to pay it off if he ever got the money. He wasn't a criminal. He wondered why his loan officer had suggested the credit-card idea. He thought back to when his mother was dying of cancer. Jack wanted to put his mom in a hospice so she could live out her remaining short time in comfort and die with some dignity. She had met her inevitable demise almost four years ago, and Jack felt fortunate that she had not seen him end up in this situation. Certainly his mother, a widow, would have died of a broken heart had she seen her son go to jail. She had loved Jack, her only child, and had never asked anything of him. She was a self-assured, proud, independent woman, who had worked two jobs to put Jack through college—Jack's father had been killed in a car accident when Jack was still a toddler—he always regretted never knowing his dad.

So far, being in jail was not at all what he had expected. Jack now wished that he had seen the Barbara Walters Special on federal prisons a few years ago. Since the airing of her Special, entitled "Club Fed," the public was outraged at the soft treatment federal prisoners were given. The idea that white-collar felons were doing little more than taking a vacation in a country club, playing golf, tennis, and swimming all day infuriated people. Other than taking away swimming privileges of inmates to pacify the public and the press, life in the camp, aside from endless boredom and chronic overcrowding, was in reality not that bad, that is, if one had to be incarcerated. Most of the 200,000 federal prisoners were not violent; they were drug dealers or white-collar criminals like Jack. In the prison library, Jack read that in 1848, the secretary of the Treasury had sent a circular inquiry to the United States marshals seeking to find out how many prisoners were in federal custody; there were only a total of forty-eight! Today, there were almost 200,000 prisoners in federal custody. Over eight million people were in jail in the United States when state and local prisoners were included in the count. Jack looked at the circular from 1848:

Theft or embezzlement of U.S. mails	19
Counterfeiting	8

Assault on the high seas	4
Manslaughter	4
Mutiny at sea	3
Slave trade violations	3
Forgery	2
Theft of government property	2
Assault	1
Attempting to create a revolt	1
Larceny	1

Jack smiled and wondered how many mutiny-at-sea convictions there had been in the new millennium.

❊   ❊   ❊

Jack's second lawyer, Donovan, had told him to lie, to claim he had a substance-abuse problem, and to apply for the drug assistance program that the Bureau of Prisons had started in 1994. Jack had received the good news last week. He had been accepted. This meant that his sentence would be cut by a year and that he would receive six months at a halfway house in Chicago and be back home in eighteen months, sooner than he'd expected. Jack would be transferred to the Robert F. Kennedy Center in Morgantown, West Virginia. Jack had already served six months of his thirty-seven-month sentence. He would be immediately transferred to Morgantown to begin the nine-month drug program and then be released almost a year and a half early. Jack was grateful. His lawyer had done a good job. However, what about the million dollars he was supposed to get after he was out of prison? He put it out of his mind for now, figuring it was probably bullshit anyway.

Everyone knew his lawyer, Donovan, and respected him, or at least feared him. It was no secret that he was connected to the underworld. He was the Outfit's lawyer. Rarely did he lose a case. As far as negotiating deals in the best interest of his clients, he was "Numero Uno." Jack had met Donovan through Jenny, his loan officer; a gorgeous knockout who worked at his bank, and Jack was immediately impressed with Donovan. He was very affable and Jack took an immediate liking to him in the first few minutes of their meeting. But Jack apologized for wasting Donovan's time, explaining that he had no money to pay for such a high-priced attorney. Jack had already given all of his money to his first lawyer, Bill Sinclair, who had obviously fucked everything up.

"That's okay," Donovan told Jack.

"What do you mean?" queried Jack, quite surprised.

"I'll do you a favor, and it won't cost you a dime," Donovan said.

Jack sat in disbelief. He was incredulous. Then Donovan told him how he could use a bright honest guy like Jack and would be willing to pay him one million over a five-year period for his help. Donovan told Jack how he respected him for not cooperating with the government—which would have kept Jack out of jail in the first place.

"Who do I have to kill?" Jack asked in jest.

"Nobody. It's nothing like that. Everything is *pretty* legal, *mostly* on the up-and-up," replied Donovan. What an oxymoron; *pretty* legal, *mostly* on the up-and-up? Jack thought.

"Oh, c'mon. Why me?"

"Because we've checked you out and we like you. You shouldn't be in jail in the first place; your first lawyer, Sinclair, was a putz. We know you've got a lot of medical bills from your mother's prolonged illness, and it's not going to be easy once you're out of jail to pay off your debts. So, you help us—we help you. It's that simple."

"Okay," Jack replied before he had time to change his mind.

"Don't worry, trust me," Donovan calmly said.

Jack knew there had to be a catch. But after a lifetime of playing it straight, he was tired—tired of being in debt—stupidly resolute in his pride that would not let him go to his boss, Mark Goodwin, for money—tired of going nowhere. He was disillusioned with the government, with the whole damn country. He had worked hard his whole life and where did it get him? Jail. What crime had he committed? Whom had he hurt? He still couldn't understand why Jenny had tried to help—why had she suggested he falsify his income on his credit-card applications? He realized now, in rueful retrospect, that it had been a bad idea. But at least, Jenny, obviously feeling guilty about getting Jack into trouble, had introduced him to Donovan.

But now that someone had attacked his contact, Pete, which he witnessed in the prison visiting room, and saw Pete's head surrounded by blood, obviously dead, what should he do? Since coming to prison, he had been thinking about a new business he should start, called LRI (Limited Risk International). He had not put a lot of time into this venture. After all, he was going to be working for Donovan with Pete, or now Pete's replacement, doing whatever it was he was called upon to do. Whatever it would be, it had to be big. Jack only hoped it wasn't too illegal or too dangerous. He surmised that the plan had something to do with prisons. But what? Was it a prison break? That didn't make much sense. There were no fences or walls in the camp. Everyone was on an honor system. If you wanted to escape, all you had to do was walk out. But even fenced-in high-security prisons were not immune to the possibility of escape.

Federal prison escapes had been done before. In the prison library, Jack had read a lot about prison escapes. For example, back in 1973, the most sophisticated escape in U.S. history took place when five prisoners walked out the main entrance of Marion, Illinois, one of the toughest prisons in the country. Through use of a complex tone generator that the inmates had constructed, a continuous tone was emitted that activated a mechanism in the control panel making all three sally port doors open simultaneously. Prison policy had always mandated that only one sally port could be opened at a time. Again, in 1978, another escape attempt was made at Marion. A woman named Barbara Oswald tried to take an inmate out of the rec yard aboard a helicopter she had chartered in St. Louis. The pilot wrestled away her gun, then shot and killed her moments before they were to land inside the prison. Jack remembered reading about the first successful helicopter escape in 1986 at the Pleasanton Co-Correctional Institution in California. A prisoner, who had been a helicopter pilot in the military, escaped during his transfer to another institution, hijacked a helicopter, landed inside the prison for a few brief seconds, picked up a woman, and flew away. They were caught later that month while shopping for a wedding ring. And in January 2001, seven inmates had escaped from a Texas penitentiary. Jack let his mind wander. He was trying to guess what the "plan" was; he really had no idea, though. Maybe he was to act as a conduit and get or give information to some high-profile inmates. The prisons were full of them and always had been.

Ever since the passage of the Three Prison Act by Congress in 1891, with the inception of the first three federal prisons, there had been many high-profile, famous people who had made Club Fed their residence. Governors, senators, congressmen, mayors, judges, and movie stars had all been sent to the Club—some of them more unique and interesting than others. Jack had read about Robert Stroud, "Birdman of Alcatraz," who was sentenced at nineteen years old to federal prison for a murder committed in Alaska. Carl Panzram, the most sinister criminal of all time, born in Minnesota in 1891, began his life of crime at the ripe old age of eleven. He had murdered twenty-three people during his criminal career. After Dr. Karl Menninger interviewed Panzram, he said: "The prisoner does not pretend to have had justification for these murders but says that he killed because he enjoys killing." Perhaps one of the most memorable of all, Al Capone, entered the Atlanta Federal

Penitentiary in May 1932 with eleven years to serve for income tax evasion, but he died of syphilis and insanity before the end of his sentence.

Jack was tired of trying to figure out what he was going to be called upon to do to earn a million dollars over five years. Since Pete was no longer around, certainly someone else from Donovan's office would contact Jack. Anyway, Jack was to be transferred soon. He had been at the camp at Terre Haute for six months and was anxious for a change of scenery. The place was old, dirty, and depressing. Jack was glad he was going on to Morgantown in West Virginia. The Robert F. Kennedy Correctional Institute, the only one in the system named after a person, was the darling of the federal system. Built into the middle of the Blue Ridge Mountains, it had the breathtaking Chapel of the Ark, a gymnasium with an indoor Olympic-sized pool, recently covered by a basketball court, and separate housing units with massive stone fireplaces. The place was sweet. There was a five-year waiting list to get into Morgantown. Jack was somewhat surprised that he was being transferred to the most magnificent institution in the country. Was he just lucky? Had someone at Terre Haute put in a good word for him? He knew that his lawyer, Donovan, and the Outfit had probably arranged everything. Jack was growing more nervous. Obviously, these people had a lot of power. What were they going to ask him to do? Why had he said yes so quickly to Donovan? He just wanted to do his time, stay out of trouble, and get his life back on track again. In fact, he had already signed his plea agreement with the government before he had fired his first lawyer, and sought out Donovan at the suggestion of Jenny from the bank.

Jack knew that considering the nonseriousness of his crime, he was given a pretty stiff sentence—only because he would not cooperate with the Feds. Jack had really gone to Donovan to get a second opinion. Donovan had told Jack that since he had already signed the plea agreement, there was not a lot he could do to change things. Donovan had told him that Sinclair could have done a better job. But by then it was too late to do anything. Donovan, unlike Sinclair, oozed confidence. He would represent him at the sentencing, he told Jack. Because he knew the judge, Donovan would make sure that Jack would get the best deal. He also told Jack about the drug treatment program, and that if accepted, he would get eighteen months knocked off his sentence. With Donovan's offer of a million bucks and no fee to represent Jack at the sentencing, it seemed like the best thing to do. Maybe not the right thing, but the best. Considering the state of Jack's mind at the time—scared, uncertain, and vulnerable—he now wondered if he had acted in haste. What if Donovan had not really done anything to help Jack; what if it was all lip service? The sentencing guidelines were thirty-seven to forty months. By pleading guilty, the assistant U.S. attorney had agreed to recommend the low end of the guidelines, and the judge had done just that. Now that he had been in the prison camp for six months, physically healthier and thinking clearer than he had in years, he wondered if he had again been set up. Since his incarceration, Jack had sent a letter to Kathleen Hawk Sawyer, director of the Bureau of Prisons who was supervised by the soon-to-be-replaced Janet Reno, outlining his business proposition, which Jack called LRI, Limited Risk International, to help rehabilitate ex-offenders. He wondered if he should pursue this legal way to potentially make some decent money and also help people, or forget about it, now that he was obligated to Donovan and obviously the Mob. Jack could not shake his gut feeling that there were other reasons why Donovan was helping him. When he had first met Donovan, there was a look in Donovan's eyes, if only for a brief microsecond, that seemed to tell Jack this man truly cared about his well-being. Jack quickly rationalized that this feeling was his own projection of something that was not really there. Maybe, subconsciously over the years, because he had never known his father, he had secretly wondered how he would have turned out if he had had a father in his life. Jack had no way of knowing whether Donovan was trying to help him or hurt him.

Chapter 21

THE PLAN

FEDERAL TRANSFER CENTER, OKLAHOMA CITY, OKLAHOMA

The seven-story high-rise was built on the grounds of the airport. The brand-new building had been costly to build. The Federal Transfer Center (FTC) at the Oklahoma City airport did not look like a prison or a jail. The exterior looked more like a modern office building. The interior, majestically painted and decorated in mauves, magentas, and aquas, looked more like a South Beach art deco hotel than a federal institution. Most prisoners being transferred by the U.S. Marshal's Air Lift Division would spend a couple of weeks at the FTC, en route to their new destination. Each floor of this structure had three pods; each pod could hold 120 men or women. Upon deplaning and slowly walking down the jetway, handcuffed and shackled, all prisoners were ushered into "holding cells" for five or six hours before being processed and taken to their cells.

Pete was one of about 100 prisoners in Jack's holding cell, sitting on the floor against the wall in the rear of the large room. Jack had seen him only briefly at Terre Haute but could still remember his face in that bloody scene of what looked like a gallon of cheap red wine pouring out of the back of Pete's brain, covering the clean, white, freshly waxed linoleum floor. Pete also instantly knew who Jack was as he sat down next to him.

"Are you okay? You looked pretty bad at Terre Haute. I thought you were dead," Jack began.

Pete laughed heartily. "Yeah, I'm fine. That was all an act. Fake blood, the whole bit staged." Jack's face registered total disbelief. "The doctor was going nuts trying to figure out where all the blood came from when there wasn't a scratch on me."

"But, I don't understand!" Jack exclaimed.

"It's simple," said Pete. "We knew you were being transferred, so I had to be creative. One of the inmates and me got into a fake fight so I would get a disciplinary transfer and have a chance to fill you in on the operation." Everyone goes through Oklahoma when they are transferred.

"You're going to Morgantown, too?" Jack asked.

Pete laughed, "No pal, when you get in a fight, your classification goes up. I'm going behind the fence, probably to Atlanta or Lewisburg. Makes no difference to me; I've got plenty of work to do no matter where they send me. To be truthful, I'm glad to be getting back to a real joint, away from all you candy-ass, pussy-campers."

"So what am I supposed to do?" Jack asked nervously.

"Have you heard of Julie Stewart?" Pete asked.

"Yes," Jack nodded. He had heard about her when he was in the camp in Terre Haute, Indiana.

Years ago, Julie Stewart's brother, Jeff, had been sentenced to five years in prison for drugs. Because of this, Julie had started an organization called FAMM in Washington, D.C.: Families Against Mandatory Minimums. FAMM was trying to fight, with some success, the draconian sentencing laws for drug dealers and users. Jack knew from being at the camp at Terre Haute that over 50 percent of the inmate population was made up of people involved with drugs. Jack also knew that most of these people didn't belong in jail. The sentences were ridiculous. Twenty-year-old kids were being incarcerated for ten years for having a small amount of rock cocaine. It made no sense. In fact, a survey of prison wardens found that half of them didn't support mandatory minimum penalties for drug offenders, and 85 percent thought that elected officials had failed to offer effective solutions for crime. Former Senator Paul Simon released the survey of 157 wardens from eight states on December 21, 1991, more than eleven years ago. FAMM's membership had mushroomed to over 100,000 inmates of the federal prison population. Julie, in trying to right a serious wrong, continually urged her members to keep writing to Congress to change the laws, but she had achieved little success.

Congress, and even the United States Sentencing Commission, had recommended that sentencing laws were too strict, but President Clinton had vetoed any reduction changes. President-elect George W. Bush, with his even tougher views on crime based on his track record of executing prisoners while governor of Texas, seemed unlikely to lighten up, either. If John Ashcroft, as expected, replaced Reno as attorney general, he would only reinforce Bush's tough stance on crime. More people were going to prison, and more prisons had to be built to handle the demand. Kathy Hawk Sawyer, the director of the Federal Bureau of Prisons had recently issued a statement, which in part stated that: "…Congress also mandated that 50 percent of the District of Columbia's inmates coming into our prison system be placed in private prisons by 2003…"

Pete went on: "Since 1986, federal law has set a five-year mandatory minimum prison term for anyone caught with crack cocaine and ten years to life for those found with more than ten grams. The number of inmates held by federal, state, and local governments has exploded to well over 8 million over the past twenty years. They don't have enough prisons to hold all the people, so if even more people keep getting sent to prison, the system will collapse. They will have to let people out."

Jack wondered if this might be true. He had seen Marc Mauer from the sentencing project in Washington, D.C, on television. Mauer criticized the escalation in the number of men and women being sent to prison. He told how 35 percent of all black men between the ages of twenty-nine and thirty-five were in jail. The government was spending over $6 billion a year just for the supervision of black males in their thirties; Pete hadn't told Jack this, but Jack already knew it. Because of the increase in the number of people being sent to prison, there was a lucrative multi-billion-dollar-a-year private for-profit prison industry, growing at 115 percent per year. There were more than fifty private companies providing housing for hundreds of thousands of prisoners, up from only 1,345 just twelve years prior. Many states allowed corporate-managed prisons. One company, CCA, founded by the same financial backers of Kentucky Fried Chicken, ranked, at one time, among the top five performing companies on the New York Stock Exchange. The value of its shares, according to PaineWebber, had soared from $50 million to over $3.5 billion. Jack wondered if Pete knew about the private prison business—if he did, he was not talking to Jack about it.

"Well," said Pete, "Julie and her FAMM organization are on the right track, but the wrong train."

"What do you mean?" asked Jack.

"They've tried…," Pete continued in hushed tones so as not to be overheard by the other inmates. "They've made some progress but not enough. So we've taken it a few steps further. We are being more aggressive in our efforts to get all these people out of jail."

"Who's 'we?'" Jack questioned.

"Oh, c'mon," Pete smiled. "Us. You and me, and others like us, and we are backed by thousands of heavy-duty criminal attorneys, judges, politicians, and Mafia Bosses. You name it, everyone's in on it," Pete concluded.

"But who's in charge of this operation?" Jack asked, fascinated.

"Some guy in Chicago," Pete replied.

"You mean Donovan?" Jack asked, not really surprised.

"Well, no," replied Pete, "his name is Marty; he works for Donovan. Donovan works directly for the Don in Miami. But, hey, that's between you and me, okay?" Pete had Jack's undivided attention as he continued. "It's crowded, and we're going to make it worse. If we double the population every six months until it's so bad, the Feds will have to consider a bill that would take all nonviolent white-collar criminals out of federal prisons and put them in halfway houses or home confinement. We're just trying to speed it up; make sure that it happens as soon as possible." Jack had read that it cost $100,000 to build a new prison cell, $200,000 over twenty-five years to pay the interest on the construction debt, and $22,000 a year to operate the cell. Since 1980, the country was opening the equivalent of three new 500-bed prisons every week, but 84 percent of the reason for the increase in the prison population was due to the incarceration of nonviolent offenders. Jack wondered if Pete knew this.

"But how are you going to double the prison population every six months?" Jack asked, perplexed.

"Simple," replied Pete, who, obviously from his confident, self-assured statements, had all the answers.

"Do you know what the Feds' conviction rate is?" asked Pete.

"High, like 90 percent or something," responded Jack.

"Close, but no cigar," Pete stated. "It's 98 percent. Do you know why? I'll tell you why. It's because everybody cops a plea. They know they can't fight the Feds. So, everyone makes a plea agreement to avoid the high legal cost and risk of going to trial, maybe losing, then getting an even higher sentence."

Jack knew this was all true; he had done the same thing, but he was still waiting for Pete to explain how he was going to double the prison population. It was as if Pete were reading his mind. He continued, "If we can get 98 percent of the people, hell, if we can get only 25 percent of the people to go to trial, it will totally fuck up the entire justice system. The courts will be tremendously overworked. Not enough judges, not enough prisons, not enough probation officers. It will cause havoc."

This seemed to make sense to Jack; seven years ago, after reading Robert Shapiro's *The Search for Justice*, he remembered what Shapiro had said on page thirteen: "Ninety percent of the cases are resolved by pleas. Imagine if they all went to trial. The court system would bog down almost instantly, and cases would be systematically dismissed, one after another." Pete said 98 percent; Shapiro had said 90.

"But, why will defendants risk going to trial and possibly getting severe sentences instead of copping a plea?" asked Jack. "And how does this benefit the Mafia?"

"It's simple," Pete replied, matter-of-factly, "Money." Pete could see that Jack was confused. He elaborated: "People under indictment inevitably run out of money to pay for their legal defense. If they can prove they're indigent, they can get a public defender, but that's a tough way to go." Pete went on: "However, if we pay the lawyers for people, they can afford to go to trial and fight."

"But, what if they lose?" Jack asked Pete.

"We cover them," Pete said. "We will even give them money for the time that they may have to spend in prison." Jack was trying to take it all in. Pete could see that he was dubious. "We'll pay the inmate, or his wife, family, friend, or his private account in the Bahamas, Liechtenstein, Switzerland, or the Cook Islands, whatever they want. We loan them money for every year they're in prison." Pete stared directly into Jack's eyes: "It's a great deal," Pete continued. "And we will give them money to pay their lawyers and fight in the first place, so odds are they won't go to the Can."

Jack thought about the million bucks he was going to get over five years and realized that Pete was probably right. He wondered how much interest he was supposed to pay Donovan; probably more than the principal. He wished now that he had questioned Donovan on some of the specifics.

"Obviously," Pete continued, "when the people get out, they owe us the money, plus favors. Realistically, after we spread the word and help people out, getting them lawyers and *giving them money while they are in prison—which is your job; that's why Donovan hired you*—in a couple of years at most, the government will not be able to hire enough prosecutors, or build enough courts, or find qualified judges, or build enough prisons to house everybody. They'll all have to be let out."

"But how can it be affordable?" Jack asked.

"Let's just say," Pete said, "the drug cartels and the Mob have enough money. It's a win-win situation for the boys. You know there are too many lawyers; one for every 250 Americans. Japan has only one lawyer for every 35,000 citizens, but in our country they can't find enough work, and with proposed tort reform, even the personal injury lawyers will have a tough time making it. Organized crime will become the single largest employer of attorneys in the country, and you know what happens to lawyers, don't you? They become senators, congressmen, mayors, and even presidents, like Clinton. The Mob had plenty to do with getting so many pardons." Pete concluded incorrectly.

Jack still had a lot of questions. Pete could see that Jack still wasn't totally sold. Pete could certainly empathize with Jack. Pete remembered only too well when he was first told about this ambitious plan. It seemed unreal, totally fantastic, and almost ridiculous; a wild, harebrained scheme that could never work. After several meetings and learning more about the plan, it seemed to make sense. There was still a lot of it that he had not been told, but he understood the most important part, that the money had to be repaid. Jack still wondered about the million bucks he was supposed to get over five years for helping promote this plan. When was he supposed to pay it back, or wasn't he? He had a bad taste in his suddenly dry mouth. Jack waited for the right opportunity to ask Pete, but for the next five hours in the holding cell

Pete laid out the plan in detail, explaining exactly what Jack was supposed to do.

It was an elaborate plan. Jack had to admit that the Outfit seemed to have thought of everything. They even had a network of beautiful women and young gay men who worked for the Outfit, offering sexual favors to politicians and business people to benefit the Outfit's interests. If and when more people started going to prison, these women and men would pay regular visits to make sure the inmates were happy and to exchange information, and make sure that money was being sent to the inmates and/or their families.

Jack was not totally clear on all aspects of this plan. Some of the ideas seemed to make sense, but he wasn't so sure about other aspects. In one sense, the plan seemed like a way to simply enrich out-of-work or hungry attorneys. God knows there were plenty of them who would do anything to get business. They had to love the plan and the opportunity to make money. The notion of lending money to inmates also made sense. In jail, their income obviously would cease. As far as being a credit risk, the ex-cons would faithfully repay their loans. They had too much to lose if they didn't pay up. Since they knew the source of the loan and even though there would be no papers to sign, they would happily pay. Jack was not forgetting the most important aspect to the plan: thousands and thousands of people would be released from federal prison, obviously greatly indebted to the people who helped them gain their freedom. Jack nervously pulled his sock up. The bulge was clearly there. He patted his ankle with his hand, feeling the copy of the letter to Kathleen Hawk folded in thirds inside his sock. Jack had successfully managed to smuggle in the letter past the marshals. He was only to be involved in one part of the plan; which was to help the inmates get money sent to them in prison. He wondered if Pete's plan really made sense. Jack knew that building new prisons was one of the biggest growth Industries of the new millennium. Would the government really let people out of jail or simply continue to build new ones?

Pete seemed to think that the government would let people out of jail. But Pete had not been told the real plan. The Mob actually wanted more people *in* prison, not *out*. They wanted to see more and more prisons, which were being built every week to handle overcrowding, thus ensuring 100 percent occupancy rates—which meant more and more prisons—and the whole privatized prison system would continue to grow. The Mob was planning on this and had already started to make sure that they were going to be the largest player in this incredibly profitable business. This scheme of lending money to help get lawyers was pure bullshit. And as far as what Jack was going to be doing; i.e., getting money to the inmates, that was merely a part of the plan devised by Marty to make usurious loans to prisoners. Marty didn't really expect too many people to actually pay it back.

It was now becoming more apparent that privatized prisons were not actually saving the public money. In fact, study after study showed that privatization was costing more. But the Mafia would still make money by running private prisons. Maybe bad business for the public but still great for the privatizers. Jack's ultimate use to the Outfit was not made clear to Marty by Donovan, intentionally.

Chapter 22

❈

THE BIG HOUSE

LEWISBURG PENITENTIARY, HARRISBURG, PENNSYLVANIA

Jack had left the Federal Transfer Center in Oklahoma and was en route to Morgantown. He didn't know that there would be a stopover. He thought that he was going directly from Oklahoma to West Virginia; he couldn't have been more wrong.

"Thank you for flying Con Air, where you have to be indicted to be invited," the female U.S. marshal, attempting in a little humor, quipped over the intercom, as the old 727 made its final descent into Harrisburg, Pennsylvania. The thirty-year-old decrepit, barely functional silver bird's engines whined to a stop at the end of the tarmac. Pot-bellied Bureau of Prisons hacks, dressed in standard-issue gray pants and white shirts, with bulletproof vests under their blue nylon Bureau of Prisons jackets, wielding automatic rifles, surrounded the no-longer-proud bird. Half a dozen U.S. marshals, replete with combat boots, operated the airlift and directed Jack, along with twenty other federal prisoners, into a waiting prison bus. Handcuffed and shackled, they slowly made their way up the three steps into the retrofitted vehicle, which had steel bars welded over the windows.

Three hours later, the bus containing the other inmates and Jack, bladder bursting, motion sick, and emotionally unsettled, pulled up at Lewisburg Penitentiary. The place was rancid, rank, and raunchy, with garbage strewn over triple-barbed-wire coils atop the dirty gray concrete walls surrounding this sixty-year-old prison. Jack was scared and even more terrified after being strip-searched.

"Lift your balls, turn around, bend over, and spread your cheeks," the guard ordered, then deposited Jack into a small, dark, damp, roach-infested cell, which he mistakenly thought was solitary confinement.

"There must be some mistake," Jack said, "I'm supposed to be going to Morgantown."

"Shut the fuck up, asshole," the guard ordered. "You aren't dealing with fucking American Airlines. There are no direct flights. You don't get to pick your flight schedule. You stop where we say!"

Scared to death, Jack did as he was told. He was thankful that he only had to spend one night in this hellhole. Jack was handcuffed, shackled, and taken to his cell by three prison guards.

Chapter 23

A MISERABLE PLACE

LEWISBURG PENITENTIARY, HARRISBURG, PENNSYLVANIA

Jack felt like he was losing his mind. The cell had a steel bunk bed, no mattress, no pillow; just an old blanket that smelled like someone had urinated on it and then, as if that weren't enough, had vomited on it, too. The six-by-six-foot cell was dark, damp, and roach infested. The only light came from a four-inch slit underneath the steel door. There was a combination stainless steel toilet-sink, which was broken and filled with rags, feces, and toilet paper. This was the hole—solitary confinement, where campers like Jack were supposedly put for their own safety. The population of the prison was made up of violent, long-term prisoners. Jack was not supposed to have any contact with other prisoners. It was considered too dangerous. But because of overcrowded conditions, he was not alone. Jack assumed he was supposed to take the top bunk since the bottom one contained a body. And the body was alive; it was snoring and reeked of body odor and the sickening pungent smell of hot sweaty feet. Jack stared through the almost total darkness at the snoring thing. As if aware of Jack's gaze, the body farted, then coughed up some phlegm, spit it somewhere, and started mumbling something incoherent.

"What?" Jack responded, not understanding.

"I said what time is it?"

"I don't know," replied Jack.

"What day is it?"

"Thursday," Jack offered.

"Have they brought dinner, yet?"

"I don't know," Jack answered.

"What the fuck *do* you know, shithead?"

Jack didn't answer. He wanted out of this hellhole and away from this human piece of shit interrogating him. He tried breathing deeply, but silently. The last thing he wanted was to show his fear to this inmate. He figured he would try to make conversation.

"My name is Jack, I've got thirty-seven months. I'm supposed to be in Morgantown."

"My name is none of your fucking business, and I've got forty-nine."

"That's only twelve more months than me."

"Not *months*, asshole…*years*."

Suddenly, shrill sounds of screaming of what sounded like somebody being raped and tortured ricocheted off the cold concrete floors and walls.

Chapter 24

❦

CLUB FED

ROBERT F. KENNEDY CENTER, MORGANTOWN, WEST VIRGINIA

Jack finally arrived by bus at Morgantown. The dungeon-like dread of his terrible confinement at Lewisburg was quickly put out of his mind as soon as he saw his new "home." In comparison to Terre Haute or Lewisburg, Morgantown was beautiful, like a small La Costa, minus the spas, golf course, and fancy restaurants. Jack was put to work in the kitchen, which was perfect. His job was on the serving line, and he immediately became well liked and friendly with all the inmates and staff. It was easy to put the plan into effect.

As Pete had explained to him, start out small; lend only limited amounts of money. "Don't try to offer inmates big money at first," Pete lectured. "It will seem too strange. Offer them small amounts, initially." This seemed to work just as Pete had predicted. Every inmate had a commissary account with a spending limit of $165 a month. Without exception, inmates were always short of money. The word got around very quickly that Jack was the person to see if anyone needed a little extra money. The conversations were almost identical when inmates approached him, "Hey man, I heard that you're lending money. How much can I get?"

"I'll start having a postal money order for $25 to $50 sent to you each month. Then, after a while, it will be increased. You pay it back, plus a small amount of interest, when you get out."

"Great, sure man, thanks," was the common response from the inmates.

Jack collected the inmates' names and register numbers, as Pete had instructed him to do; when Jack would have his first visitor, he would be able to give her this information. Pete had told Jack to expect a young woman named Janet to visit him soon—nothing more was explained or said.

Chapter 25

❈

GETTING NERVOUS

ROBERT F. KENNEDY CENTER, MORGANTOWN, WEST VIRGINIA

Business was brisk for Jack at the Kennedy Center. Apparently, a majority of the 1,200 inmates there were in need of money. Jack had a visit once a week from Janet, Marty's girl, who would smuggle out a list from him of inmates' names and register numbers. Within days, the inmates were receiving postal money orders and thanking Jack. But instead of being happy at doing his job, he was getting nervous. He was afraid that the guard in the visiting room would catch him secretly passing the list of names to Janet, and then appropriate disciplinary action would follow. The Bureau of Prisons called it a "shot." There were different levels of shots, from minor to very serious. However, getting ready to go into the drug program, Jack couldn't afford any shots. Once in the program, one shot could deny any chance of a thirty-six-hour or five-day furlough. Two shots and he would be thrown out of the program, which would mean that he would not be out in nine months; he would have to spend nearly two more years in jail. Jack was also becoming very visible in prison. Word spread quickly that Jack was the man to see if you needed money. Consequently, he always had a crowd around him. He was getting more and more paranoid. Jack felt that it was only a matter of time before one of the guards or staff would overhear something. He was also concerned because Morgantown was full of snitches. He wished now that he had never gotten himself into this mess. He had not yet heard from Kathy Hawk or the Bureau of Prisons about his business proposal. How could they *not* like it? he wondered.

Jack wanted to help inmates and ex-inmates. He thought LRI would be great PR for the government to actually help felons. He wasn't sophisticated yet about prisons and the war on crime to realize that the government first and foremost wanted to be tougher on nonviolent offenders and put them in prison. The government had a two-fold purpose. First, it was good for the politicians to talk about tough crime bills; it made the public feel safer and allowed them to sleep better at night. Second, locking up more people was good for the prison business.

🍁   🍁   🍁

One hundred percent continual occupancy with a waiting list to get in was how the big Wall Street investment firms pitched the stock in private prison companies and the construction of new prisons. Jack had been continually reading more and more about the private prison business. He found it not only very interesting, but it also made him wonder if Pete's plan really made sense. If on the average, as he had been reading, three new prisons were being built each week, then inmates, albeit faced with overcrowded conditions were not, as Pete preached, going to be let out of prison.

Chapter 26

❦

NOT LIKE CAMP

ROBERT F. KENNEDY CENTER, MORGANTOWN, WEST VIRGINIA

Prison life was quite different at Morgantown. Jack wished he were still back at the camp in Terre Haute, Indiana, where it was much more laid back. Sure, there were many similarities, like the count. Every prison—whether an FPC (Federal Prison Camp); an FCI (Federal Correctional Institute) like Morgantown; FTC (Federal Transfer Center) like Oklahoma City; an MCC (Metropolitan Correctional Center) like Chicago, New York, or Miami; or penitentiaries like Atlanta or Marion—all had counts throughout the day and night. Every institution in the country had a 4:00 P.M. daily standup count. The results of the census were then sent to the Bureau of Prisons in Washington, D.C. Even though the Kennedy Center at Morgantown was the only FCI in the country that didn't have a fence around it, Jack found the place much more restrictive than the camp at Terre Haute; which had only one or two guards for 400 campers, Morgantown had hundreds of guards for the same number of inmates. There were guards in most housing units twenty-four hours a day. Inmates had to sign out of their dorms even if they were just going for a five-minute walk. At Terre Haute, Jack spent the day in sweats or shorts playing tennis. At Morgantown, he had to have his khakis washed and ironed every day except weekends. Jack's biggest dislike was his fellow inmates. The majority of them were snitches and rats, like his bunkie, who, to reduce his sentence, testified against another person who was subsequently sentenced to thirty-one years in prison. Jack trusted nobody. He grew more paranoid in his money-lending business. He knew he had to stop. He had tried to phone Donovan at his office. Jack really wanted to talk to him, to explain his fears, but Donovan's secretary had politely explained that she had given her boss the messages and that he was out of town. But, even if Jack had reached Donovan, he couldn't have talked freely, as all calls were monitored and recorded.

Obviously, there was no way Donovan could return Jack's calls. Jack couldn't mail Donovan a letter. It was too risky. Mail was opened and sometimes read. Jack knew of Marty through Janet and Pete, and that Marty had sixty-seven special employees who could easily visit Jack, getting messages in and out—like Janet, who was visiting Jack once a week to pick up names and numbers of inmates to have money sent to them. Jack had repeatedly asked Janet to get a message to Donovan, but she had lied and said she didn't know who Donovan was. She said that she had told Marty, her boss, who had said he would see what he could do. The truth was, Donovan had no time for Jack. Jack was surprised one afternoon when he got a letter from Jenny, the officer at his bank, who had given him the introduction to Donovan. She said she wanted to visit him. Jack had always liked Jenny, an attractive brunette. He felt no hostility toward her even though she had suggested that he lie, or, as Jenny had put it, "exaggerate a bit" about his income when he was applying for some credit cards. Jack really needed money for his dying mother, and the bank where Jenny worked and where Donovan was on the board had turned him down, which he didn't understand because he had excellent credit. He still had a hard time accepting the fact that he was in prison simply because he had lied on some Visa and MasterCard applications and was not willing to cooperate with the government and be a snitch.

In order for Jenny to be able to visit, he had to put her on his visiting list and then get her approved by his counselor. It would be good to see her. Maybe he could tell Jenny about Limited Risk International (LRI), his plan that he had sent in a letter to Kathy Hawk. Jack, through LRI, had wanted to have some of the millions of dollars given as grants. He knew there were various grants available from the government—hundreds of millions of dollars, in fact, having to do with prisons and crime, which Jack had been interested in since his incarceration. And so, he had come up with what he thought was a great idea. That's why he had sent his proposal to Hawk, director of the Bureau of Prisons, with a copy to Janet Reno, attorney general of the United States. Jack hoped that one of these administrators would like his idea. LRI would help inmates and ex-inmates. His plan would help parole officers, prosecuting attorneys, and halfway houses. It would accomplish a wide range of beneficial things.

In his proposal of LRI to Reno and Hawk, Jack had explained in great detail how he could help change the system. He wanted to make things better for inmates and their families upon their release from prison and hoped that Reno, and her soon-to-be successor John Ashcroft, and Hawk would want him to spearhead LRI. But, he had heard nothing and was beginning to give up on the idea. At least it would be nice to talk to Jenny and maybe get her reaction to LRI. She would be honest with Jack and either tell him to forget about the whole idea and stop being a dreamer or perhaps offer some words of encouragement. Jack, like many people sent to prison, even if not really criminals, wanted to give something back—to somehow make it easier for people to cope with what he had been through so far—to eliminate some of the fear and uncertainty.

Jack vividly recalled the day he found out that he was going to do some prison time. He had spent the entire day at The Harold Washington Library Center in Chicago—he was trying to do research or at least find some books to help prepare him for his upcoming incarceration; there was nothing. He had read more than a dozen books that he thought might offer some insight into his soon-to-be new life. All the books he read dealt with the most stressful situations in a person's life and how to cope with them. Some of these books even listed the top ten stressful events that could occur in anyone's life, like divorce, loss of a job, IRS audit, or the death of a loved one. But nowhere in any book or magazine was there anything about prison. No one wrote about the fear and devastation of preparing for this unknown—or what it would be like once in prison. There was also nothing that would prepare the millions of inmates to readjust once they were back in society. Nothing—not a damn thing! If there was any information on this, Jack couldn't find it; neither could the library staff. Even his lawyer couldn't be of any help. Again, he thought of what a need LRI could fill—if only to inform and educate inmates and their families. But, obviously, it was not that important to most people.

In fact, Jack was too naïve to realize that the government wanted people to be scared. That was the great deterrent. The government and the Bureau of Prisons did not want people to think that serving federal time, at least in camps or low-security facilities, was in many ways like being on vacation—free room and board, a cot, and three hots a day.

CHAPTER 27

❁

THE MOB IS ALIVE AND WELL

CHICAGO, ILLINOIS

Contrary to what the government wanted people to believe, the Mob, Mafia, La Costra Nostra, underworld, Outfit, organized crime, or whatever name you preferred, was alive and well, especially in Chicago and New York. While it was true that the Mafia may not have been what it was years ago, organized crime was still thriving. Organized crime had its new favorite legitimate business—private prisons. One of the fastest growing sectors of the prison industrial complex was private correctional facilities. The investment firm of Smith Barney had been part owner of a prison in California. American Express and General Electric had invested in private prison construction in Oklahoma and Tennessee. Even communication companies like AT&T, Sprint, and MCI were in the prison business, charging inmates seven times the normal rate to call home. For the Mob, private prisons and prison labor were a pot of gold—no strikes, no union organizing, no unemployment insurance to pay, and no Workers Compensation to worry about. Prisoners were doing data entry for Chevron, making telephone reservations for TWA, and taking lingerie orders for Victoria's Secret—all at a fraction of the cost of "free labor." For example, an American worker who may have made $8 an hour loses his job when the plant is relocated to another country, and the pay rate is dropped to $2 an hour. That person, now unemployed and feeling destitute, becomes involved in the drug business or another outlawed means of survival—he is arrested and put into prison. His new salary is now $.22 per hour. From worker, to unemployed, to criminal, to convict laborer, the cycle had come full circle. And the only victor was big business. The Mob *was* big business. The Mob was, of course, still involved in other enterprises, too, such as "Operation Uptick," which involved the U.S. Justice Department unsealing indictments on June 14, 2000, against 120 defendants showing the inside story of how a stock-fraud scheme controlled by New York's five Mafia families—Lucchese, Bonanno, Gambino, Genovese, and Colombo—had destroyed an aspiring dot-com called Financial Web.com. But, more and more organized crime had become involved in the private prison business. CCA, one of the companies that controlled 50 percent of the private prison business was, at one time, one of the five most profitable firms on the New York Stock Exchange.

Without a doubt, the Mob was still thriving, even after the first shake-up or real erosion of the old Mob's power that had occurred with the Appalachian big bust in 1957 of sixty-three major Mafia Dons at Joe Barbara's palatial home in upstate New York. Then in 1963, Joe Valacci, the first and most notorious Mafia songbird, provided the Feds with the first detailed account of La Cosa Nostra. The average person thought that the Feds were actually cracking down on the Mafia, even severely curtailing the activities of organized crime, possibly eliminating this sinister group, but this simply was not true. Bill Roemer, an FBI agent who had successfully worked against the Mafia, told how, after the death of Sam "Momo" Giancana, the Outfit was losing power, which was true, but they still had plenty of power—Sam Giancana was the Chicago Mafia headman who had, by 1960, ordered 200 torture-murders of men who had crossed him or gotten in his way. Giancana controlled all the bookmakers, prostitutes, loan sharks, and extortionists in Chicago, and owned interests in the Riviera, the Stardust, and the Desert Inn hotels in Las Vegas. Arrested over seventy times, Giancana had served time in prison on a variety of charges, including murder, assault with intent to kill, contributing to the delinquency of a minor, burglary, and bombing. He had been a small, dapper man who wore sharkskin suits, Fedora hats, silk shirts, and alligator shoes, some of which were gifts from Frank Sinatra.

Many people believed the Mafia, or organized crime, was a thing of the past. Though not nearly as powerful as the old days, nothing could be further from the truth; the Mob was still going strong. The Mafia, in 2001, was still solidly involved in one of its favored, time-honored traditional businesses—the pension fund racket, like the New York City Police Detectives' Endowment. And, of course, the Mob was involved in drugs, too. There was just too much money not to be a player in the drug market.

Marty Serachi knew firsthand about the power the Mob still wielded. He reflected on it as he puffed away on a Macanudo, staring out of his window at the Board of Trade building, overlooking LaSalle Street. His title was president of TMA (Transportation Merchants Association). The company issued surety bonds for the construction of Mob projects, especially the construction of new prisons. This was a huge business. Nearly 30 percent of all construction in the United States went through TMA or one of its affiliate companies. From hotels in New York to shopping centers in Los Angeles, the Mafia was very much alive. TMA was just one of thousands upon thousands of now-legitimate businesses that had nefarious origins. Of course, there still were the Teamsters. Again, another common misconception was that years ago when Jimmy Hoffa mysteriously disappeared, the largest union in the world would be legitimized. Ron Carey, one of Hoffa's predecessors, as recently as February 2001, had been sentenced to a long term in prison. Yes, it was certainly true that a few Sicilians named Guido, Carmine, and Vito did not control the underworld. But, the reality was patently clear; there definitely was organized crime. Making money in the Mob had gone through a sophisticated metamorphosis: from the inception of its infamous crime families and clandestine meetings to the full spectrum of high-tech computerized big business; and in no place was this truer than the Chicago Outfit. There still were institutions that were holdovers from the days of Al Capone. O'Bannon's Flower Shop, for example, which had catered all Mob funerals back in the roaring twenties, still had its clientele of underworld figures and factions, but they were now legitimate—a part of the worldwide FTD network. One could even browse on the World Wide Web for anything from a bouquet of roses for a wife or mistress to a full-blown, elaborate $20,000 arrangement for a daughter's wedding or son's Bar Mitzvah. Chicagoans, as much as they publicly acted as though they were embarrassed by the city's bloody history, privately loved it and continually perpetuated and were fascinated with the Mob myth and its mystique. On Lincoln Avenue, the Biograph Theater, recently designated as a landmark by the city, where notorious gangster, John Dillenger was gunned down, was a popular tourist attraction. Chicago's legacy of crime was as deeply rooted and solid as the massive caissons that were driven into the bowels of the earth to support the huge 100-plus-story Sears Tower. Chicago's reputation was international. Chicago natives could remember the questions asked of them on their trips to a foreign country or another state. Whether it was Mexico, London, Jamaica, or Tennessee, the scenario was always the same. When getting in a taxi, the driver would inquire,

"Where are you from?"

"Chicago," the passenger would respond.

"Oh, Chicago. Al Capone, right?" Then the driver would point his finger like a gun and render his version of the sounds of a machine gun.

Many restaurants in the Windy City still had that unique Chicago decorum of photographs of Chicago's infamous history adorning their walls, fully visible at the Vernon Park Tap near the University of Chicago, which had been a favorite hangout of the Capone group in the old days, at Gibson's on Rush Street, home of the rich, famous, and infamous, which had formerly been called Sweetwater, and before that, Mister Kelly's. It was the same everywhere—irrespective of Chicago's vivid and lurid past, the city maintained a semblance of pride that was intimately tied to the origins of organized crime.

Marty Serachi loved Chicago. He loved the fact that Chicago had the most beautiful women in the world. Marty loved the power that, not too long ago, before Janet, he wielded in Chicago; he desperately wished that he had not fucked up so badly. Though he was short in stature, he felt big because of his position. The Outfit rarely used guns or violence anymore in handling their affairs. In Chicago, drugs were still a big business for them. There were too many kids making designer drugs like "X" in their basements. As long as they were small dealers and they were flying under the Outfit's radar, they were left alone. But, once they got big and started turning large profits, the Outfit demanded "security" fees; basically, dues for being allowed to do business in Mob territory. There were also many legitimate businesses to be involved in that also offered great opportunities and promises of wealth and power, such as the private prison business. Loan-sharking or vigorish (vig) was still a big business, too. People always needed money. The Outfit had an overabundance of funds that they were only too happy to lend out at 3 percent interest per week, which equaled 156 percent interest per year. Lending money followed the simple rule of community property mathematics. Huge, enormous profits were reaped, no matter how big or small the loan, and there was a never-ending myriad assortment of people in desperate search for money. Maybe it was the bar owner who was running short but needed to pay his liquor bill by Saturday so as not to be blacklisted by the Liquor Commission and be cut off from buying any more booze. Or, maybe it was the travel agent who needed to make a weekly deposit to the ARC/IATA Bank by 2:00 P.M. Tuesday to cover the cost of two first-class tickets to Geneva for the company's best corporate client who had net thirty to pay, unlike the travel agent who had to settle once a week. Many people had money problems. Most people borrowed from the bank or, when in debt, ran up their credit cards. But, some people had no choice, and, thus, borrowed from the "boys." They could default on a bank loan, go bankrupt, and not pay their credit cards, but everybody paid the boys. One way or another. *Always!*

Marty was involved in vig, or loan-sharking, TMA, and the pension funds racket, but the majority of his time and energy was focused on "corporate and political espionage" to help the Mob's private prison interests. That was a fancy euphemism for high-class prostitution. From Kansas City to Miami, Marty was in charge of a network of beautiful women who, like Janet, would be strategically planted to gain or disseminate inside information for the Outfit. This enterprise was massive and intriguing. Comprising only sixty-seven women and five young men, Marty's little sex-CIA, as he liked to refer to his organization, was as powerful as the United States Senate. Sex was, and always had been, the ultimate weapon. The Outfit had in its pocket, to name but a few, bank presidents, senators, congressmen, CEOs of Fortune 500 companies, doctors, lawyers, judges, police captains, FBI agents, newspaper reporters, TV anchor persons, movie stars, and school-board members. The gamut of people and variety of occupations that the Outfit had influence over was truly unbelievably extensive.

The president of a big bank, for example, would not make a questionable loan when he had to answer to the board of directors, or feared an investigation by the Feds, if the loan was not soundly within the bank's lending parameters. But, when it was explained to the president of a bank, who was usually a pillar of the community, that if he didn't approve a certain loan and do a favor, it would become public knowledge that for the last three and a half years he had been having an affair with a girl twenty-five years younger than he—that would usually be enough to convince him to accommodate the Outfit. If not, the next day, he would be in shock as he opened a plain brown envelope delivered by special messenger, filled with hundreds of sexually explicit photos of him and the Outfit's mistress, along with a copy of the lease for the apartment in which the man had set up his mistress. There would even be the canceled checks for the rent from the secret account that his wife never knew about because the statements were only sent to his office.

Likewise, with attorneys and judges, the ongoing scandals in Chicago made most of the judges more careful, if not downright paranoid, so oftentimes it took a little longer with them. Sometimes it could take years for Marty's gorgeous operatives to accomplish their goals. Success was never a question of *if*, but simply *when*. And Marty Serachi was very good at what he did. That was, until he brought Janet into the Outfit—because of her and her "magic pussy," he had fucked up too many times and knew that his days were numbered.

🍁   🍁   🍁

Marty had promoted Janet rapidly, rising quickly through the ranks of his little operation of illicit Charlie's Angels. Janet was the best. Within six months of her inception with Marty, she had clearly demonstrated, with a vengeance he had never seen before, how tremendously talented she was—a natural. More than just her insatiable thirst for "big money" and all the nice things that came with it, Janet thoroughly enjoyed her work. This was to be expected. She had spent her entire life, in one way or another, preparing for this. She was fulfilling a lifelong dream. She had amassed power, wealth, and respect; something she never had growing up in Berwyn, the daughter of a small-time bookie and tavern owner in one of the city's less-affluent white suburbs next to the town of Cicero, once the suburban headquarters for Al Capone. Janet had money now, a fancy car, furs, diamonds, and a beautiful condo. When Janet would drive out to her family's house in Berwyn for Sunday dinner, her parents never thought to question the extravagant gifts she would shower on them. Her baby sister, Wendy, loved Sundays. She would wait in excited anticipation for Janet's arrival. Tantamount to early and weekly Christmases, Wendy was in awe of her big sister. Janet had put her older brother into the Projectionists Union. Years ago, this had been a very tightly knit closed group with incredible pay. The only person who was not impressed with Janet was her older sister, Carole, Mark's new wife, who was a successful boutique owner on fashionable Oak Street in Chicago. Janet wanted to make Carole proud of her, but Janet always felt so inferior to her; she knew deep down that Carole would never respect her. Carole knew that whatever Janet was involved in was not good. There was no way any legitimate job could pay as much as Janet was making. Janet spent money like she was printing it herself. When she would shop at Carole's boutique, Janet would drop $7,000 or $8,000 in the blink of an eye. Carole knew Janet had a drug problem, too. As much as Carole didn't want to believe it, she knew that Janet was involved with the wrong people. She knew Marty was definitely "wrong people!" She had met Marty only once while waiting to meet Janet for a drink; Marty had stopped by the table and told Carole that Janet would be late—Janet never did show up. Carole had met Marty last night for the second time, and now she was being held hostage somewhere.

 Yes, the Outfit, although not nearly as powerful as it used to be, was very much alive and well in Chicago. Marty Serachi had been a key figure in the underworld, and Janet, under the watchful tutelage of Marty, had risen quickly in the hierarchy of the Chicago Mob, but she was in way over her head. A woman in the Outfit always was. Janet was confused. She had always fantasized about the power, money, and mystique of being an Outfit mistress—to be strong, important, powerful, and rich. Yes, the Mafia was alive and well, and she was right in the middle of it. So, why did Janet suddenly feel weak, unimportant, and powerless now that she had it all? Why did she now feel that she had no control over her own life? The answer was obvious—because Marty controlled whether Janet would live or die and also now held her sister, Carole, hostage, doped up, and would probably kill her, too. Compared to the old days, the Mafia was a shell of its former self. However, its continued secret involvement with the CIA in taking out unsavory characters, including a number of terrorists in the middle-east, and its growing involvement in the privatization of prisons all over the world, promised to restore the Mob's power. Marty could have made a lot of money—that is, if he hadn't fucked up.

Chapter 28

EARLY THURSDAY EVENING

FORT LAUDERDALE, FLORIDA

It was a beautiful night in Fort Lauderdale. Seventy-nine degrees outside, sixty degrees inside. Mark had turned up the air conditioner and lighted a fire. Glass of wine in one hand, remote in the other, he watched one of his favorite movies, *Dr. Zhivago,* on his sixty-one-inch Sony. Mark lay on the couch in his bathrobe, two pillows under his head, and one pillow under his feet and promised himself that he would stop drinking soon.

Hard as he tried, he couldn't help thinking about Carole and the wild scene he had walked in on less than twenty-four hours ago. Mark had given in and tried to call Carole earlier in the day, but there was no answer at the Chicago apartment. When he had checked in with his office, both with his secretary and the answering machine on his private line that he had installed just for Carole, there were no messages from her. Mark had called Lisa, who managed Carole's boutique on Oak Street. Lisa had not heard from Carole today, but this was not unusual. Carole seldom came into her shop or even called, preferring instead to spend most of her time traveling around the world on buying trips for the boutique. Lisa did tell Mark that she had phoned Carole yesterday at their apartment.

"I called her to find out when our fall collection would be arriving from London. Carole told me she wasn't sure and said she'd try to locate the number of the supplier and call me back. Is something wrong?" Lisa asked with some concern over the fact that Mark had never before called to check up on Carole.

Mark didn't want to alarm Lisa. "No, nothing is wrong. It just seems that we keep missing each other."

"When I talked to Carole yesterday, she said that her sister, Janet, was coming over and after that, she was expecting you to be home from the club around 7:00 and that she was looking forward to having dinner with you. Carole said that she wanted to get rid of her sister as quickly as possible," Lisa responded, a little confused. "Didn't you have dinner with Carole?" Lisa questioned.

Then it hit Mark like a ton of bricks. Carole's sister, Janet! Mark had forgotten all about Janet.

"No, we never did meet for dinner. Thanks for your help. I've got to go." Mark slammed down the phone.

"Holy shit!" he screamed at the television. "Oh God!" he yelled out. Could it be? Was it possible that Carole was not having sex with Marty, that it was Janet? He had just remembered the one and only time Carole had unhappily told Mark about her sister, Janet. Carole loved her sister, but had distanced herself from her. Janet was trouble. She was a druggie and obviously involved in something illegal because for the last couple of years, out of the clear blue, she was rolling in money. Carole had never understood her younger sister. She felt sorry for her, but had given up trying to help. Janet had always been so insecure and jealous of Carole, always trying to emulate her and win her approval and be respected by Carole. Yes, Mark had forgotten about Carole's younger sister, Janet, born seventeen minutes after Carole—her almost-identical twin sister. He jumped up from the couch in Ciel Bleu, but before he had time to think, there was a loud knocking at the door. He opened it and saw her; nose bloody, tears running down her face; an obviously drunk Connie Cook fell into his arms.

Chapter 29

❦

MOMENTS LATER

FORT LAUDERDALE, FLORIDA

Mark wiped the blood from Connie's nose with his shirt. "Is it broken? Do you want to go to the hospital?"

"No, I'm okay," Connie replied, her head pressed against Mark's hairy chest. Connie was wearing Obsession, reminding him of Carole, who also wore that fragrance.

"Don't cry, I'll get some ice for…"

"No, just hold me for a minute, I'll be okay."

"What happened?" Mark asked.

"Bill hit me," replied Connie.

"Who's Bill? Your boyfriend…?"

"Who's Bill?" Connie replied, as if everybody should know Bill. "Alderice, Bill Alderice, my fiancé. Everybody knows who Bill Alderice is, don't you?"

"No," replied Mark, getting irritated. "Why the hell did he hit you?"

"Because I hit the bastard first," Connie replied in anger.

Mark tried to console Connie; at least he wanted to, but he didn't have time to worry about Connie or get sidetracked since he had to get back to Chicago to find Carole, or her sister, Janet. He didn't exactly know what he was going to do, but he had to do something, and right away, now that he realized it was Janet, and not his wife, Carole, who was having sex with Marty and Renée in his apartment! He had his own problems. "Uh, look Connie, let me take you to your room. I have to get back to Chicago. I have an emergency."

"What's your name?"

"Mark."

"Please take me to Chicago with you, Mark," Connie whispered. "If I don't get out of this town, I'm afraid Bill is going to kill me!"

CHAPTER 30

❀

JACK'S LETTER

THE JUSTICE DEPARTMENT, WASHINGTON, D.C.

The Justice Department was no stranger to organized crime. Janet Reno's staff was more than capable of handling the majority of responsibilities that the Justice Department was charged with. However, when she had received this top-secret folder from the Bureau of Prisons, she wisely decided that she'd better handle this matter herself. Maybe she could make up for her Waco screw-up.

The attorney general of the United States of America carefully reread the file. She had never seen anything like this. The four-inch-thick file contained Jack's letter regarding LRI, the money lending and the Mobs increasing involvement in the prison industry. Reno picked up the red phone. After the third ring, a woman answered.

"The president's office, how may I help you?"

"I need to see him."

"Certainly Ms. Reno, how about next Tuesday at 10:00?"

"No, right away, Madge."

"Can you be in the Oval Office in forty-five minutes?"

"Thanks, I'll be there."

Reno would not be the attorney general much longer and desperately wanted to be thought of ten years from now as having been effective. Maybe solving this problem now would help establish a solid place for her in history and hopefully serve as a tribute to her in the future. Clinton would soon be replaced by Bush, so Reno had to move fast.

Chapter 31

❦

THURSDAY NIGHT

ALDERICE MANSION, FORT LAUDERDALE, FLORIDA

"There's plenty more where that came from," Bill Alderice yelled, as he threw $20,000 worth of $100 bills into the air. Everyone clapped and cheered wildly as Bill stood atop his pool table in all his cocaine-induced euphoric glory, looking down upon his loyal followers, friends, and suckups. "I love you all."

"We love you, too, Bill. You're the greatest!" his flock cheered wildly, as they grabbed, shoved, and pushed each other to get the $100 bills. The wild scene looked like a ticker-tape parade.

"We broke all the records. Eight hundred thousand dollars came in yesterday," Bill lied. It was only $600,000, although still a record—$50,000 more than the previous record of $550,000. But Bill was so happy and so coked up by the end of the night that even he started to believe his own lies. "We are going to be the biggest fucking company in the history of the universe!" Bill wildly exclaimed, punching the air with his right hand like some hyped-up television evangelist, while swallowing sloppy swigs from a Jack Daniels bottle, which he caressed in his other hand like a skid-row bum.

Bill's small black eyes had a drunken, hazy look; his speech was slurred and strained as he screamed to be heard over "Eric Clapton," which was blaring from the huge floor-model JBL speakers hooked up to the $20,000 custom-designed Bang and Olufsen stereo system.

"We are the greatest! We are the greatest!" Bill cheered, parroting Mohammed Ali to his loyal followers. The cocaine, Louis Roederer Cristal, and Dom flowed endlessly, as it did every night at Bill's mansion on the Intercoastal. Bill looked out over his crowd of admirers that came to party and pay tribute, sharing in the buzz and spectacle of his meteoric rise to success.

He had made it. He was Numero Uno, the top dog. He certainly felt that he was on his way to becoming one of the richest and most famous men in the world. He knew he was doing too much cocaine, but he could stop any time he wanted to. He just didn't want to, not yet anyway. The drug made him feel so good. He thought that everyone envied him. He had it all. He could do or have anything he wanted except for one thing: Connie. Sure, they were engaged; maybe they would be married, but still Bill couldn't control Connie like he could everyone and everything else in his life. Granted, he cheated on her, lied to her, and at times treated her badly, but with someone as great as he in her life, Bill narcissistically reasoned, why did she have to be so goddamned difficult? He hated, and at the same time loved, her violent temper. She was so much like him. Suddenly, he felt a sharp pain in his chest…it must be bad coke, Bill thought, as he clutched his heart, fell off the pool table onto the Italian marble floor, and slipped into unconsciousness.

Chapter 32

EARLY THURSDAY NIGHT

FORT LAUDERDALE, FLORIDA

"I can't do that," Mark replied.

"Why not?" asked Connie.

"What do you mean, why not? Because I don't even know you," Mark shot back, becoming increasingly irritated at this woman.

"So? Let's get to know each other on the plane to Chicago."

"You don't understand. I'm married."

"I'm engaged," Connie offered matter-of-factly. "Believe me, Mark, I'm not trying to hit on you." Mark said nothing as Connie continued talking. "You say you have some emergency, and you definitely look like you have a problem. Maybe I can help."

Mark stared hard at Connie. How could this woman he just met possibly help him?

"Look, I appreciate your concern. I really do, but..."

Connie interrupted Mark as if reading his mind. "I realize you don't know me. You probably think I'm some wacko hysterical bitch who is just having a lover's spat." Mark was going to reply in the affirmative, but he wasn't given a chance. "But I can help you. I'm a lot smarter than

I look. I helped my fiancé, Bill, quickly build a $200-million-a-year business, and it didn't happen because I have big tits and a nice ass. I've got brains and balls, too," Connie said confidently, without a trace of arrogance.

"I'm sure you do," Mark replied, not wanting to argue with this woman. He didn't have time for this, physically or emotionally. He wished Connie would go upstairs to her room at Ciel Bleu, so he could get going. But where should he go? What should he do first? He had not talked to anyone about this living nightmare he was experiencing. Maybe he *should* talk to Connie. No, that was pointless. What good would that possibly do? He wanted to call the police, but the note he found in his room at the Ritz this morning had warned him that something bad would happen if he did. The note also said that he was being followed. He hadn't understood the meaning of the note when he first read it, but it was all starting to make sense now—sort of. Connie grabbed Mark by his shoulder, shaking him out of his thoughts.

"Look Mark, don't be so damn macho. Let me try to help you."

"Why would you want to help me?" Mark asked, his doubts about women surfacing. He thought of how his first wife had hurt him, and also his reaction last night when he walked into his condo and thought he had found his new wife being unfaithful to him. He was further agitated by his own guilt, now realizing that he was totally wrong about the episode.

"Because I can tell you're a nice guy," said Connie.

"How do you know that?" Mark asked, sarcastically.

"Because when I pulled up before, you didn't ask me any questions. When I came in a few minutes ago crying with a bloody nose, you were kind and caring, holding me, and even wiping my nose. I can see it in your eyes; you're a kind person."

"But…," Mark began, then was cut off by Connie as she put her finger lightly over his lips, silencing his objections. She then grabbed Mark's hand and gently squeezed it. Mark's pent-up emotion of last night's events suddenly released itself like a breaking dam. Mark could no longer hold back his tears. It was Connie who now returned the favor, holding Mark in her arms as he sobbed.

"It's okay, it's all right," Connie whispered.

Chapter 33

EARLY EVENING THURSDAY

FORT LAUDERDALE, FLORIDA

"What's that?" Mark felt Connie vibrating as she hugged and consoled him.

"That's my beeper. Where's the phone?"

Mark showed Connie to the phone and acted as if he weren't listening. Connie hurriedly punched in some numbers. "When?" Connie frantically queried. "No, don't call a doctor. I'll be there in five minutes."

"What's the matter?" questioned Mark.

"It's Bill. I've got to get home right away. Please drive me. I'm too upset."

"But I've got to get a reservation to fly back to Chicago tonight."

"I don't care. I need you now," Connie sweetly but adamantly demanded.

Mark realized Connie needed help; he could see that she was visibly shaken by the call. "Let's go," he replied and led Connie by the arm into her smashed but drivable red Ferrari.

They pulled up to the house and Connie jumped out of the car before it even came to a full stop. Mark parked the car, then followed close on Connie's heels. Bill was laid out on the floor of the billiards room with a blanket over his body and a pillow under his head. The color was drained from his face. Worse yet, he was turning blue.

"What's the matter with him?" Connie screamed.

Someone from the crowd answered. "He did too much coke, then passed out. He probably just needs to sleep it off."

Mark told the people hovering around him to move. He felt for Bill's pulse behind his ear—nothing. He put his ear over Bill's mouth to hear if he was breathing, but he was not. Mark started mouth-to-mouth resuscitation; still nothing. "Call an ambulance," Mark ordered.

"No! He's on probation," Connie screamed. "If he's taken to the hospital and they find coke in his blood, his probation will be violated, and they'll put him back in jail," she nervously explained.

"Do you want him to die?" Mark asked.

"No…do something…help him…don't let him die," Connie pleaded.

Mark knew a little CPR; the practice of applying and releasing pressure on a person's chest in hopes of squeezing enough blood to the brain to keep the person alive for a few more minutes until help arrived. Against Connie's objections, someone called an ambulance. Fifteen minutes later, Bill was in the ER at Broward Community Hospital. In rare cases, though for reasons no one quite understands, one can actually provide almost normal blood flow just by pumping rhythmically on the chest. Bill's heart monitor showed ventricular tachycardia, which was a relatively good sign. At least it wasn't V-Fib (ventricular fibrillation), which is rapidly fatal if not corrected by electroshock.

"He's in critical condition, but stable," the doctor informed Connie and Mark. "If everything remains stable, we'll move him out of ICU in twenty-four hours."

Connie, with the permission of the doctor, was allowed to see Bill. She took Mark with her into the ICU. Connie saw that Bill was doing much better and gently hugged her fiancé's hand.

"Who's this?" Bill weakly muttered, looking at Mark.

"The person who saved your life," Connie replied.

"Whatever you need is yours," Bill said in appreciation.

"Mark's in a lot of trouble. I should go to Chicago with him." Connie replied.

"Go. I'll be fine," Bill spoke softly and slowly. "Give him whatever help he needs."

The trauma of the near death of Bill had made Mark temporarily forget about the situation with Carole. But now that Bill seemed okay, his mind instantly resumed its panic mode. He had to find Carole and make sure she was all right. He regretted acting so hastily in assuming that she was just another failed romance. He had to find her and know that she was okay.

"C'mon," ordered Connie. "I've got Bill's Lear standing by at Butler Aviation. Let's go to Chicago and kick some ass."

Connie was more than just indebted to Mark for coming to Bill's rescue. She thought that maybe she was falling for him, but knew that Mark could not have similar feelings. His thoughts were focused solely on his wife. She cared deeply for Bill and didn't want to see him in any trouble, but she wondered if she truly loved him; he had so many vices. Connie was grateful that the doctor accepted the generous stack of $100 bills she handed him as payment not to call the authorities; Bill could not afford to violate probation.

Chapter 34

THE THURSDAY AFTERNOON DINNER AT LITTLE MAMA'S

CHICAGO, ILLINOIS

The meeting was being held on West Grand Avenue in the old Italian neighborhood. The food was excellent, as were the homemade wines. In attendance were Donovan, the most influential Outfit lawyer in the country, heir apparent to the Don in Miami, Deemis Whitacre, the Rhode Island connection, and Marty Serachi, the local Chicago connection. Janet was also at a separate table with some low-level Outfit soldiers. Janet had not spoken to Deemis since she got back to Chicago, after seeing him late last night in Rhode Island, and was resigned to do whatever Marty wanted in order to protect her sister. Marty assured Janet again that Carole was okay.

🍁   🍁   🍁

Carole, still in captivity, was allowed to call Mark; after reaching his answering machine at home she called his office. His secretary said that he was out of town but didn't know where he could be reached. This really upset Carole. She had been kidnapped and was now being held hostage. She naturally assumed that Mark would be waiting by the phone going out of his mind, consumed with worry and concern for her welfare. How could he be so cold, so uncaring? Had she made a mistake in her marriage to Mark? Carole was still being drugged and felt totally disoriented.

Little Mama's restaurant, on Grand Avenue, was picked for its privacy and security. Prior meetings had been held at more convenient Loop restaurants, such as the now demolished Counselors' Row, or the Randolph Inn, but places like these were no longer safe; bugs had been planted by the Feds and unfortunately discovered too late. Indictments had been being handed down, and some local politicos and Outfit members had been prosecuted or made plea agreements and subsequently ended up in jail.

As was the custom, no business was discussed until the meal was finished. The decor of this family-owned restaurant (circa 1950s) was quaint and cozy. The eatery had only six tables, with plastic, red-checkered tablecloths and old white linoleum floors long in need of replacement. The garish red, worn wallpaper was adorned with pictures of the old country: Venice, Sicily, Naples, and Palermo. Unevenly hung photographs with cracked glass displayed pictures of Al Capone, Meyer Lansky, "Momo" Giancana, Frank Sinatra, the pope, and three generations of the Balernos, the proprietors of Little Mama's. The dim lighting created a rather romantic atmosphere enhanced by the empty bottles of Chianti covered in wicker with little burning candles stuffed in the necks gradually covering the bottles with polychromatic wax drippings. The old Wurlitzer, requiring no coinage, played only Sinatra, Tony Bennett, and Pavarotti. The entire Balernos family made all of the homemade Italian delicacies. For starters, there were huge antipasto platters with prosciutto, provolone, grilled garlic, red peppers, and green olives. They made two different soups: pasta é fagioli and straticella with spinach and egg. In addition, there were trays of breaded and baked garlic clams and raw oysters with homemade red sauce so hot it could easily burn the insides of the stomach. Plentiful platters of three-cheese garlic bread, with bottles of imported virgin olive oils for bread dipping, further ensured clogging of the arteries. Then, for the pièce de résistance, there were six-inch-thick lasagna, spaghetti with homemade meatballs, and homemade Italian sausage seasoned hot, hotter, and burn-your-mouth-out. And, as if there were not enough food, out came Fettuccine Alfredo à la instant coronary, shrimp Dijon, Caesar salad, and mashed potatoes and gravy to kill for. No matter how fat the patrons were, Grandma Balerno incessantly piled more food on all the plates, saying that everyone looked sickly, too skinny. "Mange, mange," was her continuous admonition to this group of killers, mobsters, hookers, and lawyers. Daughter Balerno kept circling the table with freshly grated parmesan and romano cheeses. Papa Balerno kept busily poured an endless stream of three choice homemade wines that he had brewed carefully in the basement.

Donovan began to speak after the coffee and pastries were laid out. He motioned for all the women, including Janet, to go back into the kitchen so the men could discuss business. The women were not insulted. This was simply the way it was. Donovan, with deep-set black eyes, big jowls, and a prominent nose exuded an air of confidence and authority. His appearance seemed totally natural, as if he were born to be a Don. His suntanned face belied his age of sixty-three. He wasn't handsome, but rather good-looking, in a mean, stern, and intelligent kind of way. Everyone had kidded for years, but never to his face, that Donovan was born looking like a gangster. He had that kind of mug and the demeanor to match.

"My doctor tells me I got to stop eating all this rich food," Donovan began. "Fucking doctors, they have no heart. He also told me I got to quit smoking and drinking, too," Donovan complained as he lit up his big Macanudo cigar and sipped his wine.

Donovan, although a lawyer, was the consigliore for the Don, which was kind of a misnomer, because the real godfather was a small Sicilian man in his eighties, who, although involved in all Mafia business, was too old and too tired to really care passionately about anything anymore, with the exception of the Mafia's increased involvement in the privatization prison business and his grandchildren, with whom he played every afternoon in the garden of his mansion in Miami. The Don had just made a rare flight earlier that day from Miami to Chicago to lay down the law with Marty Serachi and then had met with Donovan. Donovan was, for all intents and purposes, the main man. Everyone knew this and respected him accordingly. He was well liked, not just feared because of his position in the Mafia. He was the heir apparent to becoming Numero Uno when the Don died or retired, which was expected to be soon.

"Okay, gentlemen," everyone gave their undivided attention to Donovan as he spoke. "Let's get down to business. Deemis, I understand there may be some complications with the racetrack deal in Pawtucket. Is this true?"

"Well, yes, Mr. Donovan. According to the chairman of the racetrack, K. Calden Rooley, it seems as though some rival family is going to attempt to outbid us at the stockholders' meeting tomorrow. Worse yet, instead of closing the track and building a development, they intend to keep the track open…and you know what will happen if that occurs, sir."

"Deemis, first of all, I am not aware of any rival family trying to interfere with your operation out there, and second…"

Deemis cut him off. "Mr. Donovan, before I flew to Chicago, I got this information from very good sources while I was at the board meeting this morning in Rhode Island," Deemis nervously added, regretting that he had interrupted Donovan.

Donovan seemed to be in deep contemplation before he spoke again to Deemis. "We have invested almost two years and a helluva lotta money in this operation. Is it possible we have a rat?" Donovan stared at Deemis, who tried to show no emotion.

"No way, Mr. Donovan," Deemis answered quickly, knowing that his answer was a lie. He wished to God that he had never betrayed his people. What had he been thinking? He knew without the slightest doubt that in his anger to get back at his father-in-law, and his crippled, frigid wife, as well as his own self-loathing and self-destructive personality, he had made a stupid, fatal mistake. His world seemed to be closing in on him. Even Janet had not talked to him since she left his apartment late last night. She had flown back to Chicago this morning without a word or a call to him. Janet was firmly back with Marty now. At least Deemis took some solace, some small measure of relief, not comfort, hoping that Janet had not betrayed him in his plan to let the racetrack deal out of the bag. She wasn't stupid. If Donovan or Marty were to learn that Janet was part of the betrayal, no mercy would be spared her.

Donovan's next words to Deemis seemed almost like a bad Nixon imitation, "Let me make this perfectly clear, Whitacre…I will hold you personally responsible if this racetrack deal gets fucked up."

Deemis Whitacre turned pale as chalk. He could taste the fear in his mouth and the disgusting bile in his throat.

"Do we understand each other?" Donovan asked.

"Yes sir, Mr. Donovan," replied Deemis, thinking of nothing else to say. Even if he had, it would have been futile. He felt faint, deathly scared. He couldn't even form a thought, let alone emit another sound. He was being strangled by his own paranoia. Deemis sensed that Donovan already knew all about Deemis's betrayal in telling Janet about the racetrack deal. Now, because Janet had leaked the information about the track to someone, actually Bill Alderice, many associates were probably going to end up in prison. Donovan then turned to Marty. "Now, what do you have to report to me, Serachi?"

"Things seem to be going pretty well, considering, sir."

"Considering what?" Donovan barked back, clearly not hiding his anger at Marty.

"Well, I am sure that you know there was a little problem with Janet, but that is solved now."

"Explain what you mean, Serachi, and don't leave anything out. I know from the Don in Miami that, against our wishes, you were personally involved with the girl. She decided she wanted out of the organization, ran away somewhere last night, then came back today because you're supposedly holding her sister hostage to make sure she stays in line."

"Yeah, well that's exactly right, Mr. Donovan. But everything is okay now," Marty repeated, desperately hoping that everything *really was* okay.

As if reading his mind, Donovan spoke: "This all sounds kind of messy to me. Where are you holding her sister hostage? How long do you plan to keep her? What about this hotshot real estate husband of hers who is obviously looking for her? How do you know Janet will stay in line once we let her sister go and not screw up our plans with our growing involvement in the privatization of prisons and the racetrack deal I've been working on with Deemis?"

"Trust me," replied Marty, unconvincingly, "I've got everything under control."

"You're quite sure, Mr. Serachi?"

"Yes, absolutely. There's nothing to worry about, Mr. Donovan."

"Then I have your word on that, Marty?"

"Yes, of course, sir. You can trust me completely."

"Good," replied Donovan, who smiled broadly.

Not only couldn't Donovan trust Serachi completely, but also the truth of the matter was—he couldn't trust the man as far as he could spit. How could Marty be so stupid as to blatantly lie to him? Didn't he know it was foolish, no—dangerous, no—deadly, to bullshit him? Donovan scratched his head and wondered. Had Marty always been this dumb? Donovan's supposedly "key" people were all fuckups. How could they all be so stupid? The Mob's plan was that the majority of their money, for at least the next ten years, would come from privatized prisons. Sure, the racetrack deal was important, as were other Mafioso ventures. But to risk everything was incomprehensible to him. Did Janet have the magic pussy? No woman could be worth it, ever! thought Donovan. Too bad Marty and Deemis had done their thinking with their dicks.

After Donovan concluded the meeting, Janet returned from the kitchen with the other woman. Marty discreetly escorted Janet to a private table and began explaining to her that she would be going to Washington, D.C. that evening.

Chapter 35

THE DINNER CONCLUDES

CHICAGO, ILLINOIS, AND WASHINGTON, D.C.

When Marty had finished explaining to Janet that she would be going to D.C. in a few hours, she wished that she had never met him. He never did anything unless he was going to get something in return. Marty used people and obviously enjoyed doing so. Why hadn't Janet been smart enough to understand that when she first met him? Why had she let herself act so foolishly—or had she always been prone to foolishness? How, she wondered, could there actually have been a time when she loved him? She was smarter now. But when she had first met Marty she had been so affected by him, really taken in. He seemed to represent everything she had wanted and was desperately searching for her entire miserable life—power, money—the good life. Marty was the embodiment of everything she had always dreamed about. Janet had decided what she wanted when she was a young girl. More importantly, she knew beyond a shadow of a doubt what she *didn't* want. She had seen her mother always drunk, always unhappy, always struggling to find herself, to no avail. Janet's mother was always depressed, especially when she drank, which was all the time. She wasn't a good-looking woman, but she wasn't ugly, either. She just didn't seem to care about herself or her family. Her mom dressed in old, ill-fitting clothes. Her hair was unruly and unkempt. She was severely overweight and over the years had become complacent as far as her appearance was concerned. Janet's father was a miserable man. He was always solemn and uncaring; one of the casualties of an unhappy life. A loser. At first Janet didn't understand why her mother stayed married to him, and then as she got a bit older, she began to understand. Where would her mother go? What would she do? She had no goals, no aspirations, and no dreams. She was miserable, and misery loved, or sought out, misery. Her mother found it, embraced it, and was lost in it with her father. They were both bust-outs. Two unhappy human beings who seemed to have long ago been passed over for any hope or happiness that life offered most other people. Often, Janet tried in vain to understand why they even wanted to keep on living. The answer, she concluded, was that it would take too much effort to kill themselves. Her parents were much too apathetic to change their ways and made no attempt to break out of the perpetual malaise that immobilized their lives.

Consequently, Janet spent her whole life wishing that she could be somebody else, anybody else. She vowed to fight with every ounce of her soul not to become like her parents. She envied her happy friends. Why had she been cursed to be born into this family? When she would go to one of her friend's houses after school or on the weekends, she longed to be like them. It was so different from her own home. She was jealous of what everyone else had. The more she wanted what everyone else seemed to take for granted—little things like laughter, encouragement, and the feeling of being wanted and appreciated—the more depressed she would become. She was far too embarrassed to ever ask friends over. Sadly, as Janet progressed into her teens, all of her friends stopped associating with her. As a child, she had been plain, unattractive, and gawky.

Then she went through a pronounced metamorphosis and became a real beauty. Still, she was awkward and didn't know how to handle this sudden change. She was both disappointed and hurt that her friends, instead of accepting her, had actually become cold to her. Janet's good looks and developing full breasts intimidated them. The boys in her class were constantly staring at her well-developed chest. She felt terribly self-conscious. She wasn't interested in boys, not sexually anyway. Her mother didn't help her prepare for the problems and uncertainties that she would be facing during adolescence. Janet didn't know how to cope with what was happening to her mind and body, and she didn't want to be viewed as a sex object. Her greatest hope was just to be liked, as was her almost-identical twin sister, Carole. Sadly though, it was not just her physical appearance that made the other girls dislike her and the boys lust for her; she didn't know how to be happy. She never had any experience at being happy. So, Janet found herself becoming more reclusive. The more she tried to fit in and be like everyone else, the more it became patently clear that she was *not* like everyone else. She was different. As much as she wished this were not so, it made no difference; there was no denying it. What is wrong with me? She continually wondered. Her sister Carole, whom she idolized, seemed to be in the catbird seat. Everything for Carole seemed to be wonderful. She was happy, popular, and seemed to have a purpose to her life, unlike Janet.

Her older brother, always trying to act normal, had a drug problem. He shot morphine. Janet would hide in the closet of her brother's bedroom and watch him inject the drug. Janet had viewed this frequent ritual of her addictive brother many times. Then one Sunday, out of curiosity, she snuck into her brother's room when everybody was away for the day visiting a relative. Nervous and excited at the same time, she carefully opened the bottom drawer of the dresser; she pulled the works out and duplicated everything that she had seen her brother do far too many times. After she had carefully injected the morphine into her arm and undone the tourniquet, she noticed a book in her brother's drawer as she was putting the hypo and other paraphernalia back in place. She picked up the book and found that she couldn't put it down. As her drug-induced euphoria kicked into her brain, she spent the entire day reading, relating, and empathizing with the book's protagonist, Frankie Machine, a morphine addict. The book, *The Man with the Golden Arm*, by famous Chicago author Nelson Algren, dealt with the sordid and horrible victims of Chicago's Polish-American ghetto in the Division Street and Damen Avenue area of Chicago after World War II. While other girls Janet's age were reading *The Catcher in the Rye*, by J.D. Salinger, she had found a surreal, strangely comfortable niche in reading about the tragic lives of desperate people, feeling that she was one of them. It seemed to justify her need for shooting up drugs.

🍁 🍁 🍁

"Where are you? You seem like you're a million miles away," asked Marty, sounding a bit annoyed.

"What?" Janet replied, not realizing that she had been lost in her thoughts. "I was just thinking."

"About what?" queried Marty, somewhat interested.

"Oh, nothing in particular; I was just daydreaming. I didn't mean to be rude."

"No problem, I just want to make sure you're okay, and that everything is all right."

"I'm fine, Marty, really. Everything is fine," answered Janet, wishing for an instant that Marty *did* care about her, although she knew that wasn't the case. He had proven that by taking her sister hostage. Janet blamed herself. Obviously, if she had not been involved with Marty, the Mob, or the Outfit, none of these problems would be happening. Janet had paid a high price for talking to Marty about Carole, about her admiration for her almost-identical twin sister, and how she envied Carole, wishing she could be more like her. Unfortunately though, that would never happen—not now. Janet had gone too far and there was no turning back. She had made her bed and could do nothing but lie in it, literally and figuratively. She was a whore—albeit, a high-class one—but nevertheless, a whore. Why, Janet wondered, had she ever confided in Marty about Carole?

Marty smiled at Janet. Was she wearing underwear? he wondered. Probably not. She never did. God, how he missed fucking her. He missed the way she used to look at him as if he were the most important and virile man on the face of the earth. Marty thought again about his decision to send Janet to Washington so she could be at the same party as former Mayor Marion Barry tonight. He knew he couldn't trust her or be completely honest with her about Barry. All Janet had to know was that she was supposed to get close with the former mayor. And "close" didn't mean standing next to him; it meant she had to get him in bed; get him into a compromising situation. Janet was the best seductress there was. She had trained countless girls in the art of seduction. In fact, one of the girls that Janet had trained was already in D.C., and ready to go to the party tonight. Marty called her and told her she was being replaced by Janet. She was to leave the hotel key at the front desk for Janet to pick up. Marty realized that even though Janet was the best, it was unlikely that she could accomplish her mission in one short night. Consequently, Marty had made arrangements to have a closed-circuit TV rigged up in a suite at the Omni Shoreham Hotel, where Janet would stay. The party that Barry was going to attend was also at the Omni Shoreham. Various drugs had been planted in the room already by the girl Janet was replacing.

Years ago, when Marty would go to Washington, D.C., for business or pleasure, the first night spot he would visit after he checked into his hotel was George and Catina Harris's place, The Camelot, the best titty bar in D.C. The Camelot, with its distinctive yellow canopy outside and full-sized knight-in-armor replica by the cigarette machine, was owned by George and Catina and their three kids, Petie, Leo, and Cookie. The club was kind of an institution in D.C. Everybody went there. It was one of Marty's favorite places. Steve, the doorman, a big, black, burly 210-pound man, had been there for as long as Marty could remember, at least twenty years. Steve always gave Marty a warm reception whenever he walked into the Camelot. Steve was kind of an institution, too. He knew everybody and everything. The reason he had been the doorman for over twenty years was that he knew how to be discreet. Steve had introduced Marty to a fellow who used to work for the CIA. After a long CIA career, instead of being promoted, he had been thrown out. He now spent his time being employed by husbands, wives, and jealous girlfriends who didn't trust their spouses or lovers. His years with the CIA had taught him a lot about covert and clandestine operations. What the CIA man did now was far less glamorous. He was bugging phones, using video surveillance, and following unfaithful husbands to their young mistresses' love nests. Even though the sordid jobs were menial, the pay was excellent. When Marty called him after not seeing him for years, the man had assured Marty that for $5,000 he would record everything that happened in the suite.

Donovan needed to have an in with the former mayor. He had delegated this task to Marty. Barry had been caught and videotaped years earlier by the Feds with a young hooker smoking crack cocaine in a hotel room. Although the former mayor had been busted, he was reelected because of his popularity with the blacks in D.C., and because he believed in patronage jobs, which he freely handed out to his friends and cronies. The fact that Washington, D.C., had one of the highest crime rates in the country did not stand in the way of his being reelected. The fact that the Washington, D.C., police force probably had the nation's worst morale and conviction rate, on a par with New Orleans, also meant little. For years the federal government had been talking about taking over a lot of the District's power, to hopefully do a better job. Any change would have been an improvement. The fact remained, though, that the former mayor still wielded a tremendous amount of power. His reputation for taking care of his friends was legendary. The Outfit figured he would be easy to influence for their benefit. When he was mayor, he had been awarding prison contracts to CCA, Corrections Corporation of America. Knowing the former mayor's record and his propensity for money and young girls, Donovan and the Don had hoped, through Marty and his little sex-CIA operatives, to share in the wealth and carve out an even bigger niche in the prison business by acquiring more stock in CCA and other competitors, thereby becoming the largest player in the private prison industry by adding Barry to the Outfit's team.

Donovan had explained to Marty that the former mayor was what he categorized as a potential repeat offender. In other words, if Barry had been dumb enough to let his dick and his desire for addictive drugs fuck him up before, he would probably do it again. Plenty of "good drugs" had been stocked in the hotel room to give Janet an arsenal of ammunition to use with the former mayor.

Marty carefully explained to Janet what she was supposed to do. As far as she knew, she was simply supposed to seduce Barry. Marty had told her nothing about the Outfit's real plan.

"Hopefully you will be successful tonight," offered Marty matter-of-factly.

"But what if I can't do it tonight?" asked Janet.

"I'm sure you will," Marty shot back.

"But what if I'm not able to?" repeated Janet.

"Then you will keep going to Washington until you are," stated Marty.

"I'll do my best, Marty."

"I know you will, sweetheart."

"Will I be able to talk to, or see, my sister soon?"

"Yes, of course, dear."

"Even if I am not successful tonight?"

"Yes, Janet, I promise," and for once Marty was going to keep his promise. He knew Janet couldn't take the strain, the worry, and the uncertainty about her sister much longer. He was going to resolve this issue finally and do it very soon. He made a note to call Dr. Bernstein again and handle this Janet/Carole situation.

Janet went home, packed a small bag, and caught a plane to Washington, D.C. As soon as the plane landed at Ronald Reagan Washington National Airport, the FBI picked her up for questioning.

CHAPTER 36

LATER THURSDAY NIGHT

FORT LAUDERDALE, FLORIDA

The Lear 35 jet ascended effortlessly from Butler Aviation at Fort Lauderdale Hollywood International Airport. Mark was used to nice things. Occasionally, with his frequent flyer miles he would upgrade to first class, but the experience of taking off in Bill's private jet, Mark's first time in a Lear, was truly remarkable. He was like a little kid in awe of the power and the magnificence of this sleek, $3 million, silver sexy bullet. He had images of the old Quaker Oats Puffed Rice commercial he had seen as a kid—the lighter-than-air, fluffy white stuff being shot out of a cannon. Being in the Lear 35, although an older jet, was an experience; he was not embarrassed to admit to Connie he was truly enjoying. When he was younger, he had read a great article about John Glenn, the astronaut and senator who ran for president. The article gave the reader the inside view of what it was like to be a test pilot, like Glenn or Chuck Yeager. Mark could now relate to the endless stories Glenn had shared about the exhilaration, the natural high of his experiences as a test pilot, and then an astronaut. Mark and Connie talked about everything and they talked about nothing. Conversation with Connie was easy and exciting, as if they had known each other for years. They were unexpectedly brought into each other's lives, each with their own crisis. The cabin smelled of leather and Connie's perfume. There was sexuality between them, but Connie doubted if Mark was aware of it. There was an intellectual chemistry, two splendid minds in sync, and insatiable curiosity. Mark did feel it too, but he quickly put it out of his mind. Having thoughts like this made him feel guilty. It was inappropriate in light of his wife, Carole.

Chapter 37

AFTER THE DINNER AT LITTLE MAMA'S

CHICAGO, ILLINOIS

Donovan had been around too long; he knew he was being lied to by Marty and Deemis. It was more than just a gut feeling based on his life experience. Part of his intuition was, no doubt, a result of where he lived. He kept a condo at Water Tower Place in Chicago but was rarely there. Instead, he chose to make his home at the beautiful La Costa Country Club thirty miles north of San Diego. Donovan fit in perfectly with many of the residents there, namely mobsters. Years ago, *Penthouse* had published an investigative article by Jeff Gerty and Lowell Bergman that explained in detail how the beautiful resort was constructed and run by friends of top organized crime figures. The infusion of money came from the scandal-ridden Teamsters Central States Pension Fund. Moe Dalitz of the infamous Purple Gang in Detroit, along with Merv Adelson (ex-husband of Barbara Walters), and Irwin Molasky, the two founders of Lorimar Studios responsible for such shows as "Dallas" and "The Waltons," had developed this home for the Mob. Donovan loved La Costa and was considered to be, more or less, the resident senior statesman. Adelson, Molasky, and friends had built the resort from money supplied by the Mob's friendly Teamsters Central States Pension Fund. La Costa was an incredible place and the financial arrangements quite interesting. The Teamsters' loan agreement with La Costa bought them a 15 percent interest in the resort at a bargain price. They made millions when they later sold their shares. The guest list at La Costa read like a Who's Who of Mafia big shots: Donovan, Meyer Lansky, Sam "Momo" Giancana. Momo had a meeting in 1960 at La Costa with Jimmy "The Weasel" Fratianno, who attempted and failed three times to execute Desi Arnaz, who produced the television show "The Untouchables," which Sam Giancana objected to because of the show's portrayal of Chicago mobsters. La Costa was a Mob hangout that Donovan enjoyed while he pursued his associations with other mobsters.

Donovan knew that Deemis was lying about the information leak, but compared to Marty's answers to Donovan's questions, Deemis seemed like a saint. Marty was definitely lying through his teeth. Donovan didn't wait for Marty to answer his questions about Janet: "Where have you got her sister hidden? What will make Janet stay in line once we release her sister?" Donovan didn't need to know the answers to these questions. He already knew, and he was nothing less than livid that Marty had underestimated Donovan's intelligence so severely. How dare that stupid Jew bastard son-of-a-bitch treat him like a fool.

Chapter 38

LATER THURSDAY EVENING

CHICAGO, ILLINOIS

The Lear touched down at Palwaukee Airport. The town of Wheeling, once known as the garbage-can capital of the world, was located next to Palwaukee. The town's claim to fame was that it once produced more galvanized steel garbage cans than anyplace else in the world. Now it had quite a reputation for fine dining, like Weber's Restaurant, where everything was cooked in gigantic Weber grills. Others included on the fine-dining list were Wheeling's Cy's Crab House, formerly named Harry Caray's Steakhouse after the legendary Chicago "Holy Cow" sportscaster, who had been hired by Hall of Fame broadcasting icon, Jack Brickhouse, and Bob Chinn's Crab House, where there was always a two-hour wait rewarded with a 5,000-calorie superb meal. These eateries were located on Milwaukee Avenue. Connie and Mark drove the brand-new Cadillac, courtesy of Bill, that was waiting for them at Palwaukee. They headed north and then turning east on Dundee Road, drove toward the great elm trees that were everywhere throughout the affluent town of Glencoe where Mark grew up. Connie listened with great interest as Mark, totally engrossed in nostalgia, pointed out the familiar sights of his childhood. Once through the town of Glencoe, they continued east to Sheridan Road, driving south to Chicago through the towns of Hubbard Woods, Winnetka, Wilmette, Kenilworth, Evanston, and then to the world-famous LSD—Lake Shore Drive; ten short minutes later they were at Mark's apartment. He pulled the Cadillac down into the underground garage and parked in a visitors spot, giving the attendant a $10 bill. When they got off the elevator and Mark opened the door to the apartment, he was at once struck with a feeling that something wasn't right. Everything had seemed to be as he had left it, but something was peculiar. He scrutinized the apartment, walking around from the den through the living room, dining room, kitchen, bedroom, and finally the bathroom. Connie stared out of the floor-to-ceiling windows of Mark's apartment in the sleek Mies van der Rohe building, overwhelmed by the breathtaking panoramic cityscape of the parks, Lake Michigan, and the traffic flowing smoothly north and south on Lake Shore Drive. What a beautiful sight, she thought. Then Mark realized what was bothering him. The scent of Carole's Obsession perfume was overpowering, almost like she had been there while Mark was gone, but that couldn't be. Obviously, the pleasant scent of Obsession was also coming from Connie. However, the strong smell of Carole's perfume was everywhere, in every room, and Connie had only been in the living room. Strange, he thought, maybe the lingering scent of Carole's perfume was always that strong, and maybe because he had been away, it just seemed more prominent. Still, he wondered if maybe she could have been back, but that made no sense either. Mark saw the little red light blinking, an indication of ten messages on his answering machine. He pushed the playback message button. A caller ID box displayed the date and time of each message, along with the name and number of the caller.

"Mark, this is your Mom. Just calling to see how you're doing, honey. Give me a call when you get a chance."

"Mr. Goodwin, this is Margaret from Bank One. Nothing urgent. Please get back with me at your convenience. Thanks."

"Mark, this is Jason from Marshall Field's. The shirts you ordered came in. Please let me know whether you want me to have them delivered, or if you'll be in to pick them up. 'Bye."

"Mark, it's Bob calling. Just wanted to say hi. Talk to you later."

"Mr. Goodwin, this is Ms. James from American Express. We had sent you a preapproved application for a Platinum Card. I just wanted to make sure you received it. If you have any questions, please call me at 1-800-323-4600, extension 29, thank you."

"Mark, this is Johnnie. We had court time today at the club, and since you didn't make it, I just wanted to make sure everything is okay. Give me a call, buddy."

"Hi Mark, it's Amy. Roger and I are having a cocktail party at 8:00 next Friday. Hope you and Carole can make it. We're dying to meet her."

"Hey Mark, it's Lenny. I tried you at the office, and your girl said you were out of town. Give me a holler when you get back."

Call number nine was a hang up. Mark was getting nowhere, and Connie sensed his frustration as he looked at the answering machine. Mark looked at the caller ID box that displayed the numbers of the people who had called. Call number nine, the hang-up call, indicated "Private," which meant someone had pushed *67 so as not to reveal their number.

Mark advanced the caller ID box to number ten. That last message, which came in a minute after call number nine, also displayed "Private." As Mark pushed the playback button on the answering machine, he fully expected that it would also be another hang up. But surprisingly, it was Carole.

"Mark, honey, something terrible has happened. I can't explain it all now. I'm okay; I am being held hostage to ensure that my sister, Janet, who's in big trouble and in way over her head, will cooperate and do whatever she's supposed to do. I love you so much, darling, and miss you terribly. The people holding me told me that I'd be home in a couple of days. There is nothing you can do. Don't try to find me, or these people—they are bad people, Mark—they will only make things worse."

Mark sat in shock while he listened to the message. Connie seemed a million miles away, lost in her own intense thoughts.

"I wish I knew where that call was made from," Mark sighed in defeat, "but it won't do any good. The number was blocked on the caller ID. There is no way to know."

"Maybe there is," Connie said as she focused on Mark again.

"What do you mean?" Mark asked skeptically.

"Do you have automatic recall?"

"What's that?" Mark asked.

"You push *69, and the phone automatically dials the last number that called here," Connie explained.

"Go ahead," Mark said.

Connie dialed *69, and the phone rang on the second line from the bedroom.

"Carole called from here?" Mark exclaimed. "I don't understand."

"I think I do, and I think I know why!" Connie said. Connie didn't want to explain anything to Mark until she was certain of her hunch. But, after looking at the picture of Mark and Carole in the silver frame on the nightstand next to the phone, she knew she had seen Carole somewhere before. And, she was 98 percent sure she knew where.

Chapter 39

THE PLOT THICKENS

WASHINGTON, D.C.

Janet Reno had met with the president of the United States. She updated him with everything she knew to date. He wanted her to take immediate action, concerning the Outfit's involvement in the prison issues. He would worry about the rest. The President understood the real threat to the United States at this point, but wasn't quite sure where the most immediate danger was coming from. Was it terrorists or was it the Mob/prison or the Mob/CIA issue? There was still too much he didn't know, too much going on. Bill Clinton swore to himself and wondered, as he had for years, if God really hated him. Thank God he wasn't going to be president much longer. Reno took off on the next flight to Illinois. She had precious little time to get there. Janet Reno was going to meet Representative Henry Hyde, who was on the Judiciary Committee that oversaw the Bureau of Prisons.

She was going to find out, once and for all, if the government in its efforts to downsize and increase the privatization of prisons, was actually selling prisons to the Mob? Was it just a coincidence or part of the

Mob's plan to have Jack write a letter to Hawk about wanting to help the ex-cons? The letter explaining LRI and Jack's ideas and intentions seemed—on the surface—to be real. But, the fact that Jack's lawyer was Donovan, who was the number-two man in the Mob, gave them great concern. There also seemed to be strong evidence, through various reports, that the Outfit was involved in some aspects, including financial, with terrorists. But if the Mob was involved in terrorism, the Feds did not have enough information, at this point, to know any specifics, and were totally confused. The CIA's involvement with the Mob just made it more complicated. The President realized it was probably time to brief President-elect, George W. Bush, on what he could expect in the coming months and the lack of information being shared by both the CIA and the FBI.

Chapter 40

EVEN LATER THURSDAY EVENING

MARK'S CONDO, CHICAGO, ILLINOIS

Connie's portable Motorola flip-phone was chirping.

"Hello?...oh that's great. I was so scared."

Mark was paying no attention to Connie's conversation. He was still trying to figure out her last statement just before the flip-phone chirped. How could she possibly know what was going on with his wife? Mark was lost in his own dichotomous thinking. He heard Connie talking, but wasn't really focusing on her conversation.

"Tomorrow or the next day they will let you out of the hospital?" Obviously, Connie was talking to Bill, and he was okay. "Yeah, he's right here," Connie said as she handed the phone to Mark. "Bill would like to talk with you."

"Hi, Bill. How are you feeling?" Mark asked tentatively, not quite sure why Bill wanted to talk to him, knowing that Bill was still in ICU.

"I'm fine, thanks to you," Bill replied.

"I'm glad to hear that. Connie was really scared," Mark said, feeling a little awkward talking to Bill, trying to say the appropriate things but not quite sure what. "I owe you big time," Bill continued. "You saved my life."

"I'm just glad I was there to help," Mark replied in his traditionally modest way. "I really appreciate your letting Connie try to help me, and thanks for the Lear."

"Listen, Mark, Connie filled me in on your situation there, and Connie and I can help you. In fact, as soon as I hang up with you, I'm going to get a few of my top people and some contacts that I have in Chicago to work on this." Bill exuded confidence and authority.

"I appreciate your offer of help, Bill," Mark began, wondering how long Connie had been talking to Bill and how much she had told him. "But Carole's message said not to do anything; it will only make the situation worse, and that she would be home in a couple of days, safe and sound," Mark said unconvincingly.

"Connie told me all that, Mark, but you can't just sit on your ass hoping everything will work out."

"Bill, I know you're probably right, but…"

Bill interrupted Mark again. "But, nothing, listen, number one, I owe you. Number two, you need our help, and number three, Connie's got a hunch. She won't tell me what it is, but she's a damn smart broad, and I've learned to trust her intuition."

"So what should I…I mean we, do?" Mark asked.

"Put Connie back on the phone for a minute."

Mark handed the phone back to Connie. Connie said very little for the next fifteen minutes, as she listened to Bill. "Yeah, I understand. Love you, too," Connie said, as she handed the phone back to Mark.

"Listen," Bill said, "Connie tells me you're pretty smart when it comes to real estate."

"Well, I do okay," Mark replied, never comfortable accepting compliments and not sure how to respond to Bill's rhetorical question.

"Well, I need a little help on a real estate deal, and I need it by tomorrow. Actually, you will have to leave for Rhode Island tonight to get started."

"What kind of deal?"

"Connie will fill you in. I'll pay you $100,000 up front, and if you can pull it off successfully, you'll get a 6 percent commission on a $6.6 million deal."

Mark figured, why not? Maybe if he had a distraction—a diversion—he could stop obsessing about Carole. Her message said not to do anything or it could cause more trouble. To be honest, Mark didn't know what to do anyway. The last twenty-four hours had been too much for him; everything had happened so quickly—meeting Connie, then Bill, his heart attack, their offer of help with Carole, and now some mysterious real estate deal. Connie seemed to be taking control of everything, from the enigma of Carole, to explaining Bill's real estate deal that was being presented to Mark as if Mark were some magician or consummate deal maker—another Donald Trump, who could pull out of his hat in the eleventh hour whatever it took to succeed in Bill's venture. It was a combination of Connie's confidence and take-charge attitude and the idea of a tremendous challenge that excited Mark; also, some good money, but mainly because Mark believed that Connie and Bill were on top of his wife's situation. Mark, excited, scared and nervous, listened attentively as Connie quickly spoke about Carole and about Bill's real estate deal in Rhode Island. Twenty minutes later they were on their way to the airport. Bill wanted them to fly commercial, not in his private Lear, in order not to attract attention. Attract whose attention? Mark wondered.

Chapter 41

❀

THURSDAY

KEY BISCAYNE, FLORIDA

The Don had just returned to Florida after seeing Marty and Donovan in Chicago.

"Watch the situation very carefully," the Don told Donovan, speaking quietly into the phone while gazing out over Key Biscayne and its verdant surroundings. Two young girls continued to give the Don a massage. "Use KT immediately if you feel it's necessary," the Don concluded and gave the phone back to one of the bathing beauties, who was putting massage oil on his emaciated body browned from the Florida sun. Even though the Don had his phone checked three times a week for bugs, he used code words like "KT" just in case someone was listening. He believed in being careful. You could never be *too* careful. That's why he had lived so long.

Donovan heard the line go dead, and he placed the receiver back on the phone. KT was the abbreviation for "Kill Talk." The meaning was simple: if anyone wasn't being straight or telling the truth, kill them. If you think anyone might have talked or maybe will talk to the Mob's enemies, kill them! Contract, hit, trunk music, or swim with the fishes, it was all the same to Donovan, and he knew what to do. He smiled to himself. As cold-hearted as it was, at least he would save some money and get a good price or discount for the multiple hits he would order. They had all fucked up and deserved what they had earned. Killing Marty, Deemis, and Janet at this point was no big deal to the Don or Donovan. It was simply business.

CHAPTER 42

❦

THURSDAY EVENING

CHICAGO O'HARE AIRPORT

Once they boarded the plane, Connie was amazed at how Mark seemed to change. He was like a different person—calm, cool, collected, and in control. The flight attendant in first class gave Mark the air-phone as soon as they took off and continually made a fuss over him, ignoring Connie. The phone seemed like a natural appendage to Mark's ear. He was talking nonstop—not fast, but slow, deliberate, and confident as he gave instructions to various people and explained what he wanted done and how they were to carry out the tasks they were given. Connie watched and listened to Mark in awe as he talked on the phone. He was like an accomplished orchestra leader, directing, leading, cajoling, easily but meticulously putting a plan together; a complex one, and making it appear as though it were simply second nature, no big deal. Connie could easily see why Mark was so successful. He was confident. His charm was addictive. One could not help but be drawn to his magnetism and, unlike her fiancé, Bill, Mark didn't seem to be the slightest bit egotistical or narcissistic. It was crystal clear to Connie that unlike other people who had been involved with Bill in this real estate deal, Mark knew what he was doing. If only Bill and she had met Mark sooner, they surely would not be in this frantic, eleventh-hour crisis situation to pull off this racetrack deal.

Chapter 43

❀

LATE THURSDAY EVENING

PROVIDENCE, RHODE ISLAND

The plane landed, and Mark and Connie hurriedly walked through the jetway into the terminal. Mark looked up at the ceiling for a private airport club. He belonged to them all. He saw the arrow pointing to the Admirals Club, gently grabbed Connie's arm and stepped inside the double oak doors. Mark greeted the pretty blonde behind the desk and then gave her their baggage claims, along with $20. They exchanged a few pleasantries. Connie went to the ladies' room, and Mark settled into a couch using the phone, fax, and computer provided by the club. A lovely, buxom young redhead with sensuous, dark-green emerald eyes and a perfect mouth filled with perfect teeth took Mark's drink order and returned a couple of minutes later with a tray of drinks, pretzels, peanuts, and little Goldfish crackers.

"What's the first move? What do you want me to do?" queried Connie.

"Use the phone over there and book us three connecting rooms on the highest floor available at the Marriott downtown."

"Okay," replied Connie. "How soon are we going to be there?"

"Tell them to have the rooms ready in twenty minutes. We'll leave as soon as I finish with the press conference."

"What press conference?" Connie asked Mark.

Connie didn't have to wait for an answer to her question. She looked up and saw five or six people approach with television cameras, notepads, and microphones. Mark was incredible, Connie thought, as she eyed the press from ABC, CBS, NBC, and the *Providence Journal*. Mark had obviously arranged all this while they were on the plane. What else had he done? Connie excitedly wondered, gazing at Mark, wishing he were not married and that she were not engaged.

"Mr. Goodwin," one of the reporters began, "could you explain who you are and what you are doing here?"

"Of course," Mark smiled. "First of all, I want to thank you all for coming this late on such short notice. I appreciate it very much and will not waste your time. I will get right to the point. But please," Mark continued, with his infectious smile and good-looking boyish charm, "call me Mark." He pointed to Connie. "And this is Connie."

"Is she your wife, Mark?" one of the reporters asked.

"No, an associate," Mark replied, not noticing the disappointment on Connie's face. "I am here representing a group of investors who want to buy the Narragansett Racetrack in Pawtucket."

"Aren't you a little late Mr. Goodwin?...uh, I mean Mark. The city has already made an offer to the board, which is going to be voted on and most likely accepted by the stockholders tomorrow afternoon at 2:00 in the ballroom of the Marriott," a short, fat, badly dressed reporter shouted.

"What's your name?" Mark asked the reporter in a tone and manner that showed he thought the reporter was important. Mark knew how to instantly encourage people to like him. He treated everyone like they were millionaires.

"Bob, Bob Petit, CBS-TV."

"Well, Bob," Mark said, as though he had known this reporter his whole life, "the city has offered $5.6 million. I am offering *$7.6 million.*"

"That's $2 million more," another reporter said incredulously.

"That's right," said Mark.

"Have you formally made your offer to the board or the stockholders yet?" Bob Petit from CBS asked.

"No, not yet."

"When are you going to?" asked another reporter.

"I hope to meet with the board early in the morning; then I plan to be at the stockholders' meeting in the afternoon."

"Whom do you represent?"

"Investors who think that the shareholders are entitled to $2 million more than the current offer," Mark said matter-of-factly.

"What are your plans for the racetrack?"

"I think the bottom line here is how much the shareholders will get, not what we are going to do with the property," Mark answered, aware that he was being evasive.

The reporters had more questions, but Mark politely cut them off, then excused himself and Connie. "Thank you all, and I'll see you tomorrow," Mark said, as he walked with his arm around Connie toward the reception desk in the Admirals Club. The pretty blonde smiled at Mark, then gave him a piece of paper that had the license plate number of the limo waiting outside to take them and their luggage to the Marriott.

"That was tremendous," Connie said to Mark as they left the terminal and went outside to where the stretches were parked.

"Thank you. I thought it went pretty well." Mark added cautiously, "Let's hope they have enough time to get the story in the morning edition of the paper, or at least on all the TV stations for the 11 o'clock news."

"What's next?" Connie asked as they got into the limo.

"Call the hotel and get me fifteen people who need a job, and get a conference room with seventeen phones."

"When do you want them to start?"

"ASAP!" Mark replied.

"Okay," said Connie, "but Mark, just one thing…"

"Just one?" asked Mark, smiling.

"Just one right now," replied Connie.

"Shoot," said Mark.

"Bill only authorized you to offer $1 million more than the present offer, not $2 million."

"Trust me, Connie…tomorrow I am going to offer $2 million more, but the shareholders are only going to want $1 million more."

"I don't understand," Connie said, showing that she was definitely confused. "How do you expect…?"

Mark cut Connie off by putting his fingers over her mouth. "Don't worry," Mark whispered. "I know what I'm doing."

Connie accepted without hesitation that Mark knew exactly what he was doing, but as smart as he was, she wondered if Mark understood her feelings toward him. She didn't think so. That was part of the attraction. Mark was gorgeous, clever, and bright, yet seemed totally unaffected. He seemed to have no idea how attractive he was to the opposite sex.

Chapter 44

❁

THURSDAY NIGHT

THE CHICAGO BOARD OF TRADE (CBOT), CHICAGO, ILLINOIS

Marty Serachi stepped out of the taxi in front of his office at the Board of Trade building. He was still visibly shaken from his big dinner meeting earlier on Grand Avenue. He stopped just before entering the building and looked up at her—enigmatic and mysterious. She had no mouth to tell what her eyes had seen—a fitting representative for the closed, private, clannish society she symbolized. Ceres, weighing 6,000 pounds, the Goddess of Grain, stood fifty-one feet high atop the Chicago Board of Trade, once the city's tallest building. The brushed aluminum art deco icon had the financial world by the throat. Each year, contracts worth trillions of dollars passed through the traders at the Board of Trade and its cousin, the Chicago Mercantile Exchange, the Merc. The Board, steeped in tradition, was composed of mostly fourth-generation Irish grain traders from the lakefront suburbs. The Merc represented the new guard: ex-cops, lawyers, taxi drivers, and the young Turks—mostly Jewish hustlers raised on the streets of Chicago. Marty purposely chose to have his office at the CBOT instead of the more modern Merc. The Merc members were too much like he was. Marty felt that the Board was made up of the old guard, the blue bloods. Marty craved all the respectability he could get. Having his office at the CBOT made him feel more respectable. He dreaded the thought that Donovan would probably kill him soon. Along with the fear, he felt sadness at the prospect of missing all the action. He was addicted to the action and the lifestyle of both exchanges. It was not just because he made money from running book; the pool for the Super Bowl alone exceeded $500,000 each year. Marty was an amateur student of wheeling, dealing, and gambling history, which the Board of Trade and the Mercantile Exchange were all about, always had been, and always would be. Both exchanges had a vivid and controversial past, uniquely Chicago in nature, which began over 150 years ago. Marty knew that Donovan realized he was lying at the dinner meeting. Fearing his imminent demise, he tried to distract himself by recalling some of the vivid history of Chicago's two main exchanges.

In 1848, eighty-two grain merchants on the banks of the Chicago River met on South Water Street to organize the Chicago Board of Trade, the nation's first futures exchange. In 1929, after the stock market crash, the Merc's total net profit was only $12,000, and shortly after moving into its new location at 110 North Franklin, it was unable to pay the mortgage. Prominent Chicago real estate and construction tycoon, Colonel Henry Crown, bought the building and leased it back to the Merc. In 1958, the Congress abolished the onion market after Sam S. Siegel, a Merc onion trader and owner of a Chicago suburban produce company, manipulated the price of a fifty-pound bag of onions from $2.50 to $.10. The onions were worth less than the string bags that held them.

In 1964, Anthony "Tino" DeAngeles was sentenced to ten years in prison when his firm, Allied Crude Vegetable Oil Refining Company, ripped off the soybean market for almost $24 million.

In 1977, brothers Nelson Bunker and William Herbert Hunt, heirs to the H.L. Hunt oil fortune, were fined $500,000 for manipulating the soybean market. In January 1980, the Hunts were up to something big in the silver market, controlling 50 percent of the supply for delivery at the Comex in New York and 70 percent in Chicago, representing 200 million ounces. On January 21, the Comex ordered that the trading in silver was over and that no one else could buy silver. The Hunts had manipulated the price from $9.00 to $52.50. Silver dropped to $44.00 dollars that day, and to $31.00 the next day, and kept dropping, leaving the Hunts and their banks to clean up the mess amid years of litigation.

In 1985, Donald and Richard Schleicher's First Commodity Corporation of Boston was put out of business for excessive churning of customers' accounts. Burlas Commodities was put out of business for similar tactics. Richard Mitchell, who had been a top advertising executive at Meyerhoff, the agency for William Wrigley gum, joined and took over Burlas after his brother-in-law, Len, needed constant cash infusions to keep the churn-and-burn operation going. That is where Marty Serachi had met Pete. Pete was a street-smart hustler who was running the futures options division of Burlas. When it was closed down, Pete went to work for Marty full time, after the Don and Donnovan approved Pete by meeting him privately in Florida—Marty never knew about this meeting.

Marty was friendly and well liked by everybody at the Mercantile Exchange—from the garage attendants to the bigwigs, like Leo Melamed and Jack Sander at the Merc, who regularly exchanged greetings with Marty. But so what, he sadly reflected—that wasn't going to help him now. Leo, the self-proclaimed father of financial futures, was the only child of Hebrew teachers who fled Poland in 1939 just before World War II started. He polished his oratorical skills in amateur Yiddish theater. Leo attended John Marshall Law School, worked in a factory, and drove a cab until 1953, when, at age twenty, he borrowed $3,000 from his father to purchase a seat on the Exchange. Melamed, in

1976, stepped down as chairman of the Merc and assumed the new unelected post of special counsel, allowing him to rule the Exchange throughout the eighties and nineties.

Jack Sander was even more of a success story. At fifteen, he dropped out of high school and hung out on the mean streets of Chicago's South Side. In his first boxing match in a Catholic Youth Organization gym he was beaten badly. The legendary 1940s middleweight world champion, Tony Zale, discovered him. Zale coached Sander through sixty matches, of which he lost only two. He returned to high school, got a boxing scholarship for college, then entered Notre Dame Law School, dealt blackjack in Vegas in the summer, became head of the Chicago Board of Trade, then later the Merc. Everybody liked Jack. He was always nice to everybody, and his good looks and broad smile seemed ageless, similar to Dick Clark.

Marty liked to compare himself to Melamed and Sander, but there was no comparison. Even though the heads of the Merc and the Board might be guilty of self-dealing and manipulation for their own interests, they didn't kill people or break the law. Marty Serachi did.

Marty walked into his office and grabbed the phone before the first ring had finished.

"Yeah."

"It's me," the caller stated. "Is everything taken care of?"

"All done."

"Are your people where they're supposed to be?"

"Absolutely."

"Where's the girl?"

"In a hotel in D.C., getting ready for the party tonight."

"What if she fails?"

"She won't."

"But, what if she does?"

"It won't happen. I guarantee you."

"I don't have to remind you how important tonight is."

"Don't worry. You can count on me."

Marty hoped Donovan didn't know he was lying again. How had things gotten so out of hand? he wondered. If only he had kept his dick in his pants. But he couldn't help it with Janet. She was so damn sexy. It wasn't really his fault. After all, she had blatantly pursued him. She was always wearing those low-cut blouses and supershort skirts, and never wearing any underwear. She said it was too restrictive, made her feel uptight, inhibited, not a free spirit. Bullshit, Marty thought. She knew exactly what she was doing and what effect she had on him, and for that matter, on all men. That's why she was so good at what she did. He was fifty years old and certainly knew better. Janet was going to cost him his life. How could he be so taken with a woman? He couldn't help himself. More than just seducing politicians and whoever else Marty had instructed her to take care of, Janet became the leader of his little sex-CIA. She trained the others. She worked closely with them, meticulously instructing them in all the facets of seduction.

Janet trained them how to walk, talk, dress, kiss, smile, suck, and fuck. In the beginning Marty could not have been happier with her performance. But he had made the fatal mistake of getting involved with her, almost falling in love with her. He treated her well, like a beautiful woman instead of the whore she was. Furthermore, Janet had fallen in love with Marty. She wanted more than Marty was willing or able to give. She wanted to be special, different, not just one of Marty's Outfit girls. The timing couldn't have been worse. She knew about, and was involved in, the bullshit plan to overcrowd the court and prison systems. It all seemed to make sense to Janet from what Marty had told her. Instead of accused people copping a plea, they would plead not guilty and go to trial. If they didn't have enough money to pay an attorney, Marty's group would provide one and defer the cost, thus obligating the person to Marty and his people. If only Janet hadn't changed her mind and decided that she wanted out. Marty realized now that she was acting out of fear. Even though she said she was sorry and would toe the line, Marty was not so stupid as to believe her. He couldn't afford to. There was far too much at risk.

The big meeting in Washington tonight was just hours away. That's why he had decided to send Janet to replace the other girl. Marty was understandably nervous. He had just assured Donovan on the phone that everything was okay for tonight's meeting but he didn't mention that he had decided to send Janet. Donovan knew anyway. Janet didn't know about the Mob's real plan to take over or, if necessary, put the Nashville-based Corrections Corporation of America out of business. CCA was, at one time, the country's largest private prison company; it was renamed Prison Realty Trust and was listed on the New York Stock Exchange: (NYSE: PZN). According to its own internal public relations department, it billed itself as the world's largest private-sector owner of correctional and detention facilities with global interests in all aspects of incarceration. It bought or leased prisons from cash-strapped states and municipalities and ran them on a for-profit cash basis. Corrections Corporation of America did not know that the Mob was planning on being their largest shareholder. The Mob even had inmates start lawsuits against CCA to cause financial losses for the company, thus lowering the stock price so that it could acquire more shares at discounted prices.

The Mob's key players laughed among themselves at the supposed plan to screw up the court system and keep people from going to jail or getting inmates out; this was nothing but a smoke screen. The boys actually hoped and planned on the fact that the prison population would continue to grow. That was why they were becoming the largest privatizer of prisons. It was an incredible business, which had been continually growing, and with President-elect, Bush's tough stance on crime, the Mob knew that investment in the prison business was a safer bet for them than any other investment. Marty's girls had been working diligently to establish relationships with contractors, politicians, and Bureau of Prisons state, city, and county correctional people all over the country. Marty's group of sixty-seven women and five gay men had no idea why they were given these assignments. Even Janet didn't know. Marty was glad that he had not told Janet what the real purpose of the operation was. To Donovan, the Don, and Marty, getting into the private prison business was tantamount to the Mob involvement in Las Vegas and drugs. The only difference was that this was legal! All over the country, even as far away as Hawaii and Puerto Rico, new prisons were being built or old ones were being modernized everyday. Local, state, and federal facilities, in an effort to downsize and save money, were increasingly turning to privatization. And the profits were enormous, but most importantly, unlimited. The ancillary or secondary businesses offered additional benefits for the Mob to make more monies. Food, medicine, clothing, bedding, shampoo, towels, and toilets, soup to nuts—the list was endless. Even when the federal government had shut down, or the city or state employees went on strike, the prisons were not affected. There were over fifty companies involved in prison privatization, but the Don's, and eventually Donovan's, interests would be the biggest. It was just too bad that Marty and Deemis had to be killed. Donovan was excited though. What had started just five years ago was promising to ensure the Mob's place in history by controlling one of the largest growth industries in the world. The privatization of prisons was the true financial rebirth of the Mob. Donovan remembered once, long ago, one of the major Dons making the statement that the Mob, La Costa Nostra, would be bigger than General Motors. The privatization of federal, state, county, and local prisons would make the Mob financially and politically more powerful than all of the thirty companies that made up the Dow Jones Industrial Average.

Marty felt more than sad, realizing he had fucked up and would not be a part of the prison deal. The only thing he would be a part of was soil somewhere. He had just lied to Donovan on the phone, assuring him that the girl who had been sent to Washington, D.C., would hopefully hit a home run with Barry tonight. But Marty didn't have the same confidence in that girl as he did in Janet. That was why Marty had decided to send Janet to Washington D.C. Marty realized that Donovan would be furious that he had sent Janet instead, but—and this was a big but—if Janet was successful, then maybe, just maybe, Marty's life would be spared. He was taking a big chance. However, Marty had nothing to lose at this point. And maybe she could pull it off. God, he hoped he was right!

Chapter 45

❈

THURSDAY NIGHT

PROVIDENCE, RHODE ISLAND

The limo pulled up to the Marriott Hotel. The driver popped the trunk open and put their luggage on the cart as the doorman opened the door for Connie and Mark. Mark gave the driver a $100 bill and told him to keep the change. The $50 tip overwhelmed the driver and he gave Mark his card with his beeper and home number, telling him that he was available twenty-four hours a day. The doorman was also impressed with the generous $40 tip Mark gave him. Mark was normally frugal with his money, but wanted to appear as if he was loaded, to impress the Rhode Islanders.

"What's your name?"

"Johnnie, sir," the doorman answered Mark.

"I'm going to need some special help."

"Anything at all, sir. Just name it."

"Please don't call me sir. The name's Mark."

"Yes, sir, I mean Mark. How can I help?"

Ordinarily, the doorman thought that when someone gave him that kind of tip, he was looking for something really "special", usually a hooker. But Mark was quite a handsome man who obviously didn't have to pay for sex. Moreover, the young woman he was with was very attractive with terrific breasts, tremendous legs, and a fabulous ass.

"Help me, I mean us, get checked in quickly." Mark gave Johnnie, the doorman/bellboy, his American Express card. Connie and Mark sat down on the couch and watched as Johnnie went up to the two girls at the registration desk. They were pretending that they were not staring at Connie and Mark. They were embarrassed and nervous when they realized Mark was aware that they were staring at him. Mark quickly got off the couch and walked up to the registration desk.

The girls were visibly shaken, wondering if Mark was going to be upset with them. Mark smiled broadly.

"My name is Mark Goodwin. What are your names?"

"I'm Rebecca, Becky," the short, squat, pleasingly plump redhead replied.

"I'm Mindy, the assistant manager." The tall, lanky brunette with deep black eyes set too closely together smiled, showing slightly crooked teeth.

"Welcome to the Marriott, sir," they both said in unison.

"Please, ladies, call me Mark." They melted over his infectious smile and could not contain their excitement as Mark put a fresh $100 bill in each of their hands.

"We can't accept this, Mark," Mindy began. "It's against policy and it's totally unnecessary. It's our job to do whatever it takes to make you happy and ensure that your stay with us is a pleasant one."

"If you don't keep the money I gave you, I will be very unhappy."

"Sir, we could get fired for taking your money," Becky said.

"What money? I didn't give you any money. What are you girls talking about? Is this how gorgeous Rhode Island women treat a guy from Chicago? Accusing me of giving you money? I'm sure I don't know what you're talking about."

"Thanks, Mark," Becky said.

"I appreciate it very much," replied Mindy, fantasizing what it would be like to go to bed with Mark.

"We have three connecting rooms for you, Mark. Are there other people you are expecting?" Mindy asked.

"Yes," replied Mark, "A Mr. Ron Jaffe and his wife should be arriving from Chicago soon."

"We have some of the people at the hotel who are getting off work in the next fifteen minutes, Mark, and they were wondering if you could use them for whatever work you need done."

"Absolutely Mindy, that would be wonderful. Have them all meet in the conference room that you reserved for me as soon as they're available," replied Mark.

The bellboy took the plastic credit-card keys for the rooms. "Mark, I'll show you and the young lady to your rooms."

"Fine," replied Mark, planting another $20 bill in his hand. "Take Connie up, and I'll be there in a few minutes."

The bellboy and Connie got into the elevator and pushed the button marked "Penthouse." When the door opened, he held it, telling Connie to go to her left. He wheeled out the luggage cart, walked a few steps, then inserted the key-card into the slot and as the little light turned green, he opened the door.

"I'll open up the suitcases and hang up your clothes for you, ma'am."

"That's okay, I'll take care of it," Connie said, a little too quickly. She really didn't think it was any of the goddamned bellboy's business that they were staying in separate bedrooms. She wished it were different. Even though Bill had never been faithful to her, she had always been faithful to him. But Connie knew now that she would readily end her relationship with Bill to be with Mark. Connie knew that Mark would not come on to her. More than his just being a gentleman, Mark was in love with his wife. What a waste, Connie thought. She could make him a lot happier than Carole could, but he was loyal, in love, and deeply concerned about her. On the plane, Mark had been like a Spanish

Inquisitor. What did Connie know? What did Bill know? What was the hunch Bill said Connie had about Carole? What did it mean that maybe Carole had called from the second line in the bedroom? and on ad infinitum. Connie was not totally sure, but she would be by tomorrow. Then she could tell Mark. And it wasn't going to be easy.

Mark walked into the room as the phone started to ring; Connie picked it up. "Hello, yeah, hold on, he's right here," she gave the phone to Mark.

"Hello," Mark said.

"It's me," said Ron Jaffe.

"Where are you?"

"In the police station."

"What the hell are you doing there?"

"I don't know if it's safe to talk."

"Okay," Mark said, "I'll be right there."

"No," said Jaffe forcefully. "It's too dangerous."

"What do you mean? What in the hell is going on?" Mark asked frantically.

"All I know," Jaffe began, "is that Jill and I got off the plane, got our baggage, and went outside to wait for Senator Donaldson to pick us up and drive us to the Marriott."

"Go on...," Mark said, trying to keep calm.

"Well, we waited about fifteen minutes and he didn't show, so we got into a cab. After we traveled about a mile, we were pulled over by the cops and taken into the station."

"What's the charge? Have they arrested you?"

"I don't know, Mark. They won't tell us anything. They're holding us for questioning, but it's a setup; someone tipped them off and they wanted to make sure we couldn't meet you. It's a warning from them, so you better be careful."

Before Mark could say anything he heard the line go dead.

CHAPTER 46

FBI HEADQUARTERS

CHICAGO, ILLINOIS

The government Lear landed on the far side of O'Hare Airport in the restricted area used by the Air Force. The V.I.P. passenger was driven in a blue Chevrolet to downtown Chicago. The car stopped in front of the Dirksen Federal Building, where she got out and took the elevator to the eighth-floor conference room of FBI Headquarters. Janet Reno, only weeks away from being replaced by John Ashcroft, was confused. She couldn't be absolutely certain but was fairly confident that there was a leak somewhere. She was certain that at least one member of the House or Senate was crooked and on the take. Surely, it would not be the first time that high members of the government were guilty of double-dealing. Reno, of course, understood that the committees that had first crack at all proposed sentencing changes were the Senate Judiciary Committee and the House Judiciary Committee. These two committees decided which bills would be allowed to go to the entire Congress for a vote. In the House of Representatives, there was a subcommittee of the House Judiciary Committee that held tremendous power over which bills would go forward. It was called the House Sub-Committee on Crime. Reno knew Henry Hyde, the powerful Republican from Illinois on the House Judiciary Committee; he was someone she trusted. She had to start somewhere. Flying to Chicago to brief Henry seemed like the best move. She exchanged pleasantries with Hyde. Reno told him that she was not at liberty to discuss the problem yet. All that she would tell him was that something clandestine was going on with the criminal court system and the prison system. Hyde did not ask her to elaborate. "Who from this list," she asked Hyde, "might be on the take?" as they went over the lists of members of the House and Senate Judiciary Committee and the House Sub-Committee on Crime.

They reviewed the list discussing each committee member. Who would be more likely to be dishonest? New members of one of the committees? New members to the House and Senate? On the other hand, maybe it was the older committee members who were tired, disenchanted, greedy, or a combination of any or all. After two and a half hours she was more confused than ever. Then she pulled Jack's letter from the file in her briefcase, read it, reread it, and then scratched her head.

What made it even more difficult to figure out who was crooked was that it was no secret that a lot of politicians, both Republicans and Democrats, had been or were currently involved in one or more related aspects of the private prison industry—and there was nothing illegal about that—maybe self-serving, but not illegal. As long as stiff sentences remained, obviously new prisons had to be built, or new ones modernized, and people, including many politicians, would be lining their own pockets, both legally and illegally.

Chapter 47

THURSDAY NIGHT

UNDISCLOSED LOCATION

Quietly, carefully, hidden by the darkness of the night, he crept nearer to her. In the still, deathlike black shadows his eyes were filled with murder as he zoomed in on her, staying perfectly focused. Carole could not move or scream for help and struggled to breathe normally. It was as though a big wave had violently swept her into its treacherous undertow, deep below the murky, life-threatening waters, crushing her. Carole knew there was no escape. Her own mortality flashed before her with no sense of understanding or clear resolve, as she had always expected, or at least hoped for. He inched closer to her. She could hear his god-awful breathing, his feet moving, swinging his arms like hatchets slowly slicing through the cold, damp, and putrid-smelling air. The odor of death reeked, burning her nostrils. She could feel the evil intensity in his eyes, though she could not see him. Was it because it was too dark, or were her eyes tightly shut out of fear, trying to block out what was about to happen? Carole knew she could not escape this time. The hopelessness of the situation magnified her horrific trepidation even more. She could smell him; his scent, his odor, his hot breath, his sweat. He was like a tiger that had scoped out its prey with precision and was ready to make the final, fatal strike.

"I am finally going to kill you. You deserve to die. I'm going to kill you now. You must die," was the Death-like dirge he chanted as he was almost upon her. Carole was defenseless and paralyzed with terror, knowing she had no choice, knowing the end was near. Suddenly she did not want to die. Carole cried out for Mark to save her.

Chapter 48

THURSDAY EVENING

PROVIDENCE, RHODE ISLAND

The phone rang in his study.
"Hello."
"Senator Donaldson, please."
"Speaking."
"This is Mark Goodwin."
"I was expecting your call."
"Our friend, Ron, got picked up by the cops."
"I know. I was there."
"Ron said he waited fifteen minutes and you never showed up."
"I was there, but the cops had the place under surveillance, and I couldn't risk them seeing me meet Jaffe."
"Who tipped them off, Senator?"
"I don't know, Mr. Goodwin."
"Were you followed to the airport, Senator?"
"No, they were already there when I drove up."
"Can you come to my hotel? I'm at the Marriott."
"I don't think that would be smart. I'm sure you're being watched."

"Where then?"

"I'll try to meet you at the track, at midnight."

"But I need the names and numbers of the racetrack shareholders."

"You'll get them."

"When?"

"I'll have a messenger at your hotel within half an hour."

"Thanks, Senator. I'll see you later."

"And Mr. Goodwin…"

"Yes, Senator?"

"Please be careful."

"I will," Mark said as he hung up the phone.

Chapter 49

THURSDAY EVENING

PROVIDENCE, RHODE ISLAND

"Who was that, Mark?" Connie asked.

"A senator, actually a former senator who is a friend of Ron Jaffe's."

"And?"

"And what?" replied Mark, slightly amused.

"And, who's Ron Jaffe?"

"A friend of mine from Chicago who knows a lot about horses and racetracks. The former senator happens to be a shareholder of the Narragansett Racetrack and has a list of names and numbers of all the stockholders."

"And?"

"And what?"

"And why don't you cut the shit, and finish telling me the whole story. Like what is important about having a list of names and numbers of 1,800 stockholders?" queried Connie playfully.

"That's a good question, kid. Let's go down to the bar. I'll buy you a drink and explain."

Mark and Connie took the elevator down to the lobby. Mark headed toward the front desk with Connie following half a step behind. Mark gave a 150-watt smile to Becky behind the desk. She returned the smile, blushing slightly.

"Are your rooms okay, Mark?"

"Yes, Becky, everything is wonderful."

"Everyone will be in the conference room ready to go to work in a few minutes. Is there anything else you need?"

"Yes, there should be a messenger here shortly with a package for me. We'll be down in the bar. Please have the messenger bring it to me there."

"Sure, Mark," replied Becky.

Mark gently took Connie's arm and escorted her into the hotel bar. The name "Winners" was written in green neon script about a foot high and three feet across. Red horseshoes and white dice decorated the borders. The sign hung on the mirrored wall behind the bar. Mark escorted Connie to a small table in the back, away from the half-dozen pinball machines and three poker machines that had quite a boisterous crowd around them cheering wildly under their Hasbro hats as they chain-smoked cigarettes and downed endless beers.

Mark ordered a Perrier with a twist on the rocks from the cocktail waitress. He had much to do and didn't want to dull his senses with booze. Connie ordered her favorite Jamaican beer, Red Stripe. Mark looked at Connie; a look of fear suddenly replaced the cool, calm, collected look of confidence he had been displaying since they set out for Rhode Island.

"Okay Connie, it's time for you to be straight with me."

"About what?"

"You know about what."

"Yeah, okay, but I need a little more time."

"Why? What the hell is going on?"

"I don't want to give you false information."

Mark was losing his patience with Connie. "Just tell me what the hell you know already."

"But, you don't understand, I…"

Mark cut her off. "I, my ass. Where the hell is my wife?" Mark was angry.

"I'm not sure yet. Bill's people are working on it," replied Connie.

"What is the hunch you said you had about Carole?" asked Mark.

"Look Mark, you've got to trust me," stated Connie.

"Trust has nothing to do with it. I'm scared and upset. I love my wife and I miss her," Mark responded.

"I understand that, and I'm trying to help," Connie said.

"Then why won't you tell me anything?" queried Mark.

"Give me till tomorrow. Tomorrow I…"

Mark cut her off again. "Okay, okay, but tomorrow you tell me whatever you think, know, or feel. Don't hold anything back. I'm not an idiot. So, please don't treat me like one."

"I'm sorry, Mark, you're right. I just don't want to give you false hopes, or lead you on a wild goose chase, or hurt you in any way. Tomorrow I'll tell you everything. I promise."

"Thank you, and look…I'm sorry. I don't mean to be taking my frustrations and anger out on you. I know you're trying to help. It's just that I'm scared."

"I know you are, I really do. Believe me, I want your wife returned safely to you as much as you do," Connie said, sure that Mark had no idea she was lying. Well, not really lying, just kind of, sort of. Connie didn't wish any harm to Mark's wife; she just wanted Mark for herself.

"Okay, kid, I'm sorry for flying off the handle at you. Let's get back to business."

"What's our next step?" Connie was relieved that the subject was changed and that Mark seemed to have regained his confident demeanor.

"Are you Mr. Goodwin?" asked a young man in a courier's uniform as he walked up to their table.

"I am," replied Mark, as he took the envelope from the messenger, gave him $20, and thanked him. Mark carefully opened the envelope. He quickly studied the contents and then returned the papers to the big manila envelope and handed it over to Connie. "This is our next step," Mark said, as he signed the bar tab, included a 50 percent tip, then led Connie out of Winners back to the front desk where Becky was stationed.

"Mark, everyone is in the conference room waiting for you. Let me show you the way."

Mark and Connie followed Becky to the conference room. The three of them entered and found a group of eager, well-dressed, clean-cut wide age range of men and women. Each person was sitting in front of a phone, with a legal pad, pencils, pens, and coffee. Cindy and Becky had done a nice job of setting up the room. Mark walked around the big table and introduced himself to everyone. He explained what he wanted them to do as he gave each person an equal number of pages that contained the names, addresses, phone numbers, and amount of shares owned by each shareholder.

"How many people here have ever sold anything?" Mark asked.

About three-quarters of the people in the room raised their hands. Connie watched the scene curiously, wondering what Mark had in mind.

"How many people here have ever sold anything over the phone?"

Just a few hands went up cautiously.

"Okay, now how many of you sitting here have ever had someone call you on the phone to try to sell you something?"

Every hand in the room went up, including Connie's. She was fascinated by where this was going. Mark knew how to work a crowd. Instantly, everyone liked him; they were being drawn in to him because of his magnetic personality.

"What did they try to sell you?" Mark asked an attractive brunette, who was sitting immediately to his left.

"Some girl tried to sell me a subscription to a magazine or something; I don't remember."

"Did you buy it?"

"No, of course not."

"Why not?"

"Because I get enough magazines."

"Any other reasons?"

"Well, I guess, it's just that I don't like people calling me and bothering me on the phone, trying to sell me something."

"Thanks," Mark smiled. "Anyone else ever have someone try to sell them something on the phone?"

An overweight woman with a big nose and big brown eyes raised her hand.

"What was your experience?"

"Well, this man called and tried to set up an appointment with my husband and me."

"To do what?"

"Something about selling us new kitchen cabinets."

"And did you meet with him?"

"No."

"Why not?"

"Because he was way too pushy."

"If he wasn't so pushy, would you have made the appointment?"

"Yes, probably."

"Why?"

"Because I would have liked to have had new kitchen cabinets."

"Thanks," Mark said, looking smug, like the cat that had swallowed the canary.

Obviously, Mark was trying to make a point; what it was, though, Connie still couldn't figure out.

"We've got time to hear one more story."

Three hands went up. Mark called on a yuppy-looking young man in his late thirties, with longish jet-black hair and a well-trimmed Van Dyke. Mark made a point of looking at the man's name tag, and once he knew someone's name, he always remembered it.

"Go ahead, Steve."

"Well, this woman calls me up and tells me that I won $25,000."

"That would get my attention. What's the catch?"

"That's exactly what I asked her."

"What did she say?"

"She said there was none. My name had been drawn in a contest and I had been selected to win one of three prizes. First prize: $25,000. Second prize: a new jeep, third prize: three days, two nights in Las Vegas or Cancun, including airfare, but there was a little catch."

"I knew it," Mark laughed. "What was it?"

"It wasn't too bad, really. My wife and I had to go downtown and listen to a ninety-minute vacation ownership presentation."

"Did you go?"

"Yes, we did."

"Because you wanted the prize?"

"Not really."

"What do you mean?" asked Mark, although Mark knew what Steve meant.

"Well, I knew it was one of those time-share deals. They usually promise you the world, but unless you buy something, the only thing that you win is a set of salt-and-pepper shakers."

"So what happened? Why did you go?"

"We listened to the pitch, didn't buy anything, and got a free trip to Las Vegas—well, kind of."

"What do you mean, 'kind of?'"

"Well, we got a voucher for two for some hotel I never heard of, and airfare for only one, with a lot of restrictions."

"So, it didn't turn out so well, right?"
"Yep."
"Were you or your wife mad?"
"No."
"How come?"
"Because I knew it would be bullshit."
"Then why did you go?"
"Because of the woman who called me."
"What do you mean?"
"I liked her."
"Because she was a good salesperson?"
"Well, yeah, I guess that was part of it."
"And the other part?"
"I don't know exactly. It was kind of a combination of her nice voice and the fact that she seemed honest."
"Honest in what way?"
"She told me two things…"
"Which were?"
"One: that everyone won, and that 99 percent of the winners would get the free vacation for listening to the time-share pitch; Two: that she would get paid if my wife and I showed up and sat through the entire presentation."
"Thank you, Steve," Mark smiled.
"You're welcome," replied Steve politely, and then asked, "What does all this have to do with what you want?"

By now, Connie clearly knew and grew excited in admiration of Mark as he began to explain.

"Let me explain, now, why you are here, how you are going to help me, and how you will help other people make money, and most importantly, help yourself make money."

Mark had everyone's undivided attention. Mark explained that he was here representing a group of investors who felt that the shareholders of the

Narragansett Racetrack in Pawtucket were being cheated; not being paid nearly enough for their shares. Mark's people were offering $2 million more for the racetrack. Everyone's job was more than just calling the shareholders to tell them to come to the meeting tomorrow, although that was certainly an important part. As Mark explained to his attentive audience, their job was: "To make the people love you. Trust you. Feel good about you. Get them to not blow off the meeting or, if they had signed a proxy, to cancel it and come to the stockholders' meeting and vote in person for my offer and reject the city's offer that the board is trying to push through."

Mark made a couple of calls to get things rolling. If the person could not be reached within the next two hours, at 11:00 P.M. a telegram would be sent. Soon, the small conference room was a-buzz with the loud, energetic voices of fifteen people excitedly dialing for dollars. Mark offered cash bonuses to whomever reached the most people every half hour. He tacked up $20, $50, and $100 bills on the wall. The bonus money did the trick. The telemarketers were on fire—smiling, laughing, and cajoling the stockholders to come to the meeting tomorrow.

"You've got to give good phone. Pretend like you're making love to these people over the phone," Mark explained.

Connie wished that she could make love to Mark right now and not over the phone. Connie's cell phone chirped. "Hello," she answered, listened, then turned pale as a ghost. She hung up. "Mark, we've got a big problem."

"What is it?" he asked, concerned.

She didn't want to tell Mark that Bill had just called her to say he might have a big problem raising money for buying the racetrack. Connie didn't answer.

CHAPTER 50

❀

SOMETIME

UNDISCLOSED LOCATION

Where was Mark? Why hadn't he come to save her, to rescue her? She was not ready to die.

"I'm going to kill you now. You must die; you deserve to die. I am finally going to kill you," the voice of death repeated. Carole screamed, but no sound came out. She tried to jump up and run, but found she could not move. She felt paralyzed, as if she were in a dream and trying to scream. Could she possibly be dreaming? If she was, she wanted to wake up now and be safely at home with her husband.

"Mark!" Carole screamed. "Please help me, God," were her last words before she fell asleep from the heavy dose of the hypnotic drug, Halcion, they had dissolved in her water.

Chapter 51

※

THURSDAY EVENING POLICE STATION

PROVIDENCE, RHODE ISLAND

"You get one more chance, asshole," the fat cop said, glowering at Jaffe.

"I don't know what you're talking about," replied Jaffe.

"Yeah, sure, you think we're stupid?"

"I don't think you're stupid, I *know* you're stupid."

"*Is that so?*"

"Yeah, *that's so*," Jaffe replied, his fear of this big fat cop now turning into anger. He had already been in the tiny interrogation room for over two and a half hours. They had not let him see his wife, Jill. He had been allowed one phone call to Mark. He was hot, hungry, craving a cigarette, and had asked to go to the bathroom half a dozen times. What was the problem with this guy? Over and over again he kept asking the same questions.

"Who is Mark?"

"Just a friend," Jaffe told him repeatedly.

"Who does Mark represent?"

"I don't know," Jaffe truthfully told him.

"What are his plans for the racetrack?"

"He didn't tell me."

"How much is he paying you?"

Jaffe hadn't discussed that with Mark yet, but even if he had, it was none of the cop's business. "He isn't paying me anything. My wife and I just felt like taking a vacation to Rhode Island. We heard how lovely the police were here, and we wanted to see for ourselves."

"That's it, I've had it with you, asshole."

"Does this mean you're not going to ask me to go steady?"

Jaffe saw the fist coming, but it was too late—the fat cop hit him so hard he fell off the chair and crumpled onto the floor.

Chapter 52

❀

OH, FOR THE GOOD OLD DAYS

CHICAGO, ILLINOIS

Donovan knew that the Mafia, or Outfit, as it was known in Chicago, had a problem. Families all over the country had the same problem. The older Dons, in most cases, were either too rich, and therefore somewhat complacent, or were dying, or being sent to jail. And the middle-aged guys like Marty were all fuck-ups—they were spoiled and took too much for granted. The younger members were either too inexperienced or hotheaded to effectively carry on the underworld traditions of their bosses and predecessors. This was the main problem. They were a different breed. They didn't have the values that the older members had. They were undisciplined, immature, greedy, and impatient. The new generation, the young Mafioso, had no respect for the sacred institution of "omerta," or silence. When caught in a crime and faced with the possibility of perhaps twenty years in prison, they would quickly, without the slightest bit of hesitation, drop a dime, roll over, and talk to the authorities to save themselves. Also, the new young Turks in the Mafia looked to make the most money as quickly as possible. Consequently, they loved the drug trade. Older Dons had initially been against drugs. Some allowed drug trafficking, but tried to limit the business—no kids, only inner-city black people, who were considered animals anyway. The profits were so incredible that it was impossible to prohibit members from entering the drug business—Donovan recalled how fourteen years ago, Philadelphia had been the home of methamphetamines, or speed. Phenyl 2 Propanone (P2P) was purchased in raw form from either Belgium or West Germany for just over $100 a gallon.

The oil of phenyl acetone would be cooked with aluminum chloride for twenty-four hours. A strong-smelling paste would then be cut and thinned out. Twenty-four pounds could be produced from each gallon. The white powder looked like cocaine. The street price of this deadly powder in Philadelphia in 1988 was $10,000 a pound. A $100 investment would produce over $240,000 in profits. But today the drug of choice for many crime families was Ecstasy, a.k.a., X, E, MDMA, or rolls. There were independent labs run by kids making Ecstasy and other hip dangerous drugs. Ecstasy was a combination of speed and psilicibin; the drug was killing young people left and right. The popular "club drug" would increase body temperature and cause dehydration, then drinking too much water or booze would cause abnormally low concentrations of sodium ions in the blood, which would cause the brain to swell. People would get horny—then heat up and literally explode and die. Today, the profits were much greater. Obviously, as they liked to say in the investment field, the risk ratio was tremendous. Compared to the incredible rewards, the risk was negligible. Marty lent money to dealers, so they could buy drugs and distribute them. He lent money to a middleman who would, in turn, lend money to users to buy their drugs.

Initially, Marty, through the Outfit tutelage, ran TMA (Transportation Motorists Association) which wrote bonds for the

Outfit as well as legitimate construction projects. The construction business, along with the "pension fund rackets," had always been a big source of profits for the Mafia. Chicago was just as corrupt as New York and Philadelphia, although things were kept quieter in Chicago. Fewer scandals surfaced than in the East. Everyone still remembered when little Nicky Scarfo and his gang had decided to extort $1 million from successful real estate developer Willard Rouse, III. His uncle, James Rouse, was the well-respected developer of Reston, VA, and Columbus, MD. Willard had developed Philadelphia's Center City Galleries I and II, and the sixty-story Number One Liberty Place. Politicians and Mafia men—Beloff, Rego, Scarfo, and Carmanadi, a.k.a. Nicki the Crow—thought Rouse would be an easy target for extortion. But they were wrong. Rouse immediately went to the FBI. A similar situation in Chicago would have resulted in swift and immediate retribution; Rouse would have been trunk music. Donovan wished Marty could have stayed in line—he could have been so valuable.

🍁   🍁   🍁

In spite of all his shortcomings, Marty was well liked in the business trades and unions. Whether it was the carpenters, electricians, plumbers, or janitors union, the underlying theme never changed. Corruption was widespread and deeply infested, like a cancer running throughout these organizations. Marty, of course, only saw the world through his rose-colored, myopic glasses. The details and sweating the small stuff were not Marty's concern. Until recently, he had lived his life in the fast track of power. He was oblivious to the real world. Marty never paid for anything, yet his world consisted of beautiful women, outrageous never-ending sex, expensive booze, and the highest-quality drugs money could buy. The fact that he would use innocent people never bothered him. His concern was only one thing; himself. Setting up people, lying to them, even having them destroyed, meant nothing to him. One day he would be someone's best friend and a week later, if that person's usefulness was outlived, Marty showed not the slightest bit of remorse in ordering a contract and extinguishing him or her. Likewise, Marty accepted the fact that his own impending murder was simply part of the same business, nothing personal.

Donovan understood Marty and disliked him. Years ago he had tolerated him, but not now. What bothered him the most was Marty's egotistical, narcissistic demeanor. Marty was street smart, but enemies were everywhere. There was no need to make more, and Marty seemed to have a propensity for pissing people off, like Janet and Pete. Donovan was not happy with the way Marty had handled Janet. He felt that it was inexcusable that Marty had gotten involved with her sexually—acting like some lovesick teenager controlled by some young, hot, tight pussy. Donovan had heard the reports about Marty having taken Janet with him to Los Angeles recently. The trip was supposed to be for business. There were some problems with one of the major Hollywood Studios that was controlled by the Outfit. The vice president of the electrical union was not doing his job, from what Donovan was told. Marty's job was to go out there, meet with the guy, and discreetly assess the situation. Donovan wasn't sure, but he suspected that the union guy was trying to cause a strike on the lot of a major movie studio, which could cost millions. The reason didn't make any difference. If indeed the guy wasn't playing it straight, he was to be removed immediately. But Marty had never even seen the guy. Instead, he had spent the weekend with Janet and three young, wanna-be starlets, sucking and fucking, smoking pot and drinking Dom. The girls, obviously part of the Valley-Girl brain trust, thought the champagne was named after some Mafia Don. Marty had really screwed up, another reason to have Marty executed—not that he needed any more justification, thought Donovan.

Donovan had promised Pete that he would get him out of jail soon. Donovan liked Pete, as did the Don. Yes, he was young, but loyal, and knew how to keep his mouth shut. Pete had earned a promotion, and

Donovan thought that the vice presidency of the electrical union in Hollywood would be a perfect spot for him. Donovan knew that Pete's talents were being wasted helping Marty with the bullshit loan-a-con program. Donovan had purposely put Pete together with Marty to watch him and report back. Now Donovan was just trying to think of the best way to eliminate Marty, who could no longer be trusted. Marty's trip to L.A. had infuriated Donovan. Donovan had earlier written to Pete at Lewisburg Penitentiary and told him about the position in Hollywood that he would have soon, but now Donovan had written him another letter telling him to forget about Hollywood for a while. He couldn't elaborate in the letter, knowing that it could be read by the prison authorities. But the promotion would have to be delayed until Donovan could send someone else to L.A. to get a handle on the situation. Marty was supposed to have gone alone. Instead, he took that cheap, oversexed, underwearless whore, Janet, and spent the weekend in a ménage-à-trois. Janet had been so loaded up the entire time she didn't even know what was going on.

Donovan couldn't understand how Marty could enjoy sex with women who were all doped up and zonked out. It made no sense to him. More than just being stupid, Marty didn't realize the inherent danger. Furthermore, Marty had mistreated and used Janet far too frequently. Donovan feared that in her rare moments of lucidity, she could become a liability to the Outfit. Perhaps she would say the wrong thing, or talk to the wrong people. Perhaps inadvertently, perhaps unintentionally, but dangerous nonetheless. Donovan couldn't believe Marty was foolish enough to send Janet to Washington tonight. No matter, Marty would be dust soon. Yes, the Outfit had a problem, Donovan reflected—he couldn't count on people anymore. He desperately wished for the old days, knowing that it was only that—a wish.

Chapter 53

THURSDAY NIGHT

FORT LAUDERDALE, FLORIDA

Bill Alderice hung up the phone after talking with Connie. He was debating whether or not he should have called her in Rhode Island. He quickly realized that he had made a mistake. He snorted a couple of lines of cocaine. The doctor had been adamant about his cocaine habit—if he didn't stop, he would kill himself. Thanks to Connie's generous cash "donation" to the doctor, Bill was kept out of trouble with his probation officer, but the doctor was still very concerned about Bill's health. So Bill had cut down his daily intake considerably. Well, at least that's what he told himself. He was planning on tapering off any day now. He figured now was not the time to stop, not with all the pressures of his growing empire. The very thought of everything going on made him want to slip into a drug-induced state. He placed another rock of cocaine on the mirror and carefully chopped it with a razor blade; and then with the finesse of a surgeon, he carefully cut it into six perfectly formed five-inch lines. He quickly snorted three lines. Then he lightly dipped two fingers in the glass of

Jack Daniels that sat in front of him, rubbed them against his nostrils and sniffed forcefully, feeling his throat anesthetize with the Jack-Cocaine drip. It would have been better if Connie and Mark didn't know the bad news. So, why had he so impulsively called Connie and told her? Probably because he was straight at the time and had a clear head. Maybe he was even feeling a little bit guilty. But now that he was feeling invincible again, thanks to the shiny white powder, he punched Connie's cellular phone number on the keypad.

"Hello," she answered.
"It's me."
"What's the matter now?"
"Nothing, in fact, everything's okay now, babe."
"You're sure?"
"Absolutely," Bill lied. "Good luck tomorrow."
"Thanks, honey," replied Connie.

Bill was sufficiently high on cocaine and feeling no pain and no moral obligation to tell Connie or Mark the truth that the whole racetrack deal had fallen apart, and that they should leave Rhode Island as quickly as possible. Instead, he played along as if everything were running smoothly. In his drug-induced state, he had no concern for Connie or Mark's well-being. After all, he had built his entire empire on risks and very little concern for others. Bill snorted the remaining three lines.

Chapter 54

FBI

CHICAGO, ILLINOIS

Where was Kathy Hawk Sawyer? Reno wanted to talk to her. The attorney general was getting impatient. Before she told Henry Hyde anything more, Reno wanted to confer with the director of the Bureau of Prisons. Reno glanced at Jack's letter again. Something didn't make sense. Again she reread the letter he sent to Director Hawk and her. What was this guy up to? On the surface the letter seemed clear enough, but according to Kathy Hawk, there was a lot more to this letter than met the eye. When the two of them had talked yesterday, they had tried, unsuccessfully, to put the pieces of the puzzle together. Hawk and Reno, through their network of stool pigeons, were told of a plan that seemed complex. Some of the reports were about a money-lending operation to help inmates, which was, of course, illegal, but of greater concern were the rumors of plans to infiltrate the Department of Justice. These plans were what scared the hell out of them. The plans, especially the one about terrorists, although sketchy, were deep and troubling to these two women and their boss, the president of the

United States. There was a plethora of reports. Some of them seemed absurd, some very real. Their secret armies of intelligence had gathered a multitude of nefarious and clandestine stories. These reports of illicit activities ran the gamut of corruption, double-dealing, and security risks. Reno was not naïve. She knew there were judges, senators, and law enforcement people on the take. What really concerned her, though, was the idea of the federal, state, county, and city prisons being run by the Mob factions. Today the Mob was not just the Italians; now the Russians, Chinese, Columbians, and Iranians were also involved. The whole security of the United States was at possible risk. She couldn't stop wondering—was this Jack guy just some poor schmuck with a pen who signed the wrong credit-card applications and ended up in jail and was now involved with the Mob, or did he really want to help his fellow man, or was he really a lot smarter and more powerful than she initially assumed? Thank God she was not going to be attorney general much longer, she thought to herself. Reno knew that she could not count on President Clinton either; President elect, George W. Bush, would be taking over soon.

Chapter 55

❀

THEN AND NOW

DEERFIELD, ILLINOIS

The nondescript, twenty-year-old, two-story red brick office building on Lake Cook Road a quarter of a mile west of Northbrook Court was easily missed if you were not looking for it. Dr. Bernstein spent the majority of his time in the nearby suburb of Skokie. He was on the psychiatric staff and the board at Rush-Presbyterian-St. Luke's Medical Center. His main office was in the adjacent professional center. But every Thursday, from 3:00 to 9:00 o'clock, he saw patients at his small Deerfield office. Before going away to prison, Jack had come every Thursday evening at 7:00 to tell his problems to Dr. Bernstein. For forty-five minutes, Jack would speak of his anxieties. At first, he talked about the fear of being indicted, and then later, about going to jail. Dr. Bernstein would sit dispassionately, listening to Jack and then prescribe tranquilizers. That was more than six months ago. Now Janet was his main patient. Bernstein was drugging her and more or less controlling her with hypnotic suggestions he had planted in her mind.

Dr. Bernstein sat behind his desk in a big leather chair, sporting an antique pipe in his mouth smoking Mixture Number 79 and blowing smoke rings in the air. As he gazed out the window, his private line rang.

"Oh, shit," he mumbled.

He knew it probably was his wife. He loved her, but she was a pain in the ass, and was always disturbing him at work for some petty bullshit. Probably her French poodle was coming down with a cold, or maybe the landscaper was half an hour late. Did she bother him just to be annoying? Maybe he could ignore the ringing and she would hang up. No, that wouldn't work. He knew from past experience that she'd page him at the hospital, and if she didn't get him there, it would only make matters worse. He was even afraid to have another girlfriend.

His wife, a small, demure blonde, was incredibly jealous and oftentimes prone to violence. The last girl he was dating, a young, buxom redheaded nurse, had quit her job at the hospital and broke off her affair with Dr. Bernstein after his wife had slashed all four tires on her new Toyota. As if that weren't enough, his wife had also smashed out the front windshield with her shoe and then spray-painted the words "Cheap Whore!" on the hood of the young nurse's car. The fights between Bernstein and his wife were legendary throughout the hospital. Once at a Christmas party, his wife had poured lighter fluid over Dr. Bernstein's fur coat and tried to light him on fire. He didn't like scenes, and surprisingly, for a psychiatrist, didn't deal well with these confrontations. If his wife didn't know where he was, she would get in her Mercedes and search him out. The phone kept ringing. He finally picked up the receiver.

"Yes...." The color drained from his face; he felt a tight knot in his stomach and a lump in his throat, making it hard to swallow. It was not his wife or one of his former girlfriends. Only two men had his private number, and neither had called in over a month.

"Are you alone?" asked Marty.

"Yes I am."

"Good, I have some questions."

"Go ahead."

"What I want to know is, could it be wearing off?"

"What do you mean?"

"Could it be wearing off? Not working as well?"

"No," Dr. Bernstein replied, trying not to lose his patience.

"Are you sure?" the caller continued.

"Maybe I don't understand your question."

"I don't think I have to repeat myself, do I," Marty angrily replied.

"Well, no," Dr. Bernstein deflected. "Like I've told you, it's not like in *The Manchurian Candidate.*"

He had explained this at least a dozen times to Marty. *The Manchurian Candidate*, a novel written by Richard Condon in 1959, and later made into a very successful movie, exposed the brainwashing techniques employed by the Chinese and North Koreans during the Korean War. A Communist psychologist used hypnosis and mind-altering drugs to program a captured American soldier to assassinate people whenever commanded to do so. Though the film became a "cult classic," it was pure fiction. The CIA had spent years studying the use of hypnotism for subversive operations, and contrary to widespread beliefs, it did not work and never had. Dr. Bernstein realized that even now many professionals, including psychiatrists and psychologists, were still confused about hypnosis. Dr. Bernstein could not really fault Marty for being so confused. Though he found hypnosis to be very beneficial in his practice to help promote positive suggestions to his patients, there actually was no such thing as pure hypnosis, at least not as a unique state of awareness and consciousness. The term was an anachronism. Just as 200 years ago the words "mesmerism" and "animal magnetism" were used to describe suggestions of the imagination, today they were antiquated and inappropriate.

"You hypnotized Janet, right?"

"Yes," replied Dr. Bernstein.

"Can people fake being hypnotized? Do you think she is faking it?"

"No."

"Why do you say that?"

"Because she is a good subject. Janet has all the necessary attributes, both good and bad—a great imagination, an abusive childhood, mental passiveness, but most importantly, confidence in me to help her," Dr. Bernstein said without hesitation.

"You make it sound pretty simple," muttered Marty.

"No, that's not really the case."

"So, everyone can be hypnotized if they want to be?"

"Yes, that's right."

"And no one can be made to do anything they don't want to do, right?"

"That's correct. Anything she is doing is of her own free will. In other words, she wants to."

"But why would she want to hurt herself?"

"It's her nature, and obviously, I am reinforcing her self-destructiveness and insecurities and keeping her excessively medicated."

"I hope so."

"Look," Dr. Bernstein continued angrily, "not only could I lose my license for what I am doing…if anyone ever finds out, I could be put in jail for the rest of my life." Bernstein concluded, realizing that he was stupid for talking on the phone so openly.

"That's right, doc, but think of the alternative."

"I have."

"Well, just make sure you don't forget."

"How could I?" Dr. Bernstein replied sarcastically.

"You might get tired of your wife and not care if the real story comes out about how she killed that girl."

"You know it was an accident."

"Doc, all I know is, your wife was drunk or high, or whatever, and she ran the girl down and didn't stop. That's vehicular homicide."

"I know," replied Dr. Bernstein ruefully.

"Also, in case you get any ideas about leaving her, don't forget, you're now an accessory," Marty threatened, knowing that his statement was not true. But Bernstein didn't know that.

The phone went dead.

Dr. Bernstein knew how he had gotten involved with the Mob. Jack had been his patient and had been referred by Marty. At the time, Bernstein had no idea who Marty was. Actually, Jenny from the bank had heard that Bernstein was considered one of the leading psychiatrists in Chicago, and she knew how emotionally torn up Jack was over getting ready to go to prison—she felt guilty and responsible because she was the one who had suggested to Jack that he increase his credit lines by exaggerating his income. Jenny told Marty, who worked for her boss, Donovan, at the bank to get Jack in to see Dr. Bernstein. Marty followed Jenny's request immediately because she worked for Donovan. In the process, Marty had secretly found out some interesting things about Dr. Bernstein, specifically about the doctor's wife. Although Marty didn't know it, Donovan was happier than anyone else to make sure Janet was under Bernstein's control. Donovan, too, instantly recognized the advantage of having Dr. Bernstein see Janet. He needed a professional like the doctor to help keep Janet under control, since Marty obviously couldn't—Bernstein, unbeknownst to Marty, was regularly reporting to Donovan about Janet. Donovan was the other man who had Bernstein's private number.

Chapter 56

LEWISBURG PENITENTIARY

HARRISBURG, PENNSYLVANIA

Pete read the letter from Donovan.

"Who the fuck does that cock-sucker think I am?"

"What are you talking about?" asked his cellie.

"How can he treat me like this? Like some fucking piece of shit."

"Who?" his cellie asked again, nervously.

He knew Pete had a violent temper. He also knew that Pete was well connected. Pete always had plenty of money. The majority of the inmates, especially his cellie, showed deep respect for Pete; they were always bringing him cigarettes, chicken, steak, vodka, pot, special clothing items, and anything else he wanted. Obviously, Pete was important. More than just the way he was treated by the staff and inmates alike, Pete carried himself in a certain way. Although he was quiet and kept to himself, there was an evil aura about him—something in his eyes broadcast that he was not a person to mess with. His cellie could see the rage building in his face, which was turning red; the veins on his neck were popping out.

"I'll kill the bastard. No way are they going to fuck me. No fucking way am I going to put up with this shit."

Pete's cellie wisely decided to climb up to his top bunk. He put his headphones on, turned the volume way up on his Walkman, and started reading a magazine to get out of the way.

Pete angrily crumpled up Donovan's letter and flushed it down the toilet. If Donovan had been there right then, Pete would have surely strangled him with his bare hands. His cellie was listening to the radio and couldn't hear Pete's ranting and raving.

"How dare that piece of shit do me like this!"

He started kicking the door with his foot.

"The cock-sucker doesn't even take my calls anymore." Pete had tried at least half a dozen times to call him. He felt that Donovan's secretary was lying when she said he was out of town and couldn't be reached.

"I'll get the motherfucking double-crosser!" His anger was escalating. He was out of control, punching the walls with his fists, which were now covered with blood from his bruised, swollen knuckles. "I've spent all this time playing by Donovan's rules, keeping an eye on that stupid loan-a-con program for that asshole, Marty. I've been going from prison to prison, and now they think they're going to get away with fucking me out of that cushy union job in Hollywood and leave me in this goddamn prison? No fucking way!" Pete was too irrational and hot-headed to even consider for a second the possibility that Donovan wasn't double-crossing him. There was, as Donovan had said in the letter—simply a delay of plans—not a change. Donovan knew that the letter could be read by the guards, so naturally, he didn't spell out too much; he wasn't going to go into detail about the specifics of how it was Marty who fucked things up for the both of them by not taking care of business when he was sent to Hollywood.

Chapter 57

THURSDAY NIGHT

PROVIDENCE, RHODE ISLAND

"What problem do we have?" Mark calmly asked Connie.

"No problem," replied Connie quickly.

"But you just said that..."

"Forget what I said," Connie cut him off. "Bill called and thought there might be a problem with the racetrack deal."

"And what was the problem?"

"Nothing," replied Connie confidently.

"You sure?"

"Yeah, because he called right back to say everything was okay."

Connie felt anxiety after the two quick calls from Bill but decided it was best not to share her concerns with Mark. Watching him, she could see that he was charged up, definitely on a roll, and she didn't want to do anything to diminish Mark's energy and enthusiasm for the racetrack deal.

"You folks are great!" Mark said to the room of telemarketers. There was always something exciting about a room full of energetic people on the phone. There was a buzz, a kind of contagious adrenaline rush that

Mark loved. Connie had seen their people at IGBE back in Fort Lauderdale on the phone a hundred times trying to raise money. Until now she had thought that they were pretty good, but there was absolutely no comparison. After a fifteen-minute pep talk by Mark, these people seemed as if they had been doing this all their lives. The receivers seemed to be attached to their ears, like natural appendages growing out of their heads. Mark had explained that they should not put the receivers back on the phones, as this would break their rhythm. They should merely push down the switch hooks and quickly redial.

Mark kept walking around the room, giving words of encouragement, and when necessary, doing T.O.s—takeovers. When one of the telemarketers would run into a stubborn shareholder and was not getting anywhere, Mark would take over the call, pour on the charm, and get the person to agree to come to the shareholders' meeting tomorrow.

"Listen, kid, do you think you can hold down the fort for a while?"

"Sure," replied Connie.

"Good."

"But where are you going?"

"I've got to do a couple of things before I go out to the track to meet the Senator."

"Can't I come with you?"

"No. I need you to stay here and keep everything going."

"But they seem to be doing just fine."

"That's right, and I want to make sure everything stays that way."

"Okay," Connie said reluctantly. She was disappointed but could see that she wasn't going to change Mark's mind.

"Listen kid, go see Cindy or Becky up at the front desk and have three VCRs that record set up in one of our rooms."

"And then what?"

"Have them set to go on exactly at 11:00 P.M. and record all three local newscasts."

"But why?"

"Stop asking so many questions and just do what I ask, please," Mark said in a sweet, soft voice.

"All right, but will you be okay?"

"Yes, don't worry. I'll be fine."

"What time will you be back?"

"I'm not sure. Probably pretty late. Don't wait up for me. Get some sleep. Tomorrow is going to be one hell of a day."

"Are you kidding? No way am I *not* going to wait up for you."

Mark enjoyed being with Connie. She was easy to be around. She was exciting, but he wasn't sure if she was coming on to him. Maybe it was just his imagination, but she seemed to be giving out signals that she was attracted to him. Mark knew that when it came to understanding women, he was seldom on track. Not that Mark wasn't attracted to Connie—he was. She was a very striking woman, with a pretty face, a gorgeous body, and a subtle sexuality about her. Mark quickly put the lustful thoughts of Connie out of his mind. After all, he reasoned, he was in love with his wife. He missed Carole terribly and couldn't wait until she was home, safe and sound, so they could start their new life together. Why would Connie be interested in him anyway? She was engaged to Bill. Sure, Bill was quite a character, from what Connie had told Mark, but he was rich, successful, or so Mark thought, and very handsome. From the little he knew about them, Connie and Bill seemed perfect for each other.

"I'll see you a little later," Mark said, as he walked out the door of the conference room.

"Okay," Connie replied. Then, as Mark was almost out the door, Connie called out to him.

"Yes?"

"Please be careful."

"I will."

"Oh, and Mark…?"

"Yeah, kid?"

"I'm proud of you."

"Thanks," replied Mark, embarrassed. He had never learned how to accept compliments. Nevertheless, he was pleased by Connie's sentiments. "I couldn't do it without your help," were Mark's last words as got off the elevator and walked toward his hotel room. He took a short nap and then, refreshed, went downstairs and got into a cab.

"Where to, Mac?" the cab driver asked.

"Narragansett Racetrack, please," replied Mark.

"There's no one there, especially at this time of night," replied the cabby a bit too sarcastically to Mark's liking.

"I know," replied Mark, remaining pleasant.

"Okay Mac, it's your dime."

"My name is Mark, Mark Goodwin. What's your name?"

"Jimmy," replied the driver.

"Listen, Jimmy," Mark continued, "after you drop me off, I need you to come back and get me a little later, about 12:30."

"Sorry, no can do. I get off at midnight."

Mark handed Jimmy a $100 bill, which he immediately scrutinized under the dome light in his cab.

"Hey, Mark, are you getting me into something illegal?"

"No, nothing like that."

"Then what gives?"

"I'm here to try to make a deal to buy the racetrack."

"Hey," replied Jimmy enthusiastically, "you're the guy I heard about on the radio a little while ago, aren't you?"

"I'm not sure. What did you hear?"

"Just something on the news about someone coming into town today unexpectedly, planning to offer a couple of million dollars more than the city's offer."

"That's me."

"I hope you know what you're doing," replied Jimmy.

"What do you mean?" queried Mark.

"Just be careful, buddy."

"Why do you say that?"

"You're dealing with some rough people out here. There's a reason why Rhode Island is called Italian Village."

"I'd appreciate it if you could fill me in a little about what you mean," said Mark.

"Sorry, I don't want to say any more."

"Thanks anyway. I appreciate the warning."

"Listen man, I wish that I could tell you more. All I can say is, make sure you know what the hell you're doing." Jimmy warned Mark.

"I'll try," responded Mark.

"I'll be back to pick you up at 12:30," Jimmy said, as they pulled up to the main entrance of the track.

"Thanks, Jimmy. I'll see you in a little while." Mark exited the cab and headed toward the entrance, then turned to watch Jimmy's cab drive away. He wasn't sure why, but he was starting to get nervous. The night was chillingly cold and damp. Mark had an eerie feeling standing in the pitch-black darkness. There was no illumination except for a little dim light shining from the small window of what looked like an upstairs office. Mark felt as if someone were watching him, but he told himself that was ridiculous. He was alone. There was no one else around. Mark took a deep breath, then another, trying to relax. Suddenly, he heard footsteps behind him—and before he could turn around to see anything, he felt a sharp blow on the back of his head. Mark slumped to the ground, unconscious.

Chapter 58

❀

SHOW ME THE MONEY

ROBERT F. KENNEDY CENTER, MORGANTOWN, WEST VIRGINIA

Jack was amazed at how his opinion of the Kennedy Center at Morgantown had changed so dramatically since his first week of incarceration here at the Federal Correctional Institute in West Virginia. When he had first arrived, he thought the place was beautiful, but now he hated everything about it. Nothing had really changed, though, except his perception. The place was still beautiful. The 1,200-person compound was nestled at the base of the magnificent Blue Ridge Mountains. The rolling, verdant hills were like a natural wildlife refuge. There were deer, ducks, and wild turkeys on the compound, and over the years they had acclimated to being around humans. The animals would come right up to the inmates, and although cautious, would eat right out of their hands. When Jack had first arrived at Morgantown, he had spent countless hours watching the ducks swim in the natural pond in the middle of the compound. He had taken leisurely strolls along the natural stream, placidly reflecting on his life, transfixed by the gently undulating, endlessly flowing crystal-clear waters. But the more he watched the birds and animals, the more he resented them. They were free, and he was not. Jack tried to remember who it was that said: "You don't really appreciate your freedom until it is lost." He did his best not to fall into a mind-set of self-pity. Unfortunately, a lot of the inmates fell into that trap. All that did, Jack realized, was make the time go a lot harder and a lot slower. There was a common prison expression that went: "You can do your time or your time can do you." Jack had been determined not to let his time do him, but he found it difficult to follow his resolution. He experienced a wide range of mostly negative emotions. He would get depressed, then angry, then scared, and then vindictive for obvious reasons; he wasn't supposed to be there in the first place. He prided himself on being able to control his emotions. Jack always felt that it was a sign of weakness to let his feelings or negative thoughts get the better of him. Moreover, the notion of letting other people, in this case inmates, see him as weak or vulnerable, was a fate worse than death and certainly to be avoided at all costs. Jack was not into playing the tough guy, though. That simply wasn't his way. Most of the time he felt sorry for the inmates who played out a macho roll. Morgantown, after all, was not really a prison. There were no gangs, no violence, no rapes, and no homosexual acts. This was not a state or maximum-security federal penitentiary. People's concept of prison, including Jack's prior to his incarceration at the camp in Terre Haute, was totally wrong. The people who were hurt the most in federal prisons were not the prisoners but rather their families and friends. The greatest problem facing inmates was the never-ending days that slowly, like Chinese water torture, rolled into weeks, and months, then miserable years. Jack considered himself more fortunate than most. He loved to write. Jack had worked as a reporter for the school newspaper when he was in college. Although possessing nowhere near the talent of an Ernest Hemingway, he was similar to him in one way—like Papa, since he had been a young man, the ink and paper fascinated him. Jack, like

Hemingway, would feel exhilaration upon seeing his words put on paper. There was no greater feeling, no greater high, than seeing his words come to life, jump off the page, and talk to him. Jack had some moderate success as a writer. Nothing spectacular, but significant nonetheless. He had written and published some articles and a few books. He was working on a screenplay now, patterned after the wildly successful screenplay and movie, *The Shawshank Redemption*, adapted from a Steven King novella. His writing kept him busy. Although he had accepted his plight, what choice did he have? For him, the loss of freedom was devastating. He was thankful to temporarily escape reality for a few hours each day and lose himself in his writing.

"Hey man…"

Jack recognized the inmate. He was one of the people for whom Jack had arranged to have money put into his commissary account. "What's up?"

"You tell me," the inmate said with hostility in his voice.

"What do you mean?"

"How come my money stopped coming in?"

"I wasn't aware…"

"Yeah man, why did you cut me off?"

"I didn't," replied Jack.

"Then why the fuck haven't I got any more money?"

"Let me check on it, okay?"

"Yeah, sure. You do that."

"I will, as soon as I can."

"And what about the others?"

"What others?" replied Jack, not having any idea what the inmate was talking about.

"There's about a dozen guys I know who were getting money from your sources."

"And…?" asked Jack, annoyed.

"It's stopped. No one is getting any more money. Man, you should have told us."

"I didn't know," replied Jack honestly.

"Oh, c'mon man, don't bullshit me."

"I'm not," Jack, said, aware that this man didn't believe him and was pissed off.

"Look man," the inmate said angrily, "me and a lot of other people here were counting on that money."

"I'm sorry," Jack said, feeling genuinely sorry for the inmate, but more so for himself.

"Yeah, sure, Mr. big-shot money lender. I don't believe a word you're saying," the inmate said, glowering at Jack.

"Look, I'm telling you the truth," Jack offered nervously.

"And I'm telling you that money better start coming again and *soon*. I broke up with this big fat broad because I didn't need her anymore, or…." The inmate paused, thought for a second, and then continued, "I thought I wouldn't need her money anymore with your money coming in. Now I can't call her and make up. I told her that since I've been in prison she looks like shit since she gained about fifty pounds. The goddamned broad looks like she's grown a second ass and swallowed a piano."

"Oh," Jack said, not knowing what else to say.

"Oh, nothing, sport. Just get the money coming back. I don't care where you get it. Just *do* it, and do it *soon*, or you're in *big fucking trouble*."

"Shit, shit, shit!" Jack said to himself. He was up to his neck in trouble and wasn't sure what to do about it. He hated prison; he hated himself for getting involved in this money-lending program with Pete and Donovan. He hated his fucking life. Why hadn't Donovan contacted him? What was he supposed to do now? Obviously, Kathy Hawk and Janet Reno were not interested in his proposal to help people like himself. He felt himself sinking into a total abyss of futility.

CHAPTER 59

❧

A SOCIAL EVENT

CHICAGO, ILLINOIS

The champagne party at the Art Institute of Chicago was thoroughly enjoyable for everyone, especially Donovan. All of the wealthy Chicago socialites were there. Donovan felt right at home. There was Ron Gidwitz, CEO of Helene Curtis, with his beautiful fashion-model wife, Christina Kemper, daughter of James Kemper, chairman of the insurance corporation bearing his name. Ron's father, Gerald, developed Suave in 1940, the best-selling low-cost shampoo in history; then in 1950, Spray Net, the first successful aerosol hair spray. Evident in the crowd was Christie Hefner, head of Playboy, who, years ago, had helped turn the ailing company around by persuading her dad to sell the black DC-9 jetliner, the limousine, the sixty-nine-room Playboy Mansion, and his $4.5 million Jackson Pollock painting. Christie, to show that what was good for the goose was good for the gander, sold her Porsche and bought a Toyota.

Also in attendance was the matriarch of *Advertising Age, Automotive News*, and *Crain's Chicago Business*, Gertrude Crain, with sons, Rance and Keith and their wives, Merrile and Mary Kay. Ellen Rubin and Melvin Gordon, heads of Tootsie Roll Industries, were chatting with Marshall Field and his second wife, Jamee, along with Marshall's son and his wife, Clea Newman, daughter of Joanne Woodward and Paul Newman. Ted Field, owner of Interscope Records in L.A. and the second son of Marshall Field, IV was also there with his third wife, Susie. Even people who had messed up were there—Michael Butler, of Oakbrook, who declared bankruptcy in 1990 and had to sell his beloved polo ponies to pay his attorneys' fees. Michael was talking to Eric Johnson, whose father, George Johnson, was once turned down for a $500 bank loan because he was black. His product, Afro Sheen, became the most famous black health-care product in history. Eric was president of Johnson until his mother and sister ousted him from the company.

Donovan was looking at all these people and grinning. There was a common bond among all these folks, something quite similar that he was trying to understand. Yes, they were all wealthy and well known, yet there was something else rather odd about them that he couldn't put his finger on. What was it about these people? He racked his brain trying to figure it out. Then it came to him. All of these people, to varying degrees, had one thing in common: they had all inherited their money, fame, and fortunes from their parents. Not to say that these people weren't talented in their own right, but who could be certain? Obviously, Donovan thought, while hiding his look of disdain, it was a lot easier to be successful when you grew up with the advantage of having millions of family dollars and an established business.

Donovan's parents had been killed in a train wreck when he was two years old. He then went to live with abusive relatives who turned him over to the state. From there, he went from one foster home to another. When he was thirteen, he ran away. Donovan lived on the street for a short time before the authorities picked him up and sent him to an orphanage. But his short time on the street, in the real world, had taught him a valuable lesson—he didn't want to end up a bum! He made a resolution that he would become someone important. Donovan would do whatever it took to be successful, to make something of himself. So he applied himself with a vengeance to learning. He started reading everything that he could get his hands on—business, religion, philosophy—it made no difference. He became a voracious reader. Donovan excelled in high school and was anxious to go to college. The problem was that he had no money. He had applied for scholarships at a few colleges, and though his grades were good, they were not quite good enough. He was too young to get a good-paying job, but he was determined to do whatever it took. Then one day he got a letter from an uncle he had never met. His uncle, like Donovan, was Italian. Donovan was short for Donovelli. The letter stated that his uncle was moving to Chicago from Italy. Two weeks later, Donovan borrowed his friend's car to pick up his aunt and uncle at the airport. Donovan's aunt was short, and far too skinny for a woman.

She had dark black hair and small deep black eyes. She was not attractive—a flat nose, too big for her face, and lips so thin they almost looked as if they were drawn on with a black pen. Between her nose and upper lip was a full black mustache. Donovan couldn't decide whether she looked more ridiculous or pathetic standing next to her husband. The contrast between the two was striking, almost comical. Donovan's uncle was six feet two inches tall—a big burly man. He had an overabundance of good looks. In fact, he bore a remarkable resemblance to Dean Martin. His hands looked to be those of a boxer's, with thick fingers that were long enough to pick up a basketball in one hand. His smile was big and broad. There was an air about him, a certain presence that exuded confidence. He radiated a certain power and charisma that at once made Donovan respect him. Although he had a deep heavy Italian accent, he spoke English remarkably well. His uncle said he had booked a room at the Bismarck Hotel on Randolph Street in the Loop. The Bismarck had been a favorite Outfit hangout in Chicago, well known for its Walnut and Green dining rooms. Donovan was totally amazed by the opulence of the suite at the hotel. He had never seen anything quite like it before. Donovan immediately realized that his uncle was extremely wealthy. He didn't really know the extent of his uncle's riches until a week later, when he saw the palatial mansion his aunt and uncle moved into in the affluent suburb of Evanston.

The seventeen-room, six-bathroom estate off Sheridan Road sat on the shores of Lake Michigan. The Frank Lloyd Wright estate looked like something out of the movies. Even though the house had everything—a pool, tennis courts, its own dock—Donovan's uncle was not happy until he had a Bocce court built. His uncle loved playing this game. Donovan recalled reading an account of how in the early 1900s, during the country's first Red Scare, the government was rounding up and arresting everybody who was thought to be a Communist. The Feds had broken into a poor Italian family's home in the middle of the night. In the downstairs hall closet the Feds found eight small blue and red bombs that they immediately submerged in a tub of water to neutralize the explosives. Later, it was discovered that the so-called bombs were, in fact, only Bocce balls, and in their zealous paranoia, which was running rampant throughout the country at the time, they had assumed the worst. Judging by the people his uncle associated with, Donovan suspected that he might be a powerful gangster, but he didn't care. To the contrary, he was quite impressed. His uncle treated him like he was his own son. He made it clear to Donovan that he wanted him to get an education and become a lawyer. The old man was very wise. He understood that a law degree and a pen were more powerful weapons than a gun or knife. His uncle told Donovan that his education would be taken care of, so long as he abided by some very strict rules that he had set down. Rule one: Donovan had to maintain a straight-A average. Rule two: Donovan had to agree to work for his uncle for five years after completing law school; then after five years he could do whatever he wanted. And Rule three: Donovan was to tell no one that he was his nephew, expect no favors, and work twice as hard as anyone else. At first, everyone, not only the other lawyers, made a lot more money than he did. But Donovan handled legal matters for the Outfit in an efficient and quiet manner. He didn't talk. He kept his mouth shut. He understood the laws of omerta—keeping silent. He grew to love his uncle for all of the opportunities that had been bestowed upon him while being a young Outfit lawyer.

Then one day his life changed dramatically. One of his uncle's associates came to see him at his law office. It was time, he was told, to make his "bones"—become a man. He was to carry out a contract, an execution. The man explained that he had no choice. Donovan had to carry it out, or he would be through and lose everything he had worked for, not to mention the dishonor and shame it would bring upon his uncle if he weren't successful in his mission.

He was given the name and address of a sleazy motel on North Lincoln Avenue in Chicago. Donovan was told that a man would be there with a mistress. He was told what room they would be in and was given a pass-key. The job was to be done quickly. Donovan was to unlock the door and go in shooting, and he did just that. The look of fear on the woman's face, who was lying in bed naked as he opened the door and instantly fired two bullets into her neck and head, made him want to vomit. The man was in the bathroom. He heard the shots and opened the door quickly to try to grab his gun, which was sitting on the bureau, but Donovan was too quick for him—he fired three shots into his face. The man crumpled to the floor in a sanguinary pool of warm, red wetness.

Donovan ran out of the room screaming. Yes, he had made his bones that day. And he would never forget it.

No, Donovan was not like these people at the party. Nothing had been handed to him on a silver platter, unlike the rich socialites at this charity benefit at the Art Institute. Donovan had worked hard for everything. Looking around at this crowd of socialites who had been handed everything by their parents, or had married into money, he felt different, somehow better than all of them. Nonetheless, all these people accepted Donovan. They all knew he was a powerful Outfit figure. He posed an interesting contradiction to these well-heeled and proper rich folks. On the one hand, they looked down on Donovan, but on the other hand, he was secretly envied and admired. He represented something they were not. He had brass balls. He was powerful and above the law.

There was a mystique about the Mafia. The Mob and its colorful characters, like Donovan, had always fascinated people, especially in Chicago. Then Donovan saw his friend, Sidney Korshak. Donovan had always managed to keep a low profile, which was more than he could say for some of the Mob's other lawyers. Donovan vividly recalled one of his first meetings, years ago, with Sidney at Celano's Custom Tailors, then located at 620 North Michigan Avenue. Celano's, in addition to being a regular meeting place for Outfit members, had the dubious distinction of having had the first successful bug planted there by the FBI on July 29, 1959. Sidney Korshak, lawyer for the guys in Chicago, had worked as a chauffeur for Al Capone while he was attending law school. He lived at 2970 North Lake Shore Drive and had an office at 134 North LaSalle Street. He was a powerful man. It was said that he could resolve major problems with a single phone call. Korshak worked closely with Colonel Jake Arvey, one of Chicago's great fixers and politicos. Korshak, Arvey, and Donovan arranged for Chicago's gangsters, Tony Accardo and Gusie Alex, to acquire large blocks in the Hilton Hotel chain. Donovan often worked in tandem with Korshak and Arvey. Jake Arvey was responsible for Adlai Stevenson becoming governor of Illinois. Then Arvey tried to make him president. Jake Arvey surrounded himself with some of Chicago's most colorful characters: Artie Elrod, the connection man; Joe Grabiner, Chicago's biggest layoff bookie; and Tubbo Gilbert, often referred to as the richest policeman in the world. Arvey was involved with everybody from Abe Pritzker and Art Greene, longtime Capone advisors and financiers to "Momo" Giancana, Frank Sinatra, Mayor Richard J. Daley, Joe Kennedy, and son, Jack. Contrary to the idealized Camelot impression most people had of the Kennedys, Arvey knew better. Joe Kennedy's roots were deeply tied to the underworld. He made part of his fortune from bootlegging during the twenties. When prohibition came to a close, Kennedy retained the three most lucrative distributorships in the country: Gordon's Gin, Dewar's, and Haig & Haig, through his company, Somersett Imports. Arvey knew about Joe Kennedy having Giancana secretly annul his son Jack's first marriage. Arvey also was privy to the fact that when mobster Frank Costello put a contract out on Joe Kennedy, Giancana had the hit called off after Kennedy flew to Chicago and begged Momo for his life, promising that when his son, Jack, became president, Giancana and the Chicago Outfit would have JFK's ear in the White House. It was not surprising that after Jack and Bobby Kennedy double-crossed the Mob, Momo had both of their executions ordered.

Everybody at the socialite gathering stared at Donovan and his date, Jenny, the young girl from the bank, probably thinking how lucky he was to be bedding this young beauty who worked for him. If only they knew what was really going on—the real story—they would have been quite surprised.

Chapter 60

LATE THURSDAY EVENING

NARRAGANSETT RACETRACK, PAWTUCKET, RHODE ISLAND

"Are you all right?" Ron Jaffe asked Mark, as he knelt beside him on the ground.

"What happened?" Mark asked, rubbing his throbbing head.

"You tell me."

"I don't know," replied Mark. "Someone hit me on the back of the head. I guess I was knocked out."

"Who did it?"

"I don't know."

"You didn't see who did this to you?"

"No, it was too dark. Someone snuck up on me from behind and hit me over the head...What are you doing here?" Mark asked, relieved that Jaffe was there.

"I called your hotel after the cops let Jill and me out of jail, and your girl, Connie, said you were coming here to meet the Senator."

"I'm glad you're here, buddy."

"Me too," replied Jaffe.

"Did anyone follow you?"

"No way, it's impossible."

"How can you be so sure?" queried Mark.

"Because it took me over an hour just to find this fucking place. I must have gotten lost half a dozen times before I finally got here. No one could have followed me."

"That's good," replied Mark, relieved.

"What in the hell is going on anyway?"

"What do you mean?"

"I mean," Jaffe began, "I thought this was just some simple deal to buy a racetrack."

"Obviously not," replied Mark.

"No shit," agreed Jaffe.

"It seems we're not welcome here."

"To say the least," added Jaffe, sarcastically.

"That's right, gentlemen," the voice of an older man said. He seemed to appear out of nowhere. Mark recognized the voice.

"Hello, Senator," Mark began.

"Hi fellows. How you doing?"

Ron Jaffe spoke first. "Pretty shitty, Senator. I missed you at the airport."

"I know, Ron. I saw you and your wife there, but before I knew what was happening, the cops picked you guys up."

"Yeah, well, my wife and I have been guests at your local police department."

"I figured as much," the Senator said.

"They worked me over pretty good. Then they finally let us go."

"What did they want?" asked the Senator.

"They wanted to know who I was, who Mark was, and what we were doing here. You know, the whole third degree," Ron answered.

"Did they mention my name?"

"No. Your name did not come up."

"Good," replied the Senator.

"Why is that good?" Mark asked.

"Because," the Senator continued, "I would prefer that my name not be involved with you guys."

"I see," said Mark, not really seeing anything, but waiting for the Senator to elaborate, which he did.

"I can be a lot more help to you guys if I'm on the outside, as opposed to being followed, or in jail."

"They would put a Senator in jail?"

"Absolutely. They don't like me. They know I know too much."

"What exactly is it that you know, Senator?" Mark asked, slightly annoyed. His head felt like it had been hit by a ton of bricks. He was getting tired of this cat-and-mouse game.

"Follow me, gentlemen," the Senator said, as he led Mark and Ron to a side door of the racetrack. He took a key out of his pocket and unlocked the door. In the darkness he felt along the wall for the light switch.

"Someone must have been waiting for me when I got here," Mark said, rubbing the back of his head with his hand, wishing he had some aspirin, ice, or a stiff drink to ease the pain.

"How so?" the Senator asked.

"Because someone knocked him out, hit him over the head," Jaffe explained.

"I'm sorry to hear that, but it doesn't surprise me. In fact, we should hurry up and get out of here. The person who attacked you could still be here."

"I agree," Mark shot back.

"Are you okay?" the Senator questioned.

"Yeah, I'm wonderful," Mark, replied sarcastically. "My wife has been kidnapped. I'm involved in this crazy racetrack deal. Ron and his wife were locked up as soon as they flew into the airport. Ron was interrogated and assaulted by some asshole cop. I just had someone try to push my brains out of my skull! And now you're playing some kind of cloak-and-dagger game with me."

"I'm not, Mark, really," the Senator said.

"Then what's going on?" Jaffe demanded.

"Look guys, I'm in a funny position here. I'm a large shareholder of the racetrack. I'm privy to certain information that…"

Jaffe cut him off. "What information, Senator?"

"I can't directly tell you…it would be unethical."

"For Christ's sake," Jaffe angrily continued, "you're supposed to be my friend. You said you would help Mark and me. I was counting on you to…"

"Look," the Senator interrupted, "I am going to help you. I already gave Mark the list of shareholders."

"Big deal," replied Jaffe. "That list is public information. Anybody could have gotten that list."

The Senator found the light-switch and turned on the lights as they entered the side door.

"I can understand you fellas being annoyed, but if you'll just follow me upstairs, I have some information for you that will be quite revealing."

Mark and Ron followed Senator Donaldson up the stairway to the second-floor office. The Senator turned on another light and walked over to a wall of locked cabinets. He produced a small key, studied the file cabinets for a few seconds, and then unlocked a cabinet labeled "Dead Files." He went through the drawer of files quickly and deliberately, obviously looking for a particular one. He found what he was looking for, pulled the file out, then closed and locked the cabinet. "Here," the Senator said, as he handed the two-inch-thick file to Mark.

"What is it?" Mark asked.

"I'm afraid you will have to figure that out yourself."

"Look," Ron began angrily, "stop the mysterious shit, Senator. What's in the file, for Christ's sake?"

"Do you have a good accountant, Mark?"

"Yes, Senator, I do," Mark replied. He could now see that there was no point in getting upset with the man. The Senator was nervous, afraid of something, but nonetheless wanted to help. "What should my accountant do with this?"

"Just get it to him as quickly as possible, so he can go through it completely."

"Okay," Mark said.

"But what is he supposed to be looking for?" asked Jaffe, still hot under the collar.

Jaffe, as Mark was well aware from the years he had known him, had a fiery, explosive personality. Mark stepped in front of Jaffe to keep him from talking anymore.

"Look fellas, we have to get out of here. This is a dangerous place to be," the Senator said, as he led Mark and Ron down the stairway and out to the front of the racetrack.

"Thanks, Senator," Mark said, as the Senator quickly walked away into the darkness, got into his car, and drove away.

"What do we do now, Mark?"

"Let's go back to the hotel. How did you get here anyway?"

"Jill and I rented a car. I've got it parked a couple a hundred yards away."

"Is Jill in the car?" Mark asked in alarm.

"Hell no, man. I dropped her off at some twenty-four-hour diner. I didn't want to bring her out here."

"Smart thinking, Lincoln," Mark replied.

"C'mon Mark, let's get the fuck out of here before someone else tries to smash your skull."

"Not so fast, Ron."

"What do you mean?"

"What time is it?"

Jaffe looked at his watch—"12:25."

"Go get in your car and drive around for exactly five minutes."

"Then what?" replied Jaffe, confused by Mark's request.
"Come back here."
"I don't understand."
"I want to see if you're being followed."
"Okay," replied Ron reluctantly as he walked into the darkness to get into his car.

Jaffe drove away from the racetrack. He looked in his rearview mirror. There was no one following him. But he saw a car's headlights approaching, coming toward him, and heading to where Mark was waiting at the track. As the car sped past him, Jaffe could see that it was a taxicab. He immediately panicked, made a U-turn, and pushed the gas pedal to the floor. Typical of a cheap rental, there was no acceleration. Jaffe was getting pissed, swearing at the car, afraid for Mark. When he finally caught up with the cab, he was surprised to see Mark and the cab driver standing in front of the taxi, chatting, with what seemed like smiles on their faces illuminated by the bright headlights.

"Ron, this is the taxi driver, Jimmy. He brought me out here earlier."
"How ya doing, man?" Ron offered.
"Okay," replied Jimmy.

Jimmy got into the taxi first and closed his door. Just before Mark opened the back door, he gave Jaffe the file from the Senator. He didn't think the taxi driver had anything to do with his getting knocked out, but he felt he'd better play it safe. Mark made sure that he handed the file to Jaffe quickly but discreetly. Jaffe, in kind, took the folder and put it under his coat. Jimmy didn't see the exchange.

The taxi pulled out of the deserted racetrack. Jaffe followed about fifty yards behind for a few miles. He couldn't be sure whether or not anyone was following them. There was not a lot of traffic at this hour as they headed for the Marriott. Jaffe was now about a quarter of a mile behind the taxicab. Obviously, Jaffe thought, Mark was being paranoid. There was no one following. So Jaffe relaxed, lit a Kool, and tried to find a decent station on the cheap AM-only radio. He inhaled deeply and then blew three perfectly formed smoke rings against the windshield. He was listening to some trashy call-in program. The highly agitated, distraught young woman was upset because she suspected that her mother was sleeping with her boyfriend.

"What makes you think your mom is actually sleeping with your boyfriend?" the talk-show host asked.

"I just know it's true," the young woman replied.

"Do you have any proof?"

"What do you mean?" the woman asked angrily.

"I mean exactly what I said," the host intoned in an arrogant voice. "Do you have any evidence? Have you seen them in bed together?"

"No, not yet anyway."

"Then what makes you so sure there is something going on?"

"My mom's nipples."

"I don't understand," he replied, laughing.

"My mom has very big nipples," the woman began.

"I see," the host replied happily, knowing that talk like this, no matter how off the wall, would keep listeners, especially males, glued to his program.

"Well, you see," the young woman went on, "my mom always wears bandages over her nipples."

"Why?" the host asked in a tone of disbelief.

"*Why?*" the girl shot back angrily, as if he had just asked the most stupid question in the world. "Because her nipples are so big and huge. They are so noticeable that they stick out, even through a padded bra, and that's why she puts bandages on them—to cover them up."

"I've never heard of anyone doing this," the host replied, tongue-in-cheek, trying not to lose it.

"Are you crazy? If she doesn't wear bandages on her nipples, they stick out like two bullets."

"They do?" the talk-show host asked in false disbelief but true excitement.

"Of course they do. It's disgusting. Makes me want to puke. I wear bandages over my nipples, too. It's the proper thing to do."

"So how does this relate…? No, strike that. What does this have to do with your suspicion that your mother is sleeping with your boyfriend? I must have missed the point."

"My mother looks like a goddamned hooker lately—you can see her nipples—she's not putting bandages on them. She's obviously doing this to turn my boyfriend on. It's so obvious. I'm sure all of your listeners would agree with me."

🍁 🍁 🍁

The sound of a car loudly backfiring suddenly pierced the silent darkness outside. Jaffe turned off the radio and rolled down the window, trying to figure out the source of the noise. Then he heard it again and simultaneously saw a bright white flash. Jaffe quickly realized that it wasn't a car backfiring but rather the sound of gunshots! Someone was taking shots at Mark in Jimmy's cab. As Jaffe approached the taxi, he could see that the shots were being fired from a dark blue sedan. The next shot hit the rear window, which exploded and blew out onto the highway. Jaffe tried in vain to catch up to the sedan but wondered what he would do if he did—he wasn't sure. It was hopeless anyway; the damn rental had no power. Jaffe watched helplessly as another shot rang out, then another. The tires were blown out of the taxi, which started to skid out of control and then flipped over on its side as the blue sedan sped away into the darkness.

Chapter 61

※

EARLIER THURSDAY NIGHT

AIRPORT FBI INTERROGATION ROOM, WASHINGTON, D.C.

"Look lady, why don't you make it easy on yourself and cooperate with us?"

"I don't know what you're talking about."

"Listen Janet," the big, redheaded FBI man said, in a tough-spirited, raspy voice. "We know who you are, who you work for, and what you do for a living."

"Is that so?" replied Janet calmly.

"Yeah, that's so, Janet. We know everything."

"I'm sure you must have me mixed up with someone else. I am a self-employed saleswoman," Janet replied with sincerity and total conviction.

She was good, the big redheaded Fed thought. Real good, real smooth, this broad was a pro. She was not intimidated or flustered in the slightest. If she was, she certainly didn't show it. "So, you're just a salesperson, huh?"

"That's right, sir."

The FBI man laughed. "Well, I guess you could call it sales. After all, you sell yourself. You're nothing but a hooker, an expensive one, a beautiful one, but a whore just the same."

"Look, I don't know what you want, but I want a lawyer," Janet replied dispassionately.

"You are not under arrest. You don't need a lawyer."

"Then if I'm not under arrest, how can you hold me?"

"You can leave anytime you want."

"Thank you," Janet said as she started to get up and put on her coat. She walked toward the door, put her hand on the knob, and started to turn it.

"Oh, just one thing, Janet…"

"What's that?" asked Janet hurriedly. She had to get to the party where former mayor Marion Barry would be.

"You will probably be dead by this time tomorrow, so be careful," the fiery-haired Fed declared.

"What do you mean?" asked Janet, obviously startled.

"Oh nothing…it's just that Marty is planning on having you killed if you're not successful tonight at the hotel."

"Excuse me?" Janet was obviously startled by his comment.

"I thought that might get your attention," the Fed said nonchalantly.

"You've got it."

"Listen Janet, we know everything. Deemis and the racetrack in Rhode Island that he told you about—Donovan believes that you and Marty spilled the beans. He wants you killed, too. It's over, girlie. You don't have to pretend. We know all about the sixty-seven prostitutes that work for you, about lending money to convicts, trying to fuck up the court system, and trying to take over the private prison industry."

"The private prison industry?" Janet asked, not knowing anything about the Mob's prison privatization plans.

From the tone of her voice, the FBI agent began to believe that perhaps she really didn't know about the Outfit's plans for the private prison industry.

"Let me fill you in, Janet."

For the next half-hour Janet sat and listened, while the cop explained things that Janet could not believe. He seemed to know everything.

"What about my sister?" Janet asked.

The agent looked surprised, "What about her?"

"Can you guarantee her safety if I cooperate with you?"

The agent didn't answer; he just scratched his red head.

Chapter 62

※

LATE THURSDAY NIGHT

PAWTUCKET, RHODE ISLAND

Ron jumped out of the car and ran to the overturned taxicab. He bent down to the ground and looked into the car where the rear window had been blown out. There was no sound or movement inside the cab. The front window was shattered but still in place. The darkness made it hard for him to see in. Quickly, he got to his feet and dashed back to the rental car, opened the door, and hurriedly looked in the glove box for a flashlight—nothing. He pulled the keys out of the ignition, jumped out of the car, and opened the trunk. No flashlight, no flares, nothing—only a tire iron, which he grabbed and made his way back to the cab. He smashed out the windshield, not worrying about removing the glass carefully, thinking that there was no time. He expected the cab to burst into flames at any moment. Maybe he had seen too many accidents on TV or in the movies where cars exploded into balls of fire. Better to be safe than sorry, he thought. Jimmy, the taxi driver, had blood dripping from his left eye and right ear. There was just enough glare from the highway lights overhead for Ron to see that

Jimmy appeared to be breathing. A truck pulled up behind the cab. The big, bearded, fat truck driver called out to Ron as he made his way down from the cab of his Kenworth eighteen-wheeler.

"Is anyone hurt?"

"Yes," Ron said.

"I'll call the Highway Patrol on my CB."

"No!" replied Ron quickly. "No cops!"

"What?" the truck driver asked, surprised by Ron's adamant response.

"Bring a flashlight over here and help me get these guys out of the car. *Now*, goddammit! Hurry."

"All right man, I'm coming."

Seconds later, though it felt like minutes to Ron, he was shining the light inside the car. Mark's body lay upside down, smashed against the roof of the car. "Mark, are you all right? Can you hear me?"

There was no answer.

Ron and the truck driver gently maneuvered Jimmy's body out through the windshield of the taxi, moving him away from the car. Then they went to the back of the taxi where the rear window had been blown out by gunshots. There was still no sound or movement from Mark. He was covered with shards of glass. Gently, they were finally able to lift Mark out of the taxi, laying him on the asphalt next to Jimmy.

"I'm going to call an ambulance. These guys need to get help immediately," the truck driver said breathlessly, his face drenched with beads of sweat in the cold night air.

"Yes, hurry up and call," Ron Jaffe finally agreed, realizing as he bent down next to Mark's mouth to see if he was breathing that the situation was more serious than he had thought just a few seconds earlier. The driver rushed to his truck.

"No, I'm okay," Mark said, barely audibly.

"Is anything broken?" asked Jaffe, frightened yet relieved that Mark was alive.

"I don't think so," Mark replied drowsily, slowly regaining his consciousness.

Moments later an ambulance pulled up to the side of the highway. Jaffe was relieved that help was there. The ambulance driver and another man, presumably a paramedic, rushed over with a stretcher. They put Jimmy on it; he was still unconscious and his breathing was labored and erratic. They injected a hypo into his forearm, taped it in place, and attached a long tube from an IV bag that one of the paramedics held in the air. Quickly they popped up the gurney to its full height and carefully slid Jimmy into the ambulance. They came back and gave Mark a quick inspection. Miraculously, he seemed to be fine—obviously shaken up but no apparent broken bones, only some minor cuts and abrasions. Ron was adamant that Mark go with the paramedics, but he refused.

Before the paramedics left to attend to Jimmy, they warned Mark and Ron of possible head injury and made it clear that Mark should be supervised closely for the next day or two and brought in immediately if he experienced any type of severe headaches.

"I'm fine, Ron. Really, I'm okay." Mark started to get up, but was visibly shaky. He quickly sat back down.

"Look," implored Ron, "let's at least get you to a hospital so that they can check you out."

"Ron," replied Mark, sounding stronger, "I'm not trying to be a hero. I'm okay."

"But, what if you have a concussion or something?"

"I don't have a headache." Mark said, slightly irritated. "But if it will make you feel any better, I won't go to sleep for twenty-four hours in case I do have a concussion."

"Shit, man, what the fuck are you giving me such a hard time for? You were just nearly killed and you're acting like it's no big deal, like you stubbed your toe or something."

"I really do appreciate your concern, but I'm not bullshitting you. Nothing's wrong. Let's get out of here before the cops show up."

"Let me help you up," Ron said, realizing he wasn't getting anywhere with him, but Mark got up on his own. He wanted to make it clear to Ron that he was okay. Mark opened the door to Ron's rental, they both got in, and they drove off toward the Marriott. Mark was in tremendous pain but used every ounce of his adrenalin and willpower to mask it from Jaffe. He closed his eyes as he rested his head against the seat—thankful that he was still alive.

Chapter 63

THURSDAY NIGHT

CHICAGO, ILLINOIS

Marty answered the phone on the first ring. "Yeah?"

"It's me."

"Where in the hell have you been?"

"What do you mean?" asked Janet, trying to maintain her composure.

"You were supposed to call me over an hour ago."

"I know," replied Janet, trying not to sound nervous. "I got delayed."

"Bullshit," Marty shot back. "I called the airline and they said your plane got in almost fifteen minutes early."

"You're right, it did, but the traffic was terrible, and it took me a while to get a cab."

Marty was pissed. He sensed that something wasn't right, something in Janet's voice. But if she was lying, Marty couldn't tell. That was not surprising; after all, Janet, like Marty, was a consummate liar. She was trained to lie. Marty had no control over the immediate situation. He was not there to look her in the eye. As good a liar as Janet was—and she was quite extraordinary—Janet still couldn't pull off a lie to Marty face-to-face. There was something in her eyes that always, if only for a microsecond, gave her away. Maybe it was because when Marty had first met Janet, she was still somewhat innocent. Perhaps not in thought, but at that point in her life, at least in deed. Back then, Marty had not yet worked his magic on her, or corrupted, molded, and shaped Janet into the nymphomaniac Outfit seductress that she was now.

"Where are you?" Marty asked.

"At the hotel."

"How long have you been there?"

"I just got into my room a few minutes ago."

"Hang up. I'll call you right back," ordered Marty.

"But why…?" Janet started to ask, but the line went dead.

Obviously, Marty wanted to make certain that she was, in fact, where she was supposed to be. He called her right back to be sure. The phone rang thirty seconds later.

"Hello?" Janet answered.

"Sorry," said Marty, "I had to take care of something real quick."

"Oh," said Janet, knowing full well why Marty was lying.

Janet was getting nervous. Did he know that she had been picked up by the Feds? Could he tell that there was something different about her? Had she blown it? Did Marty hear the FBI man pick up the extension phone?

Chapter 64

❦

THURSDAY NIGHT

PROVIDENCE, RHODE ISLAND

Deemis had only been back home from the dinner meeting in Chicago for a few hours. He paced nervously in his living room as Penny watched.

"What's the matter with you?" asked Penny.

"What do you mean?" replied Deemis defensively.

"You're as nervous as a cat on a hot tin roof."

"It's just your imagination, Penny," retorted Deemis harshly.

"Look, we've been together a long time. Too long, I'm sure, from your point of view, but you can't bullshit me, Deemis. I know something is wrong, terribly wrong. I've never seen you act like this."

"I've got some things on my mind. Nothing important."

Inasmuch as Deemis loathed his wife, he almost wanted to talk to her. Yes, he had been miserable with her for all of these years, but the truth of the matter was, no matter how much he hated to admit it, Penny was a good woman. She had always tried, at least early on in their marriage, to be a good wife. But the more Penny had reached out to Deemis, the more he pushed her away, rejecting her.

"You can talk to me, Deemis. I'm still your wife."

Deemis wished he could talk to her, but he couldn't. All he could think of was the strangers in town who were trying to buy the racetrack. He had to do something quickly, but he felt defeated. And of course he wasn't forgetting for a second that if he hadn't told Janet about the track, this whole nightmare would not be occurring.

Chapter 65

THURSDAY EVENING AFTER THE DINNER IN CHICAGO

KEY BISCAYNE, FLORIDA

"Thank you for the information," the Don said as he hung up the phone. He was out on his porch drinking wine. It would have been a perfect day in Key Biscayne, if he hadn't spent the day traveling back and forth to Chicago, and now he got the telephone call from one of his people. He wasted no time calling Donovan on a secure line. The Don had talked with Donovan more today than he had the entire week.

"Yes," Donovan answered.

"Are you alone?" the Don asked dispassionately.

"Hold on one moment please." Donovan brusquely asked his secretary to put down her steno pad. "We'll continue with the dictation tomorrow."

"Yes sir, Mr. Donovan," his fiftyish, gray-haired secretary said as she closed the door behind her. She was thankful for the interruption. She should have been done with work at five o'clock, and it was many hours later; she wanted to go home.

"Sorry," said Donovan. "I'm alone now."

"Things have gotten out of hand."

"What do you mean?"

"I don't want to discuss it over the phone. It's not safe," replied the Don, annoyed.

"When and where do you want to meet?"

"Leave for the airport now. Call me when you land in Fort Lauderdale."

The Don hung up.

"Shit," said Donovan as he buzzed his secretary.

Chapter 66

❃

THURSDAY NIGHT

HOTEL, WASHINGTON, D.C.

"What time are you going to the party?" Marty grilled Janet over the phone.

"Soon. I just want to freshen up, fix my face, and then I'm going."

"Do you think you'll have any problem getting in?"

"None," replied Janet confidently.

"That's good, kid. I'm sure you'll do just fine," replied Marty, sounding relieved at Janet's answer. She seemed so sure of herself. Marty thought that maybe he had made the right decision after all by sending Janet. He knew that if anyone could get to Barry, she had the best chance. "Don't forget, just open the dresser drawer at least half an inch and the recorder and videotapes will start rolling. And there's a stockpile of drugs for you to share with him. Offer them to him, slip them in his drink, and do whatever you have to." Marty ordered, realizing his stupidity for talking so openly on the phone.

"I remember what to do, Marty," Janet said calmly. "Don't worry, everything will be fine. I feel lucky tonight."

Marty didn't feel so sure. Something wasn't right. He couldn't put his finger on it, but Janet sounded too calm. She hadn't even asked Marty about her sister, Carole.

"Good luck," he said as he hung up.

"Thanks," Janet replied, and put down the receiver.

"You did fine," the FBI man said to her as he put down the extension phone he had been listening in on.

Chapter 67

❀

LEWISBURG PENITENTIARY

HARRISBURG, PENNSYLVANIA

"Let's do it again," the guard said.

"Okay," replied the other guard.

Ten minutes later, the two guards met back at the control desk.

"How many do you got?"

"A hundred twenty-seven," replied the other guard.

The two guards paused for a moment, contemplating the short count.

"Let's get the bed-books and do it again," the guard ordered.

"Right," the other said in agreement.

The count of inmates in the unit was supposed to be 128. Twice they had counted only 127. They were one short. The bed-books contained a picture of each inmate. Carefully, the guards went through the unit again. They checked all inmates against their pictures. After twenty minutes, it became clear who was missing; inmate number 07578-424, Pete Ritelo. For the next two hours every guard made a thorough search of the prison. They looked in the laundry, the kitchen, the machine shop, the hospital, and the commissary. Every nook and cranny of the sixty-year-old, dark, dungeon-like prison was thoroughly searched and inspected. Pete was nowhere to be found. He had escaped, or what was more likely, one of the guards had been paid off to get Pete out.

Chapter 68

❦

THURSDAY NIGHT

DINER NEAR PROVIDENCE, RHODE ISLAND

Miraculously, Mark seemed to be all right, obviously shaken up, but okay nonetheless. Ron and Mark drove to the diner where Jill had been waiting. They went in and found Jill sitting there by herself in a small back booth, looking bored.

"What happened to you?" Jill asked, shocked at Mark's disheveled appearance.

"Oh, nothing," replied Mark, in his customary, nonchalant manner. "Just a little car trouble."

Likewise, Ron said nothing to his wife, not wanting to alarm Jill any more than she already was after being held at the police station for hours.

"Coffee?" the middle-aged, saucy, bleached-blonde waitress asked.

"Black," Ron replied.

"And you?" the waitress asked Mark, smiling and showing a mouth full of badly capped teeth.

"Just a cup of tea, please," Mark said, wondering if his pain and discomfort were showing.

"What do we do now?" Ron asked Mark.

"Nothing," replied Mark. "You finish your coffee, I'll finish my tea, and then we go back to the Marriott."

The three of them sat in silence for a short time and finished their drinks. Mark paid the check. As usual, he left a generous tip. The waitress picked up the check, then thanked them as they all got up, left the depressing eatery, and walked out to the rental car. As soon as they pulled out of the parking lot, Jill was the first to talk.

"Okay fellas, what the hell is going on?"

"What do you mean?" asked Ron as innocently as he could.

"Look guys, don't bullshit me. Mark walks into the diner looking like someone beat him up and tells me some crap about car trouble. I'm not buying it. What's the real story?" asked Jill.

Ron and Mark both knew that Jill was not some stupid, shrinking violet. They both looked at each other, realizing there was no point in lying.

"Someone on the highway took some shots at the taxi Mark was riding in on the way back from the racetrack," Ron admitted, trying to sound calm.

"Oh my God!" exclaimed Jill.

"Really, I'm okay," assured Mark.

"What about you?" Jill asked Ron.

"I'm fine. I wasn't in the car. Mark was in the taxi. I was following behind him."

"Look, I don't know what's going on, but I think maybe we should turn around right now, go to the airport, and catch the next plane back to Chicago."

"No, Jill," vetoed Mark, trying to sound reassuring as he continued. "I know this whole thing is getting pretty hairy, but hopefully, tomorrow I'll get to talk to the stockholders and make my offer. Either they will accept it or they won't. Then we're out of here."

"What about Carole?" asked Jill.

"I don't know," replied Mark, sounding solemn. "I've been trying not to spend every minute worrying and obsessing about her. "This girl, Connie, who I'm here with, supposedly knows something about where Carole is, or at least has some kind of hunch, according to her fiancé, Bill."

"Do you trust her? Do you believe her?" asked Jill.

"Yeah, I think so. I hope so. I really don't have any choice. She promised me that by tomorrow she'd tell me everything she knows or suspects."

"Why hasn't she told you anything yet?" questioned Jill incredulously.

"I'm not sure," Mark, replied nervously. "I'm kind of playing along with her. That's one of the main reasons that I agreed to jump into this racetrack deal. She's a powerful lady, and so is her fiancé. I saved his life, and they want to help me. They have no reason to lie to me."

"Then why don't they just help you? Why do you have to get involved in this dangerous racetrack business?" Jill asked angrily.

"I didn't have to get involved in this deal…" Mark began, but was cut off by Jill. "But they asked you, and as usual, Mark, you were too nice to say no."

"No, that's not really why I did it."

"Look Jill," Ron interrupted, "Mark's got enough to worry about. He doesn't need you giving him shit."

"I'm not trying to give him anything, Ron," Jill shot back angrily. "It's just that someone has to be a voice of reason around here, and I don't know why Mark would get involved in some crazy, obviously dangerous racetrack scheme when his wife has been kidnapped. Hell, I know you don't want to hear this, Mark, but she could be dead for all you know. You should be talking to the police, or the FBI, or someone."

"Don't you think I've thought of doing just that a million times already?" Mark retorted.

"Then why haven't you done something?" Jill persisted.

"I am doing something, Jill," Mark defended himself angrily. "Connie and her fiancé are trying to help me. They have no reason to lie or bullshit me. I was instructed not to go to the police, or I would just make matters worse. I'll give them till tomorrow. Besides, trying to do this deal is helping me keep my mind off Carole. I'm scared to death. The only thing that's keeping me from going insane is by putting myself totally into this thing. I can't just sit around and do nothing. I've got to keep busy. If Connie and her fiancé, Bill, have not made any progress by the end of tomorrow, then I'll take the next step."

"And what is that?" Ron asked.

"I don't know. In fact, I have no idea. I guess I'll just wait until tomorrow and take it from there," Mark finished, showing his total loss for an answer.

"Look, Mark," said Jill, "I'm not trying to be hard on you. It's just that I'm concerned about you—about your wife. I don't know this Connie girl, who she is, or her boyfriend, Bill, but you know best. And *whatever* you want to do, Ron and I will obviously support you completely, and of course, be there for you."

"Thanks, I appreciate your support. I'm not even sure that I know what's best… I'm not sure of anything anymore. I haven't been able to think clearly since this whole Carole mess happened," Mark said, still in tremendous pain but hiding it from the Jaffes.

The threesome pulled up to the Marriott. There were a dozen police and state trooper cars parked in front of the hotel. Mark wondered if the presence of all these cops had anything to do with him. That was nuts, he thought. Why would the police be here? It made no sense, but, lately nothing had; he felt that it was better to be safe and instructed Ron accordingly.

"Ron, keep driving. Don't stop here."

"Where do you want to go?" asked Ron.

"Just get us out of here so I can find a pay phone."

"Okay," replied Ron, wondering what was wrong now.

The trio drove to a convenience store that had an outside pay phone. Mark got out of the car and grabbed a phone book from the steel shelf of the modular phone unit attached to the wall. He found the number of the Marriott, dialed it, and asked for his room. There was no answer.

"I'm sorry, sir," the hotel operator said. "There doesn't seem to be anybody there."

"Shit," Mark said. Where was Connie? he wondered.

"Excuse *me*, sir," the operator said rudely.

"I'm sorry, ma'am, could you please connect me with the room next door?" Mark replied.

"I need a room number, sir," the operator replied, still annoyed by Mark's profanity.

"Please ring 821," Mark said. The phone rang five times.

"I'm sorry, there is no answer," the operator curtly responded.

"Could you please try 819 then?" Mark asked.

Still, there was no answer. Mark hung up and hoped that maybe he was just being paranoid and overly cautious. He got back in the car with Jill and Ron.

"What's up?" Ron asked anxiously.

"Hopefully nothing to do with us," Mark replied.

"Why don't we get on a plane and go back to Chicago?" Both men tried to ignore Jill's question, but they were each thinking that very same thought.

"Let's go back to the Marriott," Mark ordered, seriously questioning his own sanity.

When they returned to the hotel's circular driveway, there were still some police and state trooper vehicles present but not as many as a few minutes ago.

"We'll leave the car here with the keys in the ignition. Follow me. Don't look around, and act natural," Mark directed.

The three of them wondered what 'natural' was. There had been so much going on that it was hard to even think 'natural'. They entered the hotel lobby. It was very late—actually early morning—and the place was mostly deserted. There was a huge, mean-looking cop at the front desk talking to Becky. Mark's first inclination was to proceed directly to the elevator and ignore Becky and the cop. But he quickly reasoned that to do so would be unnatural and potentially draw suspicion to the threesome.

"Hi, Becky," Mark smiled as usual, trying not to pass out from the pain.

"Hello, Mark," Becky replied, seeming distracted. He wasn't sure whether to introduce Jill and Ron. Thinking quickly, he decided that it would be more prudent to do so. Otherwise, these two new people accompanying him might appear suspicious.

"Becky, this is Ron Jaffe and his wife, Jill."

"I'm glad you arrived safely. Welcome to the Marriott."

"Thanks," replied the Jaffes in unison, again trying to maintain their composure.

Mark asked Becky what all the commotion was about. The cop looked indifferent.

"Oh nothing, Mark," Becky replied, sounding tense, in a feigned effort to project a calm demeanor. Leave it alone, Mark thought to himself.

"Well, goodnight," Mark said as he walked into the elevator; Jill and Ron followed behind.

Mark felt somewhat relieved as the elevator door started to close. Then suddenly, a huge hand reached inside the elevator, hitting the door and causing it to reopen.

"Excuse me, sir, may I have a word with you?"

It was the big, tough-looking cop.

Shit, Mark thought to himself, feeling his pulse quicken as beads of sweat materialized on his forehead and under his arms. "Sure," Mark replied, trying to remain cool, desperately hoping that the cop could not see through his forced calm demeanor. Mark stepped out of the elevator to talk to the cop, as Ron and Jill proceeded up to their rooms on the top floor of the Marriott.

Chapter 69

❁

THURSDAY EVENING

FORT LAUDERDALE HOLLYWOOD INTERNATIONAL AIRPORT, FLORIDA

The moment Donovan got off the plane, he immediately proceeded to the nearest pay phone and deposited the required amount of coins. The Don answered on the third ring.

"I'm here," Donovan told him.

"Meet me at The Blimp ASAP," barked the Don harshly and hung up.

Donovan knew he wasn't referring to the Goodyear Blimp, or a submarine sandwich shop, but rather a twenty-four-hour restaurant that used to be owned by Joe "The Blimp" Sonken, the small cigar-chomping former owner of the Gold Coast Restaurant in Hollywood, Florida. Now under new ownership, the joint, or "The Blimp," as the boys had referred to it, had been a Mob hangout for years. Everybody who had been anybody had been there: Meyer Lansky, John Gotti, Carlo Gambino, Sam DeCaluacante, Santo Trafficante, Jr., John Roselli, Sam Giancana, a.k.a. Momo, and from Miami, Florida, States Attorney Richard Gerstein, a.k.a. Bad Eye. Surprisingly, Janet Reno had begun her political career as a personal aide to Gerstein, in spite of the fact that Reno's father, Henry O. Reno, a *Miami Herald* police reporter, had made allegations that Gerstein was on the take.

Donovan took a cab to the former Gold Coast Restaurant. When he walked in, he saw the Don, sitting by himself at a table in the corner with his back to the wall. The place was fairly busy. Most of the tables were occupied. Donovan didn't know for sure, but was reasonably certain that there were at least three or four bodyguards strategically placed in the restaurant, watching the Don. He couldn't pick them out; they purposefully blended in well with the clientele. Even at this late hour the place was jammed with assorted types of people presumably there for the good food and assumedly unaware of the former reputation of this eatery.

Donovan sat down at the Don's table. He did not look around; had he scrutinized some of the patrons more closely, he would have noticed Pete Ritelo hiding behind dark Ray Bans and a Dodger's baseball hat. Pete had just escaped from jail, and the Don had told him to be at this eatery. He glowered at Donovan.

"Ciao," the Don said.

"Ciao," Donovan replied.

Donovan and the Don quietly spoke with each other in Italian for a few minutes. Then suddenly, exploding like a volcano, the old Don slapped Donovan across the face and swore at him in Italian—the meeting lasted less than five minutes.

Donovan was infuriated; he quickly walked out of the restaurant. Yes, the Don was right. He should have had Deemis, Marty, and Janet killed days ago. The slap across the face stung smartly and left a mark on his cheek. *No one* had *ever* hit Donovan or called him a piece of shit, "pezzo di merda." No one, *ever*. Donovan knew exactly what he was going to do—to everyone. Pete, likewise, knew why he had been allowed to escape from prison. He would have liked to have gotten Donovan right there, but the Don had given Pete explicit instructions to cool it for the time being.

Chapter 70

FRIDAY

ROBERT F. KENNEDY CENTER, MORGANTOWN, WEST VIRGINIA

Jack was in deep trouble. Something was terribly wrong. There was no money coming in to the inmates, and increasingly they were giving him a harder time, even going so far as threatening him. To make matters even worse, he hadn't received his own personal money. Jack had written Donovan a letter each day telling him that he needed money on his telephone account. The only way that he could call Donovan was to ask his counselor or caseworker for permission to make a free call. The problem, though, was that he had to make the call in the presence of staff. Obviously, that wouldn't do. There was no provision for collect calls although the law had recently changed, and all prisons were ordered to let inmates make them. Jack was growing more and more depressed. He was also scared. The inmates were getting restless. What was he supposed to do? He wondered why Donovan stopped sending money to the inmates and, more importantly, to him.

What about his letter to Kathy Hawk? He had felt sure that his letter would have received some response. After all, he felt that LRI, his idea to start a nonprofit organization to help inmates, was a good one. Jack wanted to give something back, to help others like himself. His organization would fulfill a wide variety of needs—everything from assisting soon-to-be-incarcerated inmates and released inmates on job interviews, job training, and job placement to professional counseling in order to help inmates readjust to society. Jack was luckier than most. Many inmates, actually the majority, had much longer sentences. The average sentence for a federal prisoner was about ten years.

Prison was getting more and more depressing for Jack as the days dragged on. There were a number of reasons why. First and foremost was his loss of freedom. Furthermore, he wasn't a criminal. Jack didn't belong in prison. Had he played along with the government and basically lied and rolled over on people, he wouldn't be here. He had nothing in common with the majority of inmates. He was neither a drug dealer, a killer, a bank robber, a mugger, nor a thief. He was the textbook definition of white-collar crime. Jack's life had been pretty good until prison. Although he didn't have a father, his mother had raised him with a lot of love. Jack was bitter, but unlike many inmates, he didn't wear the label "Inmate" across his forehead. So many of them seemed to be consumed by a never-ending rage against the government. They blamed everybody and everything for their plight. The inmates spent endless hours talking about how rotten this country was, and that when they get out of prison how they were going to live in Mexico or Canada, anywhere but the United States. Jack thought that this talk, although in many cases true, was childish. Yes, of course, he was upset that he was incarcerated. And there was no question that many inmates, especially the nonviolent ones, did not belong in prison. But he had decided to do his bit, get out, and put this miserable experience behind him and get on with his life. Many of his fellow prisoners spent entire days in the law library working on their appeals. Jack thought that this was a total waste of time, tantamount to pissing up a rope in a strong wind. Often, by the time rulings would be reached on inmates' appeals, they would have already completed their sentences and be home. Jack thought it was just misdirected energy. There was no doubt in his mind that having a felony conviction on one's record, which meant any crime for which one served more than a year, was not a good thing, but it was not the end of the world. Many ex-felons had gone on to live productive and useful lives, which made Jack wonder what he was going to do when he was released. Until only a few weeks ago, he assumed that he was going to be working for Donovan. Now things had apparently changed. There was no money being sent to the inmates. Even Janet, the young beautiful girl who had been coming to Morgantown every week to smuggle out the names of inmates so that money could be sent to them, had stopped visiting. Jack's multiple letters to Donovan went unanswered. In a way, Jack felt that it was a blessing in disguise. For whatever reason, Donovan had decided to end Marty's loan-a-con program. This meant Jack was off the hook, and no longer obligated to Donovan. Now, all he had to do was figure out a way to deal with the unhappy inmates. On the one hand, he was madder than hell that Donovan had left him high and dry; however, the more he analyzed the situation, the more relieved he felt. Donovan had screwed him, left him up shit's creek. Donovan had only represented him at the sentencing. Jack was no longer sure whether the big-shot Outfit lawyer was really responsible for getting him transferred to Morgantown and into the drug program. He could find a job when he was released from prison, regardless of Kathy Hawk and the Bureau of Prisons, and he would put together a program on his own to help ex-offenders. He got along fine with the majority of inmates and staff in the prison. It was just that there were very few people he had anything in common with, other than their mutual incarceration. Most of Jack's friends didn't even know that he was in prison. Why should they, Jack had reasoned? It was none of their business. He had lied, telling them he had enlisted in the Peace Corps and would be out of the country for a couple of years. He was lonely. Jack didn't have anyone to call. He had no girlfriend and was not receiving any letters. He thought it best to cut off attachments to the real world. He saw too many inmates in prison going crazy trying to maintain outside relationships with their wives or girlfriends. Eventually, they would get the Dear John letter, or as it was referred to in prison, "Jody," a catch-all name that meant that they were either told or received a letter stating that there was another guy, that the wife was filing for a divorce, would no longer visit, or would refuse to take any more phone calls.

Jack was sitting in the TV room watching a basketball game, paying no attention to which teams were playing.

"What's the score?" an inmate asked Jack as he walked into the TV room.

"It's 94 to 78," replied Jack.

"Who's winning?" the inmate asked.

"The team with ninety-four," Jack replied, not meaning to be a smart-ass, but unable to control himself.

"Thanks for nothing," the inmate bristled.

"I'm sorry. I didn't mean to be rude. It's just that my mind is somewhere else."

"No problem, man. I know how it is."

"Thanks."

"Hey, aren't you Jack, the money guy?"

"Yes," replied Jack, as he said "shit" under his breath. Here we go again, Jack thought. Another inmate who is owed or wants money. He was tired of this crap already. Jack was expecting another threat or plea for money. Surprisingly, he got neither.

"I thought so. There was a page for you over the intercom about five minutes ago."

"There was?" asked Jack curiously.

"Yeah, you were paged to the visiting room."

"Thanks a lot. I appreciate it."

"No problem, man," the inmate replied.

Jack hurried to his room and quickly changed into some freshly ironed clothes. Then he stopped short; the excitement of just a few minutes ago was instantly gone. The only visitor that he ever had was Janet, the sexy girl who picked up the names and numbers of inmates. The fact that she was here could obviously mean only one thing—everything must be back on track with Donovan. "Fuck," he said, as he walked into the visiting room dreading the encounter; once again feeling stupid to think that his arrangement with Donovan could be over and berating himself for being such a putz. There was no getting away from the clutches of Donovan and the Outfit. Expecting to see only Janet, Jack's mouth dropped open in shock as he saw the three women. One of the three was someone he certainly wasn't expecting to see at all; and certainly not all three women at the same time. She was the *last* person in the world he expected to see—he couldn't believe his eyes. What in the hell was going on? He was really in big fucking trouble now, he reasoned.

Chapter 71

FRIDAY MORNING

ROBERT F. KENNEDY CENTER, MORGANTOWN, WEST VIRGINIA

What was going on? Jack wondered. Obviously, something big was going down. Seeing the three women sitting in the visiting room, he didn't know what to think. First, he saw Jenny, the girl from the bank, sitting by herself looking worried. Jack had been expecting her after she wrote a letter saying she was going to visit him. But what totally surprised him was seeing Janet with Kathy Hawk, the director of the Bureau of Prisons, sitting next to each other across the room. What also puzzled Jack was the visibility of Hawk in the visiting room. Why were they not using a private room, he wondered? What could this mean? Jack had no idea. The guard patted Jack down and marked his gym shoes with a yellow marker so that he couldn't switch them during his visit. He walked over to Jenny. She smiled nervously, as Jack put his hand out to shake hers. Instead, much to his surprise, she put her arms around him tightly and kissed him on the mouth. Jack had an immediate erection. He had not been around a woman for so long, with the exception of Janet, who was always pure business, let alone touch one; his physical reaction was instant.

"I have been so worried about you."

"I'm doing okay," replied Jack. "In fact, after seeing you, I'm doing much better."

"We don't have much time," Jenny began, speaking rapidly.

"What's going on?" Jack queried.

"The guard said I only have a little time to visit you," Jenny said quickly.

"Do you know what *they're* doing here?" Jack asked, nodding in the direction of Janet and Kathy Hawk.

"No, I don't," Jenny replied honestly.

"The older woman," Jack explained, "is Kathy Hawk, the head of the Bureau of Prisons." Jack didn't mention the letter about LRI he had written to Hawk. "The younger woman is Janet. She works for Donovan."

"Oh shit," replied Jenny.

"Shit is right," Jack said. "It's because of that girl, Janet—No…" Jack interrupted himself, "not her, but Donovan, that I'm in a world of trouble. He screwed me, he…"

Jenny cut him off. "He didn't hurt you. I'm the one who did."

"What in the hell are you talking about, Jenny?" Jack asked, totally confused.

"I know you're mad at Donovan, Jack," Jenny started to say, "but you've got to listen to me."

"No, I don't," Jack, said, angrily. "Donovan left me holding the bag with all of these inmates who were expecting the money to keep coming in, but he cut it off. Donovan is a bastard. I hate him."

"He's not a bastard," Jenny defended Donovan softly. "He's my father, and I love him."

"What?" Jack exclaimed, in shock and total disbelief.

"He's my father," Jenny repeated.

"I don't understand."

"It's a long story, and you need to hear it all, but since there isn't time right now I'll just quickly summarize; my dad asked me to have you fill out the credit-card applications—after he used his influence to get your bank loan turned down. At the time, I had no idea what my dad was doing."

Jack wasn't sure he wanted to hear any more, but he listened anyway, trying to make sense out of Jenny's rapid ramblings. He couldn't believe what he was hearing. Jack had a million questions, but he lashed out angrily with the most basic one:

"Why would your father have you do that—or, my real question is why would you try to set *me* up? What did I ever do to hurt you, or your father?" Jack exploded angrily at Jenny.

"You did nothing." Jenny's eyes became moist from the tears that were beginning to well up.

"Then *why*, Jenny?" As Jack raised his voice, the guard sternly looked in their direction. His anger at Jenny was becoming uncontrollable. He had to calm down or at least lower his voice, otherwise he would be taken out of the visiting room. As Jack tried to chill out, he realized that his rage was really a manifestation of his own pain and helplessness. He fought back his tears as he continued in as subdued a manner as possible. Quietly he asked, "Why in the hell would you and your father, Donovan, do this shit to me? Why? I don't understand."

Jenny felt Jack's pain as acutely as if it were her own and tried to explain what even she wasn't sure made sense, "Jack, listen to me…"

As much as Jack wanted to hear Jenny's answers, he found that he couldn't fully control his waves of anger. He cut her off abruptly. "Why? So you can get me in more trouble? Is that why your father sent you here?"

"Jack, please believe me. I didn't know I was getting you into trouble. I never wanted to see you hurt, in fact, I always really liked you." Jenny pleaded. "I told you to lie on all those credit-card applications because my father asked me to do it and let you think it was your idea. I had no idea it would get you in this kind of trouble. I thought my dad was trying to be helpful."

"So, why are you here?" Jack asked. "Did your father tell you to come here and make sure I was 'doing my job?'"

"No, Jack, I swear he doesn't know I'm here," Jenny stated honestly.

"After what you have done to my life, do you expect me to believe you?" Jack shouted, no longer caring what attention he brought to himself in the visiting room.

"Jack, I'm telling you the truth. I'm here to help you," Jenny pleaded in an effort to regain his trust. Jack desperately wanted to believe her.

"Why do you care about me? What difference does it make in your life? Are you simply trying to clear your guilty conscience? The only reason that I'm sitting in jail is because of you and your father, and I don't give a shit about your conscience right now; don't confess to me so you can sleep better in your cozy bed at night!" Jack rebuked. "I've got my own problems!"

Jenny couldn't fight back the tears anymore; she began to sob and blurted out, "I am here because *I love you, and always have.*"

Jack stared into Jenny's dark emerald eyes. He was shocked by her statement. He wanted to believe her, though he knew that he shouldn't. "You expect me to believe you?"

"I hope that you will—I really do, because it's true."

He couldn't believe what he was hearing. He continued to press her, "What's the real story, Jenny? Why did your father have me set up?"

"I really don't know too much, Jack," Jenny sobbed. "All I know is that Donovan, my dad, was trying to get your boss, Mark Goodwin, to do something for him. My dad made Mark a good offer, but he flatly refused. I think that it had something to do with construction or real estate, and Mark could have helped my dad, but he was too stubborn. He told my dad no, and *no one* tells my dad *no*—but your boss, Mark Goodwin, did just that."

"So, why pick on me then?" Jack asked, intently soaking it all in.

"Jack, my father knew how much Mark liked you. He figured that when you got into trouble, you would go to Mark for help. Then Mark would go to my dad for a favor, but you *didn't* go to Mark. You didn't even tell Mark about your trouble. So, his plan didn't work, and my father felt terrible, especially when he found out that the government wanted you to cooperate, or rather, lie, and say that Mark and some of the real estate clients that were doing business with my dad were dishonest. Even when they threatened to put you in jail, you still wouldn't cooperate; that's why he arranged to pay you so much money when you get out."

"You know about that, too?"

"Yes," replied Jenny. "I didn't then, but I do now."

"Well, when I get out, I'm not going to take any money, because I won't be able to pay it back. I plan to stay as far away from all of you as I possibly can."

"It's not a loan, Jack."

"It's my dad's way of saying he's sorry," Jenny continued.

"Jack, the reason I got on your visiting list and came here is that I overheard a conversation my father had with Marty, an associate of my dad, who said that he was planning to do something to Mark's wife, Carole, and I'm concerned about her safety. I thought you would want to know. In the beginning when your mother was dying and then you were turned down for the loan at the bank, I told my father about your financial difficulties, and he suggested that I tell you to lie on the credit-card applications; I thought my dad was trying to help. I was being naïve; I realize that now. I want to do whatever I can to help you." Jenny stated this with total sincerity, as Jack looked into her eyes wanting to believe her.

Jenny continued, "By what I gathered from my father's end of the conversation, they knew how valuable you were to Mark, and how devoted Mark was to the people who worked for him. The only problem was that you were too proud to tell anyone what was happening to you. As my father stated to Marty, they never expected that; in fact, they were absolutely certain you would go to Mark for help. No one thought all this would happen."

Jack tried to absorb everything Jenny was saying; he wanted to trust and believe her. *But how could he?* Indirectly or not, she was responsible for putting him in jail. At least now he understood why Donovan had agreed to represent him—*guilt*. Within this crazy plan that Jenny was explaining, he was never supposed to have gone to jail.

Janet, Kathy Hawk, and a guard started to walk toward Jack and Jenny.

"Oh shit," said Jack, "I'm in trouble now. What am I supposed to do?"

"My father's a good man; please keep him out of this if you can," Jenny pleaded.

"How can you say your father is a good man? It's because of Donovan that I'm in jail." Jack shouted.

The prison guard in the waiting room quickly began to move toward Jack and Jenny.

"I'd better go now. Please believe everything I have told you," Jenny begged. As she got up and walked away, Hawk and Janet sat down next to Jack.

Chapter 72

FRIDAY MORNING

ROBERT F. KENNEDY CENTER, MORGANTOWN, WEST VIRGINIA

"I'm Kathy Hawk Sawyer, the director of the Federal Bureau of Prisons."

"I know who you are," replied Jack, his mind racing, trying to figure out what was going on. He was still in total shock from everything Jenny had just told him.

"That's good," answered Hawk, politely. "And you have already been introduced to this young lady?" referring to Janet.

"Yes," Jack said, not knowing what else to say.

He wondered what kind of trouble he was in. He didn't know Janet's last name. He wasn't even sure of who her boss was, or to whom she reported. Jack suspected that Donovan was most likely the head boss, or one of them, but Donovan had never discussed details. Pete did all that. Jack had talked long enough with Pete when they were locked up in the holding cell in Oklahoma City to know that some guy named Marty was Janet's boss, and that he was largely in charge of this money-lending operation. Jack's deep-seated feelings for Jenny were unleashed after seeing her again a few minutes ago. He wanted to believe Jenny when she told him that she loved him. He wasn't sure, though, about Donovan's remorse over getting him involved in the credit-card situation, which led to his indictment and eventual incarceration. He knew that Donovan was an important person—a very powerful, well-connected Mob guy. Partly out of respect for Jenny's request to leave her father out of any conflicts, and partly because common sense told Jack that to mess with a powerful underworld figure was not conducive to his safety and well being, he decided, before Hawk continued, to do his best not to implicate Donovan in any way.

"Janet has told us everything," Hawk began. "We know all about it," she continued.

Jack said nothing. He had already decided that until he was asked a specific question, he would not offer any information.

"Why don't you start talking, Jack?"

"Ms. Hawk," Jack began, "I'm not exactly sure what you want from me, but I think it's probably advisable that I have an attorney present."

"That's up to you, Jack. But I really don't think that's necessary. I'm not here to hurt you—actually, I might even be able to help you out of this mess."

"What mess?" Jack asked, trying to show no emotion.

"Oh, c'mon, Jack. Janet has told us everything. We know about you passing her inmate names so Marty could send prisoners money."

Jack didn't respond.

"We also received your letter about LRI, setting up programs to help ex-offenders acclimate back into society. We don't want to make it easier for people to prepare to serve time. We *prefer* that they be scared. Quite frankly, Jack, that's what makes the idea of going to prison a deterrent against crime. Some of your ideas and proposed programs make sense. We may be able to work together on some of them, but you have to be honest with me. In fact, if you cooperate and tell me what you know, I may even be able to obtain an early release for you," Hawk concluded.

Jack prided himself on not being a snitch. He wasn't going to start now.

"Listen," Janet interrupted, "I already told you Jack doesn't know anything."

"Yes, that's what you told us," replied Hawk coolly.

"Marty was the one who came up with the idea for the money-lending idea with the inmates, and Jack doesn't even know Marty. He sent me up here to pressure Jack into doing it. Jack was just a conduit."

Jack knew that Janet was lying because there was no mention of Donovan or Pete. Janet gave Jack a look as if to say: just play along with me, and with what I say, and you'll be fine.

"Is that true?" Hawk asked Jack.

"Yes," Jack lied.

"You don't know a man named Marty Stein or Marty Serachi?"

"No," replied Jack.

"You've never heard his name?"

Before Jack could answer, Janet spoke again. "I may have mentioned his name to Jack once."

"Did she?" Hawk asked, losing patience with Janet and wishing that she would shut up and not coach Jack.

"Not that I remember," stated Jack confidently, not really lying. Pete had mentioned Marty's name, but he couldn't remember if Janet had ever said anything about Marty.

"What about Donovan?" Hawk asked.

"What do you mean?" returned Jack.

"Did he have anything to do with this money-lending thing?"

"No," Jack lied again.

"What is your relationship with him?"

"He's my lawyer," Jack told Hawk.

"Has Donovan ever talked to you about the Mob's plan to take over the prisons, or their terrorist involvement?"

"No," Jack said, genuinely shocked.

Now he was lost. He did, of course, remember Pete talking about screwing up the legal system, but taking over the prisons? No, he had never heard that, and certainly nothing about terrorist activities. He was totally surprised by Hawk's last question.

Hawk saw the look of surprise on Jack's face when she asked him about the prison plan and terrorism. Hawk realized that it was the same look that Janet had shown when the FBI had picked her up last night in Washington, D.C., and had asked her that same question. Obviously, neither of them were privy to the Mob's plan to take over the prisons, or they were both terrific liars.

Chapter 73

MOMENTS LATER

ROBERT F. KENNEDY CENTER, MORGANTOWN, WEST VIRGINIA

"Excuse me, Janet. Would you please let me talk to Jack alone for a minute?" Hawk requested.

Janet walked to the vending machines on the other side of the visiting room and got herself a cup of coffee.

Hawk began, "Look, Jack, I think you're telling me the truth."

"I am," replied Jack, trying to sound convincing but being careful not to overdo it.

"I don't think you're really a criminal."

"Thank you for that. I appreciate it," said Jack, accepting her compliment sincerely.

"And I don't think justice will be served by keeping you here any longer."

"I agree," said Jack wholeheartedly, wondering where this conversation was going.

"How would you like to get out of here?"

"To where?" Jack asked skeptically.

"Home."

"And what do I have to do, Ms. Hawk?"

"Nothing, other than let us know if Janet, or her boss, Marty, or Donovan, contact you."

"But Donovan is my lawyer," questioned Jack, still trying to figure out what the trap was.

"As long as what Donovan talks to you about is legal, you're under no obligation to repeat it to anyone," Hawk clarified.

"But how am I going to explain to Donovan how I got out of prison?"

"Oh, that's no problem. We'll concoct a story about an inmate who was on the wrong medication and attacked one of the prison nurses, and you intervened. You just helped an innocent girl. No snitching, no betraying anyone. In our gratitude for saving the nurse's life, we are rewarding you with an early release."

"Yes, but you're asking me to be a snitch once I get out."

"Not really. Just kind of pass along to us any information you get."

"What if I don't get any? What if no one talks to me?"

"Then you and I will have nothing to discuss, and we won't be talking again," answered Hawk, "unless, of course, it's about LRI, which I told you may have some potential."

Jack thought about Hawk's offer. Actually, it didn't seem like a bad deal. Jack had had enough of prison. He was anxious to get out—to get his life started again—hopefully go back to work with Mark and maybe start a relationship with Jenny. Jack was no snitch. Even if Donovan, Marty, or Janet tried talking to him, he would *not* report anything to Hawk. And he wouldn't feel bad about not fulfilling his end of the bargain with Hawk even if the situation arose. He owed the government nothing. Hopefully, he would not be put in a compromising position.

"Okay," Jack said, before she had time to reconsider, "you got a deal." He fantasized about how nice it would be to make love to Jenny.

"Great," Hawk said. "Someone will be in touch with you in a few days to work out the details. Let's keep this confidential."

"Absolutely," answered Jack.

Chapter 74

❀

VERY, VERY EARLY FRIDAY MORNING

MARRIOTT HOTEL, PROVIDENCE, RHODE ISLAND

"There was a robbery tonight, sir. I wonder if you could check your room when you go up and let the front desk know if anything is missing," the tough-looking cop politely said.

"Of course, officer," replied Mark, and then quickly got back on the elevator, thankful that the cop had not seen any evidence of the earlier violence Mark had experienced which might have aroused suspicion with the cop.

Mark reached the top floor and went to his room. He inserted the plastic key-card in the slot and, when the green light came on, quickly turned the lever and opened the door. Connie was sitting on the couch watching TV with Ron and Jill.

"Good program?" asked Mark.

"Actually, yes," replied Connie.

"At this time in the morning?"

"Yeah, some good-looking kid from Chicago is on," teased Connie coyly.

As Mark walked closer to the TV, he saw himself.

"Hey, that's you!" Jill exclaimed.

"How 'bout that?" replied Mark, laughing.

"Yeah, man," said Ron, "you look good."

"What do you mean 'good?'" countered Connie. "He looks great!"

"Thanks," Mark said in his true-to-form modest fashion. Mark then formally introduced Ron and Jill to Connie; they had just met each other a moment before Mark walked into the room. The four of them exchanged pleasantries for a few minutes. Mark was relieved that neither of the Jaffes brought up any mention of the recent events surrounding the track. Mark could see that Ron and Jill were tired.

"C'mon guys," Mark said, "let me show you to your room."

"Okay," the Jaffes replied, too tired to argue.

After Mark took them to their room, Ron made a comment to Mark. "I don't trust her," he said, meaning Connie.

"As usual, dear," Jill said to her husband, "I think your head is up your ass. I like her."

Mark smiled but didn't speak. Even though he was by no means an expert on women, he trusted their intuition. He agreed with Jill; Connie was nice, but his thoughts were fixated on only one woman, his wife, Carole. Over the last couple of days the only thing keeping Mark going was the hectic pace and an overabundance of adrenaline and endorphins that were running through his body since he had become involved with Connie, Bill, and this project. Later today, though, was the deadline. He would attempt to buy the racetrack at the shareholders' meeting, and win or lose, he wanted answers from Connie about Carole, or he was going back to Chicago. He had had enough. No matter what the risk, he was going to call the FBI and the cops and take action.

Mark walked back into his room. "Are you hungry?" asked Connie.

"As a matter of fact, I'm starved."

"I thought so," replied Connie.

"But I'm sure everything, including room service, is closed."

"I thought you might be hungry, so I ordered food for us earlier."

"You're the best, kid."

"Not the best," flirted Connie.

"You're not the best?" Mark joked.

"I'm just being modest—I'm willing to admit that there may be some woman better than me, but I haven't met her yet."

"Is that so?"

"Sit down and eat," Connie laughed.

He sat down at the table. There was a white tablecloth with freshly cut flowers and two tall candles. Connie lit the candles and poured Mark a glass of wine. He took a sip.

"Excellent," he said approvingly.

"I know," she said confidently.

Maybe it was his imagination, but it sure seemed to Mark that Connie was acting sexy and coming on to him. He was flattered, and despite feelings of guilt, was turned on, aware of an impending erection. Thinking of his wife, not to mention the danger she was in, he successfully pushed his lustful thoughts of Connie out of his mind. This was neither the time nor the place. Furthermore, Mark, unlike most men, didn't cheat. Never had, never would. That's not to say that he hadn't been tempted. He had been, plenty of times, like any red-blooded male. He certainly liked to look, but he didn't touch. It was a source of pride to him. It grew out of many years of seeing his father cheat on his mother. His father thought no one knew, but everyone did, especially his mother. She just never said anything. Instead, she resigned herself to living with the hurt and eating herself up inside. Mark didn't want to hurt women. He had seen how devastating it had been to his mom.

As they started eating, Connie asked Mark if he wanted to continue watching the videotapes of the evening newscasts she had recorded of him. She had been playing them back when Jill and Ron came into the room.

"Why don't you summarize it all for me."

Connie did.

They had just finished dinner and were moving toward the couch to sit down when there was a loud knock on the door. Mark got up and looked through the peephole. It was the big cop from downstairs. He opened the door slightly and stepped out into the hallway.

"Yes?" Mark asked.

"May I come in, sir?"

Mark wanted to tell him to go to hell, but he figured that wasn't too smart. Obviously, this cop was a pain in the ass and wanted something. Best be polite and let him in. "Sure," answered Mark.

The cop stepped in, looked around the room and stared at Connie, although he pretended to look elsewhere.

"Everything okay, folks?"

"Yes," replied Mark.

"Just fine," said Connie.

"Nothing's missing?"

"Not a thing," stated Mark.

"Sorry for bothering you. Have a good night."

"No problem, officer," Mark said as the cop exited the room.

Mark looked through the peephole and saw the cop walk away, presumably toward the elevators.

"What in the hell was that about, Mark?"

"Obviously, someone is watching and checking up on us."

"Why?"

"It seems," Mark began, "that we're not particularly welcome here."

Connie was anything but unaware. She knew that the police had picked up Ron and Jill the moment they arrived. She didn't know about Mark getting hit over the head at the racetrack or being shot at on the highway. Mark didn't want to alarm Connie.

"Look kid, do you feel like doing me a favor?"

"Sure, just name it," agreed Connie.

Mark went to his PalmPilot, punched a couple of keys, and wrote down a fax number for his accountant. He handed the piece of paper to Connie, along with the file the Senator had given him at the racetrack. "Please fax this entire file to this number, then stay downstairs, and make sure that it all transmits."

"No problem."

Twenty minutes later, Connie returned with a message given to her at the front desk. Mark read the note. Strange, he thought, the message had come in about five hours ago, but Becky had not told him there were any messages when he, Ron, and Jill had come in just a short while ago.

Meet us tomorrow at 7:30 A.M., the note read. There was no phone number, just an address of an office building downtown. The note was signed: "K. Calden Rooley, Chairman." Mark picked up the phone and dialed the Jaffes' room.

"Yeah," Ron answered, as he picked up the phone, sounding half asleep.

"We're on for 7:30 tomorrow morning," Mark reported. "The chairman of the board of the racetrack wants to have a meeting."

"Excellent," replied Jaffe. "Obviously, they've seen the news and are going to accept your offer to buy the racetrack. Good job, Mark."

Mark replied abruptly, "Don't get too excited."

"Why not?" queried Jaffe. "They're going to accept your offer, and why shouldn't they? You're offering more money, a better deal. It will mean more money for everyone."

"Logically, you're right, Ron, but there's nothing logical about this deal. There's more to this than money. A lot more. I just don't know what it is yet."

"Well, I hope you're wrong."

"Me, too, but I don't think I am," Mark responded.

"I'll be ready to leave at 7:00."

"Okay, Ron, I'll meet you downstairs in the coffee shop."

"Sounds good. Should I bring Jill?"

"Not unless you want to." Mark liked Jill, but there was really no reason for her being there. Ron was the one who knew all about racetracks, and was friends with the Senator, who was a major shareholder of the track.

"See you in the morning," Ron said and went back to bed.

"Listen, kid," Mark said to Connie, "it's time for bed. We've got to be up in a few hours. C'mon, I'll walk you to your room."

"That's okay," Connie shot back, unable to hide her anger, "I can walk next door myself. I'm a big girl." Connie walked out of the suite feeling embarrassed that she had become angry with Mark. She knew he wasn't going to ask her to spend the night. He was loyal to his goddamned wife, Carole. Ah yes, Carole. Connie had had enough of listening to Mark carry on about his beautiful, sweet, wonderful wife. Tomorrow the private investigator that she hired would make his full report. She had a hunch, and her hunches were usually dead-on accurate. She remembered all too well when she walked into Mark's condo in Chicago and saw the picture of Mark and Carole on their honeymoon. She had stared at the photo, not wanting to say anything until she was sure. But she knew she had definitely seen Carole before.

🍁 🍁 🍁

As promised, at 7:00 A.M., Ron was already seated in the restaurant of the hotel drinking coffee when Mark and Connie walked in. He greeted them with a robust, "Good morning."

"Hi," said Connie.

"Did you two sleep well?"

"Fine," replied Mark.

"Not really," Connie whimpered slightly. "I'm kind of tired."

"Oh, that's too bad," Ron smiled at Connie.

Although Ron had known Mark a long time, he never believed Mark's stories of fidelity. Probably because he had always fooled around on Jill. He loved her—she was a terrific wife and a wonderful mother—but after all, Ron rationalized, men were not put on this earth to be monogamous.

They entered the bank building and found Rooley listed on the directory. The elevator took them quickly to the top floor. Typical of large law firms, when the elevator opened, they didn't have to look for his offices; they were in them; they spanned the whole floor. An old, matronly looking woman was sitting behind the reception desk. She had a magazine opened but was not reading. Instead, she looked up over her half-glasses that rested loosely on the bridge of her nose.

"Yes," she said, in a stern voice that seemed to fit perfectly with her unpleasant, cold, hard demeanor.

"We're here to see Mr. Rooley," Mark said flatly, realizing that it was quite hopeless to try to charm this mean-looking lady.

"The Colonel is expecting you; follow me." Mark, Ron, and Connie followed the unpleasant, gray-haired woman down a long hall. Her walk was stiff and formal as if she had a broomstick securely lodged up her ass. "In there," she ordered, pointing to a set of double doors.

They entered and at once were struck by the scene they saw. It was as if they had walked onto the movie set from *Citizen Kane*. The conference room, though expensively done in oak and teak, was too old to look elegant. Twelve of the most unhappy looking, geezerly men sat in high-backed leather chairs too big for them, making them look more like decrepit, old midgets. They all stared dispassionately at their visitors as they entered.

Rooley, sitting at the head of the table, glowered at them. "What do you want?" he barked.

"To buy the racetrack," answered Mark.

"We're not interested," Rooley said as he scowled at the threesome.

"How can you *not* be?" Mark asked incredulously.

"We're just not," confirmed another old board member.

"I'm offering a lot more money," Mark argued angrily, losing his temper with these assholes.

"We don't care," snarled Rooley with a look of hate and disgust.

"But you have an obligation to accept, or certainly entertain, any and all offers, especially higher ones, on behalf of the stockholders you represent."

"Go to hell; get out of my office and out of my town! Now!", barked Rooley.

Ron Jaffe couldn't hold back anymore. "Listen you bunch of pathetic losers, we have tried to be nice to you assholes, but now you can all go to hell. We'll be at the shareholders' meeting this afternoon, and when we take over the racetrack, you'll all be fired."

"Show up at that meeting, and I'll make sure you're all thrown in jail. You're not shareholders, so you're not allowed in there." Rooley threatened.

"Go to hell, you rotten bunch of bluehairs," Connie shot back at the assortment of decrepit old men as the three of them took their leave.

Deemis merely stared into space and got more depressed. If only he had not told Janet about the track, all this shit wouldn't be happening now. But he had screwed up, and it was too late to undo what he had started.

Chapter 75

❈

FRIDAY

CHICAGO, ILLINOIS

Marty nervously paced back and forth in his office at the Board of Trade building. "Shit," he muttered to himself. He felt like he was going nuts, starting to lose his edge. He had always prided himself on being cool, calm, and in control but not now. Far too much shit was happening. In fact, just about everything in his life was in turmoil, and he knew it. There was no denying the mess he had gotten himself into. He knew better than to try to bullshit himself, or tell himself that things would be okay. Marty knew that the situation was only going to get worse. How much worse though, he didn't know.

Janet had come back to Chicago from Washington, D.C, and, unbeknownst to Marty, her detour to West Virginia too. When they met for coffee at Starbucks, she told Marty that she had been unsuccessful in trying to seduce former Mayor Marion Barry. Marty could handle that. He had not really expected Janet to hit a home run on her first attempt with Barry anyway. What had bothered him though, was Janet's reluctance to talk about what had happened, but more than that, she seemed different. He couldn't put his finger on it, or pinpoint exactly what the change was, but something was different about Janet. He could tell. Had he known that she was cooperating with the Feds he would have made a quick escape out of the country. He had enough money stashed away to hide out somewhere and live comfortably. Janet, at their short meeting, much to his surprise, had not even asked about her sister. She didn't even start to wax philosophical about wanting to get out of the Outfit. What in the hell was with her? What was going on? He didn't like Janet's strange, reclusive demeanor one bit.

To make matters worse, everything else seemed to be turning to shit. He had spoken to Deemis in Rhode Island by phone today. The news had not been good. Some people from out of town were all over the news with a proposal to buy the racetrack for a lot more money than Donovan's Rhode Island Mob associates had worked out with the city. Adding insult to injury was the fact that the kid who was making the offer, obviously fronting for somebody, probably a rival Mob family, was that hot-shot real estate guy, Mark Goodwin. How did he get involved? What made the situation even more embarrassing for Marty was that he was having Mark watched. Marty had done this simply as a precaution in case Mark had tried to find his wife, Carole or make contact with the police. But Mark hadn't contacted anyone. As soon as Donovan found out that the person who was fucking up the racetrack deal was Mark, Marty would be in even bigger trouble, if that were possible—not only with Donovan, but with the Don, as well. And the way Marty found out gave him a double shock. As Marty sat in his office, his surveillance guy had called to say that he still had Mark under watch, and he had followed him out of town. Just then his fax machine started. As Marty pulled the fax showing the front page of the *Providence Journal* out of his machine, he saw the picture of Mark Goodwin.

"Don't you want to know where we followed the kid to?" his guy asked.

"Providence," Marty blurted out through the phone, enraged.

"How did you know that?"

"Never mind," Marty said, as he slammed down the phone and read the article about Mark on the front page of the *Providence Journal*.

Although Marty's main job was running the bonding company for mostly Outfit construction projects around the country, Donovan and the Don had also given him a piece of the racetrack deal and the private prison industry. Marty had stopped sending money to the prisoners because he had lost interest in them and had put a stop to the loan-a-con program—it was bullshit anyway, just a smoke screen. Now, Marty had more important things to worry about—most importantly, not getting murdered by his bosses. He hoped that they would just kill him quickly, but he had been around too long to really believe that. He was sure his death was going to be long and torturous.

Chapter 76

FRIDAY

KEY BISCAYNE, FLORIDA

The Don was, as usual, on his fifty-eight-foot Sea Ray in Key Biscayne. He was sitting comfortably on a deck chair in the sun, partially shaded by a big straw hat. In one hand, he held a Bloody Mary; in the other, a Mafia novel. On a little table in front of him was a silver platter filled with fresh stone crabs, lemon slices on a bed of ice, and a little dish of hot mustard sauce. The Don reflected happily on his empire. He controlled one of the biggest crime families in the country. Business was good, and the future looked even brighter—there were more billions to be made in the private prison industry. The Mob already owned a lot of companies related to the industry and were acquiring more. He couldn't even begin to count the number of politicians and influence peddlers he had in his pocket. The Don knew that it was just a matter of time before he was the biggest player in the prison business. In spite of many problems; such as Deemis leaking the racetrack deal to Janet and Marty's mishandling of Janet; there was, nevertheless, a bright future ahead for the Mob, a future that he would pass on to Donovan when he retired, assuming Donovan was still around. His grandchildren would never have to worry, financially, when he was gone. He wanted them to go to college and not be involved in any way in the Mob.

Suddenly, the Don started choking! He tried to call out for help, but no sound came out of his mouth. Within seconds he slumped over—dead. Donovan smiled as he sat in a cigarette boat that he had bought years ago from the legendary, also-Mob-murdered boat builder, Don Aronow. He smugly watched the Don through high-powered binoculars from a quarter of a mile away, personally verifying that his order to poison the Don's drink had definitely been carried out. Donovan's large diamond pinkie-ring reflected brightly in the sun as he put the binoculars down, pushed the throttle back, and sped away at full speed. The Don would never slap anyone again. The incident at last night's meeting at the Hollywood, Florida, restaurant was now and forever settled. Donovan gave it no more thought; he immediately went to the airport and flew back to Chicago.

Chapter 77

FRIDAY

WHITACRE HOUSE, RHODE ISLAND

Penny Whitacre usually slept late but not this morning. Deemis's wife woke up when she heard the garage door opening and Deemis's car pull out early. She knew he was going to a meeting about the racetrack. The news was all over the radio, TV, and on the front page of the newspaper. Some guy from Chicago, named Mark Goodwin, had unexpectedly arrived in Providence at the eleventh hour to buy the racetrack and, according to the reports, for more money. Her father, who at eighty-nine was in ill health and stayed home most of the time, was a major shareholder of the Narragansett Racetrack. When she and Deemis had dinner at her father's home a week ago, he was very happy about the racetrack finally being sold to the city. He had even complimented his son-in-law on doing a good job and being instrumental in bringing the deal to fruition. Rarely did the old man compliment Deemis, or for that matter, say anything pleasant to him at all.

Penny knew there would be big problems if this outsider from Chicago were to buy the racetrack. She didn't know exactly what, but it was written all over her husband's face. She had never seen him so worried. He wasn't sleeping, was drinking to excess, and was obviously scared. Her fears were confirmed that something was terribly wrong with her husband when she had wheeled her chair into his study last night. She usually knocked when she wanted to go in to see him. Last night she just wheeled herself in, hoping that maybe she could comfort her husband, especially knowing how exhausted he was after going to Chicago and returning home on the same day. As soon as Deemis saw her come in, he quickly took something off his desk and put it in a drawer. Penny looked later and saw what it was: his will.

"Hello," she answered, picking up the phone on the third ring. "Yes, this is Mrs. Whitacre…What?" she screamed. "When? How did it happen?" She was in shock, gasping for breath.

Her father was dead.

Chapter 78

EARLY FRIDAY MORNING

PROVIDENCE, RHODE ISLAND

"Pleasant bunch of people," Connie sarcastically joked to Mark and Ron, as they drove back to the Marriott, obviously upset by the way they had been treated by the board.

"No shit," agreed Ron, laughing.

"Obviously," Mark began, "those people have some very good reasons for not wanting us to buy the racetrack."

After parking the Jaffe's rental car, the threesome entered the lobby of the Marriott. Mark walked up to the front desk to check if there were any messages. He was hoping that maybe his accountant had gone through the file that Connie had faxed to his Chicago office last night. Hopefully, the accountant could supply some answers. The Senator had been confident that the file, once deciphered, held the incriminating pieces to the puzzle of the racetrack.

"No messages," the front-desk clerk told Mark after she checked.

"Thank you," said Mark as he started to walk to the elevator with Connie and Ron.

"Excuse me, sir," the clerk called out to Mark.

"Yes...?"

"There's a gentleman over there waiting to see you." She nodded toward a handsome man sitting on a lobby couch restlessly reading a newspaper.

"Thank you," Mark said. He told Connie and Ron to wait a minute and then proceeded over to the couch where the man was sitting.

"May I help you?" Mark queried.

"May I talk to you for a minute, please?" Deemis asked Mark as he motioned for him to sit down.

"Sure," Mark agreed and sat down in a straight-backed upholstered chair facing the man whom he immediately recognized to be one of the board members from the meeting moments earlier.

"What's your name?" Mark asked him.

"It's not important," Deemis said, coolly avoiding the question.

"Well, what can I do for you?"

"It's what *I* can do for *you*, Mark."

"And what is that, sir?"

"I have an envelope in my pocket that contains $50,000 in cash."

"I don't understand."

"It's yours," promised Deemis.

"Either it's my lucky day or you want something!"

"Perhaps it's both."

"And what might you want from me?"

Deemis was smiling. "I want you to take this money and your friends, go to the airport, take a plane home, and forget about trying to buy the racetrack."

"Thanks, but no thanks," Mark replied without hesitation, stood up and walked back toward Connie and Ron, wondering if he should take Deemis's suggestion. He really didn't have any idea what Bill and Connie had gotten him into.

"What did he want?" Ron asked.

"Oh, nothing," said Mark nonchalantly. "He just wanted to give us $50,000 to get out of Dodge."

"I hope you said no?" interjected Connie.

"I did," replied Mark, "but maybe I should have taken the money."

"No," Ron said. "You did the right thing. If they're offering us $50,000 just to leave, imagine how much it must be worth to stay."

"That's what I'm hoping. But somehow, I can't help feeling that maybe we're in way over our heads here. I mean, let's try to look at this situation logically."

"What do you mean?" Connie questioned Mark.

"Oh, c'mon, kid," Mark started, "look at all the trouble we've had so far."

"Just some minor glitches, that's all," countered Connie confidently.

"Minor glitches? I would say that we've had more than just some minor glitches. First, Ron and Jill are picked up, then a cop punches Ron out..."

"He was probably being a smart ass," Connie jokingly interrupted.

"Well, what about my being knocked out at the track, then shot at when I was in the taxi on the way back?" Mark revealed, instantly regretting that he had told Connie.

"What?" Connie exclaimed, "You didn't tell me about any of that!"

"I didn't want to worry you," Mark apologized.

"Worry me?" Connie said angrily. "I thought that we were in this together!?"

"We are."

"Then how could you keep that from me?"

"I didn't think it was that big of a deal at the time."

"Not that big of a deal?" Connie said, still irritated.

"Well, I guess maybe..."

"Look, Mark," Connie interrupted, "I want to get this racetrack more than you do, but it's not worth risking our lives over."

"I agree," said Jill, walking up to her husband, catching the last bit of Connie's declaration. Jill was getting to like Connie more and more. Not only was Connie making sense, but she could also tell that Connie had strong feelings toward Mark. But it was obvious to Jill that Mark had not picked up on Connie's feelings. Men were so unaware, she mused, they didn't seem to have that sixth sense. Even though Mark had just married Carole and was going nuts worrying about her, Jill didn't care. She liked Connie. Jill had met Carole once, only briefly, and even though she was a gorgeous, stunning woman whom Mark was madly in love or lust with, she didn't like her. There was something about her. Jill couldn't put her finger on what caused her negative feelings toward Carole. There was just something she didn't trust about her, and the way Mark fell head over heels for Carole, like a lovesick puppy, made Jill mad. Mark was a good guy. He was kind, honest, generous, and caring. Jill had seen how hurt Mark was when Patty, his first wife, had left him for his best friend. She didn't want to see Mark hurt again. She wanted to protect Mark, but she knew that there was little she could do.

"Look folks," Mark began, "I'm not saying I disagree with any of you. In fact, you're probably right, but the fact of the matter is, I've put too much time and effort into this project to turn back. And more importantly, it's a personal thing now. I refuse to run away and hide. That's not what I'm about."

Typical male macho bullshit, Connie and Jill both thought without saying anything.

"Let's go upstairs for a while. The stockholders' meeting is only a few hours away, and I need to prepare," Mark concluded.

Chapter 79

BEFORE FRIDAY'S MEETING

MARRIOTT HOTEL, PROVIDENCE, RHODE ISLAND

Mark's father, Art, was a partner in a very successful real estate firm in Chicago. Mark had once considered going to work for his father, but after careful deliberation had decided against joining his firm. Mark was his own person and did not want to be under anyone's thumb. Mark and his father had always had a very close relationship, with mutual respect and love for one another. Part of Mark's decision for choosing not to work with his father was that he didn't want to do anything that would jeopardize their excellent relationship. But from time to time, Mark would seek out his advice and counsel on both personal and business matters. His father, a very wise man, always gave good advice, which Mark usually accepted. Like any parent and child, they did not always agree, but their love and admiration for each other was unwavering. Mark's father had given his son subtle warnings about marrying Carole.

"Why don't you take it slower? Are you sure you know enough about her?" were some of the friendly, fatherly admonitions Art had given Mark. Mark chose to ignore his dad's advice.

When Art found out through some friends that Mark was in Rhode Island trying to buy a racetrack, he realized that his son was in serious danger. His kid obviously had no idea what he was getting into. Art had been told that the racetrack was controlled by the Mob out east. His son was in way over his head, involved in a dangerous deal that could get him killed. Art was shocked. What was his son doing out there anyway? He had assumed that Mark was in Chicago with his new bride. Mark had not wanted to tell his dad about the disappearance of Carole. He was afraid he would get the usual "I told you so" from his father. Art had been frantically calling the Marriott. Mark's secretary told his father where he was staying, but every time Art called, his son was not in. He didn't want to leave a message; this was too important. Art wanted to be certain that he got in touch with his son and decided that the best course of action was to send a fax. So he did:

> *KID, I DON'T KNOW WHAT IN THE HELL YOU ARE DOING OUT THERE,*
> *BUT YOU MUST LEAVE IMMEDIATELY. I REPEAT: GET OUT OF THERE!*
> *YOUR LIFE IS IN DANGER. THESE ARE BAD PEOPLE YOU ARE MESSING AROUND WITH. GET OUT, NOW!*
> *LOVE, DAD*

The Marriott was currently under a multi-million-dollar renovation program, which was almost complete. A new phone, computer, and fax system was the last thing left to install. The existing fax machine was an old curly-roll fax, not the newer, plain-paper fax machine. When Art's fax came in, it happened to be at the end of the roll and as the paper came out of the machine off the cardboard spindle, it curled up and fell to the floor, becoming partially concealed underneath the fax machine cabinet—hidden from view.

🍁 🍁 🍁

Mark's accountant had stayed up all night going over the information that Mark had Connie fax to him from Rhode Island. This was the second time the accountant had gone over the file. Every time he went through it, he found more. He was shocked; he had never seen anything like this before. He kept meticulously double-checking and triple-checking his figures. But figures don't lie. He couldn't believe what he was seeing. This was unbelievable—absolutely amazing! Although Don Griffin, Mark's accountant, really needed many boxes of information and not just the file that had been faxed to him in order to be really thorough—he was certain of what was going on from what he had already examined.

Chapter 80

Late Friday Afternoon

Dr. Bernstein's Office, Deerfield, Illinois

Dr. Bernstein had read with great interest the article in the paper about the Don's death. He was happy to know he was gone. Unfortunately, the demise of the Don didn't change things for him, he ruefully thought in retrospect. Dr. Bernstein still had to protect his wife. Granted, it had been an accident when she struck the woman with her car. She had not meant to kill anyone. She was drunk—got scared, so she fled. But no one would ever believe that it was an accident. She would be charged with vehicular homicide. Dr. Bernstein wrongly believed that he could be charged as an accessory. The Mob had covered it up for him, and now he was indebted to them forever. He hated with a passion what he had to do to keep them from going to the police. But he had no choice; he had to protect his wife. He blamed himself, too. Dr. Bernstein knew that the reason his wife got drunk that night was because she had caught him cheating again. Only three people knew about the accident: one of those persons, the Don, was now dead, but as long as Donovan and Marty were still around, the doctor was trapped. There was nothing he could do. Dr. Bernstein knew, regrettably, that the odds of Donovan and Marty being killed and then no longer being a threat, were a million-to-one long shot. He felt terrible about what he was doing to Janet, but he had no choice.

Chapter 81

❦

LATER FRIDAY

WHITACRE HOUSE, PROVIDENCE, RHODE ISLAND

The lawyer sat with Penny, trying to comfort her. He explained that the way she was feeling about the death of her father was quite normal. "You will go through many stages," he began. "First there's shock, then anger, then denial, then disorientation, followed by depression, despair, and detachment. You will then go through a process of reorganization, develop new coping skills, and then finally you'll recover. It may take years, but time always heals."

Penny was taking her father's death harder than she expected. After all, she should not have been so surprised; death for the old man was inevitable.

The lawyer continued to console her by reminding her that her father had died quietly in his sleep. No pain, no suffering. The lawyer went over Penny's father's will. Everything was much as she expected it to be. All of his assets were left to her. There was, at the end of the will, a notarized statement from her father, signed almost thirty years ago. Penny read the document.

"Did you know?" her father's lawyer asked.
"No. I had no idea," she replied.
"Do you think your husband knows?"
"I'm pretty sure Deemis doesn't know," Penny replied.
"Are you going to tell him?"
"I don't know," she pondered, lost in her thoughts.

Chapter 82

❀

FRIDAY

FORT LAUDERDALE, FLORIDA

John Rieton prided himself on being one of the best private investigators in the business. His services were not cheap, either. When Connie had hired him to track down the whereabouts of Mark's missing wife, Rieton had told her what it would cost: a $10,000, nonrefundable retainer plus $1,000 a day, *not* including expenses. While he had told Connie that he couldn't guarantee results, he had assured her that very seldom, in the twenty years since he had left the police force, had he ever failed to successfully complete his assignments. He was determined that this case would be no exception. As usual, he had gotten to the bottom of the situation. Rieton had to admit, though, that this was one of his most unusual cases. He had never had an assignment quite like this before.

Connie had told him she would double his fee if he was successful and quick in resolving this case, and he had done just that. He called Bill Alderice, whom he had met when he went to Bill's house to pick up his $10,000 retainer.

Rieton was leaving Fort Lauderdale in the morning for an extended vacation in Europe with his girlfriend. He would not be reachable once in Europe and wanted to drop off his report to Alderice before he left and also pick up the balance of the money owed him. Rieton called Bill and arranged to stop over at his Intercoastal mansion later, which he did. Alderice paid Rieton, who thanked Bill and left.

Bill Alderice opened the big folder and smiled as he read through the report and looked at the photographs. "So that's where Connie got her hunch from," he said, surprised. He had to call Connie in Rhode Island right away, but at that moment he had an overwhelming urge to snort some more coke. So he put the envelope away in a safe place. Within five short minutes he was totally coked and doped up in a state of euphoria, totally forgetting about the envelope and his intent to call and inform Connie what he had just learned from Rieton's report.

Chapter 83

FRIDAY

NORTH MIAMI, FLORIDA

Pete had a hangover. He had spent the night with some high-class hooker whom he had met at the bar at the famous Turnberry Isle Resort Club. Why had he been so stupid to drink tequila all night? When he woke up in the morning, the girl was already gone, but her pungent perfume still filled the hotel room. He had been so drunk he didn't even remember if she was a good fuck. No matter, Pete said to himself. He had plenty of work to do. Last night, Pete had met with the Don at the former Gold Coast Restaurant after Donovan had left. His orders were simple; there was no code or kill talk used by the Don—kill them all, if Donovan wasn't successful: Marty, Deemis, and Janet. Now this morning, Pete had found out that one of the crewmembers on the Don's boat had found him dead. Pete was in shock. At first, the young deckhand had denied any involvement, but after Pete had tortured him, he made a full confession, admitting that Donovan had paid him $25,000 to poison the Don. Pete then killed the deckhand. He would get Donovan last. Pete would get even with him for screwing up his job in

Hollywood, and for killing the Don. But what he really didn't know was that Donovan had not been his enemy. When Pete met the Don last night at the restaurant, the Don had not bothered to tell Pete what really happened regarding his promised job in Hollywood. It hadn't occurred to the Don that Donovan was harboring thoughts of retribution after his public humiliation. If it had the Don would have added Donovan to Pete's list immediately.

Chapter 84

EARLY FRIDAY EVENING

WATER TOWER PLACE, CHICAGO, ILLINOIS

The news of the Don's death made the press across the country. Donovan, having returned to Chicago from Florida earlier in the day, was pleased with the different reports from the press as he watched the TV in his condo. The Don had died of a heart attack, according to the medical examiner in Dade County. The newspapers and television reports had said natural causes, and why should anyone think differently? After all, he was an old man; his time was up. The other major crime families summoned an emergency meeting. They were all in unanimous agreement; Donovan would take over as head of the Chicago Outfit, effective immediately. Donovan was pleased with himself. His plan had worked perfectly. There would be no trace of the poison even if they did an autopsy. He was home free, but most important—he had settled the score. When the Don slapped him and insulted him at the former Gold Coast Restaurant, he decided it was payback time. No one hits Donovan, not even the Don.

Pete watched the account of what had happened to the Don on the 7:00 P.M. news. He had witnessed the incident between the Don and Donovan at the restaurant last night. He had heard the dying confession of the crewmember. He would kill Donovan; that was the least he could do for the Don. After all, if the Don had not arranged his escape from prison, Pete would still be rotting in that hellhole in Lewisburg Penitentiary. Pete wrongfully thought that Donovan was only using the idea of taking over the electrical union in Hollywood as bait; he didn't believe that Donovan had any intention of following through with this promise. He was wrong—the reality was that Donovan actually was going to give him the position. Pete just assumed that Donovan had double-crossed him because Donovan had the Don killed. No one had explained to Pete that it was Marty who screwed things up—even the Don hadn't told Pete that it wasn't Donovan's fault. Donovan loomed large and menacing in Pete's mind.

Chapter 85

FRIDAY–SHAREHOLDERS MEETING

PROVIDENCE, RHODE ISLAND

The grand ballroom of the Marriott was filled to capacity. Mark's telemarketers had done a good job. Also, Mark had received a lot of coverage in the press, who were present in full force. The place was packed with over 1,800 people. Mark, Connie, Ron, and Jill were upstairs in Mark's room watching what had become a major media event on TV. The meeting was scheduled to start in ten minutes, at 2:00 P.M. Many of the shareholders inside the ballroom were chanting:

"We Want Mark! We Want Mark! We Want Mark!"

It was a wild scene. The reporter inside the ballroom, who was covering the story for one of the TV stations, was visibly excited. "Ladies and Gentlemen," he began, "I am here in the ballroom of the Marriott Hotel. In about ten minutes, the shareholders will call to order a meeting. For almost two years, the board of directors of the Narragansett Racetrack has been negotiating a sale of the property to the city. The proposal calls for the closure of the racetrack, which has been unprofitable for many years, and asks that the city pay $5.6 million for the property."

The chanting was growing louder.

"WE WANT MARK! WE WANT MARK! WE WANT MARK!"

Many of the shareholders were wildly waving signs that read, "Don't Sell To The City! Sell To Mark!" The reporter had to keep raising his voice to be heard over the din of the wild and screaming shareholders. The noise level of the frenzied crowd was becoming louder by the second. The reporter now had to scream to be heard over the roar of the crowd chanting for Mark.

"Ladies and gentlemen," the reporter said loudly, sounding more like the announcer of some wild wrestling match than a TV news reporter, "the scene here is absolutely wild. This is the most unbelievable stockholders' meeting I have ever seen. This is incredible, folks. There is standing room only in this huge ballroom."

The chanting was deafening: "WE WANT MARK!! WE WANT MARK!! WE WANT MARK!!" The board members sitting at the dais on the stage were sweating profusely, showing their obvious discomfort.

The reporter continued, "What was, just a couple of days ago, scheduled to be a rather dull, if not boring, meeting has exploded into an atmosphere of what I can only describe as sensational."

The crowd's chanting was relentless, but the reporter went on, now screaming to be heard above the crowd: "This is all because of a young man named Mark Goodwin. Mr. Goodwin—I mean Mark," the reporter corrected himself. "He told me yesterday to call him Mark. Anyway, Mark arrived in town yesterday and is going to offer the shareholders substantially more money than the present deal on the table. Mark is from Chicago, and unconfirmed rumors have it that this young, personable man is going to keep the racetrack open and pay $2 million more than the city has offered."

The scene was electric—similar to the Democratic National Convention before announcing its choice for the next president of the

United States. "WE WANT MARK!! WE WANT MARK!!! WE WANT MARK!!!"

"Folks!" screamed the reporter to be heard over the crowd, "the meeting will be starting any minute!"

Mark turned to Connie, Ron, and Jill as he stood up. "Okay guys, let's go give 'em hell!" he exclaimed loudly.

"Yeah, let's go kill them!" Connie responded excitedly.

"This is your show," Ron said enthusiastically as he patted Mark on the back.

"Give them hell, love, you can do it," Jill said as she gave Mark a big kiss on the cheek. The four of them walked into the elevator and rode down to the lobby. Mark was psyched. He was ready for his big moment. He didn't even look nervous; he looked focused, serious, and intense.

On the way down in the elevator, Connie gave Mark a big hug and whispered in his ear, "I'm so proud of you, you're great." This didn't go unnoticed by Jill; she simply smiled.

When the door to the elevator opened, the expressions on their faces changed dramatically. They looked as if they had seen a ghost, shocked at what they saw—there were at least 100 state police and local cops surrounding all the entrances to the grand ballroom. Mark sized up the situation quickly.

"Look guys," he said trying to remain calm, "if they don't let us in, or if we get separated for any reason, go right back upstairs to the room, and we'll figure out an alternate plan B."

"Okay," they all said in unison as they walked off the elevator toward the entrance to the ballroom. As they cautiously inched nearer, one of the cops—the one who had come up to Mark's room last night—shouted, "There they are. Stop them. Don't let them through!" Within seconds, the cops surrounded them like a mad swarm of wild killer bees. It was like some race riot or a movie scene depicting an out-of-control angry mob. They were tossed around like pinballs, bouncing back and forth. The force with which the cops pushed them back was tremendous. They felt like bugs smashing into the windshield of a car going eighty miles an hour. The people in the lobby were standing there in disbelief, with their mouths hanging open, as they watched this tumultuous scene unfolding before their eyes.

Finally, as though making a temporary retreat, the cops backed off. Connie, Jill, and Ron were on the ground, their clothes and hair disheveled from being pushed around. They struggled to get up and made their way back toward the elevator.

"Where is Mark?" Connie screamed, glancing around quickly as the three of them got back on the elevator.

"He's probably back up in the room," Ron shouted back, out of breath. They got off the elevator on the top floor, hurriedly went to Mark's room, and opened the door, expecting Mark to be there. But he was not.

"Where is he?" Connie asked again, becoming increasingly agitated.

"Don't worry," said Jill, trying to sound calm. "I'm sure he'll be here any minute."

"Maybe they arrested him or hurt him," Connie said becoming hysterical.

"Calm down," assuaged Ron, "he's fine, don't worry."

Jill fixed Connie a scotch, which she ingested in one gulp. The drink seemed to relax her. The TV was still on. They stood there watching the wild scene unfold. The reporter was continuing his account, "Ladies and gentlemen, I have just been informed by Mr. Rooley, the chairman of the board, that Mark Goodwin has withdrawn his offer and will not be here today to speak to you."

The crowd let out a loud collective gasp and started booing Rooley, who was now at the lectern trying to talk and be heard over the tumultuous crowd. While the three of them watched this wild drama continue to escalate in the ballroom downstairs, there was a knock at the door.

"Oh, thank God," said Connie. "He's all right," and ran to open the door. It was not Mark, but rather the bellboy from downstairs.

"Excuse me, ma'am," he said politely to Connie, "the front desk told me to bring this up to you—I think it may be important."

Connie opened the envelope and read the first message. It was the fax from Mark's father, warning him to get out of town. "Oh no," Connie cried out as she passed the note over to Ron and Jill. Then she pulled the second message out of the envelope. It was a fax from Mark's accountant. The color drained from her face; she turned white as chalk as she read the second fax:

Dear Mark,

I have reviewed the figures you sent me last night. It appears that the books are cooked, so it's clear they're bogus. Actually it's worse than that. The board members have been stealing millions of dollars a year from the racetrack consistently over the last twenty years. I talked to a lawyer friend of mine from Rhode Island. He more or less figured out what is going on out there. As long as the racetrack is sold and closed, state law does not require an audit. However, if the racetrack is sold but remains open, an audit is required. Needless to say, the board members would be found guilty of multiple felonies. My friend tells me the board out there is heavily connected with the Mob. In fact, that is an understatement; hell, they are the Mob. These are murderers and very unscrupulous people. I sincerely hope that under no circumstances are you getting involved with these guys. Do not in any way try to buy this racetrack. These are very, very dangerous people. Leave town immediately, and be careful.

The faxed note was signed:

Don Griffin, CPA

"I guess that explains it," Ron said, after they all read both faxes. Connie exclaimed frantically, "Oh God, I'm so worried about Mark."

"Well, look at the bright side of this," said Jill. "At least we were not allowed to go into the meeting and make the offer. Just think of how much trouble Mark would have been in had he been allowed into the meeting."

"I guess you're right," replied Connie unconvincingly.

"Of course she's right," Ron said, trying to calm her down but realizing he wasn't doing too good of a job.

Connie was still visibly shaken, thinking how close Mark had come just a few minutes ago to possibly getting himself killed or at least in serious trouble. They continued watching the TV. They could see that Rooley was still trying to calm the crowd down because of their disappointment over Mark's absence. Rooley asked for some water to be brought up to the dais. They continued to watch on television as the waiters wheeled over a large cart covered with a white tablecloth. Just as the waiters were almost at the dais, Mark jumped out from underneath the tablecloth! The wild scene was similar to a stripper jumping out of a big cake at a bachelor party.

The crowd went wild. They were all on their feet.

"Get him out of here! Arrest him! He is not allowed to be in here!" Rooley screamed in outrage, pointing at Mark. "He's not a shareholder! He has no right to be here!"

"I'm here to offer more money!" Mark shouted.

"Get him out of here!" Rooley yelled, as a horde of police came rushing toward Mark to arrest him.

The crowd went out of control. "LET HIM TALK!" the people were shouting. "WE WANT MARK!!! WE WANT MARK!!! WE WANT MARK!!!" Total pandemonium was breaking out. The crowd made a human barricade around Mark to protect him from the oncoming police.

Connie was crying uncontrollably. "Oh, dear God, how are we going to warn him?"

"I don't know," a shaken Jill replied, also in tears.

"I don't think there is anything we can do now," Ron said sadly.

Connie picked up the phone and called Bill in Fort Lauderdale. She was livid. How could Bill have been so irresponsible to not have checked this deal out more carefully? Had Connie known how dangerous these people were, she never would have let herself get involved; and she certainly would not have involved Mark. The phone kept ringing; there was no answer. The creep had probably passed out from doing too much coke again, or was screwing some hooker, Connie reasoned.

"All right," Rooley said bitterly, realizing he had no choice. "Goodwin, you have exactly five minutes to talk."

Mark made his way up to the dais. The reception that he received was incredible. The crowd was cheering wildly, giving him a standing ovation. It was as if he were some hero, like John Glenn returning from space, or Michael Jordan making another tremendous shot and winning another NBA Championship for the Chicago Bulls with three seconds left in the game. Mark stood at the podium. He tried repeatedly to get the stockholders to quiet down and return to their seats so he could talk. Finally, the noise of the crowd subsided to a gentle roar.

"Thank you, thank you," Mark began, "I appreciate the warm reception that you have all given me today."

"We love you Mark!" a woman from the audience yelled out, excitedly waiting to hear about his offer of more money for the shareholders.

"I love you all, too!" Mark returned the compliment.

The crowd went wild again. "WE LOVE YOU, MARK! WE LOVE YOU, MARK! WE LOVE YOU, MARK!!" was the continuing mantra chanted from the crowd. Rooley had enough of this circus. He slammed his gavel on the table five or six times until the crowd finally calmed down.

Mark resumed talking. All eyes were focused on him. He had their complete attention. "Thank you, folks. My name is Mark Goodwin, and I represent some people who want to keep the racetrack open and will pay you $2 million more than the city is offering for the racetrack."

Connie watched on TV. What is he doing, offering *$2* million more? Bill had only authorized *$1* million more. After seeing the two faxes and now understanding how dangerous this whole deal was, Connie wished with all her heart that Mark was not on that dais right now.

"That sounds great," a stockholder said, rising to his feet. "But please be more specific." From the tone of his voice, it was obvious that this man was on the side of the board and very skeptical of Mark.

Rooley didn't miss his opportunity to confront Mark. "Look, we have been working on this deal for almost two years. The racetrack is losing money. We have worked very hard arranging this sale. This is a good deal and a solid one. Everyone will benefit. All of you folks will receive substantial sums of money from the proceeds of this sale." Rooley was on a roll. "Additionally, the city plans to demolish the racetrack and build a mixed-use development on the land that will create jobs and bring in tax dollars for the city. Do we really want some stranger, who we're not even sure has the money, to come into our town at the eleventh hour and get you all excited for nothing?"

One of the stockholders, who was holding a sign that read "Don't Sell To The City, Sell To Mark," spoke up. "I think," the woman said, "that we should listen to what Mark has to say."

"Okay," said Rooley, losing his patience. "Tell us exactly what you are proposing, Mr. Goodwin, and be specific."

"I have in my hand a check for $100,000 made out to the racetrack. This will serve as my binder, or down payment. I will have an agreement drawn up today that gives my investors ninety days to do a complete feasibility study of the racetrack, and then if everything is in order, which we expect it will be, we will pay you the balance in cash."

"What if after ninety days," Rooley continued, "you or your people, whoever they are, don't like the deal?"

"Well then," replied Mark, feeling the stress of the situation, "you give me back the $100,000, and you go ahead and sell the racetrack to the city."

"Are you serious?" Rooley asked incredulously. "You expect us to give you ninety days to think about this?"

"Please understand," said Mark, realizing that the mood of the crowd was starting to get a little more than negative toward him, "I was just contacted about the racetrack yesterday; my investors have not finished their final examination of all the financial and zoning details on the project."

"That is certainly not our problem. The racetrack has been for sale for quite a long time. You should have done your homework before you came here," Rooley lectured.

"I am sure," Mark, responded, "that the shareholders will not mind waiting a little longer for the chance to get an additional $2 million. I certainly feel that an extra ninety days will not hurt anybody."

"Well," said Rooley, feeling more confident and in control of the situation, "you are dead wrong. If we do not accept the city's offer today, it will be withdrawn."

Mark said nothing. A man stood up in the front. It was Senator Donaldson. "Now, now, Mr. Rooley, I'm sure that a few days' delay won't be a big problem to the city."

"Well, I don't know, Senator," mumbled Rooley, obviously pissed, showing disdain for the man.

"I agree with you fully, Chairman Rooley, that ninety days is out of the question, but maybe we could reach an alternative proposal here," Senator Donaldson continued.

"What do you have in mind, Senator?" Rooley asked, seething at his old nemesis. "Well, it's up to Mr. Goodwin. But I was thinking—what if the $100,000 check we take today is nonrefundable? Then we give Mark and his investors three days to come up with another $900,000 that is also nonrefundable, and then give them another thirty days to come up with the balance. In consideration for Mark and his people taking more of a risk, we reduce the price by $1 million. We would still be getting $1 million more," the Senator concluded.

Mark smiled to himself—the Senator had played it just like Mark, the Senator and Ron had rehearsed.

Connie watched the scene on TV; she was still scared to death for Mark but was thoroughly impressed by what she was witnessing.

"Well," Rooley began, "I don't know…"

The crowd went nuts again. Everybody was shouting wildly again, "YES!" "LET MARK DO IT!" "A LITTLE DELAY IS WORTH IT!" "IT'S STILL A MILLION MORE FOR US!" "C'MON, MARK, DO IT!" "SAY YES, MARK!"

Rooley could see that if Mark agreed, he would have no choice but to go along with the majority of shareholders. He prayed to God, as did the other board members, that Mark would say no.

"Well, Mr. Goodwin?" Rooley asked.

Mark looked solemn and was deep in thought. It was obvious to Rooley that Mark was going to decline. Rooley suspected that he didn't have the money. There was dead silence in the grand ballroom. Mark was perspiring profusely under the heat of the bright lights surrounding the half dozen or so TV cameras focused on him. He took a deep breath to try to calm himself down.

Connie was glued to the television. "Please Mark, say no. For God's sake, say no."

"Ladies and gentlemen," Mark said as he cleared his throat, "I accept."

The crowd rose to its feet and gave Mark a standing ovation again. Mark wrote out his personal check for $100,000 and gave it to Rooley, although it was not his money. Bill had FedEx'd Mark a check for $100,000, which Mark had FedEx'd to his bank. Mark tried to make his way out of the ballroom. Everyone patted him on the back, congratulating him like he was Mohammed Ali after winning his first title fight. Mark walked out of the ballroom, graciously declining to be interviewed by the press. Once outside, Deemis came up to him.

"Congratulations, Mr. Goodwin."

"Thank you," Mark said, feeling elated.

"Mark, I'll give you $100,000 to reimburse you for your check, and another $100,000 in cash to not go through with the deal," Deemis said.

"Not interested," Mark said. He was feeling invincible; he had done it. He was so high and felt as though he were walking on air. He got on the elevator, anxious to share his jubilance with his three musketeers.

🍁   🍁   🍁

Upstairs in the hotel room, the others reacted to Mark's offer:

"No," said Connie, crying.

"Shit," said Jill.

"Fuck," said Ron.

Mark walked into the hotel room feeling euphoric. "I did it," he boasted. He was so keyed up he didn't notice the strange looks on their faces. He saw that the women had been crying. He assumed it was out of joy for him—for them. Oh, what a wonderful moment. He would always cherish this victory. If only Carole was here, safe and sound, he would be really happy.

"I'm going to take a shower," Mark happily announced to the threesome. "Let's meet back here in half an hour to celebrate!" He headed for the bathroom, elated.

🍁   🍁   🍁

"Let's not burst his bubble in his moment of glory," Ron suggested, and they all agreed. "We'll tell him in half an hour."

Mark was singing in the shower. He was in ecstasy, savoring his sweet victory. He got out of the shower and dried off, changing into some jeans and a polo shirt. "I've got to call Bill," Mark said to himself, "to tell him the wonderful news." Maybe, he thought, Connie had already called. No matter, he wanted to tell Bill himself, to be congratulated by him. He dialed his number in Fort Lauderdale. "Bill, it's Mark. I've got great news."

"Oh," Bill said, sounding doped up.

"Yeah," Mark said, "I did it."

"That's great," Bill said incoherently.

"You've got three days to come up with $900,000, and a month for the rest, just like we planned."

"Oh," Bill acknowledged, sounding spaced out.

"Just 'oh?'" exclaimed Mark. "We did it, man, aren't you happy?"

"There's a problem," Bill confessed.

"What?" Mark asked, feeling his gut start to churn.

"Well…I don't have the money."

"Then, get it!" Mark screamed.

"I can't," Bill said, apologetically. "There's no way."

"What the fuck are you talking about? I already agreed to the deal. I even wrote them a personal check for the hundred grand. Thank God I deposited your check to cover the one I just wrote," Mark said angrily, not able to believe what he was hearing.

"Mark, I'm sorry, but the check I gave you is no good."

"What?" Mark exclaimed, astonished.

"I'm really sorry, man," Bill said and hung up.

"You fucking cock-sucker!" Mark screamed, as he threw the receiver against the wall. "What the fuck am I supposed to do now?" he ranted, looking at the ceiling. Mark walked over to the mini-bar to fix himself a drink. He tried to calm down. He was hyperventilating, unable to catch his breath. Then he noticed the two faxes sitting on the table. He picked them up and read both of them. He became paralyzed, suddenly in a state of utter shock and further disbelief. Now he understood the strange worried looks on Connie's, Ron's, and Jill's faces when he entered the room. "I've got to get out of here," he said to himself, fearing for his life and the lives of his three friends. Mark picked up the phone and asked for the Jaffes' room. The operator said there was no answer. "Please tell them that I have gone back to Chicago, and that they should do the same." Then he thought about calling Connie. "No, Connie can go to hell," he cursed. "If it weren't for her and that goddamned dope-addict boyfriend of hers, I wouldn't be in all this mess!" Mark, for the second time in his life, was really scared. The first time was just a couple of days ago when he had walked in on Carole's sister, Janet—thinking she was his wife and was having sex with another man, while another crazy woman held a gun to his head. Now Mark wondered if he would be able to get out of Rhode Island—or was it already too late? Just then there was a knock at the door. Mark opened it, and Jill and Ron Jaffe walked in. They all hugged each other and agreed to meet in the lobby in five minutes with their bags packed, and go straight to the airport. Jill informed Mark that Connie was still in her room crying hysterically, but Mark didn't care at this point. He wanted nothing more to do with Connie or Bill.

Chapter 86

THE ALDERICE MANSION

FORT LAUDERDALE, FLORIDA

Connie was back in Fort Lauderdale, and it seemed as if nothing had changed. Bill, contrary to doctor's orders, was doing as much cocaine as ever, probably more. Did she really love Bill? she kept asking herself. Yes, there was a part of him that she was still attracted to, but that part seemed to be less than she remembered before meeting Mark. Every day she was growing more and more disenchanted with Bill. No question about it, she liked money, the nice house, the fine clothes, and the rich-and-famous lifestyle, but Bill was in a constant cocaine and Jack Daniels stupor—Connie was quickly tiring of the situation. When she had returned from Rhode Island, she was so angry with Bill she didn't speak to him for days. Connie felt that it was bad enough that Bill had been so irresponsible not to have checked out the racetrack deal more closely before sending her and Mark there—but to leave Mark hanging like that, in danger, without any money, causing him to make a spectacle of himself, and forcing him and the Jaffe's to rush out of town like thieves in the night, was inexcusable! She would never forgive Bill for that. Connie had wired $100,000 of her own money into Mark's bank account in Chicago just to make sure the check wouldn't bounce, so Mark wouldn't get into any trouble. She hadn't told Mark.

Since returning to Fort Lauderdale, she had thought about calling Mark at his condo or office at least half a dozen times. She knew Mark would probably never forgive her, let alone talk to her again. She was sure that he hated her, and she couldn't blame him. But the fact of the matter was that she was madly in love with Mark and she couldn't put him out of her mind. She had been drinking heavily. There was nothing else to do. Bill was on his usual perpetual cocaine high, and she wanted nothing to do with that addiction. Connie had tried cocaine once or twice, and that was enough for her. She liked being fully in control of her faculties. Having spent many years gradually gaining self-esteem, she was not willing to throw it all away for some shiny white powder. Connie hated herself for drinking so much. She was so depressed. If only Mark would talk to her. But what would she say? That she was sorry, or that she was in love with him? Connie was sure Mark wouldn't listen to her. She still had her hunch about Carole from the two photographs she had seen of Carole, one in Mark's apartment and one at Bill's, but what could she do? Nothing, she realized—there was no way to prove anything. Furthermore, Connie reasoned that Mark would not believe anything she said after the Rhode Island fiasco. Unless Connie had some proof about Carole, there was nothing she could do. The situation made her feel helpless. Connie hated feeling helpless. If only that private investigator, Rieton, had done his job. She had not heard from him. Then it dawned on her—instead of waiting for Rieton to call her, she would call that motherfucker and get him off his lazy ass. Connie had promised to double his fee if he produced quick results. Obviously, he didn't need the extra money, or was he simply incompetent? She called the number on the business card. The answering service said he was not in.

"When will he be back?"

"In about a month," the woman answered.

"What do you mean, a month?" Connie demanded.

"I'm sorry, ma'am, he left word that he will not be back for a month."

"Where is he?"

"Out of the country somewhere."

"How can I get in touch with him?"

"You can't, ma'am."

"What do you mean, I can't?"

"Sorry, ma'am, we don't have a number," the operator said and promptly ended the call.

"Shit!" Connie raged. She was furious. She started throwing ashtrays and lamps at the walls. They shattered, and there was glass and parts of broken lamps everywhere.

"What in the hell's going on?" Bill asked as he rushed into the room to see Connie destroying whatever was at hand.

"I'm pissed," snapped Connie.

"No shit," said Bill, "What about?"

"That goddamned detective never called me—now he's out of the country and cannot be reached."

"He was here," said Bill.

"*What?*" said Connie, seething at Bill.

"Yeah, he dropped off a package for you." Bill handed it to Connie after retrieving it from a drawer.

Connie, eyes wide open, read everything in the report. "I'm going to Chicago," she excitedly announced.

"When will you be back?" Bill asked.

"With any luck, never!" And she was out the door.

Chapter 87

❀

CHICAGO, ILLINOIS

When Mark got home from Rhode Island, he almost had a heart attack when he walked into his condo—Carole was sleeping on the couch.

"Carole!" Mark exclaimed, waking up his wife and feeling tears of joy welling up in his eyes.

"Oh Mark, my darling," Carole shouted, as she burst into tears, jumped up, and wrapped her arms around her husband. "You have no idea how much I missed you!"

"Me, too," replied Mark, still in a state of shock at seeing his wife.

The two reunited lovers hugged each other with a fierce passion for what seemed like hours. They said nothing, just held each other tightly, neither wanting to let go, or ever be separated again, not even for a second. It was as if they were trying to squeeze their bodies together into one inseparable unit. Carole and Mark were crying uncontrollably, kissing each other, melting into each other, becoming one synergetic being. They sucked up each other's hot, salty mouth juices like ravenous wild animals. They couldn't—and didn't—stop.

"Oh, darling…God, how I missed you," whispered Carole.

"You don't know how much I missed you," Mark said passionately. "I thought I would never see you again. I was so scared. Are you all right?"

"Yes, my dear," replied Carole as she stared lovingly into her husband's eyes.

"What happened?"

"Later," Carole said. "I'll tell you all about it later." She took Mark's hand and led him into the bedroom. "God, how I've missed fucking you, Mark. I have been so horny."

"Me, too," Mark agreed breathlessly.

"Well, my love, I guess I'll have to take care of that problem right now," Carole promised seductively.

Mark started to unzip his jeans.

"No, let me," Carole said as she stopped his hand and began to slowly unzip his pants. "Oh God, I want you so much, baby. You have no idea how much I want to make love to you."

"I can't wait," Mark said excitedly, feeling his erection growing harder.

"Patience, my love," Carole purred. "Tell me how much you want me, Mark."

"More than anything in the world," he replied, growing more and more excited.

"Oh Mark, I'm getting so hot. My pussy is burning up. It's on fire."

"Oh, God…" Mark moaned.

"My pussy is getting so wet, my underwear is soaking." Slowly, like a thousand-dollar hooker on stage, Carole started to take off her slacks and shirt. She stood over Mark in only her bra and panties. "Oh look, Mark," she said, as she rubbed her nipples with her hands, "look how hard my nipples are."

"They're so big," Mark said, as he stared up at her huge nipples protruding through her scanty brassiere.

"Oh God, Mark, my pussy is drenched. Look, darling, my hot love juices are pouring down my legs." Carole put two fingers underneath her see-through panties, which were now soaking wet, and stroked her small dark triangle. "Oh God," she moaned in ecstasy, playing with herself as Mark watched, spellbound.

"I'm going to come. Oh shit, I'm going to explode," she groaned. "Oh God!" she screamed as she rubbed herself vigorously, reaching orgasm.

Mark could see her silky juices running down her legs.

Carole removed her fingers from between her legs, rubbed them over her lips and nose, and then stuck them in her mouth as she started sucking. "Mmmm," she moaned, "I taste so good, Mark. Do you want to taste my sweet hot pussy?"

"Yes, God, yes," Mark begged, growing more and more excited.

Carole put her hand on Mark's penis, stroking it gently. "Mark, I want you to fuck me," she said as she continued stroking Mark's erect member, playing with herself at the same time.

"Me, too, Carole…you're driving me crazy."

"I want you in my mouth, Mark. I want to taste and swallow every bit of your hot, delicious cum. I want you to explode in my mouth."

"Oh God," Mark moaned, his desires for his gorgeous, sexy wife now uncontrollable.

"Then I want you to come all over my face. I want all of you, Mark. I want every last drop you have in my mouth…on my nose…in my eyes. I want you to rub your hot white syrup all over my big tits. Then I want you to ram that big hard, swollen dick of yours inside my hot, dripping pussy. I want you to fuck me hard, Mark. I want your cock deep inside me. Then I want to sit on your face with my hot pussy fucking your brains out. I want to come again all over you. I want to cover you with my hot pussy juices until you're soaking wet."

"Yes, yes!" Mark screamed.

Then Carole knelt at the foot of the bed and started slowly sucking his toes.

Mark was lost in a euphoric, orgasmic trance. Their lovemaking continued non-stop for the next few days and nights. They were lost in each other's unbridled sexual passion.

🍁   🍁   🍁

Finally, Carole explained to Mark about how her sister was involved with the wrong type of people. "Janet," she said, "was trying to break free of their clutches. The only way these bad people could make Janet do whatever she was supposed to do was to kidnap me. They forced Janet to carry out their wishes. Knowing how much Janet loved me, they knew she would do anything they told her to do, as long as I was held hostage and in danger."

"Well, so what finally happened?" asked Mark after listening to this wild story in total amazement, almost bordering on disbelief.

"Janet did what she was supposed to do, I guess. So they let me go."

"Where were you?"

"I don't know where I was. They kept me drugged up on something the whole time they had me."

"Did they hurt you?"

"No, they just scared me."

"How did you get back here?"

"I don't know. They must have brought me back here and put me on the couch. All I remember is you waking me up."

"Where is Janet?"

"I don't know."

"Well, is she all right?"

"Yes, I just talked to her on the phone."

"She called here?"

"Yes."

"Well, is she out of trouble?"

"I think so."

"I'd like to meet her and thank her for saving your life."

"I don't think that will be possible."

"Why not?"

"Janet said that after everything she's been through, she's leaving the country to start a new life. She told me she might never come back."

Mark had a thousand and one questions he wanted to ask Carole. There were parts of her story he didn't understand; parts that didn't make any sense. But when he would question Carole, she would get defensive and angry. It was over, Carole said, and she didn't want the topic brought up anymore. She wanted the whole episode to be forgotten and never mentioned again. Mark could empathize with the traumatic feelings Carole had experienced. After all, he had been through hell himself—with Rhode Island, Connie, and that whole mess. Mark made Carole promise that she would go to her doctor to get a complete physical and emotional checkup to make sure she was okay after having gone through this nightmare.

Days had passed, and Carole still had not gone to the doctor. Mark was getting more and more concerned. Something wasn't right with his wife. Maybe she was suffering from Posttraumatic Stress Disorder, Mark thought. Carole was acting strangely. Mark had not been married to her long enough to know whether this was her usual behavior, but there definitely was something wrong. He knew it. He started going back to the office again. Whenever he came home, she would still be in bed, sleeping. Carole would wake up and want to make love and then go back sleep. She seemed kind of out of it, so Mark asked her if she had been drinking or was using drugs.

"No," she told him emphatically.

Mark now finally realized that he had made a mistake marrying Carole. Yes, the sex was incredible, but it seemed like that was the only thing that their marriage was about. Mark was actually lonely. He wasn't getting the intellectual stimulation he needed. He thought about calling Connie.

Mark was not mad at Connie. He knew it was Bill's fault that the racetrack deal had become so screwed up. Mark missed being with Connie. He still wondered what her hunch was about Carole. Connie was probably happily back with Bill by now and not the least bit interested in talking to him.

As he sat in his office wondering about Connie, his secretary announced that there was a young woman in the lobby waiting to see him, but she would not reveal her name. Mark prayed that it was her. He hoped he was right as he walked out to the lobby to greet this mystery woman. To his delight, it was Connie! Standing there looking at her, he realized how much he had missed her. She was so beautiful, not sexy and sultry like Carole, but Connie's eyes—it was her deep, sincere eyes. They were magnetic. There was an energy, a dazzling sparkle in them, an excitement that instantly radiated a fiery, love-of-life persona. They awkwardly shook hands and walked into Mark's office. He closed the door.

Connie placed the report on Mark's desk and told him that he needed to read it. Mark picked it up and began reading through the report. He was in shock. The detective had done his job well. It was all there. Even Connie's comments. She had told Rieton that when she was in Mark's apartment in Chicago, she saw a picture of Mark and Carole, and she knew she had seen the woman in the picture before. Somewhere, but where? Then Connie remembered. She had run across a picture of Bill with a bunch of hookers on his boat in Fort Lauderdale. Bill had the picture hidden, but Connie had found it. One of the women in the picture was Janet, Carole's almost-identical sister. Bill must have learned about the racetrack deal from Janet. The *real* surprise, though, was what else Rieton had found out. He had gone to Janet's house in Berwyn. He had talked to their parents. He had broken into Dr. Bernstein's office in Deerfield and made a copy of Janet's file.

Now, the whole situation made sense. *Janet was, in fact, Carole!* Carole and Janet were one and the same person! There were no almost-identical twins, only one woman, albeit confused and tormented. Carole represented the good aspects; Janet, the personification of evil. The psychiatrist's report explained in detail how Janet had multiple personalities. She had been struggling her whole life with this insidious duality. Janet also had a history of drug abuse. She was shooting morphine, which Dr. Bernstein had prescribed, and topping it up with dope she was getting from a local street dealer.

Mark knew what he had to do. He told his secretary he was leaving and escorted Connie to his car. They said nothing to each other, driving down the road, both in deep thought. Mark pulled up in front of his building and told Connie to wait in the car while he went up to his apartment. He walked in pensively and went straight for the bedroom, knowing Carole, or Janet—whatever name she chose to use—would still be in bed. The bedroom door was locked. Strange, Mark thought, she had never locked it before. He went to the den, frantically searching through the desk drawers for the key to the bedroom. A sense of foreboding and unexplained doom suddenly, without warning, enveloped him. Finally, he found the key and opened the door. Mark knew instantly, as he looked at her lying on the bed, that she was dead. The syringe was still stuck in her arm; the wet still-warm blood was splattered everywhere. He sadly realized that in her disoriented state she must have missed a vein and instead hit an artery. Mark didn't have a clue she was shooting up drugs. The shock and grief of what Mark was experiencing was overwhelming; yet the feeling of relief—or rather his emancipation at the demise of his wife—overtook him as Connie gently kissed the back of his neck, lightly stroking his hair, having chosen not to wait in the car.

The nightmare was finally over. It should have never begun, and Mark tried to focus his thoughts on Connie right now, knowing full well that he would have the rest of his life to beat himself up for letting his addictive and intense sexual chemistry control and almost ruin his life.

Maybe Mark had finally grown up. Obviously, he reasoned, he had learned the hard way. But, he was confident that he would never again make the same mistakes, and he would not exercise such poor judgment when it came to women. Suddenly, maybe for the first time in Mark's entire life, he knew why and what he wanted in a woman. And Connie was not only what he wanted but also what he needed!

Chapter 88

❈

PROVIDENCE, RHODE ISLAND

Deemis walked out of his office building. He was actually smiling. It had been a very long time since he had been happy. Since Mark had not come up with the additional $900,000 three days after the shareholders' meeting, the racetrack was sold to the city. Plus, for all their aggravation and trouble, the board members got an extra $100,000 from the nonrefundable check that Mark had given the board. The members of the board split up the $100,000 among themselves as a kind of bonus; a present in honor of their successful cover-up.

The pressure was off. Things were quieting down. The racetrack being sold to the city and closed meant that they were all out of trouble. There would be no audit. Deemis was more relieved than anyone. After all, if he had not had an affair with Janet and told her that the racetrack was for sale, there would not have been all this trouble. Deemis knew that Janet had told Bill Alderice about the racetrack deal while she was on his boat in Fort Lauderdale. Deemis spent his share of the $100,000 on Penny, for an expensive operation that the insurance wouldn't cover. Miraculously, it seemed to work. For the first time in years, Penny was able to walk. Although they had been told that the surgery was highly experimental and very risky, they had decided to take the chance and go for it. The results were nothing less than spectacular. Penny was doing wonderfully. She was really working hard in physical therapy at the rehab center and making dramatic improvements every day. Deemis and Penny had even made love last night for the first time in years. It was blissful. Life was good for both of them. Deemis was going to pick her up for their first date in years and was feeling really good as he left his office, and got into his Rolls Royce, realizing how much he really loved his wife. He turned on the ignition—and suddenly in one blast, it was all over. It was payback time. Deemis was history, just when everything in his life finally seemed to be going right.

Someone was watching from a vantage point two blocks away. Even at that distance, the flames were so bright and intense that they reflected off his diamond pinkie-ring. Donovan smiled and walked away.

Pete was pissed when he found out that Deemis was dead. *He* was planning on having Deemis killed, himself. He wondered if it was Donovan who had beaten him to the punch. Who else? he reasoned. It *had* to have been Donovan.

Chapter 89

A FEW MORE WEEKS LATER

CHICAGO, ILLINOIS

Jack had spent every minute with Jenny since he had been released from Morgantown. Most of the time they just held each other. They were madly in love and were both beginning to realize that they had probably been in love with each other for a long time. They were now planning a life together and were waiting for the right moment to get married. They had finished a dinner of takeout Chinese and were sitting on the couch together, contentedly watching TV. They weren't really paying much attention to the program; instead, they were holding hands and thoroughly enjoying each other's company. The lovemaking between them had been remarkable. But the relationship was on a much deeper level than merely a physical one. They had become best friends, too.

"We interrupt this program for a special news bulletin," the voice from the TV said. "Approximately thirty minutes ago, there was a fatal shooting at one of Chicago's most prestigious condominiums." The screen flashed to several police cars and an ambulance outside the

Water Tower Apartments on East Pearson Street. Jenny sat up, hoping it wasn't what she feared most. The TV reporter said what Jenny already suspected. "I am live here at Water Tower Apartments, where paramedics were called just moments ago to the penthouse apartment of a prominent attorney after a neighbor heard gunshots." The paramedics wheeled the stretcher into the ambulance. The blanket covered the body's head. Jenny began sobbing uncontrollably. She knew that her father lived in the penthouse, and there were only two penthouse apartments in Water Tower—she recognized her father's neighbor on TV; he owned the second penthouse apartment.

Pete was in the crowd, smiling broadly under his Ray Bans.

The funeral of Donovan, per his will, was private with a closed casket. Jack and Jenny decided to delay their wedding until after the funeral. At first, Jenny had wanted to call off the wedding indefinitely, but Jack convinced her to go ahead with their marriage plans.

"Your father would have wanted you to be happy," Jack convinced Jenny. Although Jack was sad for Jenny, secretly he was relieved. With Donovan gone, he felt he was pretty much home free as far as the deal he had made with Kathy Hawk. Oh sure, that girl, Janet, was still alive, he assumed, but he really wasn't too concerned about her. Jack had not yet talked to Mark and didn't know that Janet had recently died of a drug overdose. She wasn't important, he figured, just probably some messenger. Furthermore, he didn't know where Janet lived, not even what city or state she was in, and Jack assumed that Janet didn't know where he lived either.

With Donovan gone and Jack not having any family, they decided that it would be an informal wedding, with just the two of them getting married by a Justice of the Peace at City Hall. They were planning their wedding ceremony for tomorrow. Today at 3:00 o'clock was the reading of the will at the lawyer's office on LaSalle Street. Jack thought it strange that he had been requested by the lawyer to come with Jenny to the reading of Donovan's will, but he was happy to go along to offer his support.

Jenny had wanted to wait until after the reading of the will to get married. She thought it best to wrap up the affairs of one phase of her life before starting another one with Jack. He had agreed. The lawyer read the will. After the standard bequests to charities and valued employees, half of the remaining balance was left to Jenny. The other half was left to Jack. Jenny and Jack were both shocked.

"Why?" Jack asked.

"Because," the lawyer said, "you were his son."

Jack felt like a bomb had been dropped on him. He couldn't believe that Donovan was his father! The lawyer, who had known all along, explained to Jack that his mother had always been embarrassed about Donovan being part of the underworld. His mother, a proud woman, had not been married to Donovan, and even if she had been, would accept no money or help from him. Now Jenny and Jack understood why Donovan had promised to give Jack $1 million. It was his way of doing something for his son. Donovan had not wanted to get his son in trouble with the Feds at all; he had wanted to help him without letting him know that he was his father. Still, his father was no saint; he tried to use his son and his daughter to get an in with Mark Goodwin. Mark had something or knew something that Donovan wanted.

Now Jenny understood why her father had been so adamant about Jack getting Donovan as his lawyer when the trouble started, instead of going to that other lawyer first. Donovan's plan got screwed up. Had Jack gone to Donovan first, he would never have been indicted and sent to jail. But that was all water under the bridge now. The present problem was devastatingly greater....

Jenny and Jack were brother and sister—Jenny could not understand why her father had not told her that Jack was her brother. Obviously he must have planned to before he was shot to death. But they had been sleeping together! The two of them were both overwhelmed with a mixture of emotions. They loved each other, but were overcome with deep, destructive feelings of guilt and shame. They had both been raised as devout Catholics. Their guilt was eating them up alive. In a tearful farewell to each other, Jack and Jenny both knew that they could not even remain friends. Far too much had happened between them.

Jack started drinking heavily, smoking a lot of pot, and taking pills. He was on the fast track to self-destruction. He had not even called his ex-boss, Mark Goodwin, since he had been released from prison. Nothing mattered to him anymore. He was slowly killing himself, and he didn't care. Jack had tried calling his shrink, Dr. Bernstein, but was told by the doctor's receptionist that Bernstein was out of town.

Jenny was coping no better. Friends of hers, seeing how depressed she was, assumed it was because of the death of her father. She had told no one about the devastating fact that Jack was her brother. Jenny seemed to have lost her will to live. Friends tried to cheer her up and offer comfort, but she was so morose that eventually they stopped bothering with her. Her friends couldn't stand to be around her anymore—she was too depressing.

Now in their separate, desolate lives, all Jenny and Jack could do now was think about each other. The guilt continued to fester, tormenting them. Like Romeo and Juliet, if they could not be together in life, perhaps they could find each other in death.

A small story appeared shortly after the deaths of the Don and Deemis in the *Chicago Sun-Times*. "Man falls from his office window at the Board of Trade building in an apparent suicide." Police said they were further investigating the death of Marty Serachi and would not comment further.

The cops who were first on the scene wrote in the report that Marty's testicles and penis were in his mouth, which was held shut with ten huge safety pins skewered through his lips. This was not made public. This was definitely not a suicide. It was a typical Outfit murder—a strong warning to all Outfit fuckups'.

Chapter 90

A FEW WEEKS LATER

THE SOUTH OF FRANCE

Dr. Bernstein was elated. There *was* a God after all, he thought, or was he just one lucky son of a bitch? They were all dead; the Don, who had been blown up in his boat; Marty, who was thrown out of his office window, and finally Donovan, who had (supposedly) been shot to death at his condo. Since it was a closed casket, there were some rumors that Donovan was still alive, a stunt Donovan might have arranged to make everyone think that he was dead. Bernstein was finally free of the stranglehold they all had on him and at long last was out of danger.

Bernstein, as many shrinks are, was full of shit. He knew full well that the current metamorphosis in his life was simply an act for the benefit of his wife. He had not changed at all; he was still a dishonest, unethical, cheating shithead. If he had learned anything from the ordeal with Janet/Carole; drugging her, controlling her, and cheating on his wife; he had learned to simply be more careful—*don't get caught!*

The doc took his wife on a trip to St. Tropez, then Monaco. While vacationing, he dutifully pretended that he was a changed man and would be a better, more loving, faithful husband. He knew he would never change and was quite comfortable in his chameleon-like persona. But his wife was overjoyed at the seemingly profound change in her husband. While in the south of France, he gave her much attention and affection; she actually began to believe that he really did love her.

Bernstein was smugly sitting alone in his hotel room at Hôtel de Paris while his wife was shopping next door at Loew's Monte Carlo. He was trying to figure out how to explain to her that he would be away for a few hours that evening. While he was at the pool earlier that morning, he had arranged to meet a cocktail waitress/hooker. He had been faithful for too long and needed a good fuck.

Unfortunately for Bernstein, he would not have to worry about concocting an alibi…

Three men broke into his room and forced him at gunpoint to write a suicide note. In the note to his wife, he explained that he couldn't live with the guilt of cheating on her for years and that with him out of the picture, she could at last find someone who truly deserved her.

When Bernstein's wife opened the door to their hotel room and saw her husband's brains exploded all over the desk, walls, and carpet, she screamed so loudly that everyone in the hotel heard her. Hours later, after the hotel's physician had her medicated and in bed in another room in the hotel, the police brought her the suicide note. She sobbed uncontrollably as she read the note. Naïvely, she believed the note, never once considering the possibility that her husband might have been murdered.

EPILOGUE

Donovan had one of his soldiers plant the bomb in Deemis's car and also ordered Marty's murder. Donovan set up Bernstein's murder to look like a suicide—Bernstein knew too much and had to be eliminated. From what Marty had told Pete, Pete knew that Janet, a.k.a. Carole, was shooting up drugs. So, all Pete had to do was pay Janet's supplier $100 for her drug dealer to switch bags of dope and give Janet the lethal one that would do the job and ensure the quick and efficient demise. Even though Pete had arranged for Donavan to be shot, because it was a closed-casket funeral, Pete strongly suspected that Donovan was still very much alive.

All of the board members of the racetrack eventually died of natural causes. They took their secret to their graves.

The Feds indicted both Bill and Jim Alderice for fraud. They were murdered in prison. No one ever found out who killed the brothers.

Penny Whitacre fell madly in love with an old friend. At long last she finally had a tremendous love life when she discovered that she was really a lesbian. Penny made an important call; she had no choice, because she knew that she had to do the right thing.

"Hello," Jenny said, wondering who was calling her.

"You don't know me," the woman's voice said. "My name is Penny Whitacre, and my husband was your father. I thought you would like to know."

"What?" Jenny gasped for air, totally shocked by Penny's revelation.

"Your mother had an affair with my husband, Deemis, in Chicago; she died giving birth to you. As a favor to my father, and in an attempt to protect me; my father's associate, Donovan, adopted you as his own. My husband never knew; he thought you both died while she was giving birth."

🍁 🍁 🍁

So Jack and Jenny were married, and with the inheritance they received from Donovan, they started a national program to help rehabilitate ex-cons. They also became successful entrepreneurs in the private prison industry, in partnership with Connie and Mark. They were one of the few privatizers that actually made money for themselves, and their shareholders of their company. Furthermore, they were legitimate, not involved with the Mob.

🍁 🍁 🍁

Connie and Mark were married. They made the cover of *TIME* magazine, as partners of one of the most successful real estate firms in the country. Connie had just told Mark that she was pregnant. Mark was delighted and couldn't wait to become a father.

🍁 🍁 🍁

The Mafia was still going full force. Reno, no longer attorney general, and Hawk never understood how the Mob was so deeply involved in the private and federal prison systems. Informants had told them that Donovan of the Chicago Outfit had been in charge, but he was dead, wasn't he?

🍁 🍁 🍁

The plane landed on the tarmac in Buenos Aires. It was hot, over 100 degrees in the shade. The man walking off the plane was sweating. He wiped his forehead with his hand. The reflection from Donovan's diamond pinkie ring shone brightly in the Brazilian sun.

Pete, smiling, watched Donovan leave the terminal and get into his big black limousine. Donovan didn't recognize Pete, who was still smiling under a chauffeur's hat partially obscuring a pair of Ray Ban sunglasses, as he drove Donovan out of the airport...

🍁 🍁 🍁

Connie received a phone call from her private investigator, Rieton, who had just returned from Europe and had found out some additional information. It was not a coincidence that Mark had met Carole/Janet at the party. It had been planned that she meet Mark and entice him. Mark Goodwin had something Donovan desperately needed and he was willing to do anything to get it. Donovan had used everybody, from Jenny and Jack to Marty, who had placed Carole/Janet at the party to pursue Mark and get him to marry her. Donovan hadn't counted on her dying. Connie was trying to decide if or when she should tell her new husband, Mark, about the private investigators phone call. If the rumor was true about Donovan still being alive, then she and Mark were still very much in danger... and there was increased speculation that the Mob had poured a lot of money into antiterrorist groups around the world. The Mob didn't think the leaders of our country were being honest with themselves and the American public and that terrorism was a major enemy the country was not aware of or prepared for. The Mob had known for years that terrorists were becoming a real threat to mainland USA and was protecting its own interests. They were also smart enough to know that eventually the United States government would become more reliant upon the Mob's expertise when the need arose, further strengthening the Mob.

🍁 🍁 🍁

Coming soon, *KILL TALK 2*—The Sequel

"Remember me?" Pete said as he stopped the limo, took off his sunglasses and hat, turned around, and pointed his gun at Donovan.

"Pete, let me explain," begged Donovan. Quickly Donovan wrestled with how much he could tell Pete. Hopefully, he wouldn't have to divulge how the Mob had been hired by the CIA to take out Osama Bin Laden and five other key terrorists.

"Five terrorists," the voice from the radio in the stretch limo said, "have just been…"

0-595-21656-0